KNIGHT ASCENDANT

KNIGHT ASCENDANT

KNIGHTS OF THE FLAMING STAR BOOK 2

PAUL BARRETT

STEVE MURPHY

Charlotte, NC

FALSTAFF
BOOKS

WWW.FALSTAFFBOOKS.COM

FIRST DAY OF SCHOOL

Trey, still stuffed with cake from his thirteenth birthday celebration, stared out the van's side window as the vehicle glided through the open gate. A fence of iron bars topped with spikes extended to either side of this gate. As near as Trey could tell, based on how long they drove beside the gray wall, this stone barrier surrounded a tract of land at least as large as any spaceport Trey ever visited since leaving his home and traveling with the Knights. They drove past the gate, where no guard or guardhouse stopped their entry. Trey found that odd until he speculated someone certainly already watched them, either through hidden cameras or crystal balls.

He smiled as he imagined bearded old men studying large round orbs and filing reports about the campus's various inhabitants. Trey had yet to meet a preternatural scientist who was a bearded old man, and he had never seen a real crystal ball, but it still made a funny image.

The road cut through a field of short, green grass and arrowed toward a building. Gerard had called the structure a mansion, a word Trey hadn't known until he looked it up. The definition didn't do justice to the reality. Through the van's front window, he saw the largest building outside of a city he had ever encountered. It seemed built mostly of beige-colored rock, with highlights of cocoa brown wood around the windows and edging the roofline. Slabs of light gray stone covered the sharply sloped roof. The building's center portion towered above the wings extending to either side, which were themselves two stories tall, judging from the number of windows.

Beyond the massive structure, Trey spotted a tall tower ascending into the air. The pearl-colored stone glistened in the sun, and a platform circled it near the top.

"What's that?" Trey asked.

Gerard smiled. "Officially, it's the Spire Pinnacle, but unless things have changed since I went here, most people call it the Power Tower."

As they drew closer, the road turned into a roundabout, which circled a white stone fountain. Three bowls formed the fountain, each smaller than the one below it. Water from the top spilled over the bowls and collected in a pool. Trey caught glimpses of strange, mesmerizingly beautiful creatures swimming in the water. They were like the *kenquala* Hawk had in his quarters, except bigger and more colorful.

The van, driven by Hawk, circled around the fountain and stopped in front of the imposing building. Two short stairways, divided by a landing, led to a set of double doors. A pair of columns framed the steps, each with a stylized arch etched in silver: the sigil of The Order of the Sterling Arch.

Sweat gathered under Trey's arms as the day's importance began to settle on him. He was about to become an initiate to the Order and leave the only family he had known for the last two years.

The whole crew, except for Wolf, had come to see him off. A Uraxian, Wolf was far too large and heavy to fit comfortably in the van, even one meant to accommodate ten passengers. Taciturn as always, Wolf sent Trey off with a handshake, extending one massive finger, which Trey gripped and shook.

"Do well," Wolf had said.

Trey sat between Gerard, his mentor, and Laura, his adopted

mother, the one who had claimed him from the planet where his parents died. Where he had killed his parents, if he was honest.

In the front seat, Hawk turned to him and winked. "Ready?" His thick mustache quirked up as he offered a grin.

Trey brushed the brown hair from in front of his right eye in a reflexive gesture, only to find it no longer there. It had been cut short in preparation for his arrival here and now stood less than two inches long in any spot.

"I guess," he said and gave a hesitant laugh. He had never realized sweat could form above the lip. Did a mustache stop that from happening? Why was he thinking such stupid thoughts right now?

Laura, her oval face the picture of kindness and love, patted his leg. She wore her Knights' uniform, as did the rest of the crew, with the exception of Trey. With its red piping and shimmering fabric, the black outfit highlighted her brown eyes and fair skin. She was the most beautiful woman Trey knew.

"I'm a little nervous," he confessed. A little? He was a bundle of snakes trying to get away from a ferret.

"You'll do fine."

In a rapid motion that made Trey suppress a jump, Ashron exploded out of the front passenger seat and stepped onto the white stone driveway outside the van.

"Open," he said, and the side door obeyed. The Lorothian stood there in his reptilian glory, his uniform tight against his small, compact body. His light green skin gleamed where it stuck out from the black cloth. His long mouth split open in a needle-toothed grin. "Fine?" he asked. "Fine? My dear Laura, Trey will do 'filamentous!'"

Trey beamed at hearing his favorite word come from Ashron. The Lorothian's long snout let the word out like a hiss of steam.

Ashron gave a swooping bow, then held out his hand for Laura. She took the proffered hand with a glare that quickly turned into a smile. "Ashron, you're insufferable."

"Why, thank you, my lady. Hawk just seems to think I'm 'sufferable.'"

Laura slipped out of the van. Gerard gave Trey a soft nudge with his elbow. "Let's go meet your new teacher."

Trey slid across the bench seat. Gerard followed. Once they had all gathered outside the van, Gerard put his pale hands on Trey's shoulders and said, "Wait here." His colorless eyes took in the rest of the crew. "All of you wait here. I will tender our greetings and see if we are welcome."

Ashron's tongue briefly flickered from his mouth. "Oh, I love it when you get all spellburner formal."

"You might wish to be less sarcastic, considering what happened the last time you met Genray."

Ashron winced. "Good point. I still don't think my skin ever turned back to the right color there."

Gerard nodded. "I'll return momentarily."

As Gerard walked toward the steps, Trey turned to Ashron. "What happened?"

Hawk also regarded the Lorothian with a smile. "Yeah, Ashron. What happened?"

Leaving the others behind, Gerard strolled up the stairs, awash in memories from his time here. Six of the best years of his life. He came close to envying Trey. To be young again, eager for knowledge gained with like-minded friends, sounded like a blessing to Gerard. If, for some unimaginable reason, he ever left the Knights, Gerard felt confident he would end up back here as a teacher. Though he could be comfortable anywhere, the two places Gerard felt at home were onboard Ship and at this school.

He reached the first landing when he caught sight of Chavad Genray, his old teacher, descending the second set of stairs. Gerard stopped and waited. Age had been kind to his former instructor. His white hair was perhaps thinner and his skin, pale as Gerard's, more wrinkled. But he still stepped spryly. His arms in their loose-fitting, gray sleeves swung in an exaggerated manner, which earned him the nickname "Swingsticks" from his students. A name meant with respect. He reached the landing, and his pale eyes, with a hint of green that reminded Gerard of fresh grass, regarded his former student.

"Greetings, Master Genray," Gerard said. "I, Gerard of Berol, offer myself to the Sterling Arch and beseech a boon."

"What is this boon?" Genray asked, his voice deep as a cavern. Though they both knew the purpose of Gerard's arrival, terms having been agreed upon a week ago, they followed the ritual as it had been performed since the school's inception. Formalized traditions provided stability and kept the mind sharp.

"As I was trained by those on this mystical ground, I would humbly request my protégé, Trey Julien of Kel, be taken into the Sterling Arch and taught the Rules and Formulas of our Order."

"The Arch has considered your request, and I am authorized to accept this charge. Identify your protégé so he may be offered admittance."

Gerard pointed one of the seven fingers on his cybernetic arm toward where Trey stood with the other quieted crewmembers, all of them watching from the bottom of the steps. "There stands Trey Julien of Kel, the youngling with his hair shorn for his apprenticeship."

"On behalf of the Sterling Arch, I accept Trey Julien of Kel into our fellowship. He will be taught the Rules and Formulas of our Order, to the limits of his skill. Have him come forth."

Gerard nodded. He turned and motioned for Trey to join him on the landing. The crew already knew that only the young boy could come forward at first. When Genray gave permission, the rest of them would be allowed to say their final goodbyes.

Trey walked up the steps, his hesitant stride betraying his nervousness.

The formalities finished between them, Genray allowed a small smile and dropped the stentorian tone in his voice. "I'm looking forward to meeting this young man after all you've told me about him. It sounds like he has a great deal of untapped potential."

Gerard nodded. "His energy is in the range of our greatest. His mind is sharp and quick. He simply lacks the structure the school can provide and a chance to learn in peace. I've done my best to tutor him, but being on Ship isn't always the most conducive environment for structured education."

Genray's smile widened. "So, nothing's changed."

"No, Chavad, it hasn't," Gerard said, returning his smile. "I hope you will be able to help him safely explore his power."

"Will you be attending the farewell ceremony?"

The question threw Gerard until he realized his former master referred to a different occasion and not a ceremony for Trey. "We will all be here. Considering what it honors, we would have to hide in disgrace if we didn't attend."

Genray nodded, his eyes alight with approval.

Trey reached the landing and stood before Genray. The boy had grown in the past month and had a gangling stance that made him appear uncomfortable at the best moments. Now he looked positively miserable.

Gerard put a hand on Trey's quivering shoulder. "Master Genray, I offer to you Trey Julien of Kel, given unto the Sterling Arch so he may grow in the ways of the Order. Does the Order take him to their ways?"

Genray, his face grim, studied Trey. Trey shivered more. Gerard tried to send a sense of calm to the young man. He had explained this was all formality, but he empathized with Trey's nervousness. He remembered another young apprentice who had felt the same way when his parents presented him.

"Master Trey," Genray began. "Do you agree to abide by the rules of this Order, as they have been explained to you?"

To his credit, Trey kept his voice steady and locked eyes with Genray. "I do."

"And do you agree to follow all instructions given by your masters to the best of your ability, and apply the principals of this Order for the service of all universal beings?"

"I do," Trey said. Gerard had explained the meaning of the oath to Trey. It was a lifetime commitment, a promise to work for the general well-being of all sentient races. He made sure Trey understood the Oath's importance before he agreed to present the young man to the

Order for training. Trey already had a caring spirit dedicated to those he called his friends, despite the horrors he had suffered. Gerard had every confidence the boy would uphold the Oath with his entire being.

Genray held his hands above Trey's head. As he spoke, he curved his hands down until they rested beside Trey's shoulders, making an arch to encompass the new apprentice. "With the authority of the Sterling Arch and all the masters who came before me and hold covenant with me, I formally accept you into our Order. Welcome."

"I gratefully accept your welcome," Trey said, following the ritual as Gerard had coached him.

Genray clapped his hands against Trey's shoulders, then released him and stepped back. "Be welcome."

A smile bright enough to be worthy of its own planet beamed across Trey's face. The boy's happiness told Gerard they had made the right decision.

"Now that we have all the formality out of the way," Gerard said. "Trey, this is Master Genray. Master Genray, this is Trey."

"A pleasure to meet you, sir," Trey said, his voice barely shaking. He offered a hand, which shook a bit more.

Genray took Trey's hand in his. "Why, thank you, Master Julien. It's a pleasure to meet you, too. I look forward to seeing what we can make of you."

"That's us," Hawk said as Gerard waved to them from the landing. Now that Trey had been formally accepted into the Order, they could offer their farewells. They began the ascent.

This must be how a proud father feels, Hawk thought as he walked beside his crew. *Is this what Tahorton felt when Moran and I graduated?* The thought of Moran dampened Hawk's mood until he shoved it aside, refusing to let his old friend, now a babbling husk stored away in a secure Galactic Council facility, intrude on this moment.

As they reached the top, Hawk saw Trey standing there, speaking calmly with Genray, already at ease with the pale-faced teacher. A confident man in the making. *I'm going to miss him.* "Trey! Front and center!"

Trey's head snapped around at Hawk's firm voice. The crew and Genray watched as Trey strode forward to take a stance in front of Hawk, somewhere between attention and at ease. Hawk glowered down at him with his hands on his hips. Trey shifted nervously on his feet.

Without warning, Hawk grabbed Trey and pulled him into a fatherly bear hug. After a moment, he released the boy and held him at arm's length. Hawk smiled. "Never forget, you are a Knight of the Flaming Star and part of our crew. Wherever you go and whatever you do, you have a group of people who consider you family. This family will fight for you and even die for you. Hold your head up and be proud of who you are and what you have become. You make me, us, all extremely proud." Hawk hugged him again and pushed him away. "Now go say goodbye to Laura; she's going to miss you."

Trey stepped back and started to turn but jumped into Hawk's arms. Hawk staggered back. The boy had nearly become too big to do such things.

"I'm going to miss you, too," Trey said. He settled his feet back on the floor. Eyes glistening with unshed tears, he walked over to Laura and Ashron.

Trey managed to hold back his tears until he saw Laura's face. Her eyes watered like a fountain, and Trey lost his fight. When he reached her, she picked him up as if he were a small child despite him being as tall as she was. Her strength always amazed him.

"I love you, Trey," she said. "I will miss you more than you could ever know. I—"

He could tell she wanted to say more, but the tears stopped her. So, he held on and said, "I love you, too." He had trouble speaking through the flood of conflicting emotions. Had he just yesterday been nervously excited about arriving here and beginning his classes? Now all he wanted was to go back and stay with his adopted family. Only the certainty of their disappointment kept him from demanding they leave right now.

Finally, Laura set him down and said, "I am very proud of you."

He nodded. He didn't speak, afraid "take me home" would slip out, no matter what he intended to say.

After a moment, he felt a pull on his arm. "OK, you two, my turn."

Wiping his eyes on his sleeve, which usually earned a frown from Laura but didn't today, Trey turned and smiled at Ashron. "You going to cry, too?"

Ashron pointed at his long, narrow eyes. "No tear ducts. When we get weepy, we eat our young, so I'm trying to keep it in check."

Trey took an involuntary step back. He suspected Ashron was joking but didn't want to take the chance.

"Anyway," Ashron lowered his voice in a conspiratorial manner. "I got you something." He leaned forward like he was hugging Trey and slipped a small object into Trey's back pants pocket. Trey threw his arms out to embrace the scaly Lorothian. Ashron pushed him back, and Trey's arms clamped on empty air.

"Yes, yes. I'll miss you too," Ashron said. "Stop your blubbering and go say goodbye to Gerard." With a pat on the back, Ashron pushed him toward Gerard.

Gerard's pale, thin lips quirked in confusion. "What was that all about?"

"I'm not entirely sure," Trey confessed. But he didn't mention Ashron's gift. Whatever the Lorothian gave him, he suspected it might earn Gerard or Laura's disapproval.

The pale man frowned and nodded. Trey imagined a future conversation between Gerard and Ashron and shrugged inwardly. Ashron could spill if he wanted to, but Trey wasn't going to reveal his friend's secret.

"Come on," Gerard said. "Let me show you to your quarters."

The other three crew members watched as Gerard led Trey into an ornate doorway, followed by Genray.

Ashron's tongue flicked in and out a couple of times. "Well, that was less eventful than I imagined but harder than I anticipated."

"You're not as sly as you think you are," Hawk said.

"Whatever are you talking about?" Ashron said in his completely insincere, injured tone.

"I saw you slip something into his back pocket. What was it?"

"Condom."

Laura's jaw dropped, and her brown eyes went wide. "He's only thirteen."

Ashron offered his needle-toothed smile. "What, you think I should have given him more than one?"

"How dare you—"

Ashron held up a clawed hand to stop Laura's wrath. "Joking. It was something to help him feel less homesick. Trust me, it won't get him into any trouble."

<hr>

Trey followed Gerard into the mansion and found himself in a gigantic lobby with rich, brown flooring and cream-colored walls. A double-curved, wooden staircase led to an upper level, which he couldn't see because a waist-high wall of wood so dark it was almost black ran between the stairs.

An opening at the far end of the foyer became a corridor, and Gerard walked toward it. They passed through this hallway, Trey barely noting the doors on either side at regular intervals.

"Where is everybody?" Trey asked, wincing as his voice echoed from the walls.

"Classes," Gerard told him. "And this is the administration and faculty building, so you wouldn't see many students here anyway. I'll show you to your room and hand you over to your guide."

They pushed through a set of double doors and into an open area. Trey gasped as he saw the number of buildings laid out before him. The immensity of the mansion had offered no clue about how much space lay behind it. How would he ever learn where to go?

"I know it's overwhelming," Gerard said when he spotted Trey's astonished gape. Gerard remembered having much the same reaction. "You'll learn it soon, and you won't enter many of the buildings for a while."

Rose-colored quartz sidewalks split off in three directions.

Gerard took the path to the left, and they headed toward a single-story building. The stone buildings, a uniform gray color, gave everything a drab appearance despite the bright day. They strolled into the left-hand building, the corridor not as impressive as the mansion's. The walls inside were a muted shade of red that made Trey's eyes want to water. They passed four doors and stopped at the fifth on the left. Despite the building's archaic exterior appearance, this was a modern door, a lighter shade of red than the hallway, with no handle.

"Say your name," Gerard said.

"Trey Julien."

"Welcome, Apprentice Julien," a female voice said with artificial friendliness.

The door slid open and revealed a room nearly twice the size of his cabin on Ship. Trey stepped inside, delighted at the spacious interior. Gerard followed him. The chamber consisted of a couch and coffee table, an in-wall screen, and a study desk. A low wall separated the room from a kitchen, with a chilling unit and a sink. A door beside the desk led to a bedroom, which held a single bed. Another door near the kitchen opened onto a bathroom with a stand-up shower. "This is all for me?"

Gerard nodded, to Trey's amazement. When Gerard first mentioned Trey attending the school, Trey imagined sharing a large room with several students, like the soldiers on Kel living in the barracks before the war destroyed so much of his home city. He never considered he would have his own accommodations, and certainly not something so much larger than his cabin on Ship. This made the idea of being away from his home and family so much more bearable.

"Visitor seeking entrance," the door voice said. Trey had been so enchanted with exploring the quarters he hadn't realized the door had closed.

"Let them in," Trey said.

The door opened to reveal a girl in a loose-fitting yellow jumper with pockets on both sides. She stood several centimeters shorter than Trey, with wavy red hair ending at the jumper's neckline, and pale skin, though not as milky as Gerard's. Trey's heart skipped a couple of beats when he saw her.

"Hi there," she said in a voice that made his breath catch. "I'm Samantala, but everyone calls me Sam. Well, the few people who talk to me call me Sam. I'm your orientation guide."

She held a hand with graceful, long fingers out toward him. After a few seconds, a frown creased her long face.

"You're supposed to shake her hand," Gerard prodded.

Trey realized he'd been staring, and fire roasted his cheeks. "Sorry," he said and extended his hand. It seemed ungainly, with his stubby sausage fingers, when compared to hers. They shook, and the touch of the girl thrilled him. What was happening? He had seen girls before.

Gerard offered a wan grin. "I'll leave him in your capable hands, Sam."

She returned the grin and offered a slight head bow. "As you say, *ashefah.*"

"Not quite, but thanks for the honorific. Good luck, Trey."

Trey barely heard him, his attention intent on Sam. Her eyes, deep blue with small pupils, held a look Trey recognized. He had seen the same haunted expression on his face from time to time when he caught his reflection. Something preyed on Sam's soul.

A hand on his shoulder startled him, and he whirled to find Gerard staring down at him. "Good luck."

"Thanks."

Gerard nodded and left.

"So, your name's Trey?" Sam asked.

He nodded; his mouth suddenly dry now that he was alone with her.

"And you're the talkative type, I see. Ready for your tour?"

He nodded again, still afraid to speak. What had gotten into him? Seeing her made his scalp tingle and his heart thump faster. "Yes," he finally managed to croak out.

"No, you're not," she said with a smile. Her brilliant white teeth almost disappeared against her milk-colored skin. "You need to put on your uniform."

"Uniform," he asked. "We have to wear uniforms?"

Her smile disappeared, and she cocked her head. "You didn't notice how much the campus looked like a rainbow with all the students walking around."

"Everyone's in class," he told her. "You're the first student I've seen."

She considered a moment, then let out a light laugh. "Fair enough." She indicated her muted yellow unitard with her hands. "Trust me, this wouldn't be my first color choice. Take a peek in your bedroom closet."

Trey walked the short distance to the closet. "Open," he said. Nothing happened.

"You have to open it yourself," Sam said with a giggle. Trey found her joy infectious and could listen to her laugh all day. "Not as much tech here as you might be used to."

That made sense, Trey realized. He slid the door open. Six identical red jumpers and three black ones hung in the closet. "I assume I wear the red one," he said.

"Now I see why they accepted you," she said with a touch of gentle mockery. "You're sharp." She stepped into the doorway. "Yes, red for class days, and the black for your days off. This technically won't be a class day for you, but people might as well get used to seeing you as a year one."

"What year are you?" Trey asked as he pulled one of the red jumpers from its hanger.

"This is my third," she told him. "I started when I was nine."

Trey winced. "I've got some catching up to do, don't I?"

"You do. How old are you?"

"Thirteen," Trey said. "Today's my birthday."

"Happy birthday," Sam said with a grin. "Grandpa."

Trey frowned but wasn't really upset. He liked Sam, and it thrilled him to think he might have already found a friend. "Thank you," he said. Then, because it was the first thing that popped into his mind, he added, "Where are you from?"

"Here on Berol," Sam answered.

"Really? But you look, well…" he stopped. What could he say that wouldn't sound insulting or ignorant? "…different than most Berolians," he finished, almost muttering the words.

"It's the red hair, isn't it?" Sam said as she reached up and touched her locks. "And that I don't look as much like a ghost as everyone else. My father is a native, but my mother is from Kalis. They met when she came here for a research project. She's a scientist, and he's a farmer. I guess I ended up with her hair and a combination of their skin."

Though he didn't know why, Trey felt like five kinds of idiot. He wondered if the day was going to get worse. "Sorry, I didn't mean to pry. I'm going to change."

"I'll wait for you out here," Sam said, seeming to take no offense at his questioning. He breathed an inward sigh as she strolled into the living room.

Trey closed the bedroom door and began removing his clothes. As he folded his blue pants, he spotted a lump in the back pocket—Ashron's gift to him. In the exhilarating flush of meeting Sam, he had forgotten about it.

He pulled the thin, black metal box from the pocket and cautiously opened the hinged lid to reveal a small pin in the shape of a nine-pointed star with red flames leaping off the top: the crest for the Knights of the Flaming Star.

Unexpected tears stung his eyes. The reality of what he had agreed to slammed into him, and for a few seconds, he considered going to Master Genray and saying there had been a mistake. He didn't belong here. He belonged on Ship with the crew, not at a school full of strangers.

He wiped his arm across his eyes and chided himself. If he left now, after less than an hour, every one of Ship's crew would be disappointed in him. Even Ship would probably think of him as nothing but a little kid who they couldn't depend on to do anything. He wasn't a kid anymore. He was thirteen—time to start acting like a grownup.

He took out the pin and found a folded note underneath it, his name written across it. Ashron had obviously penned it. The Lorothian's handwriting was almost machine perfect.

Trey, this gift is from Sara and me. Mostly Sara. The Order is rigorous in its clothing/uniform code, with their little pocketless rainbow outfits, so always keep this pin hidden. It has bio tape, so you can stick it to your skin if you want. Wear it as a constant reminder of our love and commitment to you. Sara told me to write that part. It is a pretty cool pin, though. Anyway, she says with this pin, you can talk to her at any time. She says to be careful, however. Until you get your implant, others around you will be able to hear her also. You don't want people to hear a voice coming from nowhere and getting nosy. Plus, you don't want to make people think you are weirder than you already are by talking to yourself. Sara says she misses you already. We all do. Take care, kid. Ashron had signed his name in his native script, flowing and full of curls and switchbacks.

Trey held up the small pin. "Can you really hear me, Sara?"

"Loud and clear," came her familiar voice. "And if you ever want privacy, say 'my own time.' And to talk again, 'your time again.'"

"Filamentous! We'll talk later."

Smiling, he pressed the pin against his collarbone. As he put on the red jumper, tears of joy trickled down the side of his face. He might be far from home, but he wasn't alone.

I think I'm going to be okay.

2

BACK TO BUSINESS

A morose crew returned to Ship, each with their thoughts about Trey's departure keeping them silent. As the elevator door opened on the main deck, they found Wolf standing there. His broad body filled the large hatchway, and his blue eyes regarded them. "Tough?"

"Tougher than I ever imagined," Laura choked. "Excuse me."

Wolf stepped to the side, and she brushed past him. Though she had turned her face aside, he still saw the sparkle of tears.

"It wasn't easy," Gerard said as he tossed the Uraxian a silver, half-kilogram bag.

Wolf caught it, the bag all but disappearing in his massive hands, and brought it to his wide nostrils. He drew a deep sniff and gave a broad grin, the only kind he had. "Sin'co's coffee. Nice. Thank you."

"I have a small pallet being delivered for you," Gerard told him. "Sin'co said it was freshly roasted at her farm the day before yesterday." Gerard held up a hand before Wolf could protest. "Vacuum sealed, with a valve, slightly below room temperature, in the dark."

Wolf gave an approving nod. "Sin'co is one of the best." He took another deep sniff.

"You two want to be alone?" Hawk asked.

Wolf ignored Hawk. "The essential substance of the Universe. I'll grind a batch and brew it up. Fresh coffee in the galley in ten. That should cheer everyone up." He took one more sniff. "An aroma to make angels weep." Wolf, the crew's most taciturn member, never failed to wax poetic about gourmet food or drink. "Ship is ready for travel," he said as he turned and trundled toward the galley.

Hawk nodded. If Wolf said Ship was ready, Ship was ready. "Ship, when is our departure slot?"

"Twenty-eight minutes. Time to ripspace connection is two hours sixteen minutes after atmosphere departure."

"Excellent. Time for a little lunch and, from what I gather, an excellent cup of coffee for our travels. Good thing caffeine doesn't keep you awake for the jump to ripspace."

Four days later, as they neared the end of their ripspace journey to Delroth, Hawk sat alone on the bridge, eyes closed, enjoying what had to be his fifth cup of Wolf's coffee, the mug clenched between his hands. Those hands trembled slightly from the caffeine intake. Since giving up alcohol, coffee had become his latest addiction. He sometimes wondered if his new substance abuse was any better than his old one. A quick trip through the stupid things he had done in his drunken days gave him the answer.

Laura shuffled in, eyes downcast. The entire crew noticed the difference on-board without Trey's enthusiastic energy and cheerful demeanor, but it affected Laura the most. She tried, they all tried, to busy themselves with the various things that occupied their time in rip, but for some reason, it all felt hollow. And Trey had been part of their life for such a short period, and not related to any of them. Hawk couldn't even imagine sending off a child you raised for over a decade.

Head raised and eyes scanning the room as if she wasn't sure how she had arrived, Laura spotted Hawk. "Hey," she said.

"You miss him, don't you?"

Laura nodded.

"So do I," Hawk told her.

"We all do," Ship said.

"I'd sure like to talk to him."

Hawk shook his head. When Ashron confessed what he had slipped in Trey's pocket, Laura immediately wanted to call him one last time to wish him luck. In his firm "captain's voice," Hawk suggested it wouldn't be a good idea. At Laura's forlorn expression, he sighed.

"He can't think we're hovering. He must be his own person, and he can't do that if we call him every day because we can't handle him being gone. And hearing from us all the time won't make it any easier for him to get over his homesickness."

Laura considered Hawk's words. Understanding his logic didn't make it any easier to accept.

"We'll visit him when we return for the memorial celebration," Hawk continued. "And we'll do a once-weekly call, all of us together."

"That will be good," Laura said. She shook herself, trying to slide past the melancholy. "I guess if there was trouble, we would hear. If there was anything wrong. If—"

"He's fine," Hawk said. This seemed like a lot more than missing Trey, but Hawk had no idea what it might be. Unless... "Ship, what is the date, adjusted for Earth Standard?"

Ship told him, and Hawk nodded grimly. That made sense. "How many years does this make it?" he asked Laura.

"Nine," Laura answered as her mind replayed in far too vivid detail Garritt being pushed into the road and hit by a car.

"Trey is fine," Hawk told her, and she wanted so badly to believe it. "He's going to be okay. He's safer than being with us, and the school is a better place for a young man than Red's."

Laura couldn't help but chuckle at remembering her suggestion they leave Trey with their friend Red, a man who ran a smuggler's paradise. "Not one of my finer moments," she admitted. "I'll be okay. Just bad timing."

"That's pretty much the definition of our existence, isn't it? Always in the wrong place at the wrong time, and somehow we come out of it."

"That we do," Laura said.

Gerard entered the bridge, the right sleeve on his blue shirt rolled up to reveal his cybernetic arm. "Transition point in twenty minutes," he told them.

"Time to take a nap," Laura said. "I'm going to go prep." She gave a wan smile.

Hawk wanted to see more, but he suspected it was the best he would get. She would come out of the pit like she did every year. "On my way," he said as she left the room. "Ship, let Ashron and Wolf know." He drained the last of his coffee with a loud slurp. *Damn, that's good.*

"Nice," Ship chided.

"In some cultures, the louder the sip, the greater the compliment," he said.

"Is that same culture responsible for the loud noises you make from the other end?" Gerard asked.

"Isn't it time for you to take us out of rip?"

Gerard grinned as he dropped his lanky frame into his chair and begin plugging the slender wires into his arm. Most rip pilots had a datajack at the base of their skull connected to the pineal gland through a magically infused cable. The jack was plugged into the rip pilot, who then plugged into their vessel. Magic and technology rarely got along, but in the discovery of ripspace, the Berloians found a way to make it work. One didn't have to be a preternatural scientist, or magician, as most people called them, to be a rip pilot, but the best pilots could also manipulate equations.

"See you on the other side," Hawk said. He set his cup on the table beside his chair and headed for the bunks where the crew gathered for the short "nap" they took while entering or exiting the ethereal confines of ripspace.

He reached the bunk chamber to find Ashron and Wolf strapped into their bunks and wearing their injector cuffs. Laura stood near Trey's bunk, cuff in hand, and gave Hawk another wan smile as he slipped into his bed. Hawk returned the expression but didn't speak. They had said all that needed saying.

<hr>

After landing on Delroth, the four days spent refitting and getting Ship ready for the installation of, as their Force 13 handler, Grendarin, put it, "experimental technology" had the crew too occupied to dwell on Trey's absence. Surreptitious updates on Trey's status from Master Genray helped. According to the headmaster, Trey was settling in well.

Hawk hated the idea of letting Force 13's mad engineer put something untested in his Ship, but he had little choice. The autonomy Force 13 gave his crew came with a price.

Satisfied Ship was in top shape, an opinion confirmed by Wolf and Gerard, they made a short flight from the capital shipyard to a location known by few, far from any inhabited areas.

"You are entering restricted space," a voice full of menace announced over the bridge speakers. The entire crew sat on the bridge and watched the approach toward the high mountains, covered in vibrant red trees, many of them on the highest peaks dusted with snow. "Please veer away, or you will be shot down."

"Send the IFF, Ship," Hawk said.

"Broadcasting."

The voice returned a few seconds later, this time much friendlier. "Greetings, Captain Grey. Welcome back. Please follow the beacon to pad seven, and we'll lower you down. I owe you a drink."

"Thank you, Aman," Hawk said. "We'll make it a coffee. Locked on the beacon and tracking."

"Control out."

Ship did a slight starboard drift and continued toward the mountains.

"Bets on whether Henna has driven her latest assistant away," Hawk said with a smile.

Laura smiled back. "Depends on the bet."

"Four to one, she hasn't."

She shook her head as she tapped her pad. "I'm not that foolish with my money. Try Ashron."

"Hey," the Lorothian said, "I'm thinking I should be offended."

Ship cleared the mountains to reveal a deep valley of light gray dirt, far more level than nature would ever allow.

"*I'm* thinking we should get ready for a landing," Hawk said.

"Hello," the young Pralin said as Hawk and the rest of the crew walked into the laboratory's foyer, an area of dark stone and little else. "I'm Miara, Dr. LaRouche's new assistant."

"How many does that make now?" Ashron asked out of the side of his long mouth.

"Six," Gerard answered.

The facility, buried deep in the Tranasan Mountain range of Delroth and hidden from prying eyes with extensive—and sometimes destructive—countermeasures, was a top-secret Galactic Council research station under the control of Dr. Henna LaRouche, one of the Council's preeminent research and development scientists. But with her brilliant mind came an ego and demanding attitude, which made working with her an exercise in saintly patience and a touch of masochistic personality disorder. Her assistants rarely lasted longer than a couple of years.

"The doctor is expecting you," Miara said. Her feline eyes went to Wolf and widened, while her pointed ears flattened. A sign of surprise. A reaction Wolf often elicited.

Recovering, she straightened her ears and said, "Follow me, please." She turned and walked through the open glass doors, tail swishing.

Hawk walked a step behind her, and the others followed. "How long have you worked for Henna?"

"Two months," she answered. "And she prefers to be called Dr. LaRouche."

No wonder she's still so chipper, Hawk thought. *The cranky sleeveen hasn't latched her talons onto her yet.* He didn't bother to address her admonition about the doctor's name. Hawk had never called her Dr. LaRouche, much as Henna might want it. Though smart enough to have obtained the title, she never bothered to put in the time and work to get the degree. She had simply jumped into theoretical research and took a job with the Council over forty Standard years ago. Hawk respected Henna's intelligence, drive, and ingenuity, but if you hadn't earned the title, you didn't get the title.

They passed several innocent-looking cubicles pressed close enough together that Wolf had to turn sideways to get through. People sat at desks and worked on computers—the standard office setup Hawk had seen at corporations throughout the galaxy, drone people doing drone business. It made him happy he had never ended up in such a position.

At the end of the cubicles, they took a left and reached an alcove blocked by a pair of silver doors. As they approached, the doors opened to reveal an elevator cabin large enough to accommodate at least ten people.

After the doors closed, the Pralin said, "Miara, authorization HLR-008-ADMA. Five guests for the doctor."

A panel in the wall slid open and revealed a glassy black square. She placed her furry hand against it. After a second, a green light glowed from the panel. It dissolved away, and a voice said, "Authorization recognized. Access granted."

The doors closed, and the elevator began its descent, bringing them toward where the facility's real research took place.

"Are you enjoying working with the doctor?" Laura asked.

The Pralin's eyes flicked toward the ceiling. Hawk followed her gaze and saw the black hole in the corner of the car. Camera, he realized. So, anything the young woman said was suspect.

"She is an instructive boss," she said in a neutral tone. "I'm learning a lot."

Hawk noticed she didn't say she was a good boss.

The elevator slowed its descent after ten more seconds, and the doors opened. An industrial smell of metal and oil filled the cabin. They had descended below the biological testing levels, gone below the semi-illegal work with robotics, and stopped where the work on ship systems took place.

When he first came here eight years ago, Hawk questioned why they worked on such large systems at a depth difficult to bring in supplies and remove finished items. It had been explained to him the underground bunker was equipped with radiation shielding, blast protection, and magic dampening. Thus, if any accidents happened, it wouldn't affect the outside world and reveal the true nature of the work done here.

They stepped out of the elevator, and Miara pointed at a six-wheeled cart designed to carry large parts. "The doctor is deep inside the facility. We'll take that since it will carry your Uraxian crewman."

Wolf sat on the bench seat on the cart's back while the others took their seats.

"Destination?" A female voice asked from somewhere within the cart.

"Take us to the crone," Miara said.

Hawk arched an eyebrow as the cart pulled away from the elevator. Miara offered an enigmatic feline smile and nothing more.

They rode past a variety of bays demarcated by yellow paint where people worked on various projects. Other than they involved starcraft systems, Hawk had no idea what purpose anything served. Sparks flew from one area as a welding torch did its work. The sound of tools drilling, tightening, and cutting filled the air. Overhead lighting gave the gigantic area a sterile look, totally incongruous with the permeating oily smell, so thick Hawk could taste it.

"I always forget how huge this place is," Ashron shouted over the noise.

"And this is one of fifteen," Miara told him. "Although this facility is the largest."

Five minutes later, the cart came to rest in front of a *Wasp*, a single-seat, short-range scout ship used for planetary reconnaissance by Galactic fleets. A woman stood at a diagnostics station staring at the holographic readouts that floated in the air. Curly white hair that ran to her shoulders topped her dark, wrinkled face, which grinned at the information before her. Her nose, little more than slits, flared, and she spun to regard the crew.

"It's the Knights," she stated in a scratchy voice, although who she was informing, Hawk didn't know. "How are those new systems working? Best you've ever had, right?"

"They're pretty damn good," Hawk said. Two years ago, their previous visit saw a complete overhaul of Ship's engine drives and fuel transfer structure.

"Pretty damn good?" LaRouche scoffed. "They are some of the best work I've done and are becoming the standard for all Force 13 ships. You're lucky I chose you to be the test subject."

Wolf held up a comp pad, which looked like a credit card in his hand. "I have some thoughts on modifications."

"Really?" The engineer's tone turned solicitous. Wolf was the sole member of the crew LaRouche respected, as far as Hawk could tell, and it was okay with him if Ship benefitted from their mutual admiration. "I look forward to seeing them."

"Later," Hawk said. "Grendarin said you had some new tech you need tested, and we're the guinea pigs again."

"Is it a new laser or missile system?" Ashron asked. "Or a high-powered mustard delivery platform?"

"Still as juvenile as ever, I see," LaRouche said, her lip curling. "Why do you put up with him?"

"I've asked myself that from time to time," Hawk said. "He's pretty good in a fight though, so he's occasionally useful."

"And a *whispum* sometimes kills a *parculi*, but I wouldn't want the disgusting things near me."

Hawk wasn't sure what that meant. He saw Ashron about to offer a retort and held up his hand. "Let's not get off track. We know you're busy."

"Yes, I am."

"So, what is it and how long is it going to take?"

"Why are you still standing there?" LaRouche's dark eyes fell on

Miara, who stood nearby. "Do you not possess intelligence? Get our guests some refreshments instead of hovering like a worrisome bug. Do the job I pay you for."

"Of course, ma'am," Miara said, her pointed ears going flat and whiskers quivering. She turned and strode away. Her tail made short, agitated flicks.

"You'd talk to Tasha like that exactly once," Ashron told LaRouche with a toothy smile. Tasha was a Pralin, like Miara. Unlike Miara, Tasha was a trained covert operative and not one to put up with disrespect.

"I don't know who Tasha is, but if she worked for me, that's exactly how I would talk to her. She'd get no special treatment."

"Ever considered being polite?" Ashron asked, his tongue flicking out.

Hawk could easily see this getting out of hand. "Let's—"

"You think I'm hard on young Miara?" LaRouche asked, one silver eyebrow quirking upward.

"I think you're hard on all your assistants, which is why you don't keep them. You can be a teacher without being a bit—" Ashron stopped. His green cheeks expanded as he pulled in and blew out a breath. "Without being a bully. Not a big fan of bullies."

"We don't—" Hawk tried again and stopped when the engineer held up a weathered hand. She advanced on Ashron, and Hawk wondered if she was going to slap him.

"Very interesting someone of your barbaric culture thinks I'm a bully." She lowered her hand. "I'm not teaching my people how to be lackeys. I'm searching for someone to train to take over my position." She indicated her wrinkled face and gray hair. "I know you can't tell beneath all this beauty, but I'm old. I'd like to retire while I can still move, and I'd like someone who can carry on where I leave off. Every assistant I bring in has the smarts, or they wouldn't be here. What none of them have had so far is the backbone. I'm hard on them, but nowhere near as hard as others will be on my replacement, as they've been on me. Shooting people and blowing things up is easy. Try dealing with the backstabbing and politics of science, then you can talk to me about bullies."

A glint flashed in her hard-blue eyes, fierce enough that Ashron stepped back, but his face took on his version of irritated consideration. "You have no idea how much I know about politics and backstabbing. More than you would ever guess."

"Perhaps you two should ease away from the ledge," Laura said.

"Agreed, we're getting way off track," Hawk finally said. If he let this go any further, the whole crew would soon be on the warpath, and Hawk didn't need that. He already suspected a future communication from Grendarin about this little exchange. "Not our place." He glared at Ashron, who returned a neutral expression.

"You're right, it isn't," LaRouche said.

Gerard watched with interest as Ashron and LaRouche glared at each other, neither wanting to back down. *Unstoppable force, say hello to immovable object*, he thought. Time to step in and help. Getting LaRouche talking about her passion should smooth things over.

"What sort of new toy do you have for us? We need to get going."

She pulled her eyes from Ashron's. "Always in a hurry. If I didn't know better, I'd think you didn't care for my company."

"It's always a pleasure seeing you," Laura said in her most charming voice.

Gerard wondered how she didn't choke on such a brazen lie.

"But we have other things to do," Laura finished.

"Things more important than assisting Force 13 protocol development?"

"Yes," Ashron said. "I have to go raid a coastal village and eat some babies."

The tension held in the air for several seconds as LaRouche stared at Ashron. Hawk wondered if maybe he should punch the Lorothian.

She gave a small chuckle as her thick brows furrowed, creating wrinkles as deep as trenches between them. "Very well. I will show you 'your new toy' as you put it."

LaRouche returned to the diagnostic station, a meter-high

rectangle on wheels. She pushed on the touchscreen and flicked a bright red switch.

The air tightened around Hawk. His skin prickled, and his hair tingled. A tinge of ozone touched his nostrils.

"What's going on?" Ashron said. "My scales feel like they want to separate from my body."

"Interesting," LaRouche said. "I wonder if there are some offensive applications I overlooked. Something to think about."

"Offensive applications to what?" Gerard said. He held his golden arm up, and a high-pitched whine emanated from it. "You have a lot of power being implemented, but I see no effect."

"Because we're in the radius." LaRouche stepped away from the station and walked past the group. "Follow me."

Hawk stepped in behind the engineer, and the others followed. After roughly six meters, the tension disappeared. The hair on Hawk's neck settled back, and his arms no longer felt like they were being poked by small needles.

LaRouche spun around and held up her arms like a conductor. "Behold your new toy."

Hawk turned around. Where the spacecraft sat, he now saw an empty bay. All the equipment surrounding the craft had also gone missing.

"A cloak?" Ashron said, the disappointment thick in his voice. "That's it? Cloaking's been around since before you were born. Or you were at least a toddler. Not too impressive."

Hawk agreed. Cloaking had existed for almost seventy years, used to hide covert survey teams when they traveled to restricted planets hidden. Ship had a cloaking system with noise suppression for just such endeavors.

"We don't have cloaking like this," LaRouche said, pride eminating from her voice despite the annoyance on her face. "The existent cloaks are visual only, with separate systems for sound. Any active scanning or signature tracking from an enemy ship will reveal an anomaly. This system eliminates all that and allows the equipped vessel to do their own active scanning without revealing themselves. This system is truly invisible to any known detection techniques."

"How effective is it?" Gerard asked. "I mean, beyond the obvious of what we can see here."

"You mean not see," Ashron said.

Everyone ignored him.

"It's as effective as I can make it without field testing. That's where you come in."

"So, we get to be the sitting ducks, not knowing if we've been detected until the bad guys start firing at us?" Hawk said. "That's great."

"You don't have to test it in active combat," LaRouche said as if she were talking to a small, uneducated child. "All you need do is have nearby friendly ships try to locate you in a variety of situations."

"You could do that here," Hawk told her. "Why do you need us?"

LaRouche smiled. "Well, if you do happen to run into a combat situation, it will be nice to get the data."

Hawk, Ashron, and Wolf stood on the platform at the shuttle station, waiting for the shuttle to arrive to take Ashron to his ship.

"Eight weeks," Ashron said, his voice jubilant, the grin spread over his snout. They had already seen Gerard and Laura off to their destinations and now waited in the port for Ashron's shuttle. Hawk made Laura promise not to contact Trey before the weekly group call. Now, Wolf leaned against the wall while Ashron and Hawk sat on a bench. "I can't believe we're getting a two-month vacation. S'ssara bless Henna LaRouche." He made a mimed toast with an invisible glass in his hand.

"That's not what you were saying thirty minutes ago," Hawk growled at him. "You were ready to bite her head off."

"All a misunderstanding," Ashron said, dropping the glass and offering a dismissive wave. "And she's not wrong. We are barbarians."

"Yes, well... anyway, you can throw a little of S'ssara's blessing our way," Hawk said. "The installation is six weeks; the additional two weeks is Wolf, Gerard, and me learning the specs and having Gerard brush up with LaRouche on maintenance and troubleshooting."

"And this is why I'm glad I only have to make things blow up."

"You're welcome," Hawk told him. "Don't forget the ceremony. Make sure you're at Berol."

"Of course," Ashron said. "I wouldn't dare disgrace the Knights by not attending. I'd be more concerned with the three of you not making it. Do you even remember what it's like to go somewhere not aboard Ship? Would that be considered cheating?"

"I'll allow it this one time," Ship said.

"It is annoying," Hawk said. "Force 13 could have definitely picked a better time to saddle this on us. I hate having to break up the training and take the loss of a week traveling. It eats into everyone's vacation, too."

"Don't worry," Ashron grinned. "We're the Knights. Force 13 will call us back to duty well before our vacation is done."

"Then they'll have to wait," Hawk said. "I might travel somewhere without Ship, but we're not going on a mission without her."

"That's very sweet," Ship said.

"Sweet, hell," Ashron said. "He wouldn't remember how to function on any other craft." He rubbed his stomach. "I'm looking forward to the gastronomical delights awaiting me. You sure I can't entice either of you to come along?"

Considering the kind of things Ashron liked to eat, Hawk couldn't imagine going on a food tour with him. The thought of what they might encounter made his bowels clench. "We have to oversee the upfit," he reminded Ashron.

"Bring us some samples," Wolf said, a grin on his broad face.

"I can do that."

Hawk groaned.

"Shuttle 67A2R to Marantis 6 now arriving. Departure in fifteen minutes," a calm feminine voice said over the loudspeakers.

Ashron stood. "My ride. I'll miss you all so much," he said, fake blubbering.

"Get out of here before I decide to make you stay and clean the missile tube."

"Bye!" With his toothy smile, Ashron turned and strolled down the tunnel, his suitcase floating along behind him.

"Come on," Hawk said to Wolf. "The refit doesn't start until tomorrow. I hear some coffee and cigars calling our name."

3

DISAPPEARANCE

The past several weeks at school had been rougher than Trey ever imagined they could be.

At night, when he performed maintenance on his prosthetic arm and considered the day's events, Trey wondered why he was having so much trouble with what should have been a simple matter. He loved learning, so why was he so miserable?

The first two weeks, he understood—homesickness, pure and simple. Being on Ship gave him a home and family again, something he had not experienced for a long time. Now he was away from there, and it felt wrong. He thought speaking to Ship would make it better, but it somehow made it worse. After the second week, he told her he wanted to limit their talks to once a week, which made things better. Hearing about the crew's exploits from the previous week became a bright spot in his routine, and looking forward to the next week's conversation replaced his homesickness. They were all on shore leave, except Hawk and Wolf who were overeeing the upgrade to Ship. Trey loved hearing about everyone's adventures, even if the adventure consisted of lying on the beach and reading, like Laura. These talks left him feeling buoyed and ready to face another week.

Homesickness aside, he found it difficult to make friends. He was in the strange position of being the oldest in his first-year class made up of eager ten-year-olds. Their rambunctious silliness irritated him, and he couldn't believe he was ever so happy-go-lucky. He couldn't even remember being as carefree as the people his own age, much as he tried. Their conversations with him, especially after his discussions with Gerard and Laura, and even Ashron, seemed juvenile and unnecessary. He tried to laugh at goofy antics and fart jokes and rumors about which boy liked which girl and which teacher would let you slide by on a test, but it all felt so…so…pedestrian.

"Did you ever think maybe you're the asshole?" Sam asked him one time when he offered his litany of complaints. Sam was the one redeeming thing in this entire nightmare experience. "It's nobody's fault they had it easy and you had it rough. Blaming them only pushes them away and makes it harder for them to accept you."

"So, I'm supposed to sink to their level?" Trey had asked.

Sam released an exasperated breath, which flipped out a lock of her bright red hair that wafted across his cheek. His face tingled. "You're supposed to realize you're different than them, not above them. Try to enjoy life. From what you told me, if anyone should realize how precious it is and how easily it could be taken away, it's you." She pointed at his prosthetic arm. "And how quickly it can change."

That night, he gave a great deal of consideration to her advice, broke his rule, and made a special call to Ship to speak to her about it.

"Your friend is a wise young lady," was all Ship said. "You should listen to her."

So, Trey tried to take it from a different perspective and consider each person for themselves and what they might offer, and what he might offer them. Though challenging, it slowly grew easier. He continued to find them mostly intolerable, but he only had to deal with them in class.

Shortly after his first month at the school, Trey stepped out of his room to find Sam leaning against the wall reading her tablet, as she had every day since he'd been here. A stupid grin came to his face whenever he saw her. Her bright red hair, her brilliant green eyes that hid some sadness he couldn't understand, and her round, freckled face always made him feel better. The last thing he thought of when he went to sleep was her. And every morning, he looked forward to talking with her about whatever came to their minds. He didn't know much about love, but he liked Sam more than any other person who wasn't his extended Ship family.

As he closed the door, she released the tablet. The tether pulled it to rest against her side. She inspected him for a moment, and a frown crossed her face.

"Hi," he said. "Sorry I'm late. You been waiting long?"

"Long enough that I was going to send in a search party." Her eyes ran over his clothing, and her frown deepened. "You're a mess."

He unconsciously ran a hand over his rumpled, red first-year uniform. At least he had managed to jump into the sonic shower and put on some deodorant. He might come across as a garbage heap, but he didn't smell like one. "I had a rough night."

Sam's frown changed as she bunched her auburn eyebrows. "Again? Still hearing the voices?"

"When you say it like that, it makes me sound crazy." He had no vocabulary to describe his brain's activities for the past weeks. As if he didn't have enough to deal with in school, he had to wonder if, despite his protests, he truly was going crazy. He once read people who suffered trauma could do that.

"It's more like really vivid dreams," he told her, though that didn't quite explain it either. He didn't want to mention—and could barely admit it to himself—that now, more and more, he was often experiencing the "dreams" when he was awake. He would be heading down the hall to class, and a disturbing image would dance across his eyes. It was all he could do not to scream, and more than once he had jumped, startling the other students. Sleeping had become close to impossible, and his studies suffered. The few notable strides he made in garnering acquaintances he could tolerate were now being eroded away by his erratic behavior. It was hard to make friends when people thought there was something off about you.

"Let's go, grandpa," Sam said, giving him a gentle punch on the shoulder. "It's a new day and a new way." Her favorite expression. Trey didn't totally believe it, but he enjoyed hearing her say it.

"You shouldn't abuse your elders," Trey told her.

They strolled through the school, two unique quarks in a stream of protons. Trey's position of being too old for a freshman and too inexperienced in the arts for his age added to his ostracism, although he had begun to overcome it with Sam's help. Gerard's previous tutelage also helped him move quickly through some of the first-year classes, so with luck, he might be advanced early and get into lessons appropriate to his age, making his outcast status no longer an issue. He and Sam stuck together because of her own odd reputation within the school. The students found her unusual, even for a school full of people learning trans-dimensional manipulation. They occasionally picked on her, but from afar. Mostly they ignored her, giving her a safe distance when she passed by.

The few who would speak to either of them had their own reasons for being outcasts, and in that, they formed a loose coalition of necessity, but it didn't endure past the school day.

He had questioned her position in the student body a few days after they met. She had demurred, telling him simply they didn't like her talent. She said no more about it, and he resisted the urge to push her for more details. If she wanted to keep it a mystery, it wasn't his place to pry. She would tell him if she wanted. After all, there were things about himself and his past he didn't want her to know. Maybe someday they could share their innermost secrets, but for now, it delighted him just to call her a friend.

"How late are we?" he asked, having forgotten to put on his wrist computer. "Do we have time to stop at DM?"

"We can make time," Sam said. "As long as we hurry, and your old knees don't give out." Sam was around three months younger than Trey, but she reminded him every chance she got.

DM was Dark Matter Coffee. The only shop allowed on the campus, it specialized in fresh ground gourmet coffee and drinks. Trey didn't know much about coffee, but Wolf had told Trey before he left that the coffee was some of the best made. Tyler, a local farmer's son, attended the school a decade back. With Genray's tacit approval, he started serving his family's coffee in the morning for extra spending money. He did so well he got permission to open a store. It employed students from the school, was never closed, and was always busy. There were rumors Tyler used what he had learned as a preternatural scientist to give his coffee extra flavor, but he swore it was all-natural.

All Trey knew was that five weeks in, he was hooked on the stuff.

He fell in beside Sam, brooding on his dreams from the night before. He had told no one else about them. When they first started, he had considered mentioning it in his weekly call to Ship and the Knights, but something stopped him at the last moment. It would do little but worry the crew if he told them, and he didn't want to spoil their shore leave. It was enough that they took time from their enjoyment to reach out for a conference call and let him tell them all about what was happening in his life. But this he kept to himself. He was thirteen now. He needed to handle things alone.

He didn't know how much longer he could fight it, though. The dark monsters haunted him—he saw flashes of the hideous creatures he had seen while suspended in ripspace when Sara used his power to trap and destroy Moran. He felt as if the creatures circled him constantly, trying to reach him for some terrible purpose.

In the beginning, the dreams had been vague and sporadic, but they had become a daily occurrence, as if the forces behind them were getting more urgent and desperate. Trey decided if he couldn't get some sleep tonight, he would make an appointment with Mistress Auraglia, the counselor, tomorrow. He wanted to deal with it himself but could admit when he needed help.

Deep in thought, Trey never saw the girl as he walked right into her path. Her shoulder slammed into him and spun him as a hand clipped his tablet computer. It broke from its tether and crashed to the floor.

"Oops," the older girl said, smiling mischievously.

"You did that on purpose," Sam said as she bent to retrieve Trey's tablet. Trey was glad to see it hadn't broken. He didn't relish asking for money to buy another one.

"I did no such thing," the girl responded in a loud, indignant manner. "Your pet wasn't paying attention and ran into me."

Trey sighed as he saw who it was. Gin Attawn stood over him, hands on the hips of her blue uniform. A large black-haired girl, Gin was part of a group of fourth-year students who, for whatever reason, had taken an interest in Trey and Sam's relationship. Most people either left them alone or spoke to them in passing. Gin and the other seven of her clique, known around school as the Hellspawn, had made it their mission to harass them; it was a turn of events that the younger kids the Hellspawn usually bullied must have appreciated.

Sam handed the tablet to Trey and then glared up at Gin, though the older girl stood half a head taller. Sam's fists clenched, and her green eyes glinted with fury.

Trey gently put his arm on Sam's. "It was my fault. I wasn't paying attention to where I was going."

Gin obviously hadn't anticipated Sam's anger. Trey saw fear in the older girl's black eyes as she took a step back.

"My fault, Sam," Trey repeated.

"It was not your fault! I watched her deliberately run into you."

Trey took a firmer grip on Sam's arm. "Not worth it," he said in a low voice. "Look around."

The other Hellspawn must have been lying in wait. They were now strategically positioned around the two of them. They stood in the middle of one of the school's larger quads, and the other students gave the disturbance a wide berth. None of them wanted to end up back on the Hellspawn's radar.

Gin drew courage from her position of superior numbers. As she positioned herself a step further away from Sam, she said, "Yeah, it was your pet's fault, and I demand an apology."

"Yeah, apologize, squirt." A deep voice spoke from their right: Mark, the muscle of the group. Trey considered Mark an unusual name for a Lokathi. But then, Mark was a rare example of his race, being large and muscular instead of thin and sinewy. He outweighed Trey by a good forty kilos, and the scowl on his orange-skinned face could curdle fresh milk.

There was nothing special about the others, six in blue uniforms, two in green. Superiority in numbers was their main advantage. Trey was confident he could win against any of them individually, having trained with Hawk and Ashron, but eight of them were way too many.

They all wore condescending smirks and haughty attitudes, although their eyes repeatedly flicked to Sam. Trey again wondered what about her had them worried. And if she scared them, why did they continue to harass her? Maybe it was *because* she scared them.

Sam was fuming, her face so red it almost matched her hair.

Trey grinned and winked. "It's okay, Sam."

He returned his attention to Gin and gave her what he considered his most charming smile, learned from Hawk. "I deeply regret our current situation and must apologize for any misunderstandings taking place here today. I am ashamed you have been subjected to what could only be construed as a misstep and lack of judgment imbued upon you by some infantile form of groupthink." Without hesitation, he bowed deeply as taught by Ashron, although in this case, he meant it as sarcasm instead of respect, even though he knew none of the Hellspawn would catch the insult.

He straightened up to see a priceless expression of confusion on Mark's coral-colored face. "What...wait..."

On the other hand, Gin's face was scrunched in fury. Maybe he underestimated her intelligence. She obviously had some idea of his disguised affront. The rest of the Hellspawn waited for direction from their leaders.

"Now, if you will excuse us," Trey said. "We're late for class." He offered his arm to Sam. "Come along, youngster."

Smiling, Sam put her arm in his. "As you wish, old man." They walked across the quad, ignoring the glances from the other students.

When they were a sufficient distance away, back among the crowd heading for the first class of the day, Sam looked at Trey. "That was no apology. You basically told Gin she ran into you because of idiotic peer pressure, and it was totally her fault."

"Did I? I didn't notice."

"Where did you learn to talk like that?"

"From the same person who taught me to fight." He grinned at her and then took on a more serious tone. "Listen, Mark won't let this go. As soon as Gin tells him what I meant, he'll feel the need for revenge. We need to be more careful for a while."

Sam smiled. "I can take care of myself, but I do worry about you."

"Don't worry about me. I'm nobody, but they're legitimately afraid of you. And that worries me. I've seen scared people do some idiotic things." He stopped and turned her to face him. "I know you don't want to talk about what you can do, and I won't push you, but the whole group kept their distance from you. And I saw the hate in their eyes. You're in danger, and they want to do you harm."

She smiled sadly up at Trey. "Harm can't come to me, Trey. It comes to those around me."

Trey started to open his mouth, but she put a finger to his lips. "We'll talk later. I promise. Now let's get to class before we're up all night in detention."

Despite the encounter with the Hellspawn, Trey managed to get a cup from DM Coffee before class. He was paying for it now. Even though Introduction to Galactic Law turned out to be one of his favorite courses, at this point, he could do nothing but squirm and wait for the lecture to end. The professor currently expounded on the general covenants that allowed the Galactic Council to administer to 208 planets in relative peace. The class covered everything from trade law to different cultures's rules toward magic. He found most of it fascinating. The class was an entry-level course, but he had already made up his mind to add this thread to his course study. If it came to pass that he wasn't much of a magician, the Knights could surely use a lawyer on the team. Trey smiled to himself. All the time he'd spent with them made him positive they could.

Sam admitted she had hated the class when she took it, although she still managed high marks. She'd never been off Berol—her home —and saw no reason to leave. She told him that as soon as she "got a handle" on her abilities, she was headed right back to the farm. "Animals are easier to deal with than people, and less judgmental," she had said.

She wasn't fooling him, though. Her family owned a large *kafer* farm run by her father, but her mother was a renowned astrocartographer specializing in ripspace holes and pathways. Sam may not have the wanderlust now, but Trey knew it was in her blood.

In thinking about her, he realized he had missed some of the teacher's lecture. He needed to quit doing that. He also knew he wasn't going to get through the last twenty minutes of class without making a puddle. He raised his hand.

"Yes, Mr. Julien," Professor Allax, a rotund Maranan with drooping ears and a large nose, said.

"May I be excused for the restroom?"

"Make it quick." He waved a large hand in a dismissive gesture.

Trey nodded and pushed a button on his desk. The recorder clicked on. It would capture what he missed while he was gone.

Trey hit the empty bathroom and headed to the far stall. Hawk liked to joke about his back teeth floating; Trey knew what that meant now.

As he washed his hands, the door opened. He glanced up in the mirror, and his heart dropped. A broadly grinning Mark and four of his cronies walked in. Trey dropped his head and shook it back and forth. *Stupid, stupid, stupid,* he thought. Then he wondered why they weren't in class. Were they waiting for him on the off-chance he would have to use the restroom? *That's dedication*, he thought wryly. More than likely, they spotted him while skipping class—just his luck.

With a sense of inevitability dancing over him, Trey faced the group. "What do you want, Mark?"

"Go outside and watch the door," Mark told one of the other blue shirt boys.

"But I want in on some of this," the young man protested.

Mark's nostrils flared. "I said go," he snapped. "And don't let anyone come in. Yell if a teacher shows up."

The boy jumped back in fear and left the room. Mark returned his attention to Trey. "Your girlfriend isn't here to protect you now, squirt."

"Yes, yes. You're great, I'm not worthy, apologies all around." As he spoke, Trey slowly drifted away from the sinks. Mark's large black eyes followed every step, but he didn't try to stop Trey. "Now, why don't you let me go."

When he reached an empty section of the wall, Trey pressed his back against it and pulled up his right leg, placing the bottom of his foot against the flat surface.

"Not this time," Mark said. "You need to learn some manners." Three of them stood facing Trey, Mark in the middle, cohorts on either side. The fourth splashed water on the floor near the door.

"Speaking of manners, four on one isn't very chivalrous. What would the professors say?"

"Who cares? We're going to be your teachers today. Gin said you might want this." Mark lifted his arm. Between his thumb and forefinger, he held up Trey's communicator pin.

Trey instinctively reached up to the pin's usual position near his collarbone. The bio tape still clung to his skin, minus the pin. How had they gotten it from him? When?

Trey's eyes narrowed. "That's mine, and I want it back," he said through gritted teeth. "Now."

Mark chuckled. "I have to admit, you are cool under pressure. If you weren't so lame, you could join us. Instead, I'm going to stomp your ass and keep your little pin as a souvenir."

"This isn't going to end the way you think."

"Oh, your tough-guy talk really scares me. You're about to slip and fall on a wet, soapy floor. You should be more…"

Using his right leg, Trey launched from the wall like a coiled spring.

Allax looked up with an inquisitive slant to his bushy eyebrow as Trey returned from the restroom. His large ears twitched. "Mister Julien, may I ask what took you so long? You seem a little disheveled."

A spate of chuckles from the other students quickly went silent at a glare from the teacher.

Trey brushed at the front of his shirt, checked to make sure his pin was back in place, and ran his fingers through his brown hair, which had grown back to a reasonable length since he had been here. "It seems Mark and some of his friends were in the bathroom and fell on a wet, soapy floor."

"I see," the teacher said as he stood. "Seems to be an epidemic around here." The teacher stood. "Are they alright?"

Trey slumped into his seat with a grunt and a wince of pain. He pressed his hand against his side. "They'll survive, but Mark might need a medic."

No sooner was Professor Allax out the door than chatter broke out among the other students, many of them casting envious or concerned glances at Trey.

He sighed. No longer fueled by adrenaline and anger, he knew the fight was a mistake. There would be repercussions, certainly from the school, and possibly from the Hellspawn. He caught them off-guard this time. Next time they wouldn't announce their intentions.

Sam found him in the hallway after class. "Are you okay? What happened? I told you to be careful. Why didn't you wait for me? I—"

Trey reached up and put a finger gently to her lips. It amazed him word about the scuffle got around so quickly, although after his time here seeing the gossip network's efficiency, it shouldn't have. Smiling wearily and doing his best to hide the pain from the bruising hits to his side, he said, "We'll talk later, I promise."

Two hours later, he sat in the foyer outside of Master Genray's office. He had been summoned here as soon as classes ended. No surprise there.

More unexpected was the half-hour wait while Genray and four other administrators discussed his fate. Trey could hear the some-times-heated exchanges through the door, but nothing discernable came from the muffled voices. The longer the adults debated, the more nervous Trey grew. Sweat near dripped from his armpits, and with dismay, he realized he needed a shower. He didn't know what he would do if he got expelled. He wasn't sure which would be more excruciating: the expulsion or the disappointment of his family on Ship.

Trey jumped as the door swung open and barely suppressed a squeal of fright. The administrators filed out, none of them making eye contact. He tried to gauge his fate based on their expressions but could get nothing. Some of them seemed amused, and others appeared visibly upset. Professor Allax dared to meet his gaze. The Galactic Law instructor gave him a small smile and a wink. Trey prepared to let loose a sigh of relief until he spotted the frowning Master Genray standing in the doorway. Trey swallowed the sigh and straightened up in his chair.

"Sit right there, Mister Julien." Master Genray said. The severe disappointment in his voice made Trey's stomach drop. "I have a call to make, and then I will get to you."

After the door closed, Trey slumped back in his chair. *Crap*, Trey thought as his heart sank. *I thought Master Genray would at least be sympathetic.*

He didn't know why, but he suddenly found himself wishing Sam were there.

"Yes, apparently the ensuing beating was thorough and mostly one-sided." Master Genray said, his disapproving face looking at them in holographic projection.

Hawk, Ashron, and Gerard were gathered in the wardroom when the call came in from Master Genray. True to form, the entire crew had returned early from their vacations. They didn't enjoy dawdling, and each came back with full to-do lists. Wolf helped Ship oversee the new upgrade's software installation, and Laura was ordering supplies for the medical bay.

"I see," Hawk said, fingers steepled in front of his face. "Will the young men be alright?"

"Again, yes. They suffered abrasions and bruising for the most part, but the group leader also suffered two broken bones and a dislocation."

Damn, Hawk thought, glancing over to Ashron.

"Terrible, just terrible," Ashron said, doing his best to keep the pride out of his voice. "You know I do not condone such behavior." His grin revealed a whole snout of teeth, and his cat-like eyes sparkled.

"Clearly not." Hawk didn't hide his sarcasm.

"As his combat instructor, my interest is purely academic in nature." Ashron took a long pull from his drink, another of the concoctions he enjoyed that the rest of the crew found semi-toxic.

"I don't believe you," Hawk said flatly.

Ashron sat up in his chair, his forked tongue flicking, and held his arms out to encompass the others, including the holographic Genray. "Fine, I'll say it. I'm proud of him. From what you've told us, Genray, the leader of those boys is a bully who outweighs Trey by a sizable margin. Trey did exactly what was necessary. He was cornered in the restroom with nowhere to go, so he used textbook speed, surprise, and violence of action. Take out the biggest one quickly and decisively and in such a manner to leave no question for the others of your intent and resolve. That's why his minions had nothing more than bruising and abrasions. They lost their nerve." Ashron's tongue again flicked back and forth through his smile.

Gerard looked up from the small motor lying disassembled on the table. "If I recall correctly, someone once said, 'Bother no one. If someone bothers you, ask him to stop. If he doesn't stop, destroy him.'"

"A quote taken out of context," Hawk said with a dismissive wave of his hand.

Gerard grinned and returned to his work.

"He's one of my crew," Hawk told Genray, "so I'll take responsibility. What do you need from me?"

"I knew that would be your reaction, but I don't need anything. We will deal with the matter. He's not going to be expelled for defending himself. Nor are the other boys. But after they complete their punishment, they may wish they had been. And I suspect whoever gave him the contraband communication device will hear Trey's side of the story."

"What's going on?" Laura asked as she walked into the room.

Hawk and Ashron suddenly grew interested in looking anywhere other than at Laura.

"Thank you for letting us know, Master Genray," Gerard said. "When we return for the ceremony, we'll discuss it with Trey. Hawk out."

"Genray out," the Berolian said. The hologram disappeared.

"Discuss what?" Laura asked in irritation. Her blue eyes locked on Ashron with laser intensity. "Did Trey get in trouble because of the pin you gave him?" she asked Ashron.

"Captain, Gerard," Ship said. "Dr. LaRouche and Wolf are ready to discuss the current iteration of the software."

"LaRouche is a pain in the ass," Hawk said as he stood from his seat. "But I can't fault her timing." He grinned at Ashron. "I'll let you handle this."

"It's complicated," Ashron said, watching in envy as Hawk and Gerard fled Laura's wrath.

"I'm intelligent, and I've got plenty of time," Laura said. "Feel free to explain."

Trey almost worked himself into a state of panic waiting for Master Genray to return. It took all his will to hold back tears as the certainty of expulsion weighed on him. What other options did the headmaster have?

The office door opened a second time, and Trey looked up from staring at the floor. Genray's pale face betrayed nothing of his conversation with Ship's crew. Master Genray had said he needed to make "a call," as if setting a doctor's appointment. But Trey wasn't stupid; he knew the headmaster reached out to Hawk and the others to give them the bad news.

Master Genray motioned for Trey to enter. Trey stood on shaking legs and walked into the office.

Despite his frightened concern, Trey couldn't help but notice the immaculate cleanliness of Master Genray's office. Trey appreciated that, being a great fan of order himself. The world was chaotic enough without adding to it.

Memorabilia from Master Genray's travels occupied various areas of the office, all labeled and displayed. Trey's trips to multiple planets in his two years with the Knights taught him a great deal about artifacts, and Wolf and Gerard owned quite a collection between them from assorted worlds, but the headmaster's put theirs to shame.

Exotic flora extended from pots or hung from planters on the ceiling. The riot of colorful plants threatened to engulf Trey's already overwrought nerves. Some of the plants seemed to follow him as he crossed the room. It gave him the creeps.

Stop it, he told himself. He had survived on a planet where death ruled the day. He could handle expulsion. It would hurt, but he would endure it.

It surprised him to realize that as when he first arrived, he might have preferred expulsion since it would have sent him back to Ship. Now he dreaded it and how letting the crew down made him feel.

He reached Master Genray's desk. In contrast to the rest of the room, the desk, made of dark-colored wood and covered with intricate carvings of mystical symbols, was a mess. Books and papers covered it, along with readers, various types of rocks, and writing utensils. Two chairs, deep blood red, sat in front of the desk. They were fashioned from animal skin, but Trey had no idea what sort of beast it might have been. He chose the one on the right.

As he slipped into the chair, the smooth fabric did nothing to soothe his nerves. It wasn't an overly large seat, but he felt like a small child sitting in it, which had nothing to do with the chair's size and everything to do with the situation. How had Hawk and the others reacted when Genray told them their prized cabin boy—no, he was more, he reminded himself—was going to be expelled? He was a member of the crew. Had been officially made a Knight of the Flaming Star. Now he was a disgrace, a failure at his first assignment. Were they disappointed with him? Of course they were. How could they be anything but? Would they expel him from the Knights too? Take away his uniform?

The idea made him want to cry. Frustration at his inability to control himself raged in him. He wanted to be a magician. No, he wanted to be a Preternatural Scientist, like Gerard. After getting rejected from the best school, would any others even consider him?

He thought about Sam. They became fast friends within the first week, both outcasts in their own way. Over the weeks, their friendship had grown. They had no need for anyone but each other. Early on, she confessed she had no friends before he showed up, everyone afraid to either befriend or offend her. Everyone but the Hellspawn, and even they pushed things only so far. What would Sam do when he left? As tears threatened to overwhelm him, Trey let out a heavy sigh and slumped back in his seat.

Master Genray took a seat at the desk, his colorless eyes regarding Trey. "Sit up, young man."

Trey did so and wiped at his eyes. He would not cry in front of the headmaster. Knights didn't cry. At least not when people could see them.

"You have put me in a predicament, Mister Julien. Are you aware of who Mark's parents are?"

"No, sir."

"No reason you should be. Suffice to say, they have power and influence and money. Those three things have been the bane of sentient existence since the first living being spoke to the second. And they are a bane for me. Mark's parents want you expelled. And according to our charter, you must be expelled."

Trey nodded, his chin jutting out and quivering. "I understand, sir." He moved to stand up from his chair.

Genray held up a hand. "But I'm not a fan of bullies. Or of bullies' sons. Some of my staff are not in agreement with me on this. They feel we must stick to the letter of the charter. For myself, I think we must stick to the spirit."

Trey sat up straighter, afraid to believe what he heard. Was Master Genray offering the possibility Trey could stay? He didn't dare smile yet, much as he wanted to.

"I know your history," Genray continued, the expression on his pale face grave. "Or as much as Gerard has shared with me. You've seen things I would wish on no one, much less a child. Things Mark or his parents wouldn't begin to understand. I explained this to the disciplinary board, which was the people you saw leave here. I convinced all but one of them. My decision will saddle me with a great deal of grief from certain quarters, but I can handle that. Before I give your punishment, for there must be some atonement, I have one question, and I want you to answer me truthfully. Can you do that?"

"Yes, sir."

"Did you act in self-defense?"

"Yes, sir." Trey swallowed, knowing he had to tell the whole truth. "But I could have stopped before I did. I kicked Mark after he was down. I couldn't stop myself. I just—"

Now Trey broke down, and the tears came. He couldn't help

himself. During the fight, Mark represented everything Trey thought he left behind on Kel. The death and destruction; the need to defend himself or hide from bigger, stronger things. To kowtow to bullies. Mark became all those things, and Trey couldn't stop hurting him. Hurting *them*, as if his past tormentors could feel what he did to the unconscious boy at his feet.

If Mark's cohorts hadn't interfered, taking their own bruises and scrapes, Trey didn't know how far he might have gone. It scared him to consider what might have happened, and he cried harder.

Genray sat and watched the weeping boy. He had not meant to push him into such a breakdown. According to Gerard, the boy's time with the Knights worked wonders for him, but this display showed Genray the child still needed a great deal of help. With some others, Genray may have followed through with the expulsion to avoid the repercussions. As much as he didn't like to admit it, some students weren't worth the extra effort or potential headaches. Trey was worth it. He could face the wrath for someone as gifted and in need of guidance as the sobbing child sitting before him. Genray couldn't do otherwise and consider himself a teacher or molder of minds.

He opened a drawer and reached inside, where he kept a box of tissues. Trey wasn't the first student to shed tears in his presence. He sat the box where Trey could reach it, leaned forward, and placed his hands on the desk. "Trey, I've spoken to Hawk. You're not going to be expelled, but –"

POP!

A wave of force pushed Genray back against his chair and rolled it backward. Before it stopped, he had jumped to his feet with a formula on his lips.

Trey was gone.

He had disappeared. No light, no movement. A sound like a firecracker had gone through the room, and the boy wasn't in his seat.

Genray closed his eyes and spoke a formula, different from the one he had prepared. An alarm sounded, and a dome of blue light descended on the school, closing it off to the outside world. Nothing would be able to come or go unless he gave the order. Knowing he needed to confer with others in the school to determine what the hell had happened, he headed for the door.

4

METAMORPHOSIS

"All systems operational and within parameters," Ship said. "Do you concur, Dr. LaRouche?"

The crew stood on the bridge and stared at several displays of numbers, waves, and graphs floating in the air. Hawk had no idea what most of the displays meant, which was why he had a crew that did. They still had a week of fine tuning and stationary tests before heading out to do a shakedown and spec study overseen by Gerard and Wolf.

"I concur," LaRouche said, her hologram staring at all of them from above the displays. "You understand the engagement protocols, Wolf?"

"I do," Wolf said in his deep voice. "Although I'm not comfortable yet. Henna, your team are masters of blurring the tech magic line, but this seems at great risk of causing a rift."

"And I'm not certain I understand what I've let you strap on to my ship," Hawk said.

"The basic concept is simple enough even you should be able to understand it," LaRouche said, taking on the pedantic tone that made Hawk want to punch her, female or not. "It's a combination shield and cloaking device that leaves no mechanical or magical signature. It's true invisibility and partial invulnerability on a large scale."

"The basic idea is fine," Gerard responded. "I'm still not convinced the process is correct."

"What's wrong with the process?" Ashron asked.

Gerard offered him a flat expression. "Do you really want me to explain?"

"I guess not, since my eyes would cross after three words."

"The process is within acceptable risk," LaRouche said. "And there are safeguards should anything go awry. But it's a prototype, which is why we're testing it on a small vessel such as yours. And why we are having these debates now, before you head out." She arched an eyebrow at Hawk. "And don't think of it as 'letting' me, Captain. As a Force 13 operative, your hands were tied."

"I could have lodged a protest," Hawk said.

"And miss the chance of being on the cutting edge?" she asked. "That's not the Knights I know."

"I see a few things we can optimize," Gerard said as he made notes on his datapad. "Let me write them up and get them to the lead engineer. Should only take them a day to implement."

LaRouche sighed. "If we must. I guess I shouldn't complain; we're ahead of schedule. Which is unusual for the idiots I've got working for me."

Hawk said in his most disarming voice, "A team is only as good as their leader."

"Right," LaRouche answered in a tone that showed she missed none of Hawk's sarcasm. She turned her gaze to Ashron. "Did you receive the package I added for you?"

"I did," Ashron said. "I assume it's the same idea on a smaller scale."

"It is."

"What is—" Hawk started.

"Sorry, Captain," Ship said over the speakers. "But Master Genray is on the comm, and he said it's urgent."

Hawk frowned. "Patch him in."

Genray appeared on a hologram next to LaRouche. One look at

the troubled expression on the man's pale face told Hawk something was—

"What's wrong?" Laura blurted out, voice tense as she stared at the headmaster.

"Trey has disappeared. And before you ask, no, he didn't run away."

"Then what do you mean, 'disappeared?' Did someone kidnap him? Did those boys—"

Genray held up a hand to stop her. "I mean he disappeared. One moment he was sitting in my office and the next he was gone. I sealed off the school, and the staff and I performed both a physical and magical search for him. We also questioned the students, especially the ones who participated in the recent altercation. They were as baffled as us. And in any case, none of them are near advanced enough to do something like that, even if we taught it to students so young."

"Then where the hell *is* he?"

Genray shrugged, and his face became a mask of misery. "I wish I knew. We're considering every option and coming up with the next course of action."

"We're on the way," Hawk said. "Four days transit time. You'll let us know if you hear anything before we arrive."

"Of course," Genray said.

"But the optimizations and trials—"

"Can damn well wait," Hawk said, cutting LaRouche off. "Lift us to the surface so we can get into the air. Unless you want me to cut on the engines and try to blast my way out of here."

Hawk couldn't tell for sure over the hologram, but it appeared like LaRouche paled at the idea. "Of course," the scientist agreed. "I'll get you out now. But if you get a chance—"

"We'll test it if we can and make notes," Gerard said. Seeing LaRouche was not mollified, he added, "We can even do remote optimizations if circumstances permit. Now, get us out of here."

As LaRouche's hologram dissolved, Hawk turned his attention back to Genray. The man was the very picture of emotional agony, his pale face contorted. "Master Genray, this isn't your fault. You're a teacher, not a fortune teller. Keep us informed and let me know of any progress."

"Of course," Genray nodded, and he, too, faded out.

A deep *kerchunk* sound reverberated through Ship, followed by grinding gears. The vessel vibrated as the lift began returning them to the planet's surface.

"Ship, can you reach him on Ashron's pin?" Hawk asked, glad the Lorothian had slipped the contraband device to the boy, despite the recent trouble it caused.

"No, Captain. That's the first thing I tried. I pinged it and got no response. But I know he's still alive."

"How do you know?" Laura asked, her voice a heartbreaking mixture of hope and disbelief.

"I'm not certain. I've never experienced it before. I can't sense any of you, and I've never sensed anyone living before now, but somehow I can feel Trey."

"Can you pinpoint his location?" Laura asked.

"No. It's like when you hear a faint sound in a large room. You can tell it's there, but it's not always easy to tell where it came from. And there's..." she paused. "Lots of distraction to filter here. It's just a general knowledge of his essence, as if he's floating somewhere in the *aether*. Sorry, I can't explain it better."

"That's okay." Laura closed her eyes. "I'm relieved to know he's still alive."

Ship's tone changed to her more professional voice. "Captain, the port tower says Dr. LaRouche has set us for emergency priority departure. Ten minutes for the lift to reach the surface, then we have authorization to depart. After I launch, we'll be outside planetary influence and safe to rip at plus seven minutes twenty-six seconds."

"Let's get secure and ready," Hawk said. "Ship, tell LaRouche we're going to engage her device when we depart, and she can see if we're detectable. Might as well get some data that doesn't involve someone shooting at us."

"Aye, Captain."

Everyone moved to their duties. Ten minutes wasn't a lot of prep time, but his crew knew their jobs. Despite the concerned tension in his shoulders, Hawk was confident in their professionalism as he prepared to go through his pre-launch checklist with Ship.

It was time to go find their lost crew member.

Laura could not remember a longer or more nerve-frazzling time aboard Ship. Only halfway through the four-day travel back to Berol, she already wanted to beat her head against the wall. She had divided the endless hours in the starless depths of ripspace between roaming aimlessly and attending half-heartedly to any number of undone tasks. She took a strange solace in the rest of the crew's demeanor. They were in no better emotional shape than her.

She wandered into the wardroom and found Hawk sitting there, a cup of coffee on the table before him. She reflected that, not so long ago, it would have been a bottle of alcohol, and he would have spent much of the trip drunk and in his cabin. She liked this version of Hawk much better. They had received no further news from either Ship or Master Genray. Ship confirmed she could still "feel" Trey's presence, but other than that, she had nothing to report. It had been a long two days. No one knew what to do or say. Mostly they kept themselves busy on minor projects they had put off for one reason or another—anything to keep their minds occupied.

Hawk glanced up as she walked to the table and sat.

"How are you doing?" she asked.

He shrugged. "Wondering if we're ever going to be able to put that boy someplace where he doesn't get in trouble. You'd think a school full of powerful Pre Scis would be the safest place possible."

Laura nodded. "You would think," she agreed.

They sat in silence. There wasn't anything else to say. Hawk reflected on how much he usually enjoyed the quiet and blankness of ripspace, but now the time pressed on him. Even though he had no idea what they could do to help when they reached Berol, being able to do anything other than pace through Ship trying to find ways to pass the time would be a relief.

"Do you think—" Laura began.

"Everyone," Ship said over the loudspeakers. "Trey has returned. He is in his room."

"Back at school?" Laura asked.

"No, right here on board."

Laura arrived first, followed closely by Hawk, then Ashron. Trey lay curled on his bed in the fetal position. His skin was an unhealthy shade of gray, and his lips trembled.

Laura dropped beside him, placed one hand to his forehead and the other against his wrist. "He's freezing. Let's get him to the Med Bay."

Ashron scooped him up and headed for the door, with Laura and Hawk close behind. They found Gerard in the hallway, walking toward them. "Headed to sickbay," the Lorothian said as he turned sideways to slip past Gerard. Wolf stepped into a side doorway as they passed, and then he fell in behind them.

The rest of the team crowded into the sickbay while Wolf stood in the doorway. Trey lay on the examination table looking frail and close to death, his breathing shallow. Monitors spelled out his condition as Laura ran a scanner over him from head to toe.

"Hypothermia and severe dehydration," Laura said as she inserted an IV in his arm. "We need to warm him up. I need someone to grab warm blankets."

"I've got them," Gerard said and left the room.

Laura turned up the temperature on the examination table. "Ship, raise the room temperature to thirty-two, leave it for ten minutes, then lower it to twenty-eight over another ten minutes."

"Done."

Gerard returned with several blankets draped over his golden arm, which let off a slight glow. Laura took them from him and, with Ashron's help, carefully wrapped Trey in a cocoon. Up to this point, Trey had made no sounds. After Laura finished the wrapping, the boy emitted a moan.

Hawk put a gentle hand on Laura's arm and wiped a tear from her cheek. "What can we do?"

"Wait. Pray." She raised her shoulders and looked at the rest of them. "He's young and strong. There's nothing physiologically wrong with him that I can detect, so I don't know why he's unconscious. I'll stay by his side and let you know if there are any changes."

"Copy," Hawk said. "Ship, contact Master Genray and let him know he can call off his search. We'll let him know what we learn as soon as we can."

"Aye, Captain."

The crew filed out of the room, leaving Laura beside the unconscious Trey.

What the hell happened? Hawk wondered.

Hawk sat in his study, trying to read without much success. The mystery of Trey's disappearance gnawed at him. He had some familiarity with magic, having once possessed the ability until he gave it all up in a failed effort to bring his beloved Sara back from death.

Ship came over the central comm. "Laura wanted to let you all know Trey is awake."

Hawk smiled. *Not a total failure*, he thought. Sara had come back, though not in a way any of them ever imagined. "On my way."

He arrived last to sickbay as his quarters sat furthest away, off the bridge's berthing area. Trey, still swaddled in blankets, rested against a stack of three pillows. Though awake, he had the appearance of someone on the losing end of a long, nasty fight. Dark circles lay under his wide, frightened eyes, and splotchy gray patches covered his visible skin.

He looks terrible, Hawk thought. *Even worse than when he lost his arm.*

The rest of the crew regarded him with uncertain expressions as

Laura ran the scanner over him and spoke to him in a low voice. Hawk couldn't tell what she said, but it seemed to be doing little to reduce the boy's disorientation. He stared at some unseen distance with wide, far-away eyes.

Hawk pushed past Ashron and stopped beside the bed. "Mister Julien," Hawk said, command in his voice.

Trey's eyes snapped to him as the rest of the crew offered expressions of shock or confusion at Hawk's tone, while Laura's face more resembled outright horror. She started to retort, but Hawk held up a hand.

Hawk continued with an authoritative voice. "Mister Julien, report. You have been AWOL for two days. You've disrupted Ship's movement and delayed trials for newly fitted equipment. That is conduct unbecoming, young man. Explain your behavior."

Hawk crossed his arms and waited. Laura's jaw gaped. She wanted to scream at Hawk for this outrageous behavior to a patient in shock. As ship's doctor, she could override him in any decision regarding care, but she withheld, hoping this tactic would help more than hurt.

After several seconds, in which Hawk had time to wonder if he miscalculated and pushed the boy too hard, Trey straightened himself in the bed. His eyes lost their frightened appearance, and he opened his mouth to speak.

Before he could say anything, Hawk smiled and winked at him. "At ease. You had us worried sick." He leaned over and gave the boy a gentle hug. The others visibly relaxed. "You seemed like you needed an anchor."

"I did," Trey said as Hawk leaned back.

"Rest some more, and when you're ready, you can tell us what happened. As you can imagine, we're more than a little curious."

"I'm downright busting with the need to know," Ashron said. "Tell us now."

"When you're ready," Hawk repeated.

"I'm ready," Trey said, his voice weak and reedy.

"No, you need to rest some more," Laura told him.

"I can rest while I talk," Trey said. "Something important and strange has happened, and all of you need to know."

Laura's frown showed everyone exactly what she thought of the idea, but she nodded. "If you're sure."

"I am. But can we go to the wardroom? I don't like it here."

"That we can," Hawk said. "And this time, I'm serving you."

5

REVELATIONS OF CHAOS

Hawk carried a cup of hot tea to Trey, who lay curled up in one of the wardroom's softer chairs, blankets still wrapped around him. Hawk was glad to see some color had returned to the young man's face. Something in his hazel eyes made him appear older, as if he had seen things he shouldn't have. Of course, Trey had witnessed horrific things men five times his age had never seen.

"Thanks," Trey said as he reached for the offered cup from Hawk. The rest of them held their drinks in hand, and Ashron had taken the opportunity to fix a snack. Hawk grabbed his coffee cup from Wolf and sat down across from Trey.

"Alright, Trey. As requested, we are all ears." Hawk sipped his coffee and waited.

Trey stared at all the eyes fixed on him, faces at turns worried and expectant. He didn't know where to begin or exactly how to tell them what happened. He downed half the cup of tea and repressed a shiver that ran through him. Though he was warmer and safe, the chill of where he had been still clung to him, unwilling to depart.

The crew waited, none of them wanting to push him. He appreciated their concern, as Ship was the one home he had known since his family's death at his hands. The Knights had become his family, and despite all that had happened to him, he considered himself lucky. Sometimes he felt more fortunate than he deserved. More than he—

He shook his head. They were waiting for him to speak, and he was drifting off track. They still watched him. Everyone but Ashron; he was too busy eating. Trey smiled, took another sip, and set his cup on the table beside his chair. Another shiver racked him as the bitter cold roiled through his body. *Ship, turn up the heat, please.*

He unwrapped himself from his blankets and started to stand up. Laura moved to the edge of her seat but stopped as Trey held up a hand. "I'm okay. You all need to see something." He got to his feet, unsteady but determined to do it himself.

"Ship, did you turn up the heat?" Hawk asked.

"I did," she said. "At Trey's request."

"What?"

Trey smiled again. That was only the beginning.

As Trey pulled his shirt over his head, Ashron said, "What are you doing?"

Trey turned around to show the crew his back.

Laura sucked in a quick breath of air. Hawk and Gerard sat up and leaned forward in their chairs so they could get a better view. Even Ashron stopped in mid-chew and stared.

"What is that?" Hawk asked in a whisper.

An intricate symbol covered the entirety of Trey's lean back. Black lines ran in random patterns, intersecting at odd angles and creating designs disturbing in their intensity. The bizarre nature was made worse by the apparent depth of the lines. As Trey shivered, the lines appeared to move in their own directions, not attached to the skin. Hawk wanted to close his eyes and turn away but couldn't.

"Trey is talking to me without his communicator pin," Ship told them. "He can hear me and speak to me without it."

"How is that possible?" Laura asked.

"That's the story he wants me to tell you."

Trey sat in Genray's office, tears staining his face, waiting for the news of his expulsion. Genray stared at him, his pale face unreadable. Trey waited, wiping at his eyes as more water poured from them.

Genray opened a drawer, took out a box of tissues, and set them in front of Trey. Then he placed his elbows on the desk. "Trey, I've spoken to Hawk. You're not going to be expelled, but—"

A chill wind blew directly through Trey's soul. His vision blurred as Master Genray folded in on himself, followed by the office, which compressed into a pinpoint and disappeared.

For the flash of an instant, nearly too quick to notice, cacophony and chaos rolled over Trey, as if all the sound, fury, pain, and joy of the universe converged on him. It squeezed, threatened to crush him.

And then it vanished, and he found himself floating in emptiness. Cold wrapped around him, numbing any other sensation. He stood on nothing, and nothing surrounded him.

"Help," he tried to say, but no sound came out. He pumped his legs and moved nowhere. He brought his arms up. Though all around him appeared dark, he could see himself. It was as if he emitted light that went no further than his immediate area.

Something moved at the corner of his vision. He spun his head to catch it, but it disappeared.

More movement, ripples in the void like fish in the water. A few at first, then more and more, until the entire surface looked alive. But still, he heard nothing nor felt anything other than the bone-numbing cold.

All at once, the ripples stopped, and creatures from his darkest nightmares surrounded Trey.

He released a silent scream.

"It was the ripspace creatures."

Ship spoke Trey's thoughts as he stood motionless, arms outstretched, back to the crew. "They called themselves Kuthrallie, as near as I can make it. They created an environment where I could breathe, but they had no concept of temperature. It was so bitterly cold I could barely think. When I recovered from the shock of seeing them, I realized they weren't going to kill me, and they hadn't driven me insane."

"Obviously, we are going to have to revise our way of thinking," Gerard said.

———

Trey stared at the creatures as they stared at him. At least, he assumed they stared at him. They had no eyes. No sense organs of any sort, near as he could tell. They reminded him of giant worms with armored, segmented rings. They undulated in place, sinuous and eerie.

"Hello," he tried to say, and again no noise came from him.

Hello, he thought.

The creatures moved, twisting around each other. A low burbling radiated around Trey. It was more a feeling that thrummed through him than a sound.

Hello, he thought again.

The worms moved faster. They were hearing him, or at least sensing his thoughts, and tried to respond.

For a moment, his sense of excitement overtook the fear and numbing cold.

———

"As I tried to communicate with them," Ship continued Trey's narrative, her voice almost machine-like in its cadence. "I began to realize what I had first thought was nothingness was more. I could see galaxies and planets, but faint and wavering. It was like when you look at something hot. Shimmering in heatwaves. They appeared far apart, and yet..." she paused as if considering. "More accessible. I'm not really getting his point across."

"I don't know how long I was there. It seemed like days. I was hungry and thirsty and cold. Always so cold. We kept talking, or thinking, to each other. It wasn't like we learned language. They don't have language, at least not like we do. It was more like we attuned to each other. As if our minds grew to know each other."

Please, Trey thought. *I'm hungry and thirsty.*

The creatures undulated in agitation. No matter how Trey tried, he couldn't get the Kuthrallie to understand those concepts. The Kuthrallie survived on the essence surrounding them. In that way, they were like fish in water. Trey could not get them to realize he couldn't survive this environment.

I must return to my home, he tried. *If I don't, I'll die.*

Die? the collective thought asked him.

Cease to exist, Trey thought. *No longer be.* Thinking of death in such terms terrified Trey, but he needed to make them understand, or the abstract concept would become a reality, and that frightened him even more.

For a long time, they offered nothing to him. Trey shivered, wanting to be home, wanting them to understand—needing them to understand.

When he thought he might scream at their lack of response, a scream that would have made no sound and accomplished nothing, they finally reached out to him.

We do not want you to cease, they told him. He wanted to cry, but the cold numbness wouldn't let him. *You are important. We need you to continue. We have not comprehended. We will return you. But first, we wish you to take a message to others of your kind.*

Trey slipped his shirt back on and turned around to find the crew staring at him, their faces a mixture of uncertainty and amazement. They looked like they weren't sure he hadn't gone mad. He flopped back into the chair, shivered, and pulled the blankets around himself, again chilled. "They said a great threat was coming to an uninhabited part of the known universe, and we needed to stop it. I can show you the way but can't tell you how to get there. It's through an undiscovered rip. It's—" He stopped, picked up his tea, and took another sip. "It's easier to do than explain."

He settled back in the chair and closed his eyes again, exhausted, cold, and nauseated. It was almost like his body had forgotten the sensation of physical matter.

Gerard spoke first. "That is a lot to digest. I have so many threads to follow; I don't know where to start."

Trey opened his eyes and gave a weak smile. "I could write a book."

"So, you can talk to Ship without a communicator?" Ashron asked.

Gerard stared at Ashron. "That's what you got out of what happened? Not that Trey apparently traveled light-years through ripspace without the use of a spaceship? Or he was suspended either in time or perhaps *aether* itself? Or even that he survived contact with beings from another dimension we always assumed were inimical to our existence?"

"Well yeah, that's important stuff if you want to think things through, I guess. But I still think being able to communicate telepathically is pretty cool." Ashron reached for his mustard and added a copious amount to his already covered snack.

"I can do that," Gerard said.

"Yeah, but could you do it when you were thirteen? And can you do it with Ship?"

Gerard shook his head with a rueful grin and glanced at Hawk, who nodded for him to continue.

"I guess I have to start somewhere," he said to Trey. "Do you know what that symbol is on your back? How it got there? What it's for?"

Trey sipped from his mug.

Hawk stood and moved over to Trey. "Here, let me warm that up for you." He took Trey's mug and headed for the galley.

Trey snuggled deeper into his blankets and yawned. "I have no idea what it's for. They applied it after I had been there for a long time. At least what seemed like a long time, it was hard to tell. Maybe after they began to understand I was dying. It's funny, I can't see it, but I know it's there."

"Does it hurt?"

Trey shook his head. "It doesn't itch, and it doesn't even pull my skin. I can't feel it on me, but I feel it here." He pulled a hand from under the blanket and pointed at his head. "I don't know how it got there. Just at some point, I could tell it was there. Not much help, am I?"

"Did you pick it up on your scan?" Gerard asked Laura.

She shook her head. "No, nothing. Something like that should have definitely shown up."

Turning back to Trey, Gerard said, "When you finally warm back up, we will want to get a closer inspection of your new artwork."

"Here you go," Hawk held out another steaming mug to Trey.

"Thanks," Trey said, smiling up at him.

Hawk sat in front of Trey. "Mind if I cut in for a moment, Gerard?"

"Not at all," Gerard replied.

"Trey, you said something about a threat we needed to stop. I'm going to assume a sense of urgency given the rather extreme tactics these beings used to deliver this message."

"The Kuthrallie," Trey told him.

"Yes, the Kuthrallie. You said it was an uninhabited area. Then why is there a threat?"

"They said it's not the location, but what they're going to do there."

"Who? The Kuthrallie?"

"No, something else. They couldn't say what, only where." He frowned. "Or if they did, I couldn't understand them. Sorry."

"It's okay," Hawk assured him. "You're handling this better than I would."

Trey didn't believe it for a second, but he appreciated the thought.

"Can you give us any insight on where to begin?" Hawk asked.

"I think so." Trey closed his eyes again and spoke out loud so they all could hear. "Ship, do you know where this is? I'm showing her a…I don't quite know how to describe it, 'picture of a location' is the best way I can come up with."

"It's a special map of a remote system. The information is incomplete, but with some triangulation, I think I can locate it... Got it. Sorry it took so long."

Hawk smiled. "You're slipping."

"It's several parsecs past explored space with nothing that would seem to indicate a reason to search further. Based strictly on location, the nearest jurisdictional claim would belong to the Berolian government."

"That's convenient," Hawk said. "We were headed there anyway. Ship, contact Grendarin and tell him we'll want to meet him at the safehouse in Berolis as soon as he can get there. I want a silent medical team available for Trey, as a precautionary checkup and to document any findings." Hawk gave Trey a pat on the shoulder. "The Ensign had a close encounter, and I want to make sure he's fit for travel."

Trey perked up. "Ensign?"

"I think recent events would rate a promotion." Hawk gave a mock frown at the boy's delighted expression. "Don't get heady; same job, same pay, fancier title."

Trey snuggled deeper into the blankets. *Ensign has a nice ring to it,* he thought.

"Is there a rip tunnel exit near the destination?" Gerard asked.

"Yes, the closest tunnel would have us traveling six standard days in rip and exit us at five hours and forty-eight minutes pre-orbit at maximum speed," Ship informed him.

Hawk whistled. "Six days. That is the middle of nowhere."

"Isn't most of space the middle of nowhere?" Ashron asked.

Ignoring him, Gerard said, "I suggest we put together a small research team to travel with us. Along with mapping a new section of unexplored space, it sounds like we're going to be engaging with two new species, the Kuthrallie and whatever this potentially invasive species is."

"I also think it's a good idea," Ship said. "Since the implications, if we find something, could be far-reaching."

Hawk nodded. "Agreed. Let's coordinate with Master Genray; he'll know who to contact in the government. I would prefer as small a team as possible, no more than three if it can be managed. Once this gets out..." He didn't finish the sentence as the diplomatic and economic consequences started to sink in.

Wolf grinned at Hawk across his steaming cup of coffee. "I know that look. You just realized how big a pile of shit we landed in." Wolf took another sip as the others turned their attention his way.

He leaned forward in his oversized chair. "Diplomatically, we have two potential races to deal with. The Berolians will be the touchpoint. Economically, every corporation will seek to leverage this. Other planetary governments may get involved. The military response could be impressive. And if the public discovers ripspace "monsters" are involved, panic will arise thanks to popular literature. We need a limited group of operatives, people who won't spill a secret." Wolf had leaned slightly forward in his chair as he spoke. He now settled back and took another gulp from his mug. "Pile of shit," he repeated.

Ashron, the last of his sandwich stopped halfway to his mouth, stared at Wolf. "I think that's the first time you've ever said more than ten words in a row."

Wolf shrugged.

Hawk flopped back in his chair and ran a hand through his brown hair. After a moment, he said, "Alright. This operation will be special access, need to know." He turned to Trey. "That means you can't say anything to anyone. Except for the people in this room, of course. No telling any of your friends at school."

The blankets moved as Trey shrugged under them. "Easy enough, I only have one."

"We'll have to come up with a plausible explanation for where you were and how you got back here. Ship, you and Laura coordinate Trey's medical needs. Make it appear routine. Gerard, schedule a private meeting with Master Genray. Let's figure out how we can go about this and keep it contained for now."

"Wouldn't it make more sense to speak to someone in the Berolian government?" Laura asked.

"When we have to," Hawk said. "I want to keep them and the GC in the dark until we know more about what's going on. They may want to step on our toes, and if it's as urgent as Trey's new buddies seem to think it is, I want to deal with as little bureaucracy as possible for now." He eyed Gerard. "That okay with you?"

Gerard nodded.

"I'm only telling Force 13 so in case we go missing, at least someone knows what happened to us and has some warning of what might be coming, even if we don't know the exact nature."

He spotted the thoughtful expression on Wolf's broad face. "I can see your wheels turning from here. You and Ship put your heads together and see how we can leverage this to our advantage. Might as well profit from this if we can before anyone else swoops in and takes the prize."

Wolf nodded.

"We'll need to maintain a level of normalcy if we don't want to attract unwanted attention," Gerard said. "We have the ceremony, but after that, I think we could disappear with little effort or notice. I'll plant rumors of us taking a contract with a new vendor. When we return from wherever this takes us and know more, we can contact my government representative and brief them. We can trust Master Genray to put together a small scientific team. He'll be discreet and, as a former Galactic operative, won't feel the need to be read into the operation."

They made the remaining two days of the travel to Berol without incident. Trey stayed mostly in his quarters recovering, still weakened from his captivity, and the others engaged their time with shipboard duties. Gerard and Wolf spent much of the trip learning about their new prototype system, including doing their own coding updates to the software based on the data they collected departing

Delroth. Gerard knew it would make LaRouche furious, but the doctor wasn't the one who would be risking her life when it came time to trust the cloak's efficacy. Ashron cleaned weapons and trained while Laura read up on the latest medical discoveries and technologies. Hawk remembered once glancing at a medical journal over her shoulder. His vision blurred by the time he reached the second paragraph.

Hawk, with Ship's help, tried to discover as much as he could about their destination. They didn't find much. Far outside traveled lanes, the system was mostly ignored. Long-range probes sent decades earlier had discovered little in the way of resources or habitable planets, so it held no interest to corporations or colonizers. Expansion went in other directions. They certainly found nothing to indicate this sector of the universe would be a flashpoint for a crisis.

A day after their arrival to Berol, Laura and Trey walked into the wardroom where Hawk sat reading an adventure novel on his datapad.

"Clean bill of health," Laura said, smiling and running her hand over Trey's bristly hair. "Healthy as a *kafer*, as Gerard's people like to say."

"And the tattoo?" Hawk asked.

Laura frowned. "Well, we can quit calling it a tattoo. It's not so much a marking on his skin as it is a part of his skin. More like a birthmark."

Trey grinned like someone offered him a bowl of ice cream. The color had returned to his complexion, and no one would ever know he had been the temperature of a popsicle two days ago. Hawk envied the resilience of the young.

"Whatever it is," Trey said, "I like it. It looks cool and doesn't hurt a bit." Trey put his bright blue eyes on Laura, "Are we done? I'd like to go see Sam. She sent me so many messages, I think my reader is full. She's been worried sick, and I told her I would see her as soon as I could."

"Fine with me." Laura regarded Hawk. "Captain?"

"Sure, just be careful what you say."

"Filamentous! Bye!" Trey ran from the room. Hawk smiled, pleased to see Trey happy.

"Ship?" Hawk said.

"On it," Ship said. "I think it will do some real good for the two of them to see each other. I'll keep a listen unless he kicks me out of his mind."

"Can he do that?" Hawk asked.

"In practical terms, no, but we've already established a code for when he wants privacy, and I would respect it."

"So," Hawk asked Laura, "anything you didn't want him to know yet?"

She sat at the table and leaned forward on her elbows. "They changed his DNA."

Hawk frowned. "Changed it how?"

"I'm not sure, and I need some time to run tests. The markings are more than a birthmark; it's his skin but different. I took a tissue sample, and when I went to administer a healing agent, the area had already healed."

"You mean closed up?"

"No, I mean healed. I couldn't tell where I took the sample. It was like he had never been cut."

"Damn."

"My thoughts exactly. I did all the lab work myself, and Ship ensured none of the results or scans are stored anywhere else but on her files. I'm not a geneticist or even a scientist, so my expertise is limited, to say the least. And we don't have the equipment on Ship to do the proper testing. We'll need to have someone other than me, an expert with the proper diagnostics tools, check over the files and the sample if we want to know what the full story is."

Hawk frowned. "Ship?"

"Yes, Captain."

"I'd like your thoughts."

"I've been mulling it over since Laura told me. The one person I can think of we might trust with this would be Dr. LaRouche. Her facility is no stranger to unusual requests, and their security level is the highest."

"Laura?" Hawk asked, looking over at her from across the table.

"I agree with Ship. She has people there who would be capable of determining what's going on. And they know how to be discreet."

"Let's run it by Wolf and Gerard and get their thoughts, but I think it's our best recourse. I want to know what they did to Trey."

"And I want Trey to know once we know," Laura said. "I'm not going to keep anything from him, but I'm not going to worry him unduly either."

"Agreed," Hawk said.

Trey couldn't believe Sam's strength. His toes hung suspended off the ground as she gave him a bear hug. "I missed you too, Sam," he said, staring down at her. He arrived during class and, after reporting to Master Genray, had sought Sam out during the period change. When she saw him, she ran up with a squeal and lifted him into the air, much to his chagrin and other students' amusement.

Sam, still holding him off the ground, stared up at him and frowned. She set him down before her, brushed off the front of her shirt, glared at him, and punched him squarely in the shoulder.

"Ow! What was that for?" He took a step back as she scowled, hands on hips.

"I was worried sick over you. Where have you been? What happened to you? Why didn't you let me know as soon as you got back?"

"I..." he stammered. "I couldn't."

"Couldn't or wouldn't?"

Trey saw tears welling up in her eyes. He didn't know what to do. Yelling he could handle. He would rather she be mad at him than disappointed and sad. He couldn't tell her anything, and he wanted to tell her everything, so long as it kept back her tears. He stammered, reached out, and took a step toward her.

She stepped back. "Oh no, you don't." She held a hand in front of her, and he stopped. "I thought we were friends, Trey. I trusted you. Why won't you tell me what's going on?"

Trey's stomach twisted, and he wanted to scream. Instead, he kept his voice as calm as possible. "I can't, Sam. It has something to do with my crew, and I had to promise not to tell anybody." He lowered his head. "Not even you. I'm sorry." Unexpected, a tear ran down his cheek. He waited for Sam to scream and walk away. To say they could never be friends again. He wouldn't blame her.

Instead, she reached up and wiped away his tear with her thumb. Trey's stomach fluttered at the touch. She tilted her head and smiled. Trey thought his heart might snap.

"I missed you too." She studied him a moment with her bright blue eyes, then sighed before saying, "Okay. What kind of friend would I be if I made you tell all your secrets? Especially when I have my own." She took his hands in hers. His cheeks burned, and he wondered if his face had turned the color of a cherry. "I trust you," she said. "If you say you can't tell me, I believe you."

Show her your back, Ship thought through their connection. Trey jumped, still not used to their awareness of each other. He wondered if she were always there and blushed until he remembered their agreement.

If you ever need me to leave, say so, and I can go until you tell me to come back, she reiterated.

"Are you okay?" Sam asked as her brows bunched. "You look like you have a fever."

"I'm all right," Trey said, abashed that she caught him being embarrassed. *Can I?* He asked.

She's worthy of your friendship and you hers. She deserves to know the gravity of what you face, and we know all too well the price of secrets kept from friends.

Okay, he thought. Sam still stared at him with bunched eyebrows and a slight frown. She probably thought he was either sick or losing his mind. Sometimes he wondered if the latter wasn't true anyway.

"I want to show you something." He scanned the hallway, which had cleared as students reached their next classes. All the nearby classrooms were occupied, but he spotted a closet. He led Sam to it and opened the door. "Trust me?"

"I said I did," she said, although she eyed the closet, which held a janitor robot and cleaning supplies, as she might a pit in the floor.

"I have to show you something, but it can't be in the open."

"Okay," she agreed warily as she stepped into the closet. Trey followed and closed the door. Darkness immediately engulfed them.

"Hang on," Sam said. He heard some fumbling, and a soft bluish glow filled the closet as she activated her datapad. The inactive robot stared down at them like some sort of statuesque monster.

"All right," he told her expectant, glowing face. "Don't freak out; I'm going to take off my shirt."

"Uh, Trey?"

"Yeah, hold that thought, Sam."

He turned around so his back faced her and pulled his red shirt off over his head. The sharp intake of her breath filled the closet. He peered over his shoulder. Her wide eyes, black in the strange light of the datapad, stared at him. She had one hand over her mouth as if holding in a scream, while the other reached toward his back. She stopped. "Can I?"

He nodded.

Her hand touched his back, sending a shiver through him. As she ran her hand across from one shoulder blade to the other, he faced the wall to hide his smile and rising laughter. Her touch tickled, but he didn't want to disturb her thoughts, which were serious based on the furrowed brow she showed before he looked away.

"What did you do?" she asked.

"I didn't do anything; this was done *to* me."

She ran her fingers in a manner that told him she was tracing some of the intricate lines. He shivered again as a feeling lurched in his stomach.

"Does it hurt?" she asked, pulling her hand away.

That disappointed him. "Nope. I can't even tell it's there."

She moved closer, and he could feel her breath against his skin. "It moves," she said, "and it looks like it's in 3D."

"I know. We can't explain it. But part of finding out what it is means we have to leave again for a while." He turned back around to face her.

"I would think so." She thought for a moment. "This is big, isn't it?"

Trey put his shirt back on. "Yeah, that's why we have to keep it secret."

"Okay, but you have to promise me one thing."

"I'll try."

"Whatever it is you are getting in to, be careful."

"I want to give you something," Trey said impulsively. He held out a closed hand to her. "And I have someone I want you to meet."

He opened his fist and dropped his communicator pin into her outstretched hand. She grinned. "Your crew pin? That doesn't mean we're a couple or anything, does it?"

Confused heat came to Trey's face as the idea both intrigued and horrified him. "No! I mean, I like you...but..."

Sam laughed. "Relax, silly; I'm kidding."

Trey took her advice and relaxed, although some part of him wished she were serious. What was wrong with him? "It's more than just a 'crew pin.' It's also a communicator."

Sam cocked her head and arched one slender eyebrow.

"Tape it there," he told her, pointing to the side of her throat, where her collarbone reached its top.

She did so, though her face showed confusion.

"Like I said, I have someone I want you to meet. Ship, this is Sam. Sam, Ship."

"Hello, Sam," Ship said.

Sam's eyes went wide. "Wow, it's like she's in my head."

Trey raised his shoulders. "It uses your collarbone as a speaker, so the volume is much lower, but other people can still hear you."

"Uh, hello, Ship. That's an odd nickname for a girl."

"Her real name is Sara, but we all call her Ship," Trey said.

"It works best for everyone," Ship said to Sam. "I thought while

Trey was away, you and I could keep in touch. That way, you won't have to worry."

"But who are you?" Sam asked.

"That's a long story Trey can tell you sometime. But for now, I'm a friend."

"And she never sleeps; you can talk to her any time you like."

"Really, you don't sleep?" Sam asked.

"It seems to be one of my many gifts. Talk to me whenever you want. But don't worry, I'm only fully aware of what's going on when you speak my name. After all, people need their privacy."

"This is so cool," Sam said. She smiled up at Trey. "Thanks, but don't you need it?"

Trey smirked. "Not really, but that's another one of those things I can't talk about."

"Sam," Ship said. "I will keep you up to date as I am allowed. Know that we all watch out for each other. I can't promise you Trey won't come to any harm. You only need to look at his back or cybernetic arm to know the danger he's seen. But I can promise you if anything happens, it will be after all efforts to protect him were exhausted. The mission we are going on is critical, and I need you to keep our communications a secret. You can't tell anyone."

Sam pursed her lips. "That shouldn't be much of a trick. Other than Trey, I don't have anyone to talk to."

A broad grin came to Trey's face. "I said the same thing."

"Well, now you have me," Ship said. "And as soon as we return, you and Trey can go back to terrorizing the school."

"Yeah, it can't come too soon."

The ache behind Sam's voice made Trey's heart almost snap. He didn't want to leave her alone, and only his love for the crew and the sense of urgency pressed on him by the Kuthrallie gave him the resolve to go.

Her deep blue eyes fell on Trey, and a smile lit up her face. "At least we get to say goodbye this time."

"Yes, we do," Trey said.

"I have to go," Ship told them. "You two say your goodbyes. Trey, we have lots to do before we depart. Sam, keep your chin up and call me anytime you feel like it. Bye for now; Ship out."

"What do you think?" Trey asked.

"I like her. Is she a computer or a real person? The whole "not having to sleep" thing is throwing me off."

Trey shrugged his shoulders.

"You sure have a lot of secrets." She punched him again, this time much softer. "But thanks. I can see why you fought so hard for this pin. I can assure you I'll protect it as fiercely."

"That reminds me," Trey said. "Did the Hellspawn try to take revenge after what I did? They didn't hurt you, did they?"

Sam threw her dazzling grin up again. "Gin and I had a talk in the ladies' room, one on one, and came to an accord. They won't be bothering us anymore."

Trey tilted his head and looked at her questioningly. "What did you say?"

She patted him on the shoulder. "You have your secrets, and I have mine." Before Trey knew what was happening, she leaned in and gave him a kiss. It was brief, no more than a second, but Trey wondered if his lips would burn forever with the touch. His cheeks burned hot again, and he suspected Sam could see the red even in her datapad's dull glow.

"Now, let's get out of this closet before someone finds us," she said, throwing him a mischievous wink. "That's how nasty rumors get started."

6

WE ARE SECOND

After a week of furious planetside preparations, Hawk thought they were as ready as possible for such a strange and mysterious mission. Gerard and Wolf, working remotely with Dr. LaRouche, had updated and fine-tuned their experimental cloaking system as much as a lack of controlled field testing allowed. Ashron had all the weapons systems prepped and ready, and Laura was locked and loaded for killing and healing.

With the help of Master Genray, who asked what they needed but not why they needed it, Gerard identified three scientists to help them on what was ostensibly a fact-finding mission around an anomaly discovered by long-range probes. It was a flimsy story at best, and Hawk hoped they found out what was going on with Trey's mysterious Kuthrallie before anyone else came looking.

The entire crew sat around the conference table in the wardroom, Wolf in his specially designed chair, the others in the seats that had become theirs by tradition.

Trey, seemingly no worse for wear after having survived in an alternate dimension, had resumed his position as Ship's steward. He sat at the table, close to the galley in case anyone needed anything, but also ready to offer any brilliant thoughts should he have them. Having been made an official member of the crew, he took his position seriously.

"I want to show you the three scientists we've settled on to help with this little covert mission," Gerard said. "Ship, give me the first photo."

The hologram in the center of the table flashed to life, showing the official Trador government photo ID of a woman who looked as if she had eaten a lemon. She had a downturned mouth with full lips and saffron-colored skin. Her black hair swam with curls. Her almost comically large ears were a common trait among Tradorians, but Hawk noticed she didn't have was the extensive ear jewelry many of the race wore. One piercing, a silver-colored hoop topped with what appeared to be a ruby, adorned the top of each ear. Her small, deep-set eyes, a disconcerting golden-blue color, combined with her dour expression to give her the appearance of someone who trusted nothing in the universe.

"First up is Dr. Hidar Prasam. As the senior member of the three, I've designated her team leader. She is an accomplished interstellar traveler and explorer. She also has the advantage of being on Galactic's payroll as a consultant, and thus already has the necessary security clearances."

Gerard glanced up from his screen to take in the entire crew. "And to get it out of the way, they all have impeccable credentials and high-level security clearances to match." He directed his attention back to his screen. "Anyway, Dr. Prasam is an Alienologist by trade."

"She looks like she's a laugh a minute," Ashron said.

"Don't let her appearance fool you. A childhood disease destroyed the nerves that allow her to smile. She is not a sour woman; however, she has the confidence and ambition to match her competence. She's a leader, and it shows." Gerard offered a broad, pale-faced smirk. "You should get along great with her, Hawk."

"As long as she does science and lets me do captain, we'll be best friends."

Gerard nodded. "I think she'll be fine with that. Ship, next."

A picture of another female popped up on the hologram. She had hair so bright red and full it almost overshadowed the face beneath it, a pale, round visage kept from being a complete circle by an exceptionally pointed chin. Her nose followed the face, button-shaped and small, her lips thin. Her blue eyes sparkled with inquisitiveness, even in a still holo.

"This is Dr. Tora Mobem."

Trey's attention riveted on Gerard when he heard the name, and the others turned their attention his way.

Gerard nodded. "I see you recognize the name. Dr. Mobem is the mother of Trey's friend, Sam. She is an Astrocartographer specializing in mapping ripspace streams, gates, holes, and highways. She'll be the most interested in what the Kuthrallie revealed. You see where Sam gets her red hair. Ship, next."

Dr. Mobem's picture flashed away, replaced by a slender Baldanian male with skin the color of aquamarine. A flat nose sat on an elongated face, above a lipless mouth, and below black eyes with no hint of pupils. The ears tapered to points on both ends and looked like croissants to Hawk. A shock of bright yellow hair stuck from his head like a short tassel of hay.

"Finally," Gerard said, "this is Dr. Bervil Griid, a Xenobiologist specializing in a variety of alien flora and fauna. He's seventy-nine years old, acts like he's thirty, and has discovered more new species than most people knew existed. We have a good team on this."

"When the inevitable happens, and the shit hits the fan, and they discover what's really going on, can we count on their discretion?" Hawk asked.

Gerard nodded. "As I mentioned earlier, they all have top-level security clearances in various areas."

"You don't get those being a blabbermouth," Ashron offered.

"You went to the local Galactic counsel," Wolf said to Hawk. "Where do they stand?"

"After we explained the situation, she agreed this should be compartmentalized and need to know. As Grendarin is our Force 13 contact, we notified him while we were in her office. He asked us to keep him in the loop. As it stands now, this is a scientific research operation with no Force 13 involvement necessary. Indeed, no government involvement whatsoever as there is no current jurisdictional sovereignty. We have a line on a new planet and are simply going to check it out."

Trey raised his hand.

"You're not in school," Laura said, smiling. "Just ask your question."

Trey gave a shy smile. "I don't understand what jurisdictional sovereignty is."

"There are vast areas of space unexplored and belonging to none of the two hundred plus planets recognized by Galactic," she said. "The coordinates the Kuthrallie gave you are such a place. So right now, no one has control of what we're going to investigate. Although technically Berol has jurisdiction based solely on distance, four systems could conceivably lay claim to it, based on planetary orbit factors and pre-existing mineral rights claims."

Trey frowned. "It sounds complicated."

Hawn nodded. "Galactic Law isn't for the faint of heart or weak of stomach, but we are also deliberately obfuscating things to keep it murky until we know what we're dealing with."

"I love it when you use big words," Ashron said. "It makes you seem almost smart. So, who's in charge?"

"Right now, us," Hawk said. "Our ship, our operation. But we are playing it as an exploratory and scientific mission to determine jurisprudence."

"Dr. Prasam has been assured she has authority over the scientific team," Gerard said. "She is a professional; we should all get along quite well."

Wolf frowned, a frightening look on his broad face. "So, none of them know the real reason we're going?"

"No," Hawk said. "They think a scout drone discovered the planet with potential military applications, so who gets control of it is a matter of utmost importance. Right now, we should leave the Kuthrallie out of it until we learn more about them and what their real agenda might be. But if things get spotty, we can fill in the science team."

"Did I just get called a scout drone?" Trey asked.

"Consider yourself lucky if that's the worst thing he ever calls you," Ashron told him.

They spent the rest of the meeting finalizing logistics, supply, and the myriad other things necessary for a long-term operation in unknown space.

"It's close to dinner time," Ashron said. "When do we leave?"

"We want to give the appearance of a routine operation," Hawk said. "The science team's equipment will be prepped and loaded tomorrow, and we'll attend the ceremony tomorrow night. Soon as we return from the pomp and circumstance, we'll depart. Any other questions?"

After a few moments in which the crew glanced from face to face and no one spoke, Hawk said, "Great, let's eat."

Hawk and his crew stepped into the Berolian Chamber, an indoor amphitheater nestled within the complex housing the planetary government for Berol. Dignitaries from all two-hundred-and-eight planets under the Galactic Council's banner were in attendance, gathered to honor the numerous magicians who sacrificed themselves defeating the traitor Moran and the corporations that joined him.

People stood around in their various groups, segregated by snobbery and perceived superiority. Hawk had no real desire to be here, but he had a personal stake in the affair, unlike most of those gathered. Moran had once been a Knight. Hawk's inability to kill him on multiple occasions had resulted in a battle with severe casualties, including the heroes being celebrated tonight. In the intervening time since that fight, Hawk had come to terms with what happened, but it had been a tough pill to swallow.

The hall was massive, as befitted the egos gathered within it. High ceilings adorned with multicolored glass chandeliers arched over the heads of the rich and powerful. Beings of all stripes mingled within a central gathering area, drinks and snacks in hand. Several races were encased in protective suits or wore masks, converting the atmosphere to something they could breathe. Hawk recognized a few people, although he wouldn't have been able to name them under threat of firing squad.

The Chamberlain, a short man with frazzled brown hair and pale-yellow skin, hurried over to Hawk and the Knights as they moved through the crowded hall.

The man had been at this job as far back as Hawk could remember. Hawk knew him only as the Chamberlain and had never heard any other name mentioned in connection with him. The Chamberlain frantically worked on his tablet, fingers flying over the screen.

"I am so sorry, my Lord," he sputtered. "I seem to have placed you and your crew in the wrong order. I am correcting the error now. If you will keep an eye on the big board, the correct order will show up momentarily. Again, my apologies for any inconvenience this may have caused."

Hawk smiled at the man. "I'm fine, really. Please don't go to any trouble. I prefer the back of the auditorium to the front anyway. Besides, the heartburn will be to the nobility, not to us."

Despite being enmeshed in it since his adoption at age seven, Hawk never grasped the archaic and convoluted caste system adopted by the Galactic Council, a hierarchal structure modified from medieval Earth. It made little sense to Hawk, both from a practical or societal perspective, but he didn't make the rules.

The Chamberlain's large violet eyes rose from his frantic tapping, his expression aghast. "My Lord Grey, I know it matters not to you, but the order is of extreme importance. You are now an Earl. After the demise of Baron Moran, you inherited all of Lord Tahorton's estate and holdings, along with those that were once your friend's."

A twinkle dotted the Chamberlain's eyes, and his shocked expression dissolved into a smirk. "My Lord Grey," he glanced around the room and lowered his voice. "Hawk, I know you don't care one way or the other. But it's refreshing to see one of the good guys work their way to the top the way it was supposed to be, by earning it through hard work and merit. Earl Tahorton had his faults, but all in all, was a good man. His estate is in capable hands. Besides, it gives me great joy to see the Blood squirm. And your objections aside, you and your crew should be honored this evening as much as those who gave their lives."

Hawk had a severe disagreement with that but didn't want to protest and make more of the matter. The Council offered them a spot of honor when planning for this event began, but the crew had rejected it to a member. They did their work in the shadows and had no desire for any recognition for doing their job.

However, he did agree with the sentiment of watching "royalty" wriggle like worms on a hook. "You know," he said. "I never did get your name."

The official's smile widened. His bright grin and light yellow skin made Hawk think of a sunbeam. "Why, it's the Chamberlain, of course."

He slipped Hawk a wink, then reverted to his officious manner and bowed. "My dear Earl Grey, I again beg your forgiveness for any discomfort this may have caused you and your crew."

Ashron snorted when he heard Hawk's title spoken out loud. The Chamberlain turned to Ashron and nodded. Ashron nodded back as if something unspoken passed between the two of them. Hawk noticed the exchange but had no time to say anything before Ashron regarded him with a grin.

"Your new title suits you to a *tea*."

"Really?" Laura asked as Hawk glared at the Lorothian. "That's what you've got?"

"What made you think I would pass on an opportunity like this? He's a celebra-tea."

"Can't you two get oolong?"

Laura grimaced. "*Et tu*, Wolf?"

Wolf's happy expression disappeared as he spotted something over Laura's shoulder. "Incoming on your six," he told the Chamberlain.

The Chamberlain and the rest of Hawk's crew turned to see a man dressed in royal red robes storming his way through the crowd, a deep scowl on his hatchet-like face. An entourage at least ten strong followed in his wake.

The Chamberlain glanced back to Hawk, rolled his eyes, put on his official face, and faced the rapidly approaching man.

"My Lord Hughes. How may I be of service to you?"

"You can be of service by telling me how this rabble of misfits jumped in the order." The man's cool gray eyes flickered to Hawk, then away, as if dismissing him.

Hawk knew Lord Elliot Hughes all too well. Hughes and his family had been on the warpath ever since Tahorton adopted Hawk and Moran over four decades ago. His adopted father had won Hawk in a card game and rescued Moran from an abusive family and formally adopted both boys two years later, when Hawk was nine and Moran eleven. Tahorton had been an Earl of considerable wealth but had no heirs. The Hughes family positioned themselves over many years to take over the estate, by hostile means if necessary.

The surprise adoption thwarted their plans, and they spent the better part of a decade in court trying to block any succession of his holdings to the two young men. Even after Tahorton's death, Hawk and Moran spent several years in court defending their position.

The acquisition of the estate would have elevated Earl Elliot Hughes to the title of Duke Elliot Hughes, as well as offering a sizable increase in the family wealth. Hawk could care less about the title, land, or money. But he would be damned if he would let someone claim and misuse his adopted father's legacy.

Eventually, a panel of judges dismissed the case without prejudice. Hawk and Moran split Tahorton's estate, and they became Barons. Ever since, Hughes did everything he could to complicate Hawk's life.

"My Lord," the Chamberlain began. "The error is completely mine; I was on my way over to assuage any troubles this may cause. I—"

"Stuff it, Chamberlain. I know where your loyalties lie. This bastard son of a crotch dropping is unworthy of any title some panel of bought off judges bestowed on him and his 'brother.' How convenient he is now an Earl, having killed off the sole other heir."

"That escalated quickly," Ashron, noting the flush of blood in

Hawk's cheeks, whispered in Laura's ear. "I think I've seen enough. I'll be right back."

"Where are you—" Laura began, only to find herself speaking to Ashron's rapidly departing back.

Hughes continued his harangue. "But that doesn't explain how he is above my house in the order, as my understanding is Blood still means something around here."

Hughes paused a moment as if considering his words. "Oh, I forgot," he continued with a flourish of his hand. "He is also a Knight, whatever the hell that means. And a commander in some secret order that may or may not be a part of our Navy." Lord Hughes's entourage —paid bodyguards and mindless sycophants—all wore broad, nasty grins as if their master was the soul of wit.

As Hughes stopped and gave Hawk a challenge-laced smile, Hawk considered his options. No one around them seemed to notice the tension, everyone intent on drinking and talking. He couldn't start a fight, much as he might want to punch Hughes in his smug face. Several cutting remarks came to mind, but such banter would do little more than escalate the situation. Hawk wasn't here for this. He came to honor the people who died saving the galaxy from Moran's insanity, not engage in verbal gunplay with a pompous jackass. The best thing to do was walk away and let the Chamberlain work his magic. Much as it galled Hawk, it was the road to take.

"Chamberlain." He nodded to the smaller man, then scanned his crew, except Ashron, who had gone missing. "Let's go," he told the rest.

Hawk pivoted on his heel and walked two steps before Hughes said, "Don't you turn your back on me, you delusional upstart."

Hawk froze. As insults went, it was a weak effort and hardly worth a response. But Hughes had said it loud enough that people nearby noticed and stopped their conversations to regard the two men. At this point, it couldn't be ignored. With a sigh, Hawk wheeled around to find Hughes smirking, backed by malicious smiles from his entourage.

"My Lord Hughes, you do your station disserv—"

Hughes pushed the Chamberlain aside as he might treat an errant dog. A few gasps passed through the crowd. Hawk's fists tightened. Not only was such action a breach of protocol, but Hawk liked The Chamberlain and didn't appreciate seeing him abused in such a manner. Hawk stepped back toward Hughes, ready to teach the arrogant bastard some manners.

A commotion at the entrance to the main hall stopped him. The crowd blocked his view, so he couldn't see the cause of the ruckus, but based on the crowd's reaction, it was either official or dangerous. Aides and court officials were scrambling. An excited murmur rolled through the gathering, and even Hughes spun with a frown to regard the disturbance.

"Wolf?" Hawk asked.

Wolf shook his head. "Too many people in the way."

Hawk glanced at the Chamberlain, whose thick brows bunched in confusion as he stared at his tablet. Then something changed on his screen, and he regarded Hughes with a gleeful smirk. "My Lords, you must excuse me for a moment. It appears we have an unexpected guest. A Royal Ambassador has arrived and requested an audience."

Lord Hughes perked up. "A Royal Ambassador? From where?"

"I'm not at liberty to say, but he is a Prince of Royal heritage and Blood."

Lord Hughes lost all interest in his squabble with Hawk. He barked some orders to his entourage about their proper place. They pushed their way past Hawk and inserted themselves between the crew and the front of the Hall.

As they brushed by Laura, ignoring her as they had during the entire exchange, she regarded Hawk, who stood with his arms crossed, a deep scowl beneath his mustache. A glance down showed his foot making a rapid patter against the floor. She tapped Gerard on the shoulder and indicated to Hawk. "What's going on?"

Gerard considered a moment and then shrugged his shoulders. "Something's bothering him, but I have no idea what."

She clicked into the private channel with Ship to keep Hawk from hearing. "Ship, do you have any idea what's going on?"

"Patience, my dear."

The Chamberlain frantically tapped on his keypad as he sidled next to Lord Hughes. Hawk continued to glare toward the commotion as more people noticed something unusual was happening. Laura joined Wolf and Gerard in waiting; the two of them seemed equally intrigued.

Before long, the crowd parted to reveal Ashron, and a thrill of surprise rippled through Laura. He wore a robe of white trimmed in gold fringe. The garment gleamed, contrasted by the jet-black cape of the Knights of the Flaming Star that flowed behind him. Dressed as he was, his head angled, his snout tilted up, he radiated royalty. His golden eyes appeared to look down on even those taller than him. Arrogance and power poured through him, projecting its own aura. Laura had never seen the Lorothian so full of confidence and control, and that was saying something. In this setting, surrounded by his peers, he seemed a different person, nowhere near the laconic, happy-go-lucky crewmate she knew. When she pulled her eyes away and noticed the stunned disbelief on Hughes's face, it took all her willpower to not laugh.

Ashron stopped before the Chamberlain, who offered a deep bow.

"My Prince," the Chamberlain said. "It is a great honor to finally make your acquaintance. You are most gracious to attend us at this solemn event. The people of Berol are in your debt."

Ashron nodded and gave a small smile, not his usual tooth-filled grin. "You honor me with your kind words. It is I and many others who owe a debt to those who sacrificed themselves in the unfortunate incident. I am honored to be here. However, I have a dilemma. I arrived with such haste I am without entourage or escort, which is highly unseemly. Would it trouble anyone greatly if I were to pull from your list of attendees and join in with one of them?"

"No trouble at all, my Prince. You may choose as your station allows. However, protocol dictates they would move to your position and not the other way around."

Ashron nodded. "I'm sure that will be acceptable. Out of curiosity, where in the order will that place me among these noble guests?"

The Chamberlain didn't glance at his tablet, and Laura suspected the man knew the answer the moment he saw Ashron in his royal attire. "Second, my Prince."

Hughes sputtered. His narrow face turned so red, Laura thought he might have a heart attack. A couple of his entourage stepped back in shock, and one's mouth dropped open, an expression Laura had never seen in real life.

"Yes, my Prince," the Chamberlain continued as if answering all the stunned looks around him. "Second. You are the Royal Blood Prince of your father's tribe. As there are no other representatives here, you must also claim duties as the Royal Ambassador of Loros. There is also your active commission as a knighted member of the Lorothian Royal Navy. Yes, my Prince, you will be entering second."

Ashron didn't speak for a moment, then he nodded. "I see. Thank you, Chamberlain. Since I am without my valet, could I bother you to let me know when it's time for entrance? I would be loath to throw off your pacing by being tardy."

"Of course, my Prince. The procession will begin in three minutes."

"Your reputation precedes you, Chamberlain. I am in your debt."

The Chamberlain bowed again deeply. "Thank you, my Prince." He straightened and hurried away to attend to other matters.

Ashron turned to find Hughes staring at him with a face the color of burning metal and an expression that said he wanted to commit murder. "My Lord, are you ill? You seem flush."

Lord Hughes's shoulders shook, and his fists were bunched so tight Ashron thought the poor man's hands might implode. "Prince? Ambassador? Second? Blood?"

"Those are all words, Sir," Ashron said with a closed-mouth smirk. "Would you like to string them into a sentence, or should I fetch my doctor?"

Hughes stepped close and lowered his voice. Hawk and Wolf moved toward him, and Ashron held up a hand. They both stopped, to Ashron's surprise and relief. No sense making this incident more disruptive than necessary.

Hughes lowered his voice. "Your race is barely this side of the primordial soup. If it weren't for us, you'd still be scrabbling about with fishing nets and spears. I will yield to protocol because I must. But you will not rate my recognition. Not now, not ever."

Ashron continued grinning, keeping a diplomatic face as his instructors taught him in his youth, though he wanted nothing more than to pummel Hughes until he reduced the man to a puddle on the floor. The insult about Lorothians was not only rude but also grossly untrue. They would have eventually developed space flight. As soon as they finished creating ways to kill each other. "I'm sorry to hear you feel that way, *Junior*. Your reputation for being a complete ass precedes you and clings to you like the stench of that body part. And as for soup, you are nothing more than an ingredient."

Hughes's crimson blush turned deeper. "You dare to insult me?"

Ashron's voice fell to barely above a whisper, though he kept the tone as casually civilized as he could manage. "I'm just getting started. You have two choices: you can walk away and not trouble my crew anymore with your self-aggrandizing bullshit." Ashron grinned, finally showing most of his pointed, mushroom-colored teeth. "Or you can challenge me, and we'll settle this the old way."

The red in Hughes's face disappeared as he blanched and took a step back. Something in his manner must have alerted his bodyguards because four of them crowded up beside their employer and glared at Ashron. He ignored them, more concerned about the frown he couldn't see but felt bearing down on him from Hawk. "Your choice," he said. "And before you turn and walk off in a huff, I suggest you offer me a proper address. Unless you want to cause a diplomatic incident with all these people watching."

Hughes scanned the crowd of people, many of whom still watched with interest. His eyes narrowed, and Ashron considered he might have pushed the man too far. No cause for concern, but it was an interesting concept.

Finally, Hughes offered the barest bow possible for protocol and said, "Excuse me, Your Highness."

Ashron offered a dismissive hand wave. "Run along."

Hughes whirled on his heels and stalked away. The bodyguards continued to glare at Ashron. He winked at them, then turned to the crew. As he suspected, a deep frown curled under Hawk's mustache.

"My Lord Grey. It would be my honor if I could join in with you and your escort to the ceremony."

Hawk gave a bow, though the frown didn't disappear. "The honor is all mine. Welcome, Prince Ashron."

Ashron sidled up beside Laura, who stared at him with the wide eyes of a stunned animal. "You appear to need a strong drink, my dear." He held out his arm. "Would you do me the honor of allowing me to escort you into the great hall?"

She slid her arm into his. "A prince? Really?" They walked toward the entrance to the hall. Hawk and the rest of the crew dutifully fell in behind them.

"I'm afraid so. One of six others in the line of succession to the throne. It's complicated and can be messy; however, we all have an equal chance."

Laura glanced back at Hawk and then to Ashron. "Who else knew?"

"On the crew, just Hawk. Well, Sara found out after she became Ship, but she only recently let me know she knew. But to be King is to serve. And the best way to learn service is to be of service, so I serve this crew. The way to learn to lead is to be led. Should the time ever come, I hope to be worthy. For now, however, I would make an inferior monarch."

"Well, I think you make a fine prince," Laura said, smiling at him.

Hawk had stepped a little closer behind the two of them. "I could have done without the attention; tomorrow, he might well be an unemployed prince."

Ashron grinned broader and flicked his tongue. "Perhaps. But today, we are second!"

The ceremony was a solemn affair, and Hawk wanted to be anywhere else. It was not that he didn't want to honor the fallen, especially considering their sacrifice had saved any number of lives and had stopped a madman from destroying the Galactic Council, an action that would have generated untold chaos. He just preferred to remember their sacrifice in his own way, with no one but his crew. But the Knights had been too central to the events to be casually absent. At least Hawk had managed, with the aid of his Force 13 liaisons, to convince the Berolian government to downplay the Knight's involvement. Instead, the gathering celebrated the Preternatural Scientists who had literally burned out their minds enacting the formulas necessary to increase the speed of numerous spaceships to outmaneuver their enemy and win the day.

Thankfully, the memorial lasted less than an hour, so Hawk managed to keep from getting fidgety. After a last farewell song from a beautifully voiced choir, the master of ceremonies called the occasion to a close. As second in line because of Ashron's shenanigans, Hawk and the crew stood and left the mourning chamber right after the Chancellor of Berol and the families of the deceased.

They walked past Hughes and company. The Earl glared at Hawk, his dark brown eyes filled with menace. His minions imitated their master. Once they had passed, Hawk sighed. "I wish you hadn't pulled rank," he told Ashron.

"Someone needed to put that asshole in his place," Ashron said. "You couldn't do it without breaching all sorts of protocol, but I could. Doesn't hurt to dust off the arrogance occasionally."

"Maybe, but he can cause us a lot of trouble if he wants. And he's not one to let an insult slide."

"Neither are we," Ashron said. "Neither are we."

7

FIRST CONTACT

The three scientists joining the crew arrived well before departure time, and the liftoff from Berol was uneventful. During the six-day trip through ripspace, the Knights and scientists familiarized themselves with each other. As a scout vessel, Ship wasn't made to accommodate many guests. Dr. Prasam, as the leader, had a room for herself, which doubled as an occasional meeting room. Drs. Mobem and Griid had to share a cabin. Fortunately, the scientists were long-time colleagues and got along well.

With the strangers on board, Ship's crew adhered to their protocol of keeping her unique nature known only among themselves. Despite their best suppression efforts after the fight with Moran, rumors had circulated about a sentient spaceship. Many of the executives of Galactic Cybernologies had made such claims after their arrest. These were pushed aside as the rantings of a lunatic Moran, meant to coax money and power from a gullible corporation. Rumors still abounded, but thanks to the work of Force 13, such musings were mostly considered outrageous conspiracy theories. After all, if the greatest scientific minds hadn't managed to create true sentience in a computer, how could a group of mercenaries, no matter how good their reputation?

So, Hawk sat perched in his chair when they had company and ran Ship's course while Wolf rested in his oversized seat and kept on eye on the craft's vital statistics. Laura monitored the crew's health, and Ashron, having nothing to shoot or blow up, sat in the galley and ate.

Even so, the scientists were bright and inquisitive, especially Dr. Prasam, and Hawk found himself often having to evade questions posed by the Tradorian. It helped that, once in ripspace, most vessels ran autonomously, so there was nothing unusual in that. The trick was not letting their guests catch them in conversation with their supposed artificial intelligence that seemed too "organic."

The cat and mouse of Ship's true nature aside, everyone got along well enough, mostly by keeping busy and at their own stations or in their quarters.

After the six-day jaunt, an exit from ripspace and a few minutes under six hours of standard travel found them approaching the mystery planet, now named Alonis Ceti Three.

Ship spoke in a bright, all-business tone. "Establishing high orbit in three, two, one, mark. Orbit established, beginning the initial planetary scan. Deploying the data collection and communications satellites. Yours was the first to deploy, Dr. Prasam; I should have a report in twenty minutes."

"I could use your computer on my research vessel," Dr. Prasam said for at least the tenth time. She stood behind Hawk's chair, watching the approach. "Her programming really is amazing." She had said that comment at least twenty times.

"Actually," Hawk said, "the credit goes to Dr. LaRouche. Her team is responsible for most of Ship's advances. Many are still much in the experimental phase, but we're getting the bugs worked out." Hawk made a similar statement every time and wondered if the scientist would ever take the hint.

"Too bad," Dr. Prasam said. "Someday, I'll have to go full-time with the Galactic Council instead of being a mere consultant. Then maybe they'll let me have good toys too. Or perhaps when this is over, you will let me study your system."

Hawk suppressed a sigh. For being so smart, Dr. Prasam played well at being obtuse. Maybe it was a mind game, and she hoped Hawk would crack and confess all. He smiled. She could keep hoping. "Perhaps," Hawk said in a neutral tone. "I would have to get clearance from the doctor to do so." It would be easy enough to make sure such clearance never came.

Dr. Prasam's large ears twitched. "Of course," she said stiffly. "I didn't mean to pry." She nodded. "I'll be in my quarters. Please inform me when we are ready to depart."

Hawk nodded. "Alright, it shouldn't be too long."

She didn't seem to know how to continue, so she simply turned and left.

"I certainly am not a *toy*," Ship said through the comlink inside Hawk's head.

"Well, I *do* remember a time in our lives..." He let the thought drift off.

"That was a lifetime ago. Still, she could be trouble if we aren't careful."

"Could be," Hawk agreed. "We'll find something to keep her occupied down there. Otherwise, she might focus her attention on you."

"She can try, but I'm pretty agile."

Hawk grinned. "Again, I remember there was a time..."

A three-meter-high black rod roughly the diameter of Wolf's arm poked out of the ground. The vegetation in a twenty-meter circle around it lay dead and brown, scrub brush crumbled to dust. A six-legged creature's bones rested near the cylindrical object, tatters of skin still clinging to it. Its cause of death was not immediately apparent.

Neither Gerard nor his scientist guests had wandered into that dead zone yet. The ambient radiation, picked up by their instruments, had led them here within a half-hour of landing on the planet. Gerard rarely cursed, but the lack of reliable, conclusive findings so far had him ready to release a stream of invective. They had no concept of the purpose or composition of this hunk of metal. They didn't know if it was native, left by some long-gone civilization, or extraterrestrial.

The whine of a motor attracted Gerard's attention. Ship's six-wheeled scout vehicle, the *Meteor*, pulled up, its balloon tires rolling smoothly over the flat land. It came to a halt just shy of Gerard. The whine subsided as the engine powered down. The side door popped open, and Hawk and Ashron strolled out.

"Well, that's kind of anti-climactic," Ashron said as he eyed the obsidian-colored monolith. "All this excitement just to find out some giant alien lost his stylus."

Hawk ignored Ashron, a skill he had gained from years of practice. "Nothing dangerous we could see on our perimeter scan. Other than some odd-looking animals, no sentient life to speak of at all. What do you make of it?"

"Too early to say," Gerard told him. "Initial scans haven't turned up much of anything. Only thing we can tell is that it's emitting a tight, focused signal."

"What kind of signal?"

"Uncertain. None of the signature patterns or waveforms are anything we recognize. Of course, nothing about this monolith is anything we recognize." Gerard scuffed his foot across the dirt, which Hawk knew as a sign of his engineer's frustration. "I have no idea what we're dealing with."

Hawk hated to push, but it was his job to ask the questions. "Any idea where it originates or what it's doing here?"

"We're backtracking with ionic patterns to see if we can get any traces of its travel path, which will at least be a start. As for the signal's recipient, the pattern is transmitting to a currently unexplored portion of space."

"You certainly have a lot of ways to say, 'I don't know,'" Ashron quipped.

Gerard gave a sharp smile. Hawk considered telling his demolitions guy to tread easy, but if Ashron hadn't learned Gerard's warning signs after five years, that was on him.

As the smile leaked away, Gerard nodded and said, "Another thing we don't know is the material components of this monolith. There are no identifying markings on it. We're running analysis now, and nothing is coming up on any databases. We're also running planetary analysis to see if there are any matches with the terrestrial composition. My early guess is we've discovered evidence of an unknown intelligent species that was either here at one time or is somewhere out there." Gerard gave a vague wave toward the sky.

"Is that a good thing or a bad thing?" Hawk asked.

"It's an exciting thing," Dr. Parsam answered for Gerard. "There hasn't been a discovery like this in at least a hundred Standard years."

"Is it possible Trey's new friends put it here as a marker so we could find where we needed to be?" Hawk asked.

"I suppose that's a possibility," Gerard conceded. "Although I think they would have mentioned it. But perhaps not. We have no true concept of how they think."

"We can ask," Hawk said. "Ship, check with—"

A wave of dizziness slammed into him. His head buzzed as if he had consumed six shots of potent alcohol in a matter of seconds.

Gerard dropped to his knees on the brown dirt and grabbed his head.

As quick as it hit Hawk, the sensation disappeared, leaving him with a throbbing head and a dry mouth. *That stinks,* he thought. *All the symptoms of a hangover without the previous night's enjoyment.*

Ashron stepped next to Gerard and held out a clawed hand for the magician to grab. "What's wrong?" he asked. Already pale-skinned, Gerard now resembled a piece of bleached paper.

"Power," Gerard said. "There is a nexus nearby, and a burst just fired off it. Almost knocked me unconscious before I could shield myself from it."

"It had to be powerful," Hawk said. "I haven't had the talent for years, and I got residual blowback from it."

"What's a nexus?" Ashron asked.

"Hard to explain without the proper background," Gerard told him. "But for ease of explanation, it's a confluence of thaumaturgic energy."

Ashron's tongue flicked out rapidly as he cocked his head. "That's the easy explanation?"

"It's a localized tear in ripspace," Dr. Mobem explained. "It releases a large amount of energy. It can be picked up by Preternatural Scientists and manipulated by them, assuming they can control the energy. Often, they will put a structure around it and sell usage rights to Pre Scis who are looking to further their studies or achieve high-caliber effects."

"The one thing I got out of that is that someone makes money off these things, which doesn't surprise me at all," Ashron said.

"Not always," Gerard added. "Sometimes they build a school around them. Sometimes, the nexus is so large that most of the planet's population has the talent to be a Preternatural Scientist."

Ashron considered this a moment, then his eyes, usually narrow slits, widened into amazed ovals. "Berol?" he asked.

Gerard nodded. "My home planet has one of the largest of the known nexuses."

"Why not the largest?"

"It's on a planet so inhospitable not even robots can land safely, so it's left alone."

Ashron nodded and turned his attention back to Dr. Mobem. "Are you a spellburner?"

She smiled and shook her head, her copper-colored hair bouncing as she did so. "I'm not a Preternatural Scientist, nor is my husband, despite being a native to Berol. But my daughter studies at the school, as I believe you know, and my studies have made me familiar with the phenomenon. The existence of a nexus automatically makes this a Class 5 Tech Restricted planet. We almost shouldn't be here with the level of tech we have, but I suspect we won't stay long enough to trigger any permanent damage." She regarded Gerard. "I guess we need to mark and survey it. Can you pinpoint the location?"

Gerard closed his eyes. "Give me a moment to focus on it."

Trey, onboard Ship as she orbited the planet, sat in his room, studying to catch up on his classes and ready to return to school. His time with the strange creatures who called themselves a name he could barely pronounce—Kuthrallie being the closest he could manage—had unnerved him, and he wanted to return to something resembling normal. He wanted to hang out with Sam and drink coffee at Dark Matter and talk about what was happening with the other students. When he was there, he had found the whole clique-based nature of school society both frustrating and not worth consideration. Now he found he missed the entire farce, and he had no idea why. Maybe the sheer ordinary nature of it appealed to him. He'd had enough adventure for a while. It was time to be a kid for once.

A barrage of images slammed into his mind, so forceful they knocked him from his chair. He landed sprawled across his carpet as a shiver of dread ran through him. "Ship, we're about to have company," he said as he pulled himself off the floor.

"What kind of company?" she asked.

"Something strange," Trey continued in a strained voice. The images assailed him at a furious pace, making it difficult to speak. He tried to project the concept of slowing down to whoever was sending him the vision, to little effect. "I don't quite understand, but it's not good. The Kuthrallie are warning me." He wished he had some better way to explain himself. The best he could manage was, "Something bad is about to happen."

"I think I found out what they want you to know," Ship said. She brought the planetside crew's comms on-line. "Captain?"

"Go."

"An unknown vessel has emerged from ripspace. It's heading toward the planet."

"Got it," Hawk said. He glanced at Gerard and saw the engineer had received the message.

He took in the trio of scientists, who didn't have the advantage of communication with Ship. "Party's over. Ashron, fire up the *Little Star* for immediate dust off. We have company, people. A large ship of unknown origin came out of rip and is heading our way. I suspect it's whoever put this marker here."

Ashron dashed toward the *Star* and began the startup sequence, recognizing the no-nonsense tone from years of working with Hawk. The mission had now gone from a scientific outing to a tactical situation. That fell under Hawk's purview. Ashron hoped the scientists were quick on their feet and willing to follow commands.

Hawk gestured with his left hand toward the shuttle. "Time to go. We fall back to Ship, go dark, and evaluate. Let's move." He saw Dr. Prasam's mouth open in preparation to say something. "Save it," Hawk told her. "We'll discuss when we're clear."

The doctor closed her mouth and nodded. She and her colleagues began to gather their equipment.

It pleased Hawk to see how briskly the scientists moved. Under his watchful gaze, they took their packed cases and returned to the shuttle with no argument. Hawk followed behind and hit the button to close the door. "Everyone, strap in," he said as he strode past the side benches and dropped into the co-pilot seat beside Ashron.

As he threw on his belt, he heard the whirr of the harnesses behind him as the scientists activated their restraints. "Everyone good?" he asked as he threw a look over his shoulder. Three upraised thumbs greeted him.

Hawk turned toward the front. "Move."

Ashron throttled the engines to half power. The shuttle leapt into the air like a bird of prey, slinging dust and debris across the dead ground. He heard a low gasp of surprise from behind. "All right?" he asked.

"Good," Dr. Griid said. "Just surprised."

Hawk smiled. When together, Ashron and the *Little Star* were full of surprises.

Ashron banked into a sharp turn. A ping from the dash informed him he had achieved prime exit trajectory to rendezvous with Ship.

He angled the craft into a nearly ninety-degree tilt and threw the engines to maximum.

"Any update, Ship?" Hawk asked as he pressed back against his chair under the increased speed.

"Not unless a complete lack of information is helpful. I know I can perform a passive scan with Dr. LaRouche's camouflage tech without giving us away. She said we can also actively scan, but I don't want to find out if it works under these circumstances. The vessel is coming in with no apparent regard for tactics or concerns they will be confronted. It's not shielded and doesn't appear to be military, or at least there are no discernable weapons. They are emitting a signal, but it's no language I can decipher. The energy signal is also completely foreign to me. I have repositioned to put us well above and away from their orbit. At least if they continue to follow their current trajectory and speed. If they maintain, they are six hours and forty-eight minutes out. Our new shields are up. I hope they work as well as promised, considering we're dealing with unknown technology on both sides."

Hawk turned back to the passenger compartment and relayed the information to the scientists. When he had finished, he continued. "As soon as we get back, I want the three of you in tactical. Leave your gear on the shuttle. You have a little over six hours to pull together thoughts, opinions, and options. Right now, we're in the dark concerning this vessel. When we get back, Laura will have a brief prepared for all of you."

"I will?" Laura quipped into his comm. Hawk ignored her.

8

OBSERVATIONS

Seven hours later, the unknown vessel settled into a geosynchronous orbit roughly thirty-five thousand kilometers from the planet's surface. Hawk had Ship draw as close as he dared to the alien vehicle, uncertain about the efficacy of their untested technology. From their vantage, they could observe and monitor the spacecraft. So far, it gave no indication of knowing they were there. Or if it did, it found them of no interest.

It was a gigantic vessel, easily ten times the size of Ship. Passive scanning had revealed tonnage and size, but all Hawk cared about was that it was a big alien ship, and he had no idea what it was doing there.

The crew and scientists sat around the conference table, studying their individual holographic projections. Despite his newfound importance, Trey fell back into his role as ship steward and busied himself passing out drinks.

"Based on the squareness of the bottom and the more standard hull line on the upper half," Wolf observed, "it's a cross between a construction platform and a cargo ship. I spotted few hardpoints or potential missile tubes. Any armaments appear strictly defensive. Science vessel?" he asked.

Dr. Prasam spoke up."I don't think so. There are not enough

obvious sensor arrays or probes for a science vessel. I like your observation of a construction vessel. But remember, we're basing this on knowledge of similar structures in our frame of reference. Their weapons may look like fuel tanks or their arrays like structural supports."

"Do we have any clues on the race?" Hawk asked. "Does it belong to any of the known societies?

The xenobiologist shook his head. "Nothing we've encountered before."

"Laura?"

"Without active scanning to determine vital statistics, or even if there are lifeforms aboard, it's impossible to tell much more," Laura said.

"We could launch a probe and see how they react to it," Ashron said.

"Could be an automated process," Laura countered. "I'd rather go to active scanning. That would at least tell us if there's anyone on board."

"Unfortunately," Hawk said, "it would alert them they're not alone out here." After consultation with Gerard, Hawk had decided this encounter was not the time to test if Dr. LaRouche's cloaking technology worked as well as the engineer claimed.

"That's assuming they don't already know we're here and don't care."

"Have they taken any interest in the satellites we deployed earlier?" Dr. Prasam asked.

"Not that I can tell. Again, they might not care. As far as they know, those satellites could have been there for years and are no threat or interest to them whatsoever."

"Nice to be ignored," Ashron said.

Hawk flopped back in his chair and ran his fingers through his hair. "Anybody remember First Contact Protocol? I sure don't."

Laura smiled. "I pulled it up because I doubt any of us have studied it since we joined Force 13. Basically, we're following it. Scan and observe, determine technology equivalence. From there, it splits into two paths, depending on if the contact possesses higher or lower technology than us. I'm going to assume from the scans and observation that we are on the equivalent or higher advancement thread."

"Anybody disagree with that assessment?" Hawk asked. The looks he got from around the table told him no one took issue with Laura's appraisal.

Dr. Prasam spoke up. "It's been several hundred years since a new race has been discovered. We are treading on new ground. Very exciting, I must say." Her ears twitched, and Hawk suspected the doctor was trying to grin and couldn't. "These protocols are out of date, but the basis seems solid. I recommend we pull back far enough to contact the Council but continue our observations. Bervil, Tora, what do you think?"

Dr. Mobem answered. "I've finished most of the mapping and updated our charts. Several of the probes we sent out have yet to report back, but I have a good understanding of the entrances and exits for travel to and from this sector. I bring this up to note that I discovered a passage that will return us to Berol in four days and is only fifteen minutes travel to orbit, not six hours."

"Nice discovery," Hawk said.

Dr. Griid looked around the room, his hands fidgeting nervously. "I'm trying to remember the last intelligent race we made first contact with that had equivalent technology. We are monitoring several lower on the scale but have not made contact. Ashron, your people were the last to join the Council, weren't they? How long ago was that?"

All eyes turned to Ashron, who flicked his tongue nervously. "Yes, well, you see, history isn't my strong suit, and neither is math for that matter. So, my answer is a qualified 'yes' with a prominent asterisk absolving me of any liability as to said answer."

"One hundred eighty-five years ago," Laura said. "The Council updated the protocols shortly afterward. Apparently, due to an 'overactive aggressiveness' associated with the Lorothian Clans."

Again, all eyes regarded Ashron. "Yes, well, worth and cooperation can be measured in various ways, can they not?"

"Let's hope this new race of people doesn't share your sense of merit," Hawk said. "Pull back where we can communicate with Galactic and tell them what we have. Preferably where we can make a quick exit if we must. We will passively monitor the situation from there. Let's stay frosty; remember, we were sent here with a sense of urgency due to an unknown danger. If that presents itself, we need to be ready. Dr. Prasam, do you and your team have enough to keep you busy for a while? I'd like to meet with my crew."

"Of course." She smiled, eyeing the giant alien platform on the big screen. "I think we will have enough work for a lifetime."

After the door closed, Hawk glanced around the table and then over to Trey. "Anything?"

Trey shook his head. "Nothing. I get the feeling this is what they were trying to get me to see, so that's why they're being quiet."

"Logical assumption," Hawk agreed. "But we can't jump to conclusions. Once we contact the Council, we'll have a better idea where we stand from the protocol side but not from the reason the Kuthrallie sent us here. I think it's safe to assume the GC will tell us to do exactly what we're doing: stand by and monitor from a safe distance, making sure we do nothing to jeopardize the situation. A diplomatic ship will be sent along with a substantial escort. All things being equal, it should arrive in about four days."

"Six days," Gerard said. "Dr. Mobem found a tunnel that will take four days, but until there has been time to double-check her calculations from a Preternatural standpoint and do a dry run, I wouldn't trust sending a vessel through the new passage."

Hawk nodded. "That's your field, so I'll defer. Six days then. Normally we'd be waiting longer, as a Diplomatic Corps vessel would not be anywhere near our location, but because of the ceremony on Berol, a diplomat is currently present on a two-week standby."

"Lord Elliot Hughes," Ashron said between clenched teeth. "Just our luck. Can you let him test run the new tunnel?" he asked Gerard.

"I like the way you think," Hawk said. "When he finds out we made the discovery, he'll pop an airlock. Under normal circumstances, I'd pull back and give them the whole operation as soon as he arrived. As far as I'm concerned, he and the Dipcore can have the credit regardless of how it turns out. Unfortunately, I'm not sure letting them know about the Kuthrallie right now is the best option."

"We sure didn't worry about first protocol there, did we?" Wolf said with a smile.

"We certainly didn't," Gerard said. "All things considered, I think we fell under their protocols instead of ours. This is an extraordinary circumstance. We have one race we know nothing about warning us about another race we know nothing about."

Ashron spoke up. "Maybe we can add an addendum to our operation manual called the 'Kuthrallie Protocol.' We can kidnap a worker from the platform over there, keep him until he is on the brink of death, tattoo our demands on his back and send him back. What do you think?"

Blank stares and headshakes were all he got from the rest of them. "What? Too soon? Trey, help me out here."

Trey grinned and winked.

Hawk smiled. "With no respect whatsoever to Ashron's Kuthrallie Protocol, I want a plan and options in case this thing goes antispinward. Wolf, learn everything you can about this ship within the limits of passive scanning; strengths, weaknesses, armament, everything."

Wolf nodded.

"Laura, same thing, only biologically. Maybe get up with Dr. Griid and Dr. Prasam and see what you can come up with. Extrapolate as best you can from what we can see."

Laura also nodded.

"Gerard, obviously you have magic and automation. See what you can find out."

Gerard raised his glass in acknowledgment.

"Trey, we need more information from the Kuthrallie. You and Sara work on contacting them, or at least making sense of what we know."

"On it," Trey said with pride. To this day, it still amazed him the Knights considered him an essential part of this crew.

With a sigh, Hawk turned to Ashron, who stared over a steaming mug of some concoction Trey had made for him. "Yes?"

"I need a plan to kill every one of them…just in case."

Ashron took a sip. "I see. All of them?"

"Yes, in case this gets out of control."

"Very well." Ashron set his cup down, stood, and calmly walked from the room.

The crew glanced around at each other with perplexed frowns. "Not the reaction I was expecting," Hawk said to no one in particular.

"Wait," Wolf said, holding up his large index finger.

No sooner did the door shut when a loud "Whoop" came from the other side, followed by an excited, "Ship, fire up the simulator! We have work to do!"

"There it is," Wolf said.

***

"Well, now we know," Hawk said. The crew and scientists were all gathered back in the galley. They had retreated to the outer rim to contact Galactic and Berol and were now discussing the response. The alien vessel hadn't changed its performance in any way, so they remained confident their dispatch went undetected. Still cloaked, Ship worked to maneuver back into a more strategic location for better observation. Trey and Ship had come up empty with the Kuthrallie. All the experiments they attempted offered no means of contact. As much as Laura tried to assure him it was not his fault, a frustrated Trey began to question his place in the scheme of everything.

Wolf and Gerard had similarly come up with nothing much. The ship carried some light defensive armaments but no visible shield points. Gerard said the ship's automation appeared straightforward, the technology perhaps slightly better than what the Council planets currently possessed. They concurred that the decision to not actively scan hampered their efforts, but they would continue passive observation with the hopes of gaining more data.

Noteworthy to Gerard's report was his inability to make any magical probe of the ship. No matter how he tried, he couldn't get any senses past the hull. He said this was also done "passively," but it was unusual none the less.

Using equipment left behind from their initial deployment, Laura and the science team had been more fruitful. A group of living creatures from the alien vessel had landed near the nexus and set up an array of large wires strung through metallic frames. As near as Dr. Prasam could tell, it was designed to gather and focus the nexus' power. Her best guess considering such a thing was not typically done since any advanced technology tended to disrupt the energy given off by such pools. She surmised this species had discovered a way to harness instead of dispelling the power provided by the *aether*.

This planet side activity allowed Dr. Griid to gather valuable information on the aliens themselves, which Hawk studied as the information came in. Their skin was various shades of subdued green, as if they were all in the middle of molting, though they didn't resemble reptiles. They resembled tall bodybuilders with broad faces, uniformly cut black hair, and oversized yellow eyes. A great deal of muscle mass covered their bodies, at least from what could be seen sticking out from the black work suits they wore, which was a single piece of fabric with various tools hanging within easy reach. Some of the tools Hawk almost recognized.

Over the chest and legs, they wore what Hawk guessed was armor, a dull shade of gray with no markings of rank or any indication of the wearer's occupation.

Also, they wore a sidearm on their hip. At least Hawk assumed it was a sidearm, and this opinion was backed by every crewmember and Dr. Prasam. Unusual pale blue color aside, there was no mistaking the purpose of something with a four-inch barrel and a trigger. When the work crew was out working on the array, half of their members would deploy an overwatch for security. So, they weren't overly concerned about this sparsely inhabited planet but were cautious enough. Perhaps they were aware of hostile animal life.

Ashron's assessment after a brief study of the creatures was short and unsurprising. He stated they were sacks of meat like any other living thing, and if the proper amount of ventilation was applied, any aggressive acts would cease.

"Let's see if we can keep that from happening," Laura said. "I'm sure Hughes and company would have a field day if something happened before they got here."

Four days later, Ashron and Laura sat in a camouflaged observation post atop a wooded ridgeline, roughly a kilometer south of the nexus. Thick trees surrounded them, five meters tall on average, with branches reaching upward as if trying to gather the most energy possible from the pale-yellow sun. The leaves were broad, rounded, and dark green with thick red lines running through them like veins.

"That thing really went up fast," Ashron said, staring at the monitors inside their temporary home. "Do you have any better idea what it's for?"

Realizing they had reached the limits of passive observation and needed to learn more about the alien creatures' activities, Hawk decided to risk letting some of the crew return to the planet using the *Little Star*. He hoped LaRouche's technology, which had also been installed on the shuttle, was as effective as the engineer claimed.

The first night on the planet, Laura cautiously slipped in as close as she dared and set up six cameras to surround the clearing, hiding them in the thick grass covering the plain. Since starting the construction, the visitors had worked ceaselessly through both the twelve hours of daylight and fourteen hours of night. Their surroundings seemed to hold little interest for them, and they hadn't ventured further than thirty meters any direction, and then to do nothing but relieve themselves, a sight Ashron could have done without witnessing.

Laura considered Ashron's question before answering. "Not any more than we did before. Gerard and Dr. Prasam still believe the array is some sort of focusing device for the nexus. But whatever its purpose, it looks like they're almost finished." She pointed at two of the monitors, which revealed something the array obscured from the other four cameras. "There's a new structure. They brought it down in their shuttle last night while you were sleeping. What do you make of it?"

Ashron studied the half-completed building, a boxy structure formed of blue-gray metal, walls attached with laser welds to ten-foot-tall square beams. It had no roof, but a pile of flat metal sheets and beams lay near the construction. "I'm guessing some sort of temporary living quarters. Maybe they're tired of the commute back and forth to the main ship and are ready to settle down and have children." He offered a wide grin.

"That was my thought also," Laura said. "Either that or a combination bivouac and control center for the array. Looks like they're thinking about staying a while."

A rustling behind them announced the arrival of one of the scientists. Ashron was glad they were a kilometer away from the array and its workers. None of the researchers knew the first thing about stealth.

He turned to see the camo netted door pulled aside. Dr. Bervil Griid walked in, various-sized containers cradled in his right arm. The labels on them were covered in the man's spidery handwriting. "Hello," he said, his face a cerulean color that showed his excitement. "Am I still good, or do we need to be leaving?"

Laura smiled. "No, you're fine. It looks like we'll be here a while longer. Just continue to observe safety protocols."

"Of course," he said in a subdued voice even as his face twitched with excitement. "I need some more collection containers." He quickly stowed the tubs under his arm into a clear spot, gathered another batch of empties from the storage bin, and almost bounded back to the wood line.

"I should have been an alien biologist," Ashron mused. "He looks delighted."

"As he should be," Laura said. "He has his life's work laid out for him. He and the rest of the team will be known as great scientists and explorers. The discoveries they make could change lives for years to come. The Serians may become the next members of the Galactic Council."

Serians, Ashron thought. *What a cool name.* As the first contact team, the scientists were allowed the privilege of giving the new species a preliminary moniker. It would change once contact was made and communication established, and the race offered their known name. But that wasn't his main concern right now.

"I'm sure the brain people will find all sorts of great things to study; I'm more curious about the unexperienced delicacies that might await." Ashron's tongue flicked in anticipation of what delightful tastes might be walking around in this strange new land.

Laura snorted. "Of course. What was I thinking? Stay alert. Dr. Griid isn't the only one around here with things to do."

"Well, I'm hungry. I hope Trey packed some goodies in with lunch."

Ashron had just started digging through the supply bag when Laura said, "Hey, something's happening over there."

"Captain, the Serian vessel has some unusual activity," Ship told Hawk through his implant. "There's a large cargo door opening aft."

"Alright, let the others know and have them meet me in the wardroom." Hawk pulled himself off his bed, where he had been catching a nap. The days and nights were full of activity and new discoveries, and the crew found sleep where they could. Observing a new, intelligent race was, if nothing else, exciting. Dr. Prasam and her team spun in a vortex of never-ending activity, taking full advantage of what was most likely a once-in-a-lifetime event.

As the team gathered, Ashron came over Ship's com system. "Uh, Captain? The bees are buzzing down here."

"Yeah, we have something going on up here also. What do you have?"

Laura's voice stepped in. "The Serians have gathered around the array, and it appears they're preparing to activate it."

"Alright, stay sharp and keep me apprised of any changes. We'll let you know what's happening up here."

Wolf entered, followed closely by Trey. "Sorry, doing shield maintenance and needed Trey for the tighter spaces. What's going on?"

"It appears they're unloading a large platform from the cargo hold," Hawk said. Wolf sat in his oversized chair, and the holo-display popped up in front of him.

"What do you make of it?" Hawk asked.

Wolf studied it for several seconds while Hawk fidgeted, and Trey stood behind, quiet and observing. Wolf nodded. "Now we know why they had such a large ship for minor construction. That platform and machinery would comprise the bulk of the ship's cargo tonnage. It's efficient. This isn't their first *trackle*."

"Their what?" Hawk asked.

"Means they've done it before."

Gerard, at his holo-monitor, added, "Consider the way it's unfolding. It's almost a work of art."

Hawk watched a moment. Whatever it was, the device was indeed unfolding like a flower, with five metal "petals" extending from a central, circular mass. The petals appeared bluish-black in the light of the planet's star, each covered in silver-colored filaments in a crosshatch pattern. The middle reminded Hawk of an ancient turbine generator, a dull gray cylinder with a thick metal spike protruding from the center. "Yeah, it's lovely," he said with none of Gerard's enthusiasm. "But what do you think it does?"

"I don't know," Wolf said as he pulled his gaze up from his monitor. "Though it's more industrial than military." His broad face regarded Gerard. "I would hazard this and the planetside array are connected. Gerard?"

"If the planet array is a focus for the nexus, it's possible this is a collector of some sort. But that makes no sense unless they have some unknown storage technology. It's not yet possible to contain *aether* like that. Ship, have you finished the analysis of the platform's composition?"

"Yes, it appears—"

"Holy shit," Trey yelped, jumping from his chair as if it had suddenly caught fire. His face flushed with embarrassment.

The others started at the young man's expletive and turned to witness him rip off his shirt. As he spun around, they saw his entire back had the ebon of deep space, yet at the same time glowed with a vibrant radiance as if starlight emanated from within his body. The lines that had been there before were gone.

Frightened, Hawk ran to the young man's side. "You okay? What can I do?"

Dots began to appear on Trey's back, pinpoints of light in various sizes.

Gerard drew near but quickly stepped back in shock. "There's enough *aetheric* energy pulsing through you to—" he didn't finish the thought. "Does it hurt?"

Trey pulled on his shoulder and vainly attempted to see his back. "It tingles, and I can feel the ends of my hair, but that's it. What does it look like?"

As he asked, the dots increased, and some grew larger while others formed in clusters. It began to dawn on Hawk that Trey's back was turning into a living galactic map.

"Like a new development," Hawk told him. "Please tell me you know what it means."

The young boy quit trying to see his back and turned to them. His somber face made him appear more adult than child. He paused a moment, and his head cocked as if he listened. His bright blue eyes stared at Hawk, and a shudder went through the captain. "It means…" Trey said in a quiet voice. "…I know what that platform is for and why we have to stop it."

"Hold that thought," Hawk said. "Unless we're going to blow up in the next sixty seconds?"

Trey shook his head.

Hawk nodded. "Ship, open comm."

"Comm open."

"Dr. Mobem, Dr. Prasam, can you join us on the bridge, please?"

"Yes, we'll be right there," Dr. Mobem's soft contralto voice said.

"Thank you. Comm off."

"Comm off."

"Ashron, Laura, listen up. Is Dr. Griid with you?"

"No," Laura said. "He's still out gathering specimens. He's like Ashron in an armory or delicatessen."

Hawk smiled. "See if you can round him up, he might want to hear whatever our Ensign is going to tell us." Since none of the science team had the internal communications of Ship's crew, Hawk didn't want to risk external communications except over short-range, lessening the chance of the Serians detecting their presence.

"Copy that," Laura confirmed. "We'll get him back."

The door to the bridge opened, and the two scientists walked in, Dr. Mobem ahead of her colleague.

"What did you—" she started, then stopped when she saw Trey. Her blue eyes widened, and her mouth fell into the universal O of surprise. Dr. Prasam's large ears twitched, and her eyebrows rose.

After the initial shock, Tora Mobem strolled across the bridge and stopped a few feet from Trey. "What's going on?"

"I thought you might want to see this, and Trey has some important information to impart to us all," Hawk told her. "Laura, do you have your wayward xenobiologist yet?"

"He'll be here within a minute."

Dr. Mobem studied Trey's back, which continued to glow with the blackness of deep space, the blue-white of stars like pinpricks on his skin. Her round face had taken on the clinical detachment of a dedicated scientist. "It's a star chart," she said, confirming what Hawk already suspected. "Though I don't recognize anything I'm seeing." She reached out toward Trey's back. When she touched his skin, he yelped.

She yanked her hand away. "It's like ice," she said. "Are you cold or uncomfortable?"

"No. Sorry I shouted. It got white-hot and searing when you touched me."

"Then I won't do that again," she said with a soft smile. "How does it feel otherwise?"

"Hard to describe," Trey said. "It goes from hot to cold, then it's like my skin is butter, then really hard. It's..." he sighed, his face a mask of misery. "I can't explain it. I'm sorry."

"Don't be," Dr. Mobem said. "I'm sure it's all as new for you as it is for all of us." She turned to Hawk, a frown on her round face. "It would appear you may have left out a few things in our briefing. Perhaps now is the time to bring us up to speed?"

"In due course," Hawk promised. "But right now, I think we have more pressing issues."

"Dr. Griid has joined us," Laura said in his ear.

"Perfect timing," Hawk said. "Open the speaker so he can hear everything, too." He put his gaze on Trey. "Okay, tell us why you called this meeting."

Trey pointed to the holo floating in the center of the bridge, which streamed a live feed of the platform unfolding like a giant metal flower behind the alien ship He offered a brief smile that disappeared as he began to speak. "If I understand correctly, this is basically a gate that gets its power from the nexus on the planet and will reach into ripspace. What you've been calling an array is a device that focuses the raw *aetheric* energy from the nexus into kinetic energy that powers the gate. How they are overcoming the technical/aetheric dissonance from such a vast energy source, the Kuthrallie don't know, but they are. Once they form this gate, it will allow them to traverse space immediately, bypassing the ripspace tunnels."

"Okay," Hawk said. "I applaud them for their efficiency, but I'm not sure why it's a problem for us."

"Because the way they focus and use the energy will produce a feedback wave that will, in turn, cause the surrounding ripspace tunnels to collapse, and we'll be trapped here with no quick way to travel between systems."

Gerard spoke up. "That is a problem. But if the Kuthrallie hadn't sent us here, we wouldn't be in a situation that required us to extricate ourselves."

"They created their own exigency," Wolf said.

"I have no idea what that means," Trey said to Wolf. "But there's more. I don't understand distances the way the Kuthrallie explain them, but the best I can get is when this gate is activated, the tunnel collapse will affect an area the same distance as Ship can travel through ripspace in ten days."

The gathered group glanced among themselves, every face carrying a shocked expression.

"That seems like a lot," Ashron said over the comm.

"I'm not going to make any assumptions as to the speed of this particular 'scout' ship," Dr. Mobem said. She offered an arch of her dark red eyebrow toward Hawk. "But using the time and distance we traveled here from our original starting point..." she paused as she moved her fingers and stared into the distance. Hawk caught the tiny flickering images in her eyes that revealed she wore compute contacts.

She blinked, and the images over her pupils disappeared. "At a rough estimate, the collapse will affect eleven known inhabited planets, including Berol." She indicated the hologram. "May I?"

Hawk nodded. Dr. Mobem touched the controls on the panel before her. The image of the unfolding platform flickered and changed to a star map similar to the one on Trey's back, but it was different enough that even Hawk could tell it wasn't the same area.

Dr. Mobem continued. "I've been triangulating and creating a coordinate map of this new sector, using Berol as the barycenter." She pointed at the holograph, and a red silhouette in the shape of Ship appeared. "That's our current position, give or take a thousand kilometers." She swept her arm in a wide arc, and a circle of blue inscribed itself on the hologram, following the path of her arm. "This is the area of effect Trey is describing. It's a rough estimate, but close enough to give you the idea."

Hawk leaned in to get a better angle. More than half of the circle covered a black mass, indicating unexplored, or at least uncharted, space. But the rest of the area encompassed well-traveled and well-inhabited travel lanes.

Dr. Mobem continued to indicate the map. "Berol is the planet marked in blue. These are the other affected planets are." Eleven planets popped up as glowing green dots as she indicated them. "Two of them are still colonizing and not yet self-sufficient. They are completely dependent on trade with Berol and their other neighbors. They won't survive if they're cut off."

Hawk turned to Trey. "Do you know how long we have before it all goes to shit?"

"I'm not sure," Trey replied, face downcast. "I don't think they understand time the same way we do."

"Clearly not. Or governmental structure, for that matter." Hawk ran his hand through his hair and over his mustache. "Why now? They couldn't have told us this a couple of days ago? Or better yet, before we got the Diplomatic Corps involved."

"Like I said, they don't consider time the same way we do. I guess they need to know about 'imminent' too," Trey said sheepishly.

Watching the Serian's progress in his monitor, Wolf said, "I'd guess we have until they get the platform set up and ready to receive a signal. The orbit is still too low, I believe. After completion, they'll tow it out and establish a better fixed location. Waste of fuel to keep it where it is."

"Best estimate?" Hawk asked.

Wolf's broad face considered a moment, then gave a deep frown. "A matter of hours."

9

PROTOCOLS

Okay, Laura, Ashron, stand by and let me know if anything unusual happens down there," Hawk said. "I'll get back with instructions soon."

"Copy," Laura said.

"May I continue my gathering?" Dr. Griid asked.

"Yes," Hawk answered, "but stay close, in case we need all of you to do a quick dust-off."

"Yes, Captain," the scientist said.

"Laura," Hawk said, his voice soft. "Go ahead and read the doctor in on everything."

"Are you sure?"

"Yes," Hawk answered. "I'm about to tell our guests here, so their colleague should know too." He looked at the two guests on Ship. "I think I owe you an apology," he paused for a second, then continued. "And an explanation. I want your input for our next course of action, and you need to know exactly why we're here."

Tora Mobem considered all the information the captain had poured on her and her team leader about the Kuthrallie and the mission's true purpose. She wasn't angry; both she and Dr. Prasam had worked for Galactic and understood 'need to know' protocols. And nothing Hawk revealed would have changed their minds about coming on the expedition.

As she studied the four crew members who were giving her time to gather her thoughts, she felt perhaps Hawk could have let the scientists know sooner. Dr. Hidar Prasam chewed at her lower lip as she mulled over the information. Tora knew her mostly by her reputation as a smart and confident woman who sometimes bordered on arrogance, and she wondered if Hidar were as impassive about the withholding of information as her expression made her seem.

Hawk wanted her thoughts on the current situation, but first, she had questions. She regarded Trey, his face open and honest and full of curiosity. No trace of fear or concern. Tora couldn't imagine how anyone could be so calm going through such an experience at any age, much less being as young as Trey. Her daughter had mentioned he was exceptional, and the past days on Ship had shown Tora why Sam liked him. Exceptional was only one of the superlatives she might use to describe the young man. Confident, smart, and respectful came to mind. And powerful, if she were to believe the reports from her contacts at the Sterling Arch. "So, you were contacted by the Kuthrallie and instructed to come out here because there is some kind of danger?"

Though she had directed the question at Trey, it was Gerard who answered.

"More abducted than contacted," the pale man said, scratching his thin white hair under his blue baseball cap. "But yes, that is the gist of it."

She pointed at Trey. "And the Kuthrallie put that on your back?"

"Yes, this and the other design."

She stared at him, confused. "Other design?"

Gerard touched a spot on the panel, and another image appeared, a vid display of an intricate pattern of wavering lines that seemed to writhe and undulate on Trey's back. Tora studied the image, fascinated. "Can you bring that one back?"

Trey shook his head. "I have no control over any of it," he said.

"Any idea what it does and why they did it?"

"Laura checked it out and said it wasn't a tattoo and my skin transformed into something else."

"Changed it how? On a cellular, molecular, or atomic level?"

Trey shrugged, and Gerard spoke again. "Laura hasn't been able to test it that extensively yet."

"Of course not," Tora said. A scout ship wouldn't have the equipment in a medbay necessary for such sophisticated analysis. Although it wouldn't surprise her, considering the areas in which this vessel went beyond the average. "We'll assume cellular for now." *And hope there were no resulting ill effects*, she didn't add.

"We can't rule out *aetheric*, either," Gerard said.

Tora nodded. Knowing the creatures involved, that made a great deal of sense. The thought put her ill at ease.

"These creatures..." Dr. Prasam began, her deep-set eyes on Trey. "Their environment is actually in ripspace."

It was a statement more than a question, so nobody answered her.

"Like another dimension that touches ours." Dr. Prasam continued, "Not in one place, but everywhere at once. Like an overlay."

Trey nodded. "That seems right."

"And our travels are through tubes that pass through their dimension?"

"An oversimplification" Gerard answered as Trey nodded. "But essentially correct."

Dr. Prasam paused a moment, her brows bunched. "And you said time isn't the same for them as it is for us?"

"As near as I can grasp," Trey said. "But keep in mind, I have very little understanding of them, and we are still learning how to communicate effectively."

"Amazing," Dr. Prasam said. "Trey, if you ever learn to fully understand the...what do you call them, the Kuthrallie? It boggles the mind what they could tell you. A different concept of time, the co-existence of dimensions. It could well turn out everything we know to be true is either wrong or so elementary as to be comical. And you will be the only one with the insight to understand any of it." She frowned, her already serious expression turning ominous. "You need to be careful, young man; you are about to become a highly sought-after commodity."

Trey's face tightened in concern, and his blue eyes went to Hawk.

"Don't worry," Hawk smiled at Trey. "We're all in this together." He turned his brown eyes toward the two scientists. "All of us."

Dr. Prasam took a step back, seeming to belatedly realize the effect of her words on Trey. "Oh, yes, of course. Your secret is safe with us. Tora's daughter, Sam, has a similar, shall we say, paradox. Rest assured, no one on this team will ever betray that confidence. Hers or yours."

At the mention of Sam's name, Trey relaxed a little.

Tora would have preferred Hidar not mentioned Sam. Tora loved her daughter, but the girl's ability frightened her. Trey didn't scare her yet, but there was no telling what a child with his power might do if persuaded by outside forces such as inter-dimensional beings. They had no way of knowing if the Kuthrallie really had their best interests at heart.

"So, then, this map is new?"

"Yes, as of today," Gerard said. He returned his attention to Trey's back. "Not sure what the purpose is, and the Kuthrallie didn't seem forthcoming on sharing information with Trey. Perhaps it's nothing more than a map of the path the Serians took to get here, to give us an idea on the dimensions we're dealing with."

Tora again examined the map, careful not to touch Trey's back, no matter how interested she was in getting a better sense of precisely what it was. She had to remind herself she was an astrocartographer, not a physician. Despite her underlying concern, the mysteries before her tugged at her inner explorer. She smiled and chuckled. "If this is accurate, there is a lifetime of study presented here. Upon observing the areas we have already mapped out, I must assume the rest are equally correct." She glanced over to Hawk. "Do we have time for me to record this, or have you already done so?"

Hawk pursed his lips together. "In the spirit of openness, I have one more revelation. Ship, would you make the mappings on Trey's back available to Dr. Mobem, please."

"Certainly, Captain," Ship said over the intercom. "Dr. Mobem, you should now be able to access them on your tablet. Please let me know if you have any questions."

Dr. Mobem watched as a series of charts appeared on her tablet. "There are more here than I currently see on Trey's back."

"Yes," Ship said. "Trey and I have been recording every event or occurrence he has experienced since his return from the Kuthrallie. Some have been other star charts of unexplored areas of space; others have been unknown equations and symbols, and still others completely indiscernible. Dr. Prasam, everything will be available to your team."

Dr. Prasam's deep eyes blinked for a moment, "She keeps saying 'I' like a sentient being. I only ask because of the rumors." She glanced questioningly at Hawk.

Hawk simply shrugged.

"So, the rumors are true?"

Hawk smiled. "Depends on the rumors. When there is more time, you can sit down and speak with Ship about it at length."

"Ship?"

"Her name is Sara, but the name stuck while we were in a state of flux as a team," Hawk said. "It also helps keep memories at bay." He gestured around the room. "Ship, may I formally introduce you to Dr. Hildar Prasam and Dr. Tora Mobem."

"A pleasure," Ship said. "I am at your service. And Dr. Mobem, your daughter and I have been keeping secrets; we should talk later."

"I suppose I shouldn't be surprised," Tora said with a smirk. "I look forward to it."

Dr. Prasam pointed over to Hawk. "I think you and I have some talking to do, also."

"Most likely. But currently, we have more pressing issues. Now that everyone is up to speed, we need to decide on a course of action."

Laura watched the monitor as the Serians, having finished assembling the secondary structure, ran several large cables from inside the building and over to the larger platform. Sparks flew as they welded or fused the silver-colored ends to black octagonal boxes beneath the platform.

A shuffling noise caught her attention, and she shifted to find Ashron digging through another supply container. "Are you still hungry?"

Ashron stopped and lifted his long snout. His green skin darkened a shade, and he glanced away. "Maybe."

Laura chuckled. "I find your metabolism somewhat enviable."

"If by enviable, you mean staying hungry most of the time, then you have strange priorities. However, it helps that I can eat pretty much anything, and I'm not particularly choosy."

"So we've noticed," Laura said with an arched eyebrow.

He ignored the snarky comment. "Good thing my species evolved on a planet rich in resources." Finding nothing but medical supplies and spare ammunition in his current container, he shoved it aside and opened another, covered with hastily scrawled words on the side.

"That's—" Laura started.

"Of course," Ashron interrupted. "A heavy slathering of mustard makes everything taste better." He grinned as he pulled out a writhing blue creature with six legs and a single horizontal black eye.

As he opened his mouth wide, Laura clapped her hands and pointed a finger at him. "No! Bad Lorothian. Put that back. That isn't food; that's one of Dr. Griid's specimen samples."

Ashron closed his mouth and narrowed his eyes in disappointment as he dropped the squirming creature back into the plastic box and closed the lid. "Glad you didn't have a newspaper to hit me with. Hey, we should get a dog for Ship."

"You take that up with Hawk," Laura said. "Who knows? He might go for it."

Ashron indicated the container. "You know he'd never miss it, right? He has more than enough samples to keep him busy for months." Movement on the monitor caught Ashron's eye. "Back on task."

Laura turned and observed that the Serians had finished running and attaching the cables. At least twenty of them stood assembled in front of a square panel with no discernable function. Or at least not one easy to determine while trying to study it through a press of bodies. "Bet you a candy bar it's a power source."

Ashron stepped up beside her. "You've got a candy bar?"

Laura rolled her eyes. "Ship, comm on."

"Comm on," Ship said.

"Hawk, are you seeing this?" Laura asked.

"Yes," Hawk said. "Wolf and Gerard are thinking power source."

Laura grinned at Ashron. "Yeah, that was our conclusion here too."

"So, they might be close to starting it up," Hawk said. "Get Dr. Griid and meet back on the *Little Star*. We've got a plan to share with you."

"On it," Ashron said as he headed for the shelter's exit.

Ashron, Laura, and Dr. Griid sat gathered in the *Little Star*, staring at the main holograph, which floated above the cockpit's control console, between the pilot and co-pilot's joysticks. The crew and scientists aboard Ship hovered before them. Hawk had just briefed the shuttle's occupants on earlier events that transpired with Trey and the scientists, and on the course of action the six of them agreed to.

"So that's where we stand at the moment," Hawk concluded. "Thoughts, comments, and criticisms cheerfully accepted."

No one spoke as everyone on the shuttle considered the plan and the implications, as far as they could see them. On the side monitor, the Serians still stood before the octagonal panel but had done nothing else. Laura wondered if it was perhaps some sort of ritual or religious service, or if they were simply waiting for some process to complete. The surveillance cameras had microphones, but none sensitive enough to hear anything at their distance other than the sigh of wind or the occasional chitter of a native animal.

When she had finished going over strategies and options, Laura spoke. "I think we should stay planetside. Once you reveal your presence to the Serian ship, they may not react well. If they don't, or you can't stop their progress or explain why they must stop before things become critical, we may have to take measures down here."

"Agreed," Hawk said. "We'll have Ship do a scan once the Serians know we're here. If necessary, you can disrupt or destroy the power supply."

"Not exactly the best way to make a good first impression, is it?"

"Good impression is up to them," Hawk said. "Best way to do that is to stop plans to open their tunnel when we tell them what will happen. If they don't, then we do what we must. I want you to keep a low profile, but be ready just in case."

"I'm always ready," Ashron said with a toothy grin.

"I know," Hawk said. "That's what keeps me up at night. We'll return contact in twenty minutes." The main holograph went dark, leaving only the images of the Serian machines on the planet and in space.

Dr. Griid looked thoughtful. "So, your ship isn't sentient, or an aware computer, but an actual person?"

"More like haunted by a ghost," Ashron said.

"You'll pay for that," Ship whispered.

"Or maybe a poltergeist." Ashron winked at Dr. Griid and Laura.

"I have cameras that can see you," Ship said over the shuttle's loudspeakers. "I also know where you sleep."

"Fair enough," Ashron said. "She's a real person who lives in the *aether*. Sort of like a big cloud of gas."

"Keep digging."

Ashron's grin widened. He stepped up to one of the shuttle's lockers and pulled out a square red case, roughly the size of a dinner platter. He placed the box on the bench, opened it, and pulled out an iron-colored cylindrical object that resembled a large metal pill. He held out the item to Dr. Griid. "This is a personal shield I want you to wear in case things go sideways." He pointed to the metal clip on the back. "Put it on your belt. It's magnetic, so you don't have to worry about it falling off. You activate it by turning the entire unit ninety degrees and pushing the little black button in the middle. To turn it off, you do the opposite."

Dr. Griid took the device from Ashron and pushed it onto his belt. There was a click as the magnetic clip connected.

"Are you familiar with any weaponry?" Ashron asked hopefully.

"Other than a personal sidearm I'm barely qualified with, not really, no. I believe Tora, er, Dr. Mobem has some training, but I'm afraid I never had the desire or inclination to learn past the basics."

"That's a shame," Ashron said, flashing back to another operative with no training who almost died because of it. Ashron had taught Thomas the basics and wondered if the confidence instilled with the training helped the man survive or contributed to his getting severely wounded. No time to consider it now. And it didn't matter in this case. Ashron suspected if something bad was going to happen, it would be hours from now, not days.

"I can fly a shuttle, though, if that would free you up."

Ashron brightened. At least the scientist wasn't utterly useless in a combat situation. "Great. The *Star* might be different than anything you've flown before, though."

"Yeah, I got that the first day we dusted off from this planet. Let me stow the rest of my samples, and I'll familiarize myself with the controls."

"Ship can help you get familiarized, too."

As Dr. Griid left the shuttle to gather his boxes, Laura looked back at Ashron. "You ready?"

"I'm—"

"I know, you're always ready." She put her hand down on the metal cylinder on her hip, like the one Ashron had given Dr. Griid. "Do these new shields work as well as the last ones?"

"Better, theoretically. They're a miniaturized version of the upgrade we installed on Ship. During the testing I did on them, they defeated every personal weapon we have. They don't last long, but they can get you out of a jam. Gerard is working on the energy source to see if he can improve it."

"How long do they last?" she asked.

"Depends on the absorption rate. Once you start taking serious hits, it's time to start falling back, but the cloaking aspect is the real plus here. Tough to hit what you can't see. That's where the power drain happens." He shrugged and activated his shield.

Laura watched as Ashron shimmered and blended into the bulkhead. If she hadn't been staring at him when he activated it, she would have never been able to pick him out.

"Wow. And it's a shield?"

"Yep. And like I said, a damn fine one too." He deactivated the device and shimmered back in to focus. "The camouflage will deactivate first. When that happens, it vibrates to let you know it's gone. Then you have ten direct hits of protection before it depletes. So, try not to get hit much."

"That's my primary objective in any firefight," Laura told him.

He paused a moment and glanced at the monitors, where little had changed. "If Hawk's plan A doesn't work, I can move in and disrupt the power source while you cover me. Clean, and no one gets hurt but the bad guys."

In addition to the observation positions they set up, they had also rigged several long-range unmanned weapons hidden within the tree line. Using a separate set of monitors and controls, Laura could cover Ashron's movements either from the shuttle or the closer monitoring position. An IFF transponder embedded within each crew would keep the weapons from accidentally shooting Ashron, should he have to get up close and personal.

Laura responded. "If it comes to that, and Dr. Griid can fly the *Star*, we should set up in the forward post, so we can jump quickly if something goes wrong. I'll get everything ready. Why don't you help Dr. Griid load up and check him out on the shuttle? Let's make sure he won't fly it into the ground. When you're in position, we'll send the all-ready to Hawk."

"As you say, Second Mate," Ashron said with a flick of his tongue. "I am yours to command. Maybe I can sneak a snack from one of the doctor's boxes when he isn't looking."

"I'm going to check inventory," Laura said, but Ashron was already exiting the shuttle.

Hawk kept his gaze locked with Drs. Prasam and Mobem, although Dr. Prasam's golden-blue eyes unnerved him for some reason he couldn't quite name. "Last chance to back out if you want. I see no reason for either of you to take any heat or responsibility for our actions. Even if all goes well, we are in complete defiance of established protocols, and the Diplomatic Corps is going to demand blood."

"Dr. Mobem and I talked it over. We both agree and support this course of action," Dr. Prasam said. "I have worked with Dr. Griid enough that I can say he will agree. Although you are free to confirm that with him."

Dr. Prasam leaned forward in her seat, her face intense and shoulders forward as if she were lecturing an incredibly dense student. "Everything up until now has been based on Trey's encounter with the Kuthrallie. And I see nothing to indicate this new information would be inconsistent with what has been delivered in the past." She turned her intense gaze on Trey. "What I'm trying to say is, near as we can tell, they haven't misled or lied up to this point; I see no reason to believe they are suddenly going to start."

"I was the holdout on that," Dr. Mobem admitted. "I feared possible ulterior, unfriendly motives."

"Any reason why?" Hawk asked.

Tora shrugged. "Human bias. Or perhaps more accurately, dimensional bias. Beings from another plane seem too strange to be up to any good. The flaw is all mine."

"Ten minutes out, Captain." Ship said.

"Thank you, Ship," Hawk replied, standing as he spoke. Wolf was already moving to his station in engineering, followed closely by Trey.

"You two are welcome to join Gerard and me on the bridge," Hawk told the scientists. "If things get spicy, I'd value your input."

"A front-row seat to a first contact," Dr. Mobem said as she stood. "I wouldn't miss this for the world."

Dr. Prasam nodded agreement. "Let's hope the only thing spicy is tonight's dinner." She turned her attention to Gerard. "You lead an incredibly interesting life for a scholar."

Gerard laughed. "You have no idea."

Hawk scanned the room to make sure everyone was strapped in. The four crew members and two scientists had taken their positions, Dr. Mobem occupying Laura's usual seat and Dr. Prasam sitting in Ashron's chair. The main holoscreen offered a close-up of the Serian ship and platform. The Serians stuck close to Wolf's estimated schedule and would soon have the now fully opened platform maneuvered into optimal position for activation. This was assuming everyone's educated guesses had been correct and the Serians weren't doing anything more sinister than opening a bizarre space resort.

"Laura, are you in position?" Hawk asked.

"In position and ready on your mark. Ashron is embedded and one hundred meters out."

Per their plan, Ashron had settled himself over the rise opposite her location. Taking as much advantage of the sparse terrain as possible, he crawled in close to the array, using both his natural stealth and tried-and-true camouflage methods, saving his new shield for when it might matter. As near as they could tell, he settled in unobserved. From his position, he could launch a limited attack on the array and disable it. That was the idea in theory, anyway. They had no way of knowing if it would work until they put the plan into action, an eventuality no one wanted to come to pass. As combat-eager as Ashron always was, it delighted him more when he could ex-fil without inci-dent. Fighting got in the way of eating.

"Wolf? How about you and Trey?"

"Ready when you are, Captain," Wolf said. He turned his broad face to Trey, who was strapped into his seat. The boy's hands, both his real one and his cybernetic one, flexed with excitement and nervousness.

Wolf winked at him. "A little different than your first encounter, yes?"

Trey offered his radiant smile. "Yeah. This is much better."

Hawk let out a deep breath, "Ship, you ready?"

"Ready," she answered. "In position and all offensive and defensive protocols prepared."

"Alright, once more into the breach. Let's hail the Serians on all frequencies and hope they're friendly."

WE COME IN...OH, SHIT

They quickly discovered the Serians weren't exceptionally agreeable to uninvited guests. Within seconds after Ship disengaged the prototype cloaking device and sent out a transmission, numerous warning lights activated on the bridge.

"I've detected a missile lock," Ship announced.

"That turned unfriendly," Hawk muttered. "Laura, sitrep?"

"Looks like you kicked a *relim* nest down here," Laura reported. "Sensors indicate a shield has energized around the entire base, and the Serians immediately went weapons hot and established a defensive perimeter around the main structure. Either they have an amazingly fast analysis computer, or we weren't as undetected as we assumed. In any case, this isn't their first dance."

"Obviously," Hawk said. "Ashron?"

"I'm about ten meters west of the energy source, inside the main shield."

Hawk nodded, though Ashron couldn't see him. "Ship, inform them we don't want any trouble. We just want to talk."

"Already done, Captain. I used the standard Diplomatic Corps phrasing and protocols in all known Galactic languages and sent both mathematical symbology, pictograph phrases, and musical intonations. If it's in the arsenal, I'm broadcasting it."

Hawk considered for a moment and decided to gamble. They had already dropped the cloaking, which is what started this whole mess. There had always been the potential for conflict, but Hawk hadn't honestly expected it to escalate this quickly. Most sentient races would at least pretend to offer negotiation. Hoping the platform had no undetected weapons, he said, "Ship, drop the shields. Wolf, weapons idle."

Though he was busy watching the monitors, Hawk caught the exchange of worried glances between the two scientists out of the corner of his eye. He couldn't blame them.

"Done," Ship and Wolf answered in unison.

"Laura, Ashron, let me know of any change on your end." He knew they would regardless, but the routine of command ran through him like lifeblood. "Ship, rebroadcast all the protocols and offer visual, too. Let them see we're laying here with our bellies up." To avoid a first contact conflict, Hawk would happily offer the illusion of submissiveness, knowing Ship and crew could change posture with the agility of a leopard if necessary.

"Aye, Captain."

"Gerard, firing solutions up to date?"

"They are," Gerard responded, not taking his eyes from his screen.

"Wolf?"

"Same here, Captain."

"Ship, they check out?"

"As good as I could manage, Sean."

Ship could easily handle all the tasks Hawk and his crew were currently performing and do them most likely quicker and with fewer errors. But on discovering Ship's uniqueness, Hawk instituted a policy that she would take over operations only in the direst circumstances. He wanted to keep his crew sharp and battle-ready. Letting Ship handle everything in every situation was a sure path to sloppiness. Plus, and Hawk didn't like admitting this, there was always the possibility something would happen to Ship, or they would find themselves on another vessel without her unique abilities. He didn't want his crew unprepared if they got orphaned.

"Ashron? Laura?"

"Good down here," Ashron said, and Hawk detected the slightest note of irritation in the Lorothian's voice. "I think we'd know by now if they had spotted me. Several of them entered the power structure a few moments ago. They looked determined, faces all scrunched up and frowning. Could be they all had gas."

Hawk couldn't help but let out a nervous laugh. Leave it to Ashron to offer a bad joke in a bad situation.

"Multiple missiles launched!" Ship exclaimed.

So much for diplomacy. "All defensive countermeasures," Hawk barked. "And throw up our new cloak."

It took all of Hawk's willpower to voice the next command. "Gerard, do not return fire." The next one was easier. "Ship, get us out of here." He wouldn't be the aggressor, but he'd be damned if he would sit and be a willing target.

"Laura, Ashron, you two stay frosty down there and keep me apprised. Ship, continue to broadcast our intent as non-hostile."

"I'm not sure if non-hostile is the proper tone to take at this time," Dr. Prasam said. Despite the tense situation, she didn't seem overly concerned—which impressed Hawk.

On the other hand, Dr. Mobem appeared ready to faint, her face pale and hands gripped tightly on her armrests.

"Maybe not," Hawk said, meeting Dr. Prasam's eyes. "But I don't want to respond inappropriately to something that may have been an overreaction by a new officer of the deck on their end."

It sounded both perfectly rational and like total bullshit to Hawk. The Serians had known they were there. Maybe not on day one, but at some point, Hawk and crew had been compromised. Either LaRouche's prototype still needed work, or they had slipped somewhere, and the Serians had lulled them in with their lack of reaction. Nothing he could do about it now. He returned his attention to the holomonitors. "Gerard, sitrep on those incoming missiles."

"Five bogies, slow-moving, ten minutes out. Unknown type. Based on the size and current technology level, which, of course, we know nothing about, they shouldn't overwhelm our defenses, even if they breach our shields."

Gerard's pale face turned up from his monitor, and his clear eyes stared at Hawk. "Of course, we're making a huge assumption on their technology level based on minimal information." Gerard glanced back to his monitor. "And they've passed the first level of countermeasures."

Before Hawk could respond, Laura's voice came over Ship's intercom.

"Hawk, it looks like they've activated the array's power supply. The roof popped open, and the whole structure is glowing a bright gold color. What do you advise?"

Yet again, Hawk was about to offer his thoughts when Trey let out a high-pitched, bloodcurdling shout.

From his vantage point, Ashron observed as two Serians exited the power structure, one obviously of higher rank than the other. Over the past days of surveillance, he and Laura had determined a rough hierarchy of the Serians. They concluded there were two castes involved in the on-planet construction: technicians and laborers. The technicians, oversized computer pads in hand and odd-shaped devices on their heads, ran around indicating various problems, chittering, and often gathering in groups of three or four and holding extended conversations. Typical middle management, Ashron told Laura with a grin. In the meantime, the poor laborers wore loaded toolbelts and turned bolts and welded seams, all while bowing to their intellectual superiors. Ashron could almost picture them at the end of the day gathering for drinks and bitching about how they should be in charge.

Now, however, he came to realize the laborers may have fulfilled that function out of necessity. The long-barreled weapons they held, and their alert posture, indicated to Ashron their primary duty was soldier. Earlier, they were digging latrines. Now, they were ready to jump into the shit.

The apparent leader exited the building with his shorter subordinate and pointed at three workers, who now sported some sort of laminate armor in addition to their rifles. He said something Ashron heard but couldn't understand and gestured at the rise where Laura and Dr. Griid hid. The three grunts nodded in acknowledgment, turned, and loped off in the direction indicated by their officer.

Damn, he thought. *I hate underestimating people.* "Heads up, Laura, you're about to have company. I count three moving from side two."

<hr>

"Copy," Laura replied as she stared at the heads-up display that presented itself in her field of view, checking the quadrant they had designated as side two. When the Serians activated their shield, something in the energy signature affected her monitoring system. It had gone fuzzy when penetrating the shield barrier. She could still make out everything as blurry shapes, with nothing in detail. It was like trying to peer through a shimmering veil of water.

Three vague silhouettes moving beyond the barrier suddenly resolved into a trio of heavily armed Serians as they left the safety of the shield and plodded toward her location.

Guess we weren't as undetected as we thought, Laura mused as she slammed the lid of the case that contained her monitoring equipment. She slipped the thick carrying strap over her shoulder, grabbed her rifle, and ran for the shuttle. "Coming in hot, Griid. Quick dust-off and fall back to our secondary location."

"Roger," came the scientist's nervous voice over Laura's comm. She hoped Griid could fly the shuttle as well as he claimed and didn't freeze up under pressure.

Laura studied her HUD as she ran. Red dots—the Serians that pursued her—played across her field of view. *A couple of Gerard's drones would certainly chase away the itching between my shoulder blades,* she thought. For now, all she could do was stay hidden in the trees, out of range and view, until she reached the shuttle.

Hawk wheeled around at Trey's shout. The others on the bridge had also turned to regard him.

"Are you okay?" Gerard asked.

Trey stared at his open non-cybernetic hand. "Yeah, this is new." A jet-black orb floated above his palm, larger than could reasonably exist within the boy's grasp, as if the globe existed elsewhere...most likely somewhere in ripspace, considering the beings had taken Trey on as their own.

Hawk walked over to Trey's side, joined by Gerard. The scientists watched from a respectful distance. Wolf, after a glance, returned his broad stare to monitoring the action. "You know what it is?" Hawk asked.

Trey looked up, eyes and brows wide with worry. "I'm pretty sure it's a timer. And it's counting down."

"How long?"

"Minutes."

Hawk let out an exasperated grunt. "Son of a bitch. We need to work on your new friends' timing and communication skills," he told Trey.

He centered his attention on Drs. Mobem and Prasam. Tora stared intently at Trey's hand, the curiosity written all over her round face. Hidar's expression was more enigmatic, her dark, deep-set eyes seeming to consider the entire situation more than merely the newest excitement. Gerard waited for Hawk to offer either thoughts or questions.

Hawk stroked his mustache a second, thinking. "Knowing their different understanding of time, minutes could mean anything, but I think we have no choice but to take it literally. Thoughts?" He asked the group.

Dr. Prasam was the first to answer. "Agreed." She turned her yellow-skinned face to Dr. Mobem. "Tora?"

"If we accept that the Kuthrallie are telling us the truth about when the platform becomes operational, and all the ripspace tunnels within the affected area we mapped out will collapse, then we must stop them. I see no other option." She offered an apologetic smile. "Looks like I picked the wrong species to be concerned about."

Hawk regarded Gerard, who, in turn, put his attention on Trey. "Do you have any reason to believe the Kuthrallie are lying?"

Trey didn't hesitate. "No. I'm so intertwined with them, I don't think they could lie without me knowing, even though I couldn't begin to explain how I know *that*."

Gerard turned his attention back to Hawk. "We are acting without authority from the Galactic Council or the Diplomatic Corps. The repercussions of any decision from this point forward are going to be exponentially worse for us."

As he spoke, he removed his blue baseball cap and scratched at his thin, white hair. "But to take no action would be criminal. If Dr. Mobem's calculations are correct, tens of thousands will die, and millions will be condemned to a life of suffering before we can re-establish new tunnels. And that's assuming doing so is even a possibility."

Hawk nodded. "Ship, what do you say?"

"Ship," Dr. Prasam said. "Why are you—" She stopped when Hawk held up a finger and fixed her with a glare that said such questions were out of order. Dr. Prasam narrowed her eyes but nodded.

"If you're taking a poll, knowing what we all know, Gerard couldn't have stated it better, and we are all in agreement. We must act." Ship said to everyone, even the two crew and one scientist on the planet. However, on Hawk's personal connection, she said, "Supernova or black hole, I'm with you to the end. Nothing will change that. The decision is yours to make, and no matter the repercussions, know I will always be at your side."

He smiled, "I know," he said quietly. "And I yours." Hawk squared his shoulders. Face grim and speaking as if was throwing himself and his compatriots off a tall cliff, he said, "Ashron, take out the array."

"On it, boss."

Hawk continued. "Gerard, you'll have to cover his movements while Laura and Dr. Griid are on the move."

Gerard nodded, walked back over to his chair and consoles, and switched control of Laura's remote firing system to himself.

"Wolf, you have weapons."

"Aye," Wolf responded.

Hawk took a seat in his chair. "Ship, activate shields, and get those missiles off our ass."

"I thought you'd never ask," Ship said with a delighted purr in her voice.

Ashron was on the move, using the natural vegetation of high dark green grasses and the gently hilly terrain to slink toward his primary target. His verdigris skin blended well with his surroundings, and he hoped to remain undetected and able to do his job without undue complications.

As he drew close to the buildings, he spotted three soldiers with their attention focused on the perimeter. One had a long rifle of some manner, covered with coils and an optical device that had to be a scope. The creature gazed through the eyepiece, making a slow scan— a sniper. *Best avoid him*, Ashron thought. His hand twitched, eager to turn on his shield, but he needed to conserve the power. He would have to rely on his abilities and coloring to keep him out of sight for now.

The other two soldiers carried smaller weapons; carbines were the closest thing Ashron could relate them to. They served as close support to protect their long-range buddy.

The other Serians, twenty or so at a quick estimate, concentrated on the array itself, still going through their strange movements, though now with a greater sense of urgency.

After their initial inspection, he and Laura had agreed the best and least destructive way to stop the activation was to disrupt the recently constructed power supply. The goal was property damage with no loss of life. If done correctly, it would seem like an accident, which was Ashron's goal. If negotiations improved—or at least commenced—it was easier to offer replacement of equipment than personnel. Machines didn't have grieving families to console.

Staying low and out of the sentries' field of view, Ashron slid up beside the structure. It hummed and vibrated, rattling Ashron in a not particularly pleasant way. His snout twitched at the odor of ozone and dirt. He suppressed an urge to sneeze. With a last glance to make sure he hadn't been spotted, he headed for the door, hoping no one had bothered to lock it.

Laura found herself impressed with Dr. Griid's piloting of the *Little Star*. He handled the craft with deft confidence, adapting well to the shuttle's controls. "As soon as we land," Laura said, "I want to set up quickly so I can take back overwatch from Gerard."

Dr. Griid raised his chin in acknowledgment and launched the craft into a tight bank toward their secondary landing zone.

"Where did you learn to fly?" Laura asked.

"Military reserves," he answered with a gigantic grin. "Back home, service is compulsory. If you're in school, you serve in a reserve component. I learned to fly duster/feeder shuttles on my uncle's farm when I was younger, so I became a military transport supply pilot. Basically, big hulking freighters to transport anything the military needed anywhere it wanted. Not a sexy job, I'm afraid, but a beneficial and satisfactory one. This shuttle is amazing. After this is over, do you think Ashron would let me take it for a joyride?"

Laura half-listened as she kept an eye on her HUD. Several red flashes popped up. "Don't put her down just yet," she told Griid. "Do another hard bank left and circle back. Act like you misread the landing and are circling for a second pass."

"Sure." Griid wavered the throttle, causing the shuttle to dip and yaw as he banked left, approximating an inexperienced or uncertain pilot. "What's wrong?"

Laura sent her HUD feed to one of the shuttle's side monitors to better view the situation. She increased magnification and studied the area.

"The LZ is compromised. Several tell tales we set have been tripped." She double-checked the monitor, looking for a clear spot outside the zone of their trip sensors. Satisfied, she stepped up next to the pilot's chair.

"There," Laura said as she pointed out the *Star's* large cockpit window. "Put down in the clearing over there, but hover two meters off the deck. I want to study the area before we commit."

"Got it." He angled the *Little Star* around to the indicated area. The clearing Laura had pointed out was barely larger than the shuttle, but Dr. Griid managed to bring it in with one minor mishap with a low-hanging branch.

"Sorry," he said over his shoulder. "Six off on my mark. Still getting used to the maneuverability of this incredible thing."

Laura smiled at the doctor's delight and grabbed her gear bag. While the shuttle maneuvered into position, Laura crouched and leaned out the side hatch, scanning the area around the shuttle over the various visual spectrums available through her HUD.

"Mark," Dr. Griid said as he settled the shuttle into hover.

Satisfied with her scan, Laura reached in her bag, pulled out a palm-sized, silver-colored sphere covered with circuitry, and tossed it into the center of the clearing.

"What's that?" Dr. Griid asked.

Laura looked over her shoulder. "One of Gerard's new toys. It covers a wider spectrum than my HUD contacts and will reveal any surprises the Serians might have left for us."

"Gerard seems to come up with a lot of useful devices. And here I thought he was nothing more than an eccentric professor who liked gallivanting around the galaxy. I need to get out more." He indicated the small orb. "Anything?"

"Nothing," Laura replied. Whatever had disturbed their markers wasn't around now and hadn't left anything dangerous. Or if they had, it was fashioned from something the crew had never encountered. From what they had gleaned of the Serians' technology so far, they were just different, not necessarily that much more advanced. Hoping that was an accurate assessment, Laura said, "Go ahead and put down."

After the shuttle landed, Laura slid into her gear harness and snagged her rifle. She held up her hand as Dr. Griid started to get out of the pilot's seat. "No, you stay with the shuttle and be ready for a rapid extraction."

She pointed over to the wood line out the craft's right side. "Ashron will be coming from that direction." She indicated the trees in front of the shuttle. "If the three Serians tracking us know about our fallback position, they will be coming from that direction. And there's no telling if Ashron will have any more on his tail.

"If anyone you don't recognize emerges from the wood line," Laura continued, "you haul ass." Dr. Griid opened his mouth to protest, and Laura held up a hand. "I hate using the words 'that's an order,' but..." She offered a sharp nod, turned, and ran into the woods.

<hr>

Ashron tested the door's oblong handle and found it unlocked. He listened a moment, trying to filter out the ambient noise. It was impossible to hear anything over the hum vibrating through the building. He steeled himself, weapon ready, and prepared to open the door.

Illumination touched the ground as a beam of gold light shot out of the top of the array, heading toward the sky. Ashron stepped back and stared up, narrowing his eyes at the intense glare. The vibration rattled across the ground and shook through Ashron. In front of the array, the Serian workers let out low-pitched ululations, what Ashron interpreted as shouts of glee.

That can't be good, he thought.

Ship calculated the five incoming missiles' speed and trajectory, set up the firing solutions, and launched. Everyone watched as the ten smaller anti-missiles fanned out in their intercept pattern. Ship continued her calculations and updated the information as the distances shrunk. As a precaution, she charged up their anti-missile beam weapons and fed the same information to their systems. "Thirty seconds to intercept," she told the crew.

As they watched, the closest enemy missile's nosecone spun around like a centrifuge and emitted a blur of lasers at the two missiles designated to intercept it. Shortly after, the other four did the same thing, destroying the ten missiles meant to intercept them.

"Never seen that before," Gerard said to no one in particular, seemingly impressed. "Nice touch. Wonder how they fit everything in such a small tube?"

Before he finished his last sentence, a series of dull thuds reverberated through Ship, indicating the launch of more anti-missiles.

"Changing course," Ship said, and everyone braced as the craft took evasive maneuvers. "Fifty AMs launched. Let's see if we can overwhelm their onboard countermeasures."

Everyone anxiously watched the holoscreen as the swarm of small missiles rushed toward the five larger incoming projectiles.

"They've tracked our course change," Gerard said. "Dr. LaRoche's cloaking system isn't foolproof."

"That's why I hate field tests," Hawk muttered. "Wonder what part of 'we come in peace' they missed."

"Thirty seconds to countermeasure intercept," Ship advised.

It was a tense thirty seconds. As the anti-missiles drew within range, the countermeasures spun up. Brief explosions flared as the laser flashes pierced and detonated Ship's missiles. But the lasers, effective as they were, couldn't finish the task before the swarm of remaining projectiles reached and destroyed the incoming weapons.

Hawk smiled when he heard an audible sigh of relief from Dr.'s Prasam and Mobem. He kept his sigh inward, but he couldn't deny the relief that flowed through him as well. "Put as much distance between them and us as fast as you can, Ship."

"Engaging thrusters. Multiple missile launches detected. I count twenty inbound from the Serian ship."

As she spoke, Hawk saw the dots appear and began closing the distance between them.

"Be advised," Ship continued, "we do not have a ten-to-one ratio left in our AM tubes."

"Thanks for the confirmation," Hawk said. He knew his craft's armaments, and twenty incoming missiles with enhanced counter-measures were way more than Ship could handle.

"We should be well out of range before intercept," Gerard said. "But these are unknown weapons, and their launch means they think they can reach us."

"I'd lay even odds they aren't wrong," Hawk said as he watched the bright dots closing on the center of the screen.

Through the optics on her rifle, Laura observed as the three Serians loped in loose formation toward the secondary location, their long, coil wrapped weapons at the ready. At that pace, they would reach the trees in less than a minute. Fortunately, their path would keep them well away from the shuttle's current location.

She took another breath, let it halfway out, and settled the reticle on the last one in line. *Bang*, she thought. She watched as the three continued on, unaware they were being tracked. She gathered her gear and angled toward her primary position when she saw the beam of golden light reaching toward the sky like a sunbeam brought close. The Serians, specks outside the view of her scope, glanced back and then continued running. Gear ready, she stepped forward.

Dr. Prasam pointed at the screen over the central console, where Ship's cameras watched both the surface and the structure that floated in space a short distance from the mothership. "Look, something above the platform is unfolding."

A bright golden beam of light lanced up from the crater dug into the planet's surface and thrust toward space like the finger of God. It struck the parabolic mirror on the bottom of the orbiting structure, the vibrant light absorbed by the curved surface.

Above the collector, a square metal structure unfolded. The sides dropped away, and a protuberance extended from the building's base. As it rose, it slowly started spinning, like a giant gyroscope. The higher it went, the faster it turned. Hawk looked at Trey, who stared at the orb in his hand, sweat on his pale forehead. "I'd say that is what the Kuthrallie didn't want to happen." A pained expression ran over his face. His back arched and body writhed as if electricity ran through his spine. "No...NOW, NOW!" he screamed. "Stop it now, or we're dead!"

So much for subtlety and making it look like an accident, Ashron thought. He yanked the door open, pulled out two grips, each smaller than his palm. He squeezed, activating the pressure-sensitive timer switches, and tossed the spherical grenades through the open door.

As he sprinted back toward the tree line, he reached down and activated his shield. His scales tightened as the energy wrapped around him, vibration replaced by pressure against the hearing membranes in his skull. The low whine of some form of magnetic weapon sounded behind him. Whatever projectile the gun fired, the shot splayed wide enough that Ashron didn't hear it pass him. Despite that, he jogged right to present an erratic target. Invisible and irregular was better than just invisible. He counted the seconds in his head, waiting for the low-powered explosive to destroy the inside of the building.

The massive explosion caught him completely off-guard, and everything went white.

Trey's nerves buzzed with pinpricks, the flood of fear from the Kuthrallie almost too much to handle. He watched the holomonitors, Ship's camera focused on the planetary surface, the beam from ground to space steady, thrumming with energy like a heartbeat. "I can't—" Trey said and paused, unable to voice what he couldn't do. "This is going to—" He stopped again when the golden glow on the surface flared, overwhelming the camera's optics. The lens dimmed down to reveal the building surrounding the crater amid an all-engulfing explosion. Debris flew in all directions.

The beam intensified again, gold turning bright white in a pulse that rocketed toward the platform. Within seconds, it struck the collector. Like ignition to jet fuel, the white light arced over and encompassed the gyroscope. The platform disintegrated, shards of metal dispersing in an upward burst. Seconds later, the mothership followed, flames flaring out and extinguishing in the vacuum of space. Before Hawk could draw in a breath, both the platform and mothership spun outward as chunks of destroyed metal.

"Ashron," Laura shouted over her comm. Smoke hung in the air, distant and silent. But there had been nothing distant or silent about the explosion that rumbled across the plain and warmed the air like a miniature furnace. Even here, she felt a brief wash of heat. The Serians had paused a moment, caught off-guard, as she was, by the unexpected detonation. They had quickly recovered and continued their jog toward their destination. "Ashron," Laura repeated. "Talk to me, damn it."

Nothing.

"What should I do?" Dr. Griid asked, an edge of panic in his voice.

"Maintain, unless you're compromised," Laura said. Her instinct was to go to Ashron; she took a step in that direction. But when the trio of Serians found their secondary location vacant, they would search the area and eventually find Dr. Griid.

"Damn, damn, damn." She kicked the ground in anger and headed to the hideout she had prepared earlier, hailing Ashron every so often as she went.

Trey slumped back in his chair and closed his eyes. The orb had disappeared from his hand.

"Well?" Wolf asked.

"Looks like we might have been just in time," he said, not opening his eyes.

"You okay?"

"Yeah. Suddenly exhausted is all."

Wolf's giant hand patted Trey's shoulder. "I'll be right here if you need anything."

"Thank you."

Gerard studied his console. "Looks like the incoming missiles lost their guidance systems when the ship was destroyed. They're no longer tracking us."

"Keep an eye on them, Gerard," Hawk said. "Ship, active scan and plot a course for that platform and ship, or what's left of them. Let's see if there are any survivors. This has turned into a rescue operation. We need to find someone to give us some answers."

Laura's voice came over Ashron's comm. Based on the insistent edge in her call, she had been trying to contact him for some time. "Ashron, answer me, dammit."

"I'm here," he told her, unsure how long she had been shouting for him and why he only now noticed her.

Other sensations came to him. He lay on his stomach, his head pressed against a solid surface, neck bent at an uncomfortable angle. He rolled over, groggy, and realized the force of the explosion had driven him against the trunk of what had once been a tree, an outlier a dozen meters before the tree line proper. The trunk was sheared off above his head. Splinters lay scattered on the surrounding ground. The scent of burnt metal and grass tickled his nostrils.

"Are you okay?" Laura asked, relief evident in her voice.

"I'm not sure," Ashron said. He tilted his head and stared down the hill; utter destruction—charred ground and devastated vegetation—spread at least a hundred meters in a circle around a deep, pock-marked crater. Smoke drifted from the hole, thin tendrils reaching up like the wispy fingers of a giant ghost. He saw nothing of the array structures or the Serians. He sat himself up with a groan. "Holy shit," he muttered as he took in the destruction. His muffled voice pounded against the inside of his skull; he shook his head and instantly regretted it.

"Talk to me," Laura said. "What happened?"

"It's all gone."

"It's all gone up here, too," Hawk told him. "I think we succeeded."

A glance down revealed a patch of clean, unscorched ground in the rough silhouette of his body. He regarded the shield generator on his belt and saw a dim red glow. It was depleted of all energy. He reflexively patted himself down, checking for injuries. When he found nothing obvious, he said, "Ship, remind me to buy something expensive for Dr. LaRouche. Something exorbitant."

"You got it," Ship said.

He gingerly pulled himself up, placing his hand on the stunted, splintered tree as a support. He studied the area, amazed at the anni-hilation. "Heading to secondary," he told Laura as he began to jog.

"Secondary has been compromised," she said. "The shuttle and Dr. Griid are a kilometer north of there, in a small clearing. Shelter and hide in place, and we'll come to you."

As if her words were a mallet between his eyes, he stopped running. His ears rang like someone struck a gong inside his head, and for some reason, everything smelled like fresh-baked bread. He tried to walk and stumbled over his stupid feet. The world had trouble keeping up with his eyes. "I might have a concussion…"

"You'd better, or I'll give you one for letting me worry this long. Three hostiles are operating in the area, so be careful."

"I'm fine; I'll work my way to you…"

"Shelter and hide in place," Laura repeated. "That wasn't a request."

Just as well, he thought. He was on his hands and knees, staring at the ground with no idea how he got there.

Laura scanned the area, but there was no sign of the Serians. Shortly after the explosion, they disappeared over a rise in the terrain and hadn't reappeared. *Maybe their priorities changed,* she thought. She checked her motion sensors: nothing. "Griid, do you show anything on the shuttle monitors?"

"Negative."

"Alright, I'm coming to you. Let's get Ashron and get the hell out of here."

Laura returned to the *Little Star,* still scanning for the Serians. Things were eerily quiet, as if the explosion had killed everything.

Dr. Griid had Ashron's location pegged on his map and was ready to go when Laura climbed in the side door. She secured her gear as the shuttle lifted off. Laura left the side door open and strapped into what Ashron affectionately called the "door gunner" chair, though there was no gun there. She checked her rifle as Dr. Griid wasted no time buzzing the treetops and getting to Ashron. It appeared he was as ready to get out of here as Laura was.

Dr. Griid's voice came through her thoughts. "He's in a large clearing about two thousand meters out. Looks like he has company; I'm picking up three other signatures."

Laura sighed. *Damn, they must have doubled back.*

Ashron lay on his back and couldn't open his eyes. The sun was too bright, and his head felt like it might split down the middle. The rocks he had fallen on felt softer now for some reason. They were wet too, and something was biting at his chest.

A shadow passed between him and the sun, so he slowly opened one eye. It wasn't a shadow. Someone stood over him, blocking the light. He couldn't focus, and he didn't know if there were one or two. They kept fading in and out. Something bit his chest again, but he still couldn't tell what it was. Laughter reached his ringing ears and echoed through the pain in his skull.

Laura looked at the scene through her scope as the shuttle passed the treetops, and the clearing came into view. Ashron was on the ground. Three Serians stood around him. One had a bronze-colored knife, which they used to poke Ashron in the chest. The other two stood and watched. She couldn't hear them over the shuttle's whine, but their facial expressions and shaking bodies were enough to tell her they were laughing. One of them kicked Ashron in the side; he didn't react.

Don't you dare be dead, she thought as she sighted in on the one with the knife. She released her breath and held it. A slight adjustment of the rifle and the scope's internal computer offered a green glow. She squeezed the trigger. A smooth recoil rocked her shoulder as the projectile left the barrel. Compensators allowed her to quickly acquire her next target and…squeeze…*boom*.

Through Ashron's cloudy vision, he saw the being that stood above him prepare to stab him again. It wasn't a bite after all, but some sort of knife. He couldn't raise the energy to care.

The creature's chest suddenly exploded, covering him with warm liquid. Ashron closed his eyes as the body fell on top of him. The rocks were softer now. Time to rest. He sighed and relaxed, uncaring about what happened next.

The other Serian raised his weapon to fire at the incoming shuttle as soon as he saw his cohort fall dead to the ground. He never got the chance as his chest imploded from Laura's second shot.

She turned her rifle on the third Serian, but he ran away at a dead sprint toward the wood line. She lowered her weapon. *So much for first contact protocol*, she thought. "Put down beside Ashron but keep the shuttle between us and where the other Serian went."

"Yes, ma'am," Dr. Griid said, guiding the *Little Star* toward where Laura had indicated. "Over eight hundred meters from a moving platform," he said as she landed the shuttle. "That's impressive."

Laura considered Dr. Griid's words and gave a solemn nod. "Yeah, I suppose we all have our gifts." Before the dust kicked up in the shuttle's wake began to settle, she grabbed her medkit, jumped to the ground, and ran toward Ashron. "Ship, you available?"

"I am," Ship answered.

"Ashron's down. I'll give you a sitrep shortly. I need you to remotely operate the *Little Star*. I need Dr. Griid with me to…"

Bolts of pale blue plasma flew from the wood line. One passed harmlessly in front of the shuttle. The other two struck and burned through the craft like a hot wire through plastic. Dr. Griid cried out.

Laura dove and rolled as a bolt struck the ground beside her. The dry odor of burned grass and baked earth hit Laura as she skidded over to Ashron and covered his body with hers.

The shuttle spun on its axis, and a hatch opened below the cockpit. Three more plasma blasts emerged from the trees. Two went wide, and the third struck a glancing blow below the windshield. The angled hull deflected the bolt, and it buried into the ground with no damage to the hull but a scorch mark. Ten micro-missiles launched from the shuttle and streaked across the clearing. The line of trees exploded and collapsed as the missiles struck. Leaves and bark plumed through the sky.

"Target eliminated," Ship said.

"Thanks," Laura said. She shoved the dead Serian off Ashron and wiped the deep blue ichor off his chest, trying to determine the extent of his injuries.

"How does he look?" Ship asked.

"Not his best," she said as she opened her medkit. "HUD, give me Ashron's vitals." She scanned the information that appeared in her visual field. "He has numerous superficial lacerations, and he's lost a lot of blood." She studied the scrolling information a moment longer. "Seems like he has internal injuries also." She pulled a bottle of sterilizer and a can of medical sealing foam from her kit. As she worked on Ashron, she shouted back to the shuttle. "Dr. Griid, I could use your help out here."

He yelled back in a scratchy, weak voice. "I, um, I've been shot. Energy bolt went through both legs…can't get up."

"Dammit." Laura glanced down at Ashron. He was unconscious, his breathing shallow and his vitals stable, if low because of his blood loss. She splashed the sterilizer liquid over his chest and, with a towel from her kit, wiped away the worst of both the Serian's and Ashron's blood. She did a quick count. Fourteen punctures, all thin and shallow. She offered a strange prayer of thanks that the Serians—or at least these soldiers—were sadists. His internal injuries worried her. She applied the sealing foam. It wasn't the full nanobot-infused repair foam, but it would do to hold the wounds together until she could give him better treatment. Right now, the goal was to get everyone back to Ship so she could heal them. "I hope you are as tough as we all think you are."

She pulled out two small needles and jabbed them into his thigh in rapid succession. His large eyes popped open, the slits of his pupils wide, and he sucked in a sizeable gulp of air. She took his head in her hands and turned his eyes to her. The pupils narrowed as the light hit them, and he took in another gasp of air.

"You've been badly wounded," she told him, louder than normal in case the explosion had damaged his hearing. "I've administered two shots; one will alleviate the pain, the other will make you feel invincible. You are not. Do you understand so far?"

Ashron nodded.

"Good." His eyes started to drift, so she gave him a soft pat on the cheek to get his attention. He turned back to her, and she continued. "Dr. Griid has been shot, and I need to see to him. I need you to get up and walk to the shuttle. Get in, strap in, and do nothing else. We are safe. Now move." She got up and sprinted back to the shuttle.

Ashron rolled over and sat up. He felt light-headed but no pain. The ringing in his ear membranes had subsided to a small, constant *ting* sound. He looked at his chest, the cuts covered with the dull gray sealing foam, and smiled. If he lived, he would have some impressive scarring. Using his hands for support, he stood up unsteadily and took a step. It felt like something moved on his left side, under his ribs, unmoored from whatever was supposed to keep it in place. He reached down and gave a gentle, probing push. Squishy, like maybe something important had been pounded with a hammer or put in a blender. He decided further self-examination might not be the best idea. He concentrated on his task and took another tentative step, and then another. He peered up; the shuttle seemed a lifetime away even though his eyes told him it was less than fifty meters. Another step. If this was how invincible felt, he wanted no part of it. Ashron knew the shot Laura had given him. *Adrenalum.* He had never used it but knew it provided a significant boost to strength and stamina. The fact it did no more than make him feel he would lose a fight to a kitten told him how close to death he had been. He clenched his jaw. He was still close, possibly as close as he had ever been, but he wasn't about to let the bastard have him yet. "Not today, Ship."

"Not today, dear," Ship agreed. "Today is not your day, my *Arongth.*"

He straightened, heartened by Ship's praise, and took several stronger steps. *Arongth* meant "guardian warrior" in his native tongue. It was a title of great honor, earned and not given lightly. It had almost religious connotations. Ship had just told him she would trust him to do everything in his power to protect her, up to and including death. Another step. He smiled. No, today was not his day. Step.

***

Laura reached Dr. Griid as he slumped forward against the pilot's steering console. She quickly lowered the scientist to the floor. She couldn't take a HUD readout because Dr. Griid didn't have the internal chip Ship's crew possessed, but she didn't need it to see the doctor was in a bad way. Blood soaked the pants on both his legs. Laura slapped an adhesive monitoring strip on Bevril's arm. The readout was as dire as Laura suspected.

The energy blast had burned much of the fabric away, so it was a simple matter of cutting away his pants to assess the damage. She grabbed another can of sealing foam and used it to cover the four holes on the scientist's legs. There wasn't enough for a proper seal, and the gray immediately began turning dark. Cauterization from the heat of the plasma blasts was the only thing that kept him from bleeding out already. Laura was going to have to go old-school. As she searched through the medkit for tourniquet straps, she said, "We need to be in medical right now, Ship. As soon as Ashron gets in, lift off." She found the straps and began to tie off the left leg.

"The shuttle has been holed. Won't maintain pressure. You will need to wear your suits."

"I don't think I can keep him alive if he's wearing a pressure suit and I'm wearing mine." Left leg finished, she started on the right leg. Laura wouldn't be able to periodically relieve the tourniquets if the doctor were in a pressure suit. He would lose his legs, assuming he survived the trip. Laura administered a thickening agent to further slow the bleeding. A momentary memory of two children killed by such a chemical touched her thoughts, and she pushed it away. The person responsible had been handled. Laura rechecked the monitoring band. "His vitals are borderline, and he's going into shock."

Ashron reached the shuttle entrance. He was starting to see double again but still didn't feel any pain. He knew that wouldn't last; pain was your body's way of letting you know to slow down and that you should stop and rest. He wanted nothing more than to do that very thing, but he apparently had a job to perform. He hoped Laura's stimulant would continue long enough to let him complete it.

"Ship, give us a soft launch and meander. I'll patch the holes before we punch through the atmosphere," Ashron said.

Laura glared at him over her shoulder. "You'll do no such thing. You have no idea how gravely wounded you are; those shots will wear off before you know it. You need to sit down and strap in." She turned her attention back to Dr. Griid and said quietly to herself. "I'll figure something out."

Ashron grinned at her back. "Today is not my day." He opened the lower-left supply cabinet and pulled out an emergency repair kit. "Ship, my eyes are doing double-duty; I need you to guide me to the breaches. The patches are self-sealing and easy to apply, so I'll do that and then collapse before Laura kills me."

As the *Little Star* began a slow ascent, the engines thrumming through the cabin, Laura finished tying off the other tourniquet. "I should have shot that Serian sonofabitch in the back when I had him sighted."

"Don't beat yourself up," Hawk said over her comm. "We had no idea what their reaction would be. We're maneuvering closer. Dr. Prasam said she has some medical training and will be able to assist you. She and Dr. Mobem are already in medical, getting things ready." He paused a moment and added, "Besides, apparently Lorothian Princes can choose the date of their death. You worry about Dr. Griid; Ashron will be fine."

"Not entirely accurate, but close enough for today." Ashron nodded as the last of the patches released the compounding chemicals and sealed the plasma burn in the shuttle's hull. "Ship, the shuttle is whole." Noticing the shuttle deck fast approaching his face, he closed his eyes and waited for impact.

He never felt it.

HOPE ISN'T A STRATEGY

Ashron slowly opened one eye to find Trey staring down at him, his blue eyes intense with concern, his short brown hair sticking up.

So, I'm alive, Ashron thought. It was a good start. As consciousness came back, he realized he was lying on a bed and not the shuttle floor—another step in the right direction. Trey wore a light blue shirt and loose-fitting gray pants, the clothing he usually wore aboard Ship, which meant they must be away from the planet. Better and better.

He opened his other eye and realized he was on his bed in his room. His pet python, Dijon, rested comfortably on his branch in the room's corner. Things were considerably better than they had been when he passed out. His eyes focused back on Trey; the boy now wore his room-brightening smile. It amazed Ashron that Trey could still flash that grin with everything he had experienced.

Then a faint scent of broth came to his nose, and he spotted the most important thing. Trey held a tray. He chuckled, a *tray of Trey*. A yellow bowl covered with a lid sat on the tray, a spoon, and napkin beside it. "Good morning. How long have I been out?"

"Afternoon," Trey said. "And almost two days. Hungry?"

"Famished." Ashron bolted up in the bed, ready to gobble down whatever Trey had, and at least four more helpings. The rapid movement made his head dance and the room spin sideways. Something inside wobbled as if it wasn't in place. He flopped back down on his pillow. "That was a bad idea."

"You have a concussion," Trey told him. "Laura said the blast should have killed you, even with the shield. She patched up your insides, but they're still a mess, and your vision may be erratic for several days; that's the good news."

"What's the bad news, then?"

Trey lifted the lid off the bowl. Inside lurked a dark brown broth that vaguely smelled of meat Ashron couldn't identify. "Liquid diet."

Ashron closed his eyes. Cutting out the bright light of the room gave slight relief to his headache. "Trey, I'll give you my Lorothian Royal Sword, the one with the family crest, if you bring me something alive, squirming and slathered in mustard."

"Um, well, Laura made me promise not to..."

"What Laura doesn't know won't hurt her."

"I know everything that happens to my patients." Laura's bright voice spoke up.

Ashron, eyes still closed, sighed. "A little heads up next time, Trey." He reopened one eye and aimed it toward Laura, who leaned against the doorway in her shipboard clothing, a light green short sleeve shirt, and dark blue slacks. "Told you it wasn't my day," Ashron said and grinned, although doing so hurt his mouth. "I appreciate you keeping me alive. How is Dr. Griid?"

"He survived, thanks to you." She walked over, sat beside him on his bed, took his head in her hands, and rotated it side to side, checking his color. "He should make a full recovery. I was able to stabilize him until we got up here, and with the help of the medbay and the other two scientists, I got him patched. He would have died before we got back if he had to go in a pressure suit." Laura set the portable monitor on Ashron's chest and watched as his vital signs played out across it. "You, on the other hand, should be dead."

"I was invincible, remember? You told me so." For some reason, his eye started pulsing so hard he thought it might pop out of his head, so he closed it again to keep it from doing so.

"You have quite the selective memory."

"Well, I either read somewhere, or someone said at one point, that selective memory might be a symptom of a concussion. Or maybe I dreamed it."

She put something warm and floral-scented over his eyes and forehead. The pressure in his eyes immediately lessened, and they now seemed happy remaining where they belonged.

"You didn't help matters by continuing to stand up and then passing out and falling back down. Your internal injuries were impressive, to say the least. The nanobots are doing their work, but I'm not ready to declare you out of the woods yet."

"I don't remember doing any of that. I'd insert a snippy comment about me being in my room and not in the woods, but I'm hungry, and I'm not as quick when I'm hungry. Trey, a spoon if you would be so kind." Ashron removed the heavy cloth and opened his eyes. They still throbbed but not nearly as bad as before.

Trey turned to Laura for approval. When she nodded, he took the spoon out of the rolled napkin and handed it to Ashron. Ashron took it, surprised at how heavy it felt. "What is this thing made off, lead?"

"No," Laura said. "But you are that weak right now. So, take it easy. You're allowed to rest."

"Blasphemy," Ashron said. "Bed, up forty-five degrees," he said. With a *whirr*, the bed shifted upward until it settled into position. "That's much better." He took the spoon and placed it into the broth.

"It might be a little thick," Trey said.

Ashron pulled the spoon out and found the "broth" was more of a stew, although he saw no chunks of anything. He put the spoon into his mouth and slurped down the hearty liquid. It tasted almost like beef, but with a fuller, zestier flavor. "Say, that's tasty. What's in it?"

"Something Dr. Mobem put together," Laura said. "She said something about farm life, your diet, and local ingredients. Honestly, she sounded more like a commercial for locally grown cuisine than anything else. All I know is that some of Dr. Griid's specimens were involved, and I will never drink another smoothie from the blender she used."

He took another long slurp. "The mustard is a nice touch."

"The mustard was my idea," Trey said with a lopsided grin. "But everything else was Dr. Mobem's. She said this should get you back on your feet in no time."

Laura put a gentle hand on his shoulder. "I know you heal fast on your own, and I said this already, but the drugs and bots are working overtime on you. Take it easy and let them do their job. Rest."

"Yes, mother."

"I mean it. Don't force me to make it an order."

Ashron nodded. "I'll take it as easy as I physically can."

Laura returned the nod and sighed while also grinning. "I guess that's the best I can expect from you. But if your third liver falls out, don't blame me." She stood and walked for the door. "Keep an eye on him, Trey; I'm going to check on Dr. Griid."

Ashron waited until her footfalls faded to nothing. To be certain, he asked, "Is she gone?"

"Yes."

He pointed at the bowl with the spoon. "As good as this is, my earlier request and stated bribe still stand." Ashron's tongue flicked out in anticipation. "What do you say?"

"Not a chance." Trey set the drink down next to Ashron's bed. "I need you healthy to continue my lessons. And there's no way I'm going to disobey Laura." Trey chuckled and headed for the door. "Hawk, Gerard, and the rest of the team are in the wardroom, so I need to go see to them." He turned back at the doorway. "Besides, right now, even I could take you."

Ashron watched the young man leave. Considering the strange weight of the spoon and his headache, he had to agree with Trey. A squirrel with a sharp acorn could take him right now.

But that would change soon enough. Laura's exceptional work and the science she employed increased his natural healing rate exponentially. He would be mobile within two days and at full strength within four—a remarkable recovery from a near-death experience. He decided then and there it wasn't an experience he wanted to repeat. He took another bite of the stew. Dr. Mobem and Trey had put together a fantastic concoction. The only thing that would make it better was a large hunk of succulent, rare meat.

Everyone other than Dr. Griid and Ashron sat around the table in the wardroom, screens in hand, drinks of various types close by. Trey perched on a stool near the galley in case someone needed something more. They were all reading the report Hawk and Ship had prepared, and silence reigned. As Hawk had explained, "This details the events leading up to our decision to make our presence known. The second attachment is the AAR or After- Action Report. That includes everything from initial contact to yesterday and has relevant video attached. That document will also contain a critical assessment of what worked, what didn't, and where I think we messed up."

Trey's reader rested on the bar. He had read the report, though not as thoroughly as he suspected others did. He was practicing the speedreading techniques he had learned at school, and, while he could read quickly, he still needed to work on comprehension.

Dr. Prasam looked up from her screen. "This is an impressive and thorough document you've put together, and I've read my share of impressive documents by some quite talented minds."

Hawk smirked. "Yes, well, I would submit that those authors didn't have Ship as their ghostwriter. Besides, we work for the government. Filling out paperwork is a second career."

"I agree with Dr. Prasam," Dr. Mobem said. "A well-written and concise report. However, you left out the discussion we had prior to making our presence known and our involvement in the decision. In this current version of events, you take all responsibility and liability for what occurred. That is unacceptable. I know you're trying to protect us, but I am a grown woman and do not need or desire your protection. We are not unaccustomed to scrutiny nor outside pressures, and I will not let you fall on your sword for this team and me. I can do my own fighting. I won't sign off on this report as written." She leaned forward with a grim look in her eye. "Do I make myself clear?"

As Trey watched the exchange, he saw an eerily grown-up version of Sam. There was no doubt his friend was Dr. Mobem's daughter. That look. The determination in her eyes. The sense of right and wrong. A pang went through Trey's gut. He missed Sam and wondered how she was doing at school. He also wondered if she missed him.

Hawk leaned back in his chair with a thoughtful expression as he stroked his mustache. No one else spoke, but Dr. Prasam nodded in agreement. Wolf smiled his broad smile and knowingly took a sip of coffee. Dr. Mobem never took her eyes off Hawk, and the fire never left. She wouldn't acquiesce. Everyone in the room watched and waited.

Finally, Hawk sighed and leaned forward. "As Captain of this expedition, I have the last say." He held up his hand to forestall any protest. "Make no mistake on where the responsibility or liability falls in any and all decisions made during this operation, irrespective of counsel given or actions taken."

Dr. Mobem tilted her head, anger still on her face, but she kept silent, waiting for Hawk to say his piece.

"Those are the realities of command," he continued. "Regardless of reports written or decisions made completely out of my control, the accountability is mine alone." Hawk smiled. "It may not surprise you that your reaction was anticipated. I will amend the report as you ask, as Ship and I already prepared a second document. Please see if it meets your approval."

"You anticipated my reaction?"

Hawk raised an eyebrow. "Maybe we did surprise you. Ship suspected the three of you would never go for the report as written, so we wrote an alternate version just in case. It should be on your readers now."

"He is giving me way too much credit," Ship said. "The second document references the discussions we had coming to our decisions and contains the transcripts of our conversations in an addendum. There will be no ambiguity or misunderstandings on your input or where you stand. And Dr. Prasam, as the science team leader, your recommendations are highlighted as well."

Tora glanced up from the newly provided documents. "Excellent. The decisions we made were as a team. I understand what you are saying, Captain, but I want people to know that, despite your reputation, you weren't some cowboy running around looking for glory."

"I have that reputation?"

The scientist nodded. "You do. But in this case, counsel was sought and given. Actions were measured and well-considered. I have no regrets and stand with you and your crew." She turned to Laura. "And I am forever in the debt of you and Ashron. Dr. Griid is both a colleague and a dear friend. I will never be able to repay you."

After a moment of hesitation, Laura offered a tight smile. "Thank you. I'm grateful for your words, but there is no debt to repay. We were lucky."

Dr. Mobem stood abruptly, walked over to Laura, and knelt. She took Laura's hands in hers. "You stop this right now. You don't say it, but I can see it in your eyes and body. You blame yourself for Bervil's injuries. You think you should have shot the creature in the back as he ran away. Hindsight is a terrible mistress. You had no idea we had been fired upon or their ship had been destroyed. All you knew was that you made first contact, and it resulted in you having to kill two of them to protect Ashron. The threat was over as he ran away. Your honor is whole, and our gratitude is genuine."

Laura didn't say anything for some time, and Trey watched, wondering if he should go to comfort her, as she had done so many times for him. He remained, deciding this was a moment for the two of them, and he shouldn't interrupt.

Finally, Laura nodded, and this time her expression was broad and genuine. "Thank you," she said.

"I told her the same thing," Hawk said. "But you said it way better than I ever could."

Oblivious to the entire exchange, Dr. Prasam raised her head from the reader. "We need to discuss how coordinated their responses were in space and on planet. I'm seeing something I don't like and would like feedback before I put together my initial sociological report."

"What is it?" Hawk asked.

"Not entirely sure, but it's obvious this wasn't their first incursion."

"And you think it might not be their last."

The alientologist shrugged.

"It seems a reasonable assumption," Hawk said. "And certainly worth discussion. For now, I need all of you to sign off on the amended report. Then we'll transmit it and see if we're going to be hailed as heroes or hung for insubordination."

In the two days since Hawk sent out the after-action report about what the crew referred to as the "Serian Gate Crash Incident," the Knights worked as hard as ever.

Ashron, under Laura's care, healed remarkably well. He still moved slower than usual, but otherwise, someone would be hard-pressed to know he had been gravely wounded so recently. It hadn't affected his appetite. Hawk envied the Lorothian's ability to heal and withstand pain and injury. He wondered if Laura could synthesize a drug from Ashron's blood they could all use.

Dr. Griid also fared well but lacked Ashron's recuperative abilities and had a long way to go. He could join them in the wardroom but needed assistance to get out of bed and travel around the ship. His spirits were high; he even joked about the scars he would eventually have to show off and how his legs had stopped the energy blast from doing more damage to the shuttle.

While the scientists compiled their initial findings for transmission, Dr. Griid studied all the new specimens. The rest of the crew spent their time looking for survivors, which was a futile effort, and gathering any debris from the wreckage that might be useful for study. They found precious little. The superheated explosion had been thorough in its destruction.

Gerard and Wolf determined the construction of the building magnified the power of Ashron's grenades. The shimmery metal was toraluminum coated with a magnesium/selenium compound. The process that combined the chemicals removed the radioactivity but rendered the resultant material highly flammable and volatile. Gerard conjectured the metal was integral to the array's operation in connection with the space platform, which was the only reason any of them could think of for the Serians to use such a dangerous material.

Hearing this, Ashron said, "If they're that stupid, maybe it's just as well we don't meet them." It also relieved him to know he hadn't misjudged his own demolitions. It had weighed heavily on him that he might be getting careless.

The crew also collected the two dead Serian soldiers shot by Laura. They found no sign of the third one that retreated to the wood line. Gerard had been particularly giddy about one salvage item from the mothership that Ship managed to scoop on-board and had spent considerable time in his quarters working with it.

***

"The armada is drawing within visual range," Ship said.

"Get everyone to the wardroom," Hawk said. "Let's see what sort of madness we've unleashed."

It took less than a minute for everyone to arrive. Dr. Griid was last, accompanied by Laura.

"Show us what we've got," Hawk said.

As the holo lit up to reveal the surrounding space, Dr. Griid let out a low whistle. "That looks like an awful lot of ships for a first contact mission."

"A full-sized carrier group," Hawk said. "With a few additions. Considering the odd circumstances, it's about what I expected. Several Destroyers, a couple of Cruisers, and two Supply Freighters. The expeditionary group is a surprise but makes sense; there is a new planet involved, after all. Then there's the diplomatic contingent, although who they're going to talk to now is anybody's guess. I count fourteen. Ship, did I miss any?"

"Your count is correct. The Carrier Group is commanded by Rear Admiral Dillings. The Diplomatic Corps is being overseen by your old friend Elliot Hughes. He has his complete retinue with him."

"What do we know about Admiral Dillings?" Hawk asked.

"Looking at his bio, he and Elliot Hughes are, what's the expression? Thick as thieves. Nearly every deployment where Hughes rates an escort, Admiral Dillings has been tapped for the job. It appears he is a political appointee with his commission sponsored by the Hughes family. The Dillings family are minor royals in the Saltus cluster, with most of their holdings attached to the fringes of the Hughes family influences. Admiral Dillings is the sole military member of the family; the rest are minor perfunctory government leeches or working within Hughes-owned companies. Fleas on a dog."

Hawk barked a laugh. "Don't hold back, Ship; say what's on your mind."

"That's enough about them. Despite that, Dillings' record is unmarked with any detractions, so maybe he's the exception to the rule. Ashron, do you know a Colonel Nassara Graf'eel?"

"I know her family, but not her personally. I didn't know she had made Colonel. Good for her. Why?"

"She is the Marine Commander of the expeditionary force assigned to Admiral Dillings."

Hawk offered him a raised eyebrow as Ashron continued. "Her family is a well-respected clan. They have a long history of military service, followed by public service. Her father is the director of security for the King."

"You mean your father?" Hawk said.

"Yeah, but I figured that went without saying."

The three scientists stared at the demolition expert with varying degrees of surprise and shock.

"Yeah, that's the expression most people have when they find out," Hawk told them. "Followed by sheer disbelief. Ship, have they hailed us yet?"

"If they had, I would have told you."

Chuckles sounded around the wardroom.

"Guess I had that one coming," Hawk said. "Probably deciding if they want to talk to us or open fire. Add Colonel Graf'eel to the communication network along with Admiral Dillings and Elliot Hughes. Send them the debriefing report we prepared for the GC and let them know we are available and at their service."

"Done."

"What now?" Dr. Prasam asked.

"We wait," Hawk said. He leaned back in his chair. "Wolf, any chance I could get a robust cup of your finest?"

Wolf smiled and stood. "Of course. Can I get anyone else some?"

All but Trey and Ashron said they would like one also. Trey busied himself fixing a concoction for Ashron and poured himself a hot tea.

Hawk turned to Dr. Prasam. "It will take Hughes a little while to go through the reports, but he and his family will be furious and out for blood." He looked over to Ashron. "Do you think we have an ally in Colonel Graf'eel?"

Ashron glanced up from enjoying the aroma of the drink Trey had prepared for him. "Yes and no. Her first loyalty will lie with the oath she took as an officer and then to any she may have through her family. As long as she is a Marine officer, she is under no obligation to any family commitments. That's part of the oath we take. Keeps things from getting messy or clouded, like what we have with Admiral Dillings." He took a pleasurable sip and sighed with contentment. "Make no mistake, she will follow orders, even bad ones, as long as they are legal."

"That's all we can ask," Hawk said.

Several hours later, Hawk sat on the bridge watching as Trey, under Gerard's tutelage, practiced finger exercises while reciting equations that would release thaumaturgic energy. Trey stopped short of stating solutions to the equations, since nobody wanted magic firing off inside Ship. Hawk compared it to dry firing a weapon to get used to it.

According to Genray, because of Trey's time learning under Gerard before coming to the school, he breezed past what most preternatural scientists considered basic equations: floating small items, making a spark, or hiding an inanimate object. What he was learning now was more complicated and potentially more destructive. So, until they returned him to school, where they had buildings set up for such training, Trey would turn in his homework incomplete.

Hawk's attention alternated between Trey and the armada as they positioned themselves to complete their tasks. No one had reached out to communicate with Ship, which Hawk had pretty much expected. They were ignoring him and his crew while they determined the best course of action among themselves. So many protocols and departments to deal with, each wanting their say. Of all the pleasant things Hawk could say about working with Galactic, the bureaucracy and political machinations weren't among them. So, he watched and waited while the various fleet elements moved to carry out their assignments. One of the freighters angled toward the debris field created by the destroyed platform, escorted by one of the destroyers. The expeditionary force transport was positioning itself into a geosynchronous orbit over the location of the now-destroyed array. Hawk surmised they were going to send a science crew and dispatch of Marines to secure and explore the area. According to Ship, a science team had already dispatched to the planet to investigate the beacon that drew their attention in the first place. Everything was standard operational procudures per Galactic regulations.

Everything except the rest of the fleet positioning themselves around Ship to block any exit route.

Gerard stepped away from Trey and peered over Hawk's shoulder at the monitors. "Not unexpected."

"No, but disappointing," Hawk answered. "I was hoping for a more measured response, although with Hughes involved, I should know better."

"You always say hope isn't a good strategy," Trey said from across the room, his fingers bent in a formation that made Hawk's hands hurt in sympathy.

Hawk smiled. "And it's not, which is why we aren't going to rely on it. Ship, how is our orbit in relation to our earlier conversation?"

"Almost there. At this drift rate, another hour or so, and we should be in position."

"Excellent." Hawk studied his chart and compared it to the fleet's positions, which Ship conveniently provided on a strategic layout. He traced his finger along their projected course. "What do you think?"

"Based on my calculations," Gerard said, "they'll have us encircled before we reach our destination."

"That's what I figured. Let's force their hand. Ship, all ahead full."

"Aye, Captain."

"'Full' for a ship of our class, not our full capability."

"Of course."

"That should get their attention," Hawk said as he continued to watch his monitor.

Trey had walked up behind them, apparently more interested in their situation than his studies. "Why are you running?"

Hawk turned to the boy's inquisitive stare and grinned. "I'm not running. They've been slowly positioning themselves to surround us, waiting until they had us trapped before they opened communications. Not sure if they think we're stupid or simply not paying attention. Anyway," Hawk pointed to a spot on the monitor. "I want to stop here. But I want them to think they forced us there."

"Captain, we're being hailed," Ship said.

Gerard laughed. "That was fast."

"Hughes must be on the bridge with the Admiral," Hawk said. He checked the updated positions of the ships. They had dropped the pretense of casual maneuvers and adjusted to Ship's dramatic course change. "Don't answer yet, Ship."

"Very well," she said.

Gerard indicated on the chart. "What do you think? About here should be good."

"That's what I was thinking, too. That way, we can decelerate all the way there and drift if we need to." Hawk drew their attention to the shifting positions of the armada vessels. "Look."

"What?" Trey asked, his brows bunched in confusion.

Gerard answered. "Two of the Destroyers and a Cruiser are accelerating to get out ahead of us and cut off our escape."

"You don't need subtlety when you have superior firepower," Hawk said.

"We're being hailed again," Ship said. "They're being more insistent this time."

"Guess it's time we talk to them, then." Hawk plopped down in his chair and faced the main screen. "Put them up."

The holo popped up to reveal a young man with short blond hair, a square jaw, and an expression that said he took his position way too seriously. He wore a Galactic Navy officer's uniform, a dark blue coat with silver highlights over a pale tan shirt. Hawk always thought it a sharp-looking outfit, although he never had the desire to try it on. The shoulder insignia gave the young man the rank of Lieutenant Junior Grade.

Hawk put on what he hoped was a disarming smile. "Good afternoon, Lieutenant. What can I do for you?"

The man did not return the smile. "You will stop at once and come to a stationary position." His voice had the bark of command, as if he were rehearsing for the day when he had a higher rank.

Hawk dropped his smile. *So that's how they want to play it.* "I see. Lieutenant, what is your name?"

The man's stern expression disappeared, replaced with confusion as if surprised Hawk hadn't immediately jumped at his order. "Um...Lieutenant Junior Grade Bannon, communications officer of the GS Carrier *Noble Sacrifice*." He quickly regained himself. "You will decelerate at once and come to a stationary position."

Hawk paused and scratched at the center of his mustache with his index finger, pretending to consider the request.

"Mr. Bannon," he said. "I didn't realize we were under any sort of movement restriction. I have received no communication from your fleet since you arrived. Are we under arrest? Or are we free to move about?"

The Lieutenant glanced off-screen and back to Hawk. "Of course, you are not under arrest; we simply request you remain here until we finish our investigation into the destruction of the alien vessel."

"Your fleet's actions would seem to indicate otherwise." Hawk leaned forward. "Let's not banter about or toy with one another, okay?" Hawk glanced over to Gerard, who looked up from his plotting system and nodded.

"Helm, all stop," Hawk said as he returned his attention to Lieutenant Bannon. "Please inform the good Admiral Dillings—although I know he can hear me since he's standing beside you out of view, along with Diplomatic Officer Elliot Hughes—that he can call off his destroyer escort. I will wait for his invitation to go over my report and will answer any questions he or others have, but I will not sit idly by while bloated egos try to intimidate me and pretend they have jurisdiction over my actions."

Hawk heard a sputter and a "How dare he..." off-screen but continued as if he hadn't. "My report is thorough and complete, with no hidden agendas. If I do not hear something soon, I will assume there are no questions and will depart. If you try to detain me, I will lodge a formal complaint with the Galactic Navy and JAG. I have my own people to report to, and I will not waste their time waiting while certain people play 'my dick is bigger than yours.' Captain Sean Grey out."

Hawk saw Admiral Dillings, anger on his broad, wrinkled face, walk into view behind the stunned Lieutenant before Ship cut off the connection.

Trey busted out laughing, and Hawk turned to see the boy's red face as he continued to chuckle. At Hawk's bluster or juvenile language, he didn't know.

"And that, Trey," Ship said, "is why our dear Captain is not part of the Diplomatic Corps."

"Well, they needed a push," Hawk said. "And I would submit that I stimulated diplomacy, as we are likely to hear something from them soon."

"I'm hearing something from the Admiral right now, but it's not family-friendly."

"See, it worked. Diplomacy. Maybe we can cross-train and transfer when we get back. Push Hughes's family out. A win for everybody." Hawk glanced Gerard's way to find the engineer shaking his head. "Ship, tell the Admiral I stepped out and will get back to him shortly. Gather everyone in the wardroom. I want to get things straight before we accept the invitation to visit the admiral's carrier."

"Are we agreed?" Hawk asked those gathered around the table in the wardroom. Heads nodded all around.

"We've backed you this far," Dr. Prasam said. "In for the prologue, in for the epilogue, as they say."

"They do?" Ashron asked.

"Cultured people do," Laura said with a smile. "So, you're excused for not knowing it."

"Okay," Hawk said. "Ship, bring the admiral up on screen before he has an aneurysm."

A holographic image appeared in the middle of the table, showing Admiral Dillings standing there with an expression as if he were ready to chew the bulkheads. The admiral was an older man with a head of gray hair worn in a buzzcut. His face carried the wrinkles of a life under stress, but none around his mouth to indicate he had ever laughed or smiled. His nose was thin and pointed, and he stared over it with dark eyes. He had the pale complexion of a man who has spent his life on spacecraft, with little time for sunshine, even the simulated kind available in any large ship's fitness room. Currently, that paleness was suffused with the red of anger.

"They've opened the line," an off-screen voice said.

Dillings glared at the monitor, his gaze seeming to hit everyone at the table at once. "Commander Grey," he said in his raspy voice.

"We've been seeking communications for the past fifteen minutes. Explain yourself."

"Issues with our comm system. Interference from the debris would be my guess."

The Admiral didn't look like he believed a word of it, but Hawk didn't care. "Fine," Dillings bellowed. "Now that you've answered, we want—"

"One moment, Admiral," Hawk said. "Record."

"Recording," Ship said so everyone could hear, including the admiral.

"The following is a conference between Admiral Dillings of the 56th Galactic Carrier Group, commanding the GS *Noble Sacrifice*, and the commander of the Galactic Scout vessel *The Flaming Star*, on special assignment and commanded by Sean Grey."

"What are you—" the Admiral said and stopped when Hawk held up a finger.

"Present at this conference are the following." Hawk listed all the crew members gathered around the table, pointing to them as he named them. The Admiral fumed, his face again turning red, as Hawk continued.

With the crew named, Hawk indicated the two scientists present, identifying them and their roles in the mission. He finished with, "Not present is Dr. Bevril Griid, who is in the medical bay recuperating from injuries sustained on the planet. He will be privy to this recorded conversation, should he wish." Hawk stared at the Admiral, whose mouth was pressed into a line so tight his lips had all but disappeared. "The recording is timestamped according to the Universal Calendar standard and begins now. Okay, Admiral, you can proceed."

"What was the meaning of all that?"

"Protocol," Hawk said. "According to both the Galactic Armed Forces Manual and the Codes of Interstellar Regulations, all official conversations between military personnel and civilians are to be recorded. To prevent any misunderstandings."

The Admiral glared at Hawk, who stared back and waited. Just because Hawk didn't like the bureaucracy game didn't mean he couldn't play it.

When it seemed the Admiral wasn't going to speak, Hawk said, "What was it you wanted, Admiral?"

"I want everyone on your ship to report to the *Noble* posthaste," Dillings said. "We have convened an official board of inquiry to question both your actions and the resultant outcomes. The bay will be waiting to receive your shuttle."

Before Hawk could respond, Dr. Prasam spoke up. "No."

"I beg your pardon," Admiral Dillings said.

"Beg all you want; you won't receive it. My team will not be coming to your ship."

"I'm ordering you to bring yourself and your team to my vessel," the Admiral's face was turning red again, and Hawk wondered at the man's health.

"Be that as it may, we are an independent science team and civilians. As we are not currently on a wartime footing in this system, we are not beholden to any emergency laws. We will remain on this ship and monitor the unfolding situation."

It took all of Hawk's willpower to keep the grin from splitting his face. The Admiral now matched the color of a tomato, no doubt from both being defied, and knowing he had no recourse but to accept Dr. Prasam's assessment.

Hughes stepped into the camera's view, his face covered with the haughtiness he had doubtless been born with. Looking at the people gathered, he offered an unctuous smile. "Dr. Prasam, I understand your reluctance, and I have nothing but the utmost respect for the sciences."

Ashron snorted, which earned him a glare and quick headshake from Hawk.

"But," Hughes continued, "your testimony will be integral to the official military and diplomatic report, as you can bear witness to the events and the rashness of both Captain Grey and his crew in creating what will certainly be a precarious situation, considering the delicate nature of first contact with an unknown race."

Spoken like a true diplomat, Hawk thought, *and totally the wrong tack to take.*

"We have filed our report, along with the report filed by the captain. It contains everything we wish to say. If you are convening an inquiry, you can submit further questions to our legal team, which can be found in the capital city on Berol."

"But—" Hughes started.

"This conversation is done," Dr. Prasam said as she stood, her voice brooking no debate. "You have our answer." She nodded to Hawk, who nodded back. Dr. Mobem stood, and the two scientists walked out.

"Don't you dare—"

Hughes was again cut off, this time by Admiral Dillings. "Let it be." He looked at the remainder of the crew. "They may be civilians, but the rest of you aren't. This is a formal request and order to attend a military inquest to investigate your extralegal actions regarding contact and engagement with the newly discovered and unclassified, unnamed species."

"We call them Serians," Ashron said.

"Do you always name things right before you kill them?" Hughes asked.

Ashron offered the diplomat a toothy smile. "Yes, I do, *Mr. Hughes.*" His grin crept wider.

Hughes stepped back at the expression. Hawk shook his head.

"You may call them what you want," Dillings continued. "Captain Grey, I want you and your entire crew heading toward my carrier within the hour. That is an order."

"Understood," Hawk said, ready for the conversation to be over. "Cut the feed."

The image of the Admiral and Hughes disappeared before either could say anything else. Hawk looked around at his gathered crew members. "I'm going," he said. "But I'm going alone."

INQUISITION

tubborn damn crew, Hawk thought as he watched from the co-pilot's chair while Ashron maneuvered the *Little Star* toward the indicated bay on the carrier. Despite his protests, the rest of the crew insisted on coming with him. If one went down, they would all go down. After some back-and-forth negotiations—and it still astonished Hawk he had to negotiate with a crew he supposedly commanded—they had agreed to have Gerard and Trey remain behind. Trey was a no-brainer. Gerard had taken more convincing, but when Hawk explained his reasoning, the rest understood and accepted. So, Ashron, Laura, Wolf, and Hawk were on the shuttle, three more people than he wanted with him.

"Automaneuver engaged," a sexless voice said over the shuttle's speakers when they had approached within five hundred meters of the carrier. Ashron released the joystick as the larger ship's computer took over, pulling them toward the bay's maw.

"Like a whale swallowing a fish," Hawk said.

They waited, Hawk tapping his fingers on the armrest as the shuttle drew closer and finally landed on the deck. With a loud mechanical *whirr* and *click,* locking clamps engaged on the craft's landing gear while the bay doors closed.

"Looks like we have a heavily-armed Marine welcoming party," Ashron said as he stared out the shuttle window. Hawk followed his gaze and saw a platoon of Galactic Marines, dressed in their black and gray shipboard uniforms, trot on to the deck and move out of sight, presumably to take up formation outside the shuttle, next to the currently retracted ramp.

"Guess I should expect that," Hawk said. "After all, why wouldn't you send twenty Marines to escort five people to an inquiry? Now I'm certain they would have fired on us if we tried to leave."

As he unbuckled from the seat, he stood and scanned his three crew members, his eyes settling on Ashron. "Do nothing that could be interpreted as a hostile move."

Ashron cocked his head in imitation of a puppy, all sunshine and innocence.

"I mean it. We all know there's more to this inquest than simple military matters. Hughes is looking to settle a score. And if he isn't, caution is the watchword anyway. Let's do nothing to set them off or give them an excuse."

"Maybe it is nothing more than a formal inquiry," Ashron said. "We did accidentally blow up equipment and kill people. Seems like they might want to know why. Maybe you need to go back to drinking; you were less paranoid then."

"Hold that thought until after this," Hawk said. "Ship, how is your reception?"

"Crystal clear, Captain. All crew cameras are active, and everything will be recorded in visual and audio. Seems they anticipated we might try this, but Gerard and I figured out how to circumvent their jamming signal."

Hawk raised an eyebrow at Ashron. "An ounce of paranoia prevents a pound of pain."

Laura winced. "You might want to leave aphorisms to the professionals."

Hawk flashed a grin, then grew serious. "Game faces, everyone. We're throwing ourselves into the pit. Wolf, open the door."

Wolf reached over with his large hand and hit the red button beside the door, disconnecting the locking mechanism. The shuttle door slid open, letting in a rush of oil-scented air. Hydraulics hissed as the ramp extended toward the deck.

Hawk stepped up to the door and, as he guessed, the Marines stood ten to a side in parade rest, spaced perfectly to allow the ramp to land. And in front of the formation, a meter from where the foot of the ramp would hit, stood Colonel Graf'eel, her uniform crisp, her boots shining. The Galactic Marines had always impressed Hawk as a force, though he found their training ethos problematic. They were a special breed, represented by every known race, and the individuality was trained right out of them. A Galactic Marine was a soldier first, a teammate second, and somewhere down the list, their personality might be allowed to emerge.

A glance at this group told Hawk they were top drawer, likely the Colonel's personal squad. He found himself wondering what it would take to be chosen to join her. He glanced over to Ashron. The Lorothian's long mouth was stretched in a tight grin, and he nodded, pride gleaming in his yellow eyes.

Hawk, determined to show well for these troops if not for their brass, squared his shoulders and strode down the ramp. He paused at the bottom and stared down at the Colonel. She was short, like all Lorothians, barely more than a meter-and-a-half tall. Her skin gleamed a lighter shade of green than Ashron's, more akin to moss than grass. Her snout was also smaller, her eyes larger and paler, and a stout ridge of bone ran from her forehead toward her back, though Hawk couldn't see where it ended.

Hawk saluted. "Captain Sean Grey and crew reporting. Permission to come aboard."

Colonel Graf'eel crisply returned the salute with her long-fingered hand. "Permission granted." She shifted her body to Ashron and offered a slight bow, then returned attention to Hawk, "I was told to expect six."

Six? Hawk thought. *She must mean Trey.* Although Trey had been sitting in the wardroom during the conversation with the Admiral, Hawk had not mentioned the boy's involvement with the Serians in his report. The people who knew about Trey's participation didn't need it reported. "My science officer elected to remain behind with the science team, and my ensign has had a stimulating couple of months and needed a break." He glanced at Laura. "His doctor insisted."

"I see," the Colonel said. "The Admiral will be…" her eyes narrowed the slightest bit. "Disappointed."

Hawk wanted to say something to the effect that the Admiral should get used to it, but he refrained. "I will explain everything to Admiral Dillings in our meeting." *If he gives me the chance.*

"Very well," she nodded. "Please follow me." She turned and spoke in a loud, authoritative voice. "First Lieutenant, on me."

Her squad executed a crisp ninety-degree turn as one and fell in beside her, flanking Hawk and his crew. She marched ahead of the procession, her steps measured and sharp.

Ashron couldn't keep the delighted grin off his face. "If the rest of her brigade are half as good as this lot, she could take the palace with one hand tied behind her back." He glanced at Hawk. "Her father would be proud."

"I take it her Prince is," Hawk said.

Ashron sized up the platoon one more time. "He is. He is, indeed."

Hawk wasn't sure if Colonel Graf'eel heard Ashron, but her back seemed to grow straighter.

Wolf looked down at Ashron. "We haven't been told as such, but you realize we are being escorted as prisoners, not esteemed guests."

"I do," Ashron said. "But we have rated the Colonel's personal squad and attention, which indicates how much the brass either respects or fears us. But more importantly, the Colonel won't allow any misunderstandings." He glanced back over his shoulder and up at Wolf. "This is no puppet goon squad that will do the Admiral or Hughes's bidding on a whim." He turned forward again and spoke louder to be sure everyone could hear him. "I'm fragile, remember? Dr. Laura said so. I don't want to inadvertently fall down a flight of stairs."

The remainder of the silent walk was a series of lifts and corridors.

The personnel they passed gave them a wide berth and openly curious stares. Hawk offered a curt nod to any who caught his eye.

They eventually reached a large hallway with a set of double doors. Six guards stood before it, three to a side. Though burly and severe-looking, they were not Marines. They wore the blue and silver of the Navy. A Lieutenant Commander stood before the door. As the group approached, he strode forward. "Thank you, Colonel. I will take it from here. You are dismissed."

Without another word, he regarded Hawk with a sneer of contempt. Colonel Graf'eel stepped directly in front of him, her eyes narrowed. All her squad glared at the man, a score of faces mentally dressing him down.

Though the Lieutenant Commander stood a foot taller than Colonel Graf'eel, her presence, backed by her platoon, left no doubt about who had taken charge of the situation.

"Lieutenant Commander, a word." With an outstretched arm, she indicated an area away from their respective troops. He looked down and opened his mouth, but she locked eyes with him before he could speak. Through a toothy grin that reminded Hawk of Ashron's smile right before he launched into a fight, she said, "It's not a request."

She wrapped her fingers, claws extended, around his bicep and guided him to the indicated area, away from the rest of the group.

At first, it appeared she and the Lieutenant Commander would have a heated discussion concerning the merits of adherence to the military command structure, but the conversation quickly turned one-sided. She spoke while he moved his mouth up and down like a fish gasping for air but never got in a word. Hawk couldn't hear what Graf'eel said, but he imagined she had no fondness for being summarily dismissed by someone two ranks below her.

Ashron smiled as he tried to overhear. "I would hate to be on the receiving end of that lecture," he told Hawk. He nodded his snout toward the black-haired man the Colonel had called First Lieutenant. "It looks like he might have an idea of what it's like."

The First Lieutenant had a knowing smirk on his long, birdlike face that reflected a fair amount of pity for the current recipient of the

Colonel's wrath. Ashron returned his gaze to the conversation. "I don't know her, but I already like her." Colonel Graf'eel moved her mouth close to the Lieutenant Commander's ear. He had stopped moving his mouth and paled considerably.

"Think she's going to bite his ear off?" Hawk asked out of the side of his mouth.

"Nah," Ashron said. "Humans are too gristly and bitter-tasting to eat."

She spoke directly into his ear for a few seconds, and he nodded rapidly. She retreated half a meter, smiled a Lorothian's tooth-packed smile, and spoke so all could hear. "Thank you, Lieutenant Commander, for your understanding."

She turned to the six guards still standing at the door, having made no real move to do anything for their commanding officer. "Gentlemen, if you would kindly open the door and move aside, I must fulfill my duties."

They deferred to the Lieutenant Commander, every set of eyes going to his face. He nodded. Four of the guards took a step back while the two closest to the wide double doors opened them by pushing the panel on the wall. It was a ceremonial gesture at best.

Hawk sensed the tension between the Marines and Naval officers. Subtle at first, it grew as the Colonel and Lieutenant Commander had their impromptu chat. He had seen rivalry between service members, but there was more here. This was personal, and it made the hair stand on his arm. He didn't want to be around if their cold war ever went hot.

"First Lieutenant, take charge."

The young First Lieutenant popped to attention and gave a sharp nod. "Yes, ma'am." With precise, quick hand gestures, he split the platoon into two units and had them enter the conference room and spread along the back wall on either side of the entry doors.

While he performed this task, Colonel Graf'eel and another Marine, a dark-skinned man with black hair shaved tight to his head and a horizontal scar on his forehead, stepped over to Hawk and his crew. "I wanted to take a moment to introduce you to my second, Sergeant Major Bishop."

Hawk returned the Sergeant Major's salute and held out his hand. They shook hands. "A pleasure."

Bishop nodded, his face impassive.

Colonel Graf'eel continued. "Sergeant Major Bishop speaks for me. If you ever need anything, his word is as binding as mine. He will escort you inside. Since you saw fit to send me a copy of your AAR, I will be on the inquest panel." She narrowed her eyes at Hawk. "That action did not win you any points with the Admiral, nor me for that matter. I will not take sides," her eyes flickered over to Ashron. "No matter who you have on your crew."

Hawk met her intimidating gaze. "Please don't misunderstand my intention in sending you our report. As the Expeditionary Force commander, I wanted you to be fully aware of the circumstances first-hand so you could draw your own conclusions. This way, you won't receive any information through a potentially contaminated filter."

Her nostrils flared, and she offered him a predatory smile. "That's an interesting way to acknowledge a probable negative agenda and declare I might be lied to in order to be manipulated. It could be argued that your filter is also contaminated, and you are attempting to do the very thing you claim you're trying to avoid."

"She's a sharp one," Ship said in Hawk's ear.

"That's true," Hawk said, answering both Ship and the Colonel. "But I at least wanted you to have our side of the story *also*, so you may judge fairly."

The Colonel considered this for a moment. "My judgment doesn't really matter, but I appreciate the consideration." They nodded to each other, and the Colonel turned and strode into the conference room.

"Oh, I *really* like her," Ashron said.

"Pull it in, schoolboy," Hawk told Ashron. To the Sergeant Major, he said, "That is one fine Marine."

"One of the finest I have ever had the pleasure of serving; she demands excellence in herself and leads by example and action." He gave a lopsided half-smile. "It doesn't hurt that she's a Lorothian, and I suspect you know how deadly they can be."

"I do."

"We'll follow her to hell if she decides she wants to go. Not blindly, mind you. But then, she wouldn't ask us to. Her bad decisions are better than most commanders' good ones." His smile disappeared. "She won't break, or even bend, the rules. For you or anyone else."

"I'm counting on it, Sergeant Major. I'm counting on it."

A Navy Lieutenant appeared at the door. "Sergeant Major, you may escort your charges in now."

"Thank you, Lieutenant." He turned to Hawk, his friendly demeanor replaced with the mien of the professional soldier. "Captain, if you and your crew would follow me." He entered, and they followed him through the double doors.

It was a military auditorium, twenty meters to a side. Several rows of chairs were set up, an aisle cutting through the middle. A long table sat at the front on a raised dais with five people behind it, facing Hawk and his crew. A smaller table and six chairs sat before it. Hawk noticed the newness of the platform which held the larger table. Someone had deliberately set this up so the people sitting at the smaller table would have to look up at the people on the dais. Intimidation 101. Hawk grinned tightly. They would have to do better than that to bully his crew.

In a loud voice that would make a drill instructor proud, the Sergeant Major bellowed, "Commander Sean Grey of the Knights of the Flaming Star, Lieutenant Commander Wofanienlapabeko, Lieutenant Commander Laura Benzing, and Lieutenant Ashron Ses Ateron." The man pronounced Wolf's name correctly without missing a beat, and Hawk was glad the Lieutenant Commander knew nothing about Hawk's standing thousand credit reward to those who managed that difficult feat.

Hawk studied the assembled panel while the Lieutenant Commander saluted and stepped over to join his unit on the rear wall. He recognized three of the five people facing him. Admiral Dillings sat in the center; Elliot Hughes was to his right, and

Colonel Graf'eel sat two seats to the Admiral's left in the outermost chair. Hawk did not recognize the other two. Another civilian sat beside Hughes in the other outside chair. Hawk could only suppose it was one of Hughes' close advisors, although he had not been present at the memorial where Hughes and Hawk confronted each other.

A Karenain Navy Captain sat directly to the Admiral's left, his frog-like, dark blue head almost disappearing in his uniform. Hawk also noted the conference room was empty except for the Marine escort and twice as many Navy Masters at Arms. Everyone lined the outside walls, the Marines sandwiched in by the Navy members.

Hawk looked at his crew. "Quite a reception committee." He waved his arm to indicate the setup at the front. "This is why I wanted to come alone. Shall we?"

He strode confidently down the aisle and heard the soft thud of feet as the others followed him across the carpeted floor. He stopped in front of the small table and saluted. "Commander Sean Grey reporting." His crew stood at attention behind him.

Hawk held his salute, waiting for the Admiral to return it. Dillings glared at Hawk for a moment and said, "Cut the display, Commander; it will get you nowhere here."

Hawk dropped his hand to his side. "My apologies, Admiral, I didn't realize following protocol was a 'display.'" He caught Colonel Graf'eel's eye and saw she also noticed the lack of proper decorum.

"Where is the rest of your crew?" Dillings said. "I specifically directed you to bring your entire staff. I don't recall allowing room for any exceptions."

Hawk remained at attention. "No, Admiral, your request was quite clear; however, regulations prohibit leaving a vessel unattended while drifting in space. Someone might consider it abandoned and either salvage it or take claim on it, demanding a handsome reward should the owners return. Not to mention, it would be a major navigation hazard, considering the number of ships surrounding her."

A flush rose in the Admiral's cheeks, and Hawk mused that Dillings would be a horrible poker player. "It would not have been abandoned, Commander; the science team made themselves available to watch over it while you were here."

"That is true, Admiral, but they are not Naval Officers nor are any of them trained in ship operations. Should an emergency arise, such as an onboard fire, or the need to maneuver to avoid an object of some sort, I felt it prudent, for their protection, of course, to leave someone behind as a contingency."

"And what of the boy? I'm sure you have a good reason why he did not accompany you."

"If you are referring to Ensign Julien, that would be doctor's orders. His encounter with the alien race has left him…scarred and—"

The red in his face getting brighter, Dillings interrupted Hawk, his loud voice filling the room. "Calling a thirteen-year-old boy an Ensign is an affront to all who wear the uniform. If he is so scarred that he needs medical attention, he should have been brought here immediately. We have a fully equipped hospital with an impressive psychological wing and a team of *real* doctors who can perform an *impartial* evaluation. Your violation of orders under the guise of protecting civilians falls well short of any legal test I can envision."

Hawk could sense Laura's tension behind him, but she kept silent. Hawk was beginning to grow irate himself but maintained his calm demeanor. He wasn't going to give the Admiral nor Hughes the satisfaction of getting him riled. "The Admiral may not be aware, as it is unusual for a ship of our class, but Lieutenant Commander Benzing is a board-certified medical doctor in good standing." *And miles above any of the trogs you might have.* "As for Ensign Julien, that would be a decision above my paygrade."

"Yes, it seems you perform a lot of functions and make a lot of decisions above your paygrade, wouldn't it? Holding the rank of a Navy Commander with only five direct reports seems suspicious at best, and perhaps illegal." Dillings leaned forward and glared at Hawk. "Now, sit down and stop with this pretense that you rate some sort of respect from a uniform and rank you did not earn."

Hawk had observed Elliot Hughes in his seat twitching like

someone with insects stinging his legs, burning to say something. The Admiral's last dig was more than Hughes could take.

"Admiral, if I may, it's the same thing with his title of Earl. Given because someone adopted him out of pity, like a stray dog. And like a stray, after his master died, he killed off the only other heir and slipped into the role as if he belonged there. He has no bloodline to claim and none to follow. It seems to be a theme with him: titles claimed and not earned. He is nothing but a common con artist. It pleases me no end that you have seen through his elaborate charade." He stared at Hawk like a victorious predator, almost tripping over his nose as he looked down it. His voice dripped condescension as he said, "Yes, Sean, do sit down."

Hawk held his arms out to his side as Ashron, Laura, and Wolf advanced. He regarded his crew, not at all surprised to see their eyes glittering with fury.

Ashron whispered, "I can take all but the Colonel before those goons along the wall ever react."

"I believe you," Hawk said. "Even if you are injured." He stepped back to encompass all three in his vision. He spoke quickly since he knew he wouldn't have much time before the panel interrupted him. "We knew this was a possible scenario, but I never anticipated it would be this overt. That's why I wanted to come alone, but I'm grateful, nonetheless. Consider the source." He winked at them. In a louder voice, he said, "Now stand down."

Before he turned to face the big table and Dillings, Hawk scanned the back of the room and caught Sergeant Major Bishop as his hands dropped away from his stun baton, and he gave Hawk a grateful nod. The Marines were professional and would maintain order if necessary, but Hawk was going to do his best to make it unnecessary. The disappointed looks shared among the Admiral's goons along the wall told him they realized they had missed a fight they were itching to have. In Hawk's experience, people who always longed for a brawl had never been in one, with Ashron being the notable exception. Based on their unchanged expressions and relaxed manner, the Sergeant Major and his Marines ascribed to this rule also. The goons along the wall had missed out on a learning opportunity; they just didn't know it.

Hawk spun back to the dais and found four smug expressions staring down at him. Five years with Ashron had taught Hawk how to read Lorothians, and he saw Colonel Graf'eel's face was a mixture of confusion and anger. She had walked into this expecting a board of inquiry and was beginning to realize she had stepped into something different and far less pleasant.

"I said sit." The Admiral's tone dripped with the same arrogance as Hughes. His implication was clear; he had latched on to Hughes' comment about stray dogs and was treating Hawk appropriately. Some of the Navy men along the wall chuckled.

Hawk smiled, though what he wanted to do was leap up and slap Hughes and the Admiral. He reflected that less than a year ago, he might have done precisely that. "Admiral, if you have an issue with my or my crew's ranking within the Galactic Military, you need to take that up with the Council. And Mr. Hughes, you may take up my lineage and my right thereof with me personally and not hide behind this panel."

Anger flashed over Hughes' plump face, and Hawk waited, hoping the aristocrat would foolishly speak the formal challenge. He opened his mouth but stopped when the Admiral put a hand on his shoulder. "Sit," the Admiral repeated to Hawk and his crew, "before my men make you sit."

As his eyes scanned the room, Hawk prepared to tell the Admiral how big a mistake that would be, but he caught a warning head shake from Sergeant Major Bishop and held off.

With a feeling he was doing nothing more than delaying the inevitable, Hawk tried a different tack. He would discover exactly how much of a sham this proceeding was.

"Admiral Dillings, you are an officer in the Galactic Navy, so I assume you or your adjutant would have done homework on my crew and me, as you had requested my whole crew attend what you claim was an inquest. Thus, you should have known that my Chief Engineer, Lieutenant Commander Wofanienlapabeko, is of Uraxian descent. Therefore, you would have provided appropriate seating for someone of his stature."

Hawk gestured to the six human-sized chairs before him. "Since you didn't, I am forced to make several more assumptions, to my regret. First, I assume the adjutant or whoever you assigned the task is either incompetent, or you never informed them. After all, there are few Uraxians in military service, so it could have been an oversight on that person's part. But what I find more likely is that it was done as a direct slight to humiliate and offset us. Similar to putting yourself and your panel on a dais to elevate your position and to project authority. I think after our first few minutes here, we all know which it was."

"How dare you? Take your seat. And that is an order."

"I will not sit comfortably while one of my crew is forced to stand. I will take a seat when the proper accommodations are provided for my entire crew, as is my right under Military Law."

Admiral Dillings had again turned that alarming shade of red, although rather than looking distressed, he seemed close to gloating. "I don't believe you are in a position to quote Military Law to me, Commander Grey. I, your superior officer, am giving you a direct order: take your seat and address this panel as you are bound to do."

Hawk grew tired of the charade. Who knew how long they could go like this, getting nowhere? Time to force the issue. "Admiral, with all due respect, I would be happy to sit before a proper inquiry board and answer any questions they may have about our actions and motives both before, during, and after our contact with the Serians. However, I don't believe it was ever your intent for this to be a proper board of inquiry. And our current exchange isn't about me sitting in a chair. It's simply a *trosh* and *trangon* show with the intent of proving my insubordination. But I say again, under Military Law, my crew is entitled to appropriate accommodations. Until those are provided, this board is not in session, and we are not required to do anything. So, either fulfill my request or carry on with your charade. In either case, I'm sick of playing around, and I stand with my crew."

A giant smirk covered Hughes's face. "You make it so easy."

Admiral Dillings turned to him with a frown. He spoke low, but

Hawk heard it anyway. "Keep quiet." He waved his hand to the Master at Arms along the wall. "Senior Chief, place these four under arrest and throw them in the brig."

A large man who nearly rippled out of his Chief's uniform advanced with a nasty grin. "A pleasure, Admiral."

Hawk watched the rest of the Navy men push themselves off the wall and step forward, evil intent in every eye and malicious smiles spread among them. This is what they had been waiting for; they had probably thought they were going to have to sit through hours of boring testimony before getting to this point. But as Hughes said, Hawk made it easy for them by accelerating the timeline. That was fine with Hawk. He'd rather go down swinging than be ground down by humiliation, especially at the hands of someone like Hughes.

"Belay that last order."

The authority in the voice stopped everyone in the room as they turned to the source. Colonel Graf'eel stood at the table, the presence of command radiating off her. She had barked the order in her battle-field voice and expected unquestioning obedience. Her thin, piercing eyes scanned the room, pinning the Navy men where they stood.

Hawk knew he would always remember the shocked expression on the Admiral's face. The red flush had receded, replaced with open-mouthed amazement and wide eyes. He was unaccustomed to having his orders questioned, much less countermanded. "Colonel, what is the meaning of this?"

She moved around the large table, indicating she no longer sided with those gathered to question Hawk. She strode over to the Admiral and stood directly before him. She kept her voice low so no one along the wall could hear what she said except those on the dais.

"Enhance hearing all," Hawk said in a low voice. Now he and his crew would also be able to hear what the Colonel said. She might not approve, but Hawk needed to know the situation they faced.

"I will not be a party to this travesty," the Colonel said. "Nor will I belittle or bring dishonor to the Navy or Marines in any way. You should have left me out of this, but that wasn't possible, was it?"

She turned and glared at Hawk. He took a half step back at the fury of her gaze. Whether she had somehow figured out he was listening or was still angry about him sending the unrequested After-Action Report, he didn't know.

Admiral Dillings didn't bother to keep his voice low. He wanted everyone to hear. When he spoke, spittle formed around the corners of his mouth. "Colonel, you will stand down. Take your squad and get off my ship before I have you and your men thrown in the brig along with Captain Grey's team."

Hawk looked around and took stock of the room. The Marines had all left the wall, their posture tense and alert. Sergeant Major Bishop and his young First Lieutenant stood on either end of the platoon, ready to give orders and offer support if necessary. The Navy Senior Chief, standing beside Sergeant Major Bishop, also took it all in. It was clear by his nervous, flickering gaze around the room, followed by a sidelong glance at Bishop, that the Chief knew precisely how this would end if it came to a stand-up fight. The Navy men had arrived geared up for a brawl; the Marines were outfitted for war. Hawk hoped Dillings didn't push things to that point. If necessary, Hawk would capitulate. He wanted to corner Dillings and Hughes; he didn't want people hurt to make it happen.

"That would be unwise, Admiral," the Colonel said, still quietly enough so no one but Hawk and the crew could hear. Then she raised her voice. Not the bark of command, but forceful. "These are my charges, and I intend to see them tried either through a formal board of inquiry or a military court of law. You placed them in my care when you had me escort them from their ship. Clearly, you never considered them anything but convicts and guilty without cause."

She waved her arm to encompass the people sitting at the table. "This was nothing but a sham. Therefore, the chain of custody never left my control. Article 104 is quite clear. I can quote it if you'd like, especially the part about Marines having jurisdiction of prisoners on Naval warships."

"This is dangerous ground you're treading on, Colonel," the Admiral said, his voice taking on a menacing edge. "Perhaps career-ending. This is a secure room, and nothing is being recorded."

Hawk spoke up. "That's not entirely accurate, Admiral."

Admiral Dillings flashed Hawk a glare. "Accidents happen to prisoners all the time, Mr. Grey. You and your crew might…"

As Admiral Dillings spoke, his holographic image appeared in the middle of the conference room, and his voice blared over the speakers hidden in the wall.

"What the hell?" Dillings said, and his face and voice echoed through the room with minimal delay. "What did you—." He stopped as the hologram again mimicked his actions and words. He glared at Hawk with a newfound hatred. "How dare you…"

"As you referenced earlier, a little something I picked up from a group of undeserving people above my paygrade. Insurance for, as you said, 'accidents.'" Though the hologram disappeared, Hawk's voice also played over the sound system.

Hughes stammered at his seat, and Hawk hoped the Earl was about to say something stupid and damning.

The Admiral held up a hand and made a shushing noise. "Silence, Hughes. Not another word." He looked back to Colonel Graf'eel with narrowed eyes. "I believe we were discussing the terms of a prisoner transfer."

The Colonel showed no sign of victory. Her face and voice remained professional. "As I said, Article 104 speaks to the jurisdiction and custody of prisoners; Article 105 to their care. I assume full responsibility for both."

The Admiral took a breath. His flush had gone, and he was now all cold business. "Article 22 details court proceedings and depositions. I insist these prisoners be available promptly for any questioning at any time."

"I see no problems with your request."

"That was not a request, Colonel. And neither is this." He glared down at her. She returned his gaze, seemingly not intimidated, or ever unduly bothered, by his angry stare. "They will be incarcerated on *this* carrier in *my* brig. As you said, Marine jurisdiction on a *Naval* warship, which this still is. Therefore, you are under *my* jurisdiction. Are we clear?"

"As the sky above."

"Good. You are dismissed." He wheeled around and stormed for the rear door. "Come, Hughes. We have much to discuss."

Yes, little doggie, follow your master, Hawk thought. Although he had to wonder who controlled who. As they disappeared through the door, Colonel Graf'eel came into Hawk's view. She stood with her hands on her hips, her pupils nothing more than vertical slits in her large eyes. Hawk caught a barely perceptible tail flick he had seen before from Ashron. He glanced over at the Lorothian, who witnessed the same thing.

"Shit list," Ashron said. "It looks like you just made it to the top."

"She'll have to take a number," Hawk said.

Colonel Graf'eel turned to her troops, dismissing Hawk for the moment. "Lieutenant, take two Marines to a secure a location in the brig that will hold these four. Keep in mind we now have a Uraxian in our charge."

The Lieutenant gave a crisp salute. "Yes, ma'am." He pointed at two of the other Marines. "You two, on me." The trio left the room.

The Colonel spoke to Sergeant Major Bishop. "Escort our prisoners to a temporary secure location until the good Lieutenant contacts you." He nodded his understanding, and she regarded Hawk. "I also want to be clear. Though you have not been formally charged, you are nonetheless prisoners, not guests. I can cite the statute that allows me to do this, but I trust that won't be necessary. Act accordingly, and you will be treated accordingly. Do not try me on this."

"We are in your debt," Hawk said.

She stared at him, her tongue flicking in and out, but nothing else indicated what she thought. She offered a curt nod, then walked toward the exit.

13

AT THE SPEED OF TIME

Gerard looked at the three scientists, who had been watching everything unfold on the wide-format holo in the wardroom. Dr. Griid was the first to speak. He winced as he shifted in the special chair they had given him to keep his injured legs elevated. "Well, that jumped the *tillick* in a hurry. What do we do now?"

"It's not as dire as you might think," Gerard said, shifting his cap back on his head. "We knew Hughes and the Admiral had something up their sleeves. We didn't know what exactly, but we had a solid idea when the Admiral insisted he wanted the whole crew on the carrier. Dr. Prasam threw a wrench in their plans by outright defying the Admiral. Dillings wanted us all on the *Noble Sacrifice* so he could control the narrative and present all his evidence to the Council without giving us a chance of rebuttal. With us divided, and especially now that he knows we have audiovisual evidence of his sham court, his only move is to impound our ship and transfer us over to the *Sacrifice*, whether we want to go or not. Ship, I assume they're still blocking our transmission capabilities."

"As far as they know, they are."

Gerard smiled. "Of course, even what we have isn't enough to do anything. What Hughes did was irregular and perhaps unethical, but he could get a savvy team of military lawyers to get him exonerated of any illegality."

"But he threatened Hawk," Trey said. "Isn't that illegal?"

Gerard shook his head. "He made an implied threat, but he could easily get out of that one with the tried and true 'I was just joking' defense."

Trey frowned. "That's stupid."

"Way of the universe," Gerard said. "But back to your question, Dr. Griid. What do we do now? We leave. We can use Dr. Mobem's newly discovered rip tunnel entrance to return to Berol. It's unlikely our captors are aware of the tunnel yet. That's why we chose this location. Right now, they probably believe we'll stay close and either wait to see what happens or try to negotiate for the crew's release. We need to move before they decide differently and send a boarding party. Go prepare for rip jump and let me know when you're ready. I'll be on the bridge."

When Gerard reached the bridge, he placed himself in the navigational chair and began hooking up for rip jump. "Any change?"

"Not yet," Ship answered. "They've maintained position and not attempted contact."

"Good," Gerard said, plugging in the last of the connections to his golden arm. "Let me know as soon as everyone is down and ready."

Gerard double-checked his connections and went over the route that would return them to Berol while he waited. Before long, Ship came back over his comm. "Everyone is in ripsleep. Dr. Mobem adjusted the dose slightly to keep them out longer than usual in case it takes us longer to escape this mess. And you are about to have company."

"What do you mean?" Gerard turned at a movement in the corner of his eye and saw Trey walk onto the bridge.

"I don't think I need to sleep during the transition anymore," Trey said as he took a seat next to Gerard.

"You don't 'think,' or you're sure? Being wrong could have grave consequences."

"Yeah, I know." He considered a moment and said, "I'm sure. I'm not afraid of the Kuthrallie anymore. Ship and I talked about this, and we think sleeping during the transition might hurt me more than help. I've done this once already one time before, and I didn't have a ship. Remember?" Trey gave Gerard a boyish grin.

"All too clearly. I also remember that it almost killed you. Speaking of which, how's your back?"

Trey shrugged. "Nothing different, so I guess things are calm for the moment." He smiled. "No imminent disasters we need to avert."

"Good," Gerard said. "I think one crisis a month is plenty. Ship, are you certain about this? Laura will kill me and scuttle you if something happens to Trey."

"More certain than I am about making this jump before a beam from one of those Destroyers over there cuts us in half."

Gerard looked thoughtful for a moment. "Alright, then. Trey, take the Captain's chair. Grab the controls and feel how they move as Sara pilots the ship. Don't fight them. Lightly wrap your hands around them, so you get a feel for the subtle nature of being a ship's pilot. You might as well learn something while we're at this."

"Filamentous!" Trey leapt over the side of the Captain's chair, caught his foot on the armrest, and fell into it headfirst.

"You okay?" Gerard asked.

Trey looked up over the back of the chair, a sheepish grin on his face. "Yeah, I'm all right."

"Not the way to instill confidence in your crew, Captain," Gerard said with a laugh. "Strap in. Let's see how serious they are about keeping us here."

Trey took a moment to adjust the seat and harness to fit his smaller frame. It was almost too big for him. He reached out and took the controls, making sure to be gentle and not move them. He hoped

Gerard couldn't tell his hands were shaking. "I'm ready," he said, and cursed internally when his voice cracked.

Gerard smiled. "We will begin on your mark, Captain."

"Me?"

"Yes, you."

"Um, er, okay," Trey sat straighter in the chair. He had seen Hawk and Laura do this a hundred times before, so why was he so nervous? "Ship, um…ah."

He glanced over at Gerard.

"All ahead full," Gerard said under his breath.

"Right. Ship, on my mark, all ahead full. Mark."

"Aye, Captain," Ship said. "All ahead full. Any bets on how quickly we hear something from the fleet?"

Trey could feel the controls move under his hands as Ship accelerated. His heart jumped into his throat, and his pulse raced. He wasn't controlling the ship, but it felt like he was. There was power beneath his hands different than anything he had ever experienced. No wonder Ashron and Hawk liked to pilot, even though Ship was autonomous. Trey was hooked. If they survived this madness, he would be asking for more lessons and chances to "pilot" Ship.

They were closing in on the recently discovered ripspace entry point Ship and Dr. Mobem had found. Gerard felt confident in his assessment; the armada knew nothing about the tunnel. Even if they had bothered to begin any sort of astrocartography—an unlikely prospect—they would not have had time to analyze the data. That would buy Ship breathing room, as Hughes and Dillings would most likely think Gerard had panicked and was running for deep space. The Naval Warships could easily keep up or outpace the smaller ship with ease. Or so they thought.

Despite Ship's assertion, Gerard wasn't unduly concerned Dillings would have Ship destroyed or even fired upon. The Knights were too high-profile to disappear in such a dramatic manner, especially with so many witnesses. The Armed Forces could be insular and tight-lipped, but something as big as the destruction of Ship would get out, no matter how hard a lid someone tried to clamp down on it. So, he wasn't worried as they approached the rip tunnel. At least, not too worried.

"They're hailing us," Ship said.

"Put them on screen," Trey said, unconsciously imitating Hawk.

"Cool your jets there," Gerard said with a smile. "We want to buy some time to get into position."

Trey's cheeks turned bright pink. "Sorry, I got caught up in the moment."

"Actually, Gerard," Ship said. "This might work in our favor."

The more Gerard considered Ship's implication, the more it appealed to him. "I like it. Trey, I want you to talk to the Admiral."

"Me?" Trey squeaked. The idea made him want to crawl under the chair. "What am I going to say to him?"

"Just be yourself, Trey," Ship advised. "Tell him you're scared, and you are running away."

"I am scared."

"That's fine," Gerard said. "Nothing wrong with being frightened. Use it. The Admiral is going to ask you questions you won't have the answers to. Say whatever comes to mind; it doesn't matter at this point."

"I don't know…"

Gerard spoke in his most reassuring tone. "After everything you've been through, dealing with the Admiral will be like first grade. You're smarter than he is by a long shot. And we're here with you."

Trey again straightened up in the captain's chair, taking courage. He had been through a lot, possibly more than someone like the Admiral had. He was a Knight of the Flaming Star. Time to prove he deserved the name. "Put them on screen, Ship."

The holographic image that popped up revealed Lieutenant Junior Grade Bannon, the communications officer they had encountered earlier. His stern expression changed to a cocked head of confusion when he saw Trey in the captain's chair. Clearly, the man had been expecting Gerard or one of the science team. "And who might you be, young man?"

"I'm Trey," he said, projecting confidence he only halfway felt. At least he wasn't dealing with the Admiral.

Bannon glanced down at something off-monitor, most likely an information console of some sort, "Yes, I see here: Trey Julien." He glanced up and quickly back down again as if something had tried to bite at his feet. He looked back up with his eyebrows raised. "Ensign, Galactic Navy?"

He heard a muffled, "Bullshit," from offscreen, easily recognizable as Hughes' voice.

Bannon continued. "Presently attending the Order of the Sterling Arch as a Freshman." He smiled, although Trey didn't think it was a particularly friendly one. "It says you are, however, currently studying abroad. Given your current situation, that might need to be amended." His not-friendly smile disappeared, and now he appeared downright mean. "Alright, Ensign," he said, contempt in his voice. "Where the hell do you think you're going?"

Trey swallowed hard. "Back to school. I'm late for class."

"I see. At your current direction and speed, you should make it back by the time you're three hundred years old. Where is the rest of the crew?"

"You arrested them."

"I was referring to the ones currently on your ship."

"They're taking a nap."

"So, all of the adults on your ship decided to let a thirteen-year-old boy pilot them back to Berol? Without making a ripspace jump?" The derision dripped from him so much Trey expected it to take on a physical presence. "You're going the wrong way."

Trey examined his plotting screen. He was still learning the details of how to read the device, but near as he could tell, the military ships were easily keeping pace, which was not a surprise considering Ship hadn't adopted a quick speed. Other ships maneuvered to intercede and force Trey to stop or crash. "I'm lining up to make a turn and head the right way."

An obviously irritated Admiral Dillings, his cheeks red and face snarling, stepped into view. "That's enough. This is Admiral Dillings of the *Noble Sacrifice*, flagship of the Galactic Navy's 56th Carrier Fleet. Your captain and crew have been put under arrest, and I am impounding your ship as evidence. You, your preternatural scientist friend, and the three members of your science team are also under arrest."

"On what charges?" Trey asked, anger overstepping his fear. Out of the corner of his eye, he caught Gerard's astounded expression.

The Admiral was so surprised his head rocked back slightly. "I don't know who you think you are that you have the temerity to ask me such a question, and I won't dignify it with an answer. I do not recognize any ridiculous rank you or your captain may think you possess. And I will not negotiate with a child who is pretending he has hijacked a military vessel. My words are for the rest of the crew who are standing where I can't see them. Cease and desist all ship operations. This is an official notification that you are hereby under arrest on the charges of first contact protocol violations, destruction of unknown personnel and equipment in relation to said violations, and anything else I can think of when I have a moment. Your ship is hereby impounded. Currently, your charges are pending a court of inquiry. You have five minutes to comply. If by that time, you choose not to obey my direct lawful order, you will be branded as fugitives, and I will give the order to destroy your ship. End communication." The hologram went blank.

Trey turned to Gerard. Sweat had gathered on his forehead. "That was no fun at all. Do you think he means it?"

"I didn't think so at first, but I do now. He knows after the conference room incident that we can record all conversations regardless of his countermeasures. It won't be long before he realizes he may not be able to stop our broadcasting capabilities. If he impounds our ship, he can erase the recordings. If he destroys our ship, he doesn't have to worry about the recordings, and he'll deal with any fallout from such a brazen act. He'll control the narrative at that point, and history becomes what he says it is. Right now, he has the Navy believing we're criminals. If we're dead, it might be hard to prove otherwise. Ship, I think it's time to go."

"Couldn't agree more."

***

"Admiral, they're accelerating."

Admiral Dillings raised an eyebrow. "The die is cast, then. Lock on and fire on my mark."

"Aye, sir."

***

The controls moved under Trey's hands as the craft responded to Sara's commands. He stared at the bridge monitor, seeing stars, other spacecraft, and the projected area of the ripspace tunnel entrance, a roughly circular-shaped void where no stars showed. Long strings of red mist streamed from the darkness, appearing like trails of vaporized blood. His back grew warm and tingled. He got a strange, not unpleasant feeling of being gently tugged toward the tendrils as if he belonged within those reaching branches. Far from the horrific dreams of monsters and destruction that usually accompanied his jaunts into ripspace, this beautiful sight comforted and soothed him.

Trey pulled his eyes away from the screen—a tougher feat than he expected—and looked over to Gerard to see if he was witnessing the same calming view, but the magician's eyes were closed, and his arm glowed red, light dancing off it in a way similar to the tendrils. Trey watched his plotting screen as Ship made a slight adjustment to their flight path.

"We are approaching the point where most people need to be in ripsleep," she told him, communicating through their newfound link, which was much better than having to hear her out loud. He was not old enough to receive the in-ear implant like the rest of the crew, but this was better. Warmth from her presence surrounded him and made him think of his mother. Rather than the heavy guilt such memories often brought, he felt a closeness to the times when they had been happy—before the war and the death.

"Watch," Ship told him. "Gerard calls to the *aether,* and it responds."

Trey watched as more and more tendrils emanated from the hole. They started to envelop the ship, and their presence inundated him as they wrapped themselves around and through every surface of the craft.

"Don't fight the *aether* when it comes," Ship told him. "Breath it in; embrace it." The mist floated toward him. Gerard was already swathed, his eyes closed, his arm glowing and sparkling with red and orange energy.

The mist crawled up his body, reaching over him like searching fingers. It was chilly but not uncomfortably so, and he had no fear. He closed his eyes as it danced over his face, and he inhaled deeply. And he saw them again: the Kuthrallie. This time was different; he wasn't cold, hungry, and afraid. He hadn't been ripped from his comfortable surroundings against his will. This time he was prepared and had invited them. They reached out, dancing through his mind, trying to communicate, not out of urgency, but curiosity. They weren't monsters attempting to devour the ship; they held it together as it approached ripspace. They kept both the vessel and the people inside it from flying apart and dispersing into the *aether.* As Trey watched, he saw two Gerards, one floating above the other, who sat in the chair. While the one in the chair didn't move, the other, more insubstantial one, moved slowly, as if he stuck in liquid. Red mist danced about both forms. Gerard's motions were deliberate, though Trey had no idea what they signified or accomplished.

Suddenly, Trey's breath caught, and he felt as if two giant hands crushed him.

"Locked on, sir."

"Fire."

Fortunately, the feeling of being crushed disappeared almost before Trey understood what was happening. He opened his eyes, which he didn't realize he had closed, and watched as the tendrils intertwined around Ship and yanked them into ripspace. It happened in a blink. One moment they were in deep space, surrounded by black and stars, and then they were in rip, encircled by swirling gray that was as close to nothingness as Trey had ever seen. A tunnel stretched both before and behind them, the way created by the Kuthrallie. Trey "saw" all this in his mind, and he could follow the full path that would take them to Berol. The one thing he couldn't sense was how fast they were moving. Nothing showed up on any of the monitors, and he had no frame of reference, nothing to see outside the bridge windows to help. His new senses gave him nothing.

At the speed of time, something whispered to him.

"What do you mean, gone?" Dillings asked.

As the red mist faded away and things returned to "normal," Trey turned and saw Gerard unhooking the wires from his arm and looking at Trey.

"Are you okay?" Gerard asked.

"Wow. That was intense." Trey started to unbuckle. "Is it always like that?"

"I don't know what you experienced, but what I experience is the same every time." Gerard finished disconnecting and pulled himself out of the chair. "I want us to compare notes later. I am curious if we encounter the same things. But for now, Ship, wake the science team."

"Already on it."

14

────────

MOTIVATIONS

Admiral Brooks Dillings stood on the bridge of the *Noble Sacrifice* and watched the entities under his command go about their work, having all recovered from the ripspace transition. While in ripspace, much of the ship functions were automated, and his crew made sure all the systems ran according to specifications.

They were a good crew, and it annoyed him that his group had been sent on this chase simply because of the whims of a man who knew the right people and had the right influence. If Dillings had his way, there would be no such thing as nobles or holdings or any of the associated trappings; the entire Council structure was based on such ridiculously complex and antiquated notions. Considering the number of planets and races involved in the Coalition of the Galactic Council, he supposed they had to come up with something all the member planets would accept. The Admiral simply wished it involved better criteria than money and land and perceived superiority. In his heart, he wanted things handled first and foremost by the military. But he had studied enough history to know the foolishness of such an idea.

"Admiral?" a reedy voice said from behind him. He turned to find his adjutant Reeksus standing there, an annoyed expression on his thin, cyan-colored face. His long, broad ears also twitched in irritation.

"Yes?"

"Mr. Hughes is in your stateroom waiting for you." At naming Hughes, Reeksus's mouth puckered as if he had eaten a lemon.

The Admiral frowned as he felt the blood rising with the familiar *thud-thud* in his ears. Hughes was going to give him a heart attack or stroke before this was over. He cursed the day he ever got involved with the Hughes dynasty, rued the day he ever accepted their help. But there was nothing to be done now other than get through this madness and hope he could extricate himself without too much damage to his career. He was looking forward to retirement soon and hoped this imbroglio didn't derail those plans. "Thank you, Reeksus. I'll see him."

Dillings strode across the bridge and entered the room that served as his quarters on the bridge. He found Hughes in there, impudently seated in one of the two high-backed chairs before the rectangular desk. Though formed from plastic, the desk had the appearance of caramel-colored wood.

Hughes was pale. Well, paler than usual. A reaction to the ripspace transition, Dillings figured. Some people didn't handle it well, and it was tougher on a large vessel like this, which didn't carry a sufficient medical contingent to administer ripsleep. Thus, ninety percent of the ship, including civilian personnel, had to let the automated system figure out the proper dosage to put them under. The machines erred on the side of higher dosages, thus occasionally leaving the unlucky recipient with a sleep hangover.

Dillings considered offering Hughes some juice to help restore him and then decided against it. "What do you want?" Dillings snapped as he sat behind his desk.

Hughes peered at him with his dark eyes. "Once we reach Berol, I want you to take custody of the remainder of Grey's crew so they can stand trial with the rest. Since you let them slip away, I've taken it upon myself to communicate with my contacts in the Council embassy in Berol. They are standing by to demand Gerard's arrest. And the brat too."

Dillings wanted to reach over and slap the man. The arrogance surrounding him put the Admiral's teeth on edge. Everything about this situation riled him up.

The most annoying part was that the man wasn't entirely wrong. Dillings had underestimated Gerard; he hadn't expected him to jump into a previously undiscovered ripspace tunnel and leave his captain and friends behind like he did. He also hadn't expected them to break his jamming signals around the conference room and record the "board of inquiry."

Dillings leaned forward, easing the pressure in his face and ears. "If the Council manages to take him into custody, they can transport him to Creron. There's no reason for us to take him on board. In fact, once we reach Berol, I'll turn the entire crew over to the Council for transport, and my part in this is done."

"Your part in this is done when I say it's done."

Something snapped in the Admiral. He had to let out his steam or explode from inside. He stood and slammed his hands on the plastic desk, causing Hughes to start back in the chair, eyes wide.

"Listen up, you arrogant little shit," Dillings said. "I've participated further in this than I wanted to. I'm not sure why you felt you needed a full carrier group to accompany you on an exploration and diplomatic mission, and I don't care, but I'm done. Your desire to take Commander Grey and his crew to trial is a waste of time and resources. Nothing more than the petulance of a scorned man. I won't have any more to do with it."

Hughes had quickly recovered from his fright once he realized the Admiral was going to attack him with words and not violence. "You came along willingly enough when you thought there was a chance for some glory, a chance to meet a new race, and maybe go to war with them. You should want to see Hawk go down. You hate him as much as I do."

Dillings shook his head and sat back down. Now that he had shouted, he felt better. The thudding of his heartbeat in his ears had lessened. "I barely know the man," he said. "I think he is insolent to the Armed Forces and doesn't take his position as a member of them seriously enough, but the reputation of the Knights is top-notch."

Hughes snorted.

The Admiral slammed his fist on the desk again. "I got this information from people I trust, not from the nobility or toady little sycophants. I also read the After-Action Report and saw the video. As near as I can tell, the Captain and his crew did everything as by the book as they possibly could have, given the situation."

"A report made from their point of view. And video can be edited."

"That's true," Dillings conceded. "And that will be for the Council trial to determine. But you have used up enough of my resources, and you should be thankful I don't launch my own investigation into misallocation of military property for this little wild *turkin* chase of yours."

Anger flashed in Hughes's eyes as he sat up in the chair, and the Admiral saw the man had some backbone in him. Whether it was real courage or the bravery of noble backing, Dillings didn't know and couldn't drum up enough energy to care. "Taking such an action would be a bad idea," Hughes said, his voice low and menacing. "You owe me."

Dillings put his elbows on the desk and leaned closer. "I owe your father, and you are not him. I went along with this because of what he did for me but make no mistake: I don't like you. I might dislike you more than I dislike Captain Grey. Your actions have driven an even deeper wedge between my men and the Marines on this ship. I don't appreciate the effect that's had on morale. The sooner I get you off my ship and pretend you never existed, the better. The charade is over. I will take the Knights to Berol, and I will hand them over to the Council. You will depart my ship and never bother me again. Are we clear?"

"I am a member of the Diplomatic Corps," Hughes said with a tone of pride as if he had earned it and not bought his way in. "I can insist your fleet remain under my control for as long as I can make up a reasonable diplomatic need. And believe me, I can do such things in my sleep. So, as I said before, you're not done until I say you're done."

"And what if I refuse and kick you off my ship?"

"Then I will see that you go on trial for insubordination and will do everything in my power to make sure you lose your pension. And word about exactly why you needed my father's help might leak to your superiors."

As they talked, both men had leaned closer and closer over the desk. Fury boiled over in Dillings, and he reached out quick as a cobra with both hands and grabbed Hughes by the shoulders. With a squeak, the man tried to pull back, but the Admiral held him firm. He locked eyes with the nobleman. "I suggest you reconsider that plan. As you mentioned earlier, that would be a bad idea. You are a civilian on a military ship, which is a dangerous place. Accidents happen."

Hughes's eyes went wide for several moments, and he fell into an expression of guile that made the hair stand on Dillings' neck stand.

"You're absolutely correct," Hughes said. "Accidents happen all the time."

15

ROGUE COFFEE RUN

Hawk, Ashron, and Wolf had been placed into a single large cell that could have easily held half a dozen people. Or two people and a Uraxian. It pleased Hawk his captors made accommodations for Wolf. He suspected Colonel Graf'eel had more to do with that than the Admiral.

Laura occupied the cell directly next to theirs; she would have been in with them if not for the necessity of separate facilities. This was not a requirement on her part, but Sergeant Major Bishop had explained that Article twenty-something included a section on the separation of the sexes when it came to prisoners. Considering the number of genders among the various races that made up the Galactic military, Hawk didn't want to think about the headaches such an outdated regulation could cause. In this respect, Hawk was surprised there wasn't an antiquated article dedicated to the separation of species also.

The cells lacked all amenities save a set of double bunk beds, a table and two chairs, and a toilet. The Knights had been placed in a brig section segregated from the other prisoners. It sat at the end of a hallway that blossomed into a large square resembling a courtyard. Empty cells lined the edges, made the old-fashioned way, with bars that looked like iron although they were made of duraluminum. It was bizarrely out of place on the modern carrier, but Hawk figured it reflected the Admiral's attitude.

Sergeant Major Bishop and three Marines had escorted them to the cell. As they moved down the hallway, Hawk saw a few other prisoners, crewmembers who had fallen afoul of various regulations. They had walked past them and been placed in these deep cells well away from the others. It was almost like being in group solitary.

"You three stay here," Bishop told his Marines. All Colonel Graf'eel's Marines were dangerous looking, but this trio gave off the aura of exceptional skill and lethality.

"Seems like an excessive guard," Hawk commented to Bishop. "I assure you my team and I will not attempt to escape or cause any trouble."

"I know that," the Sergeant Major said. "There's nowhere to go."

"We could find a way," Hawk had assured him with a tight smile. "But I respect your Colonel and have caused her enough grief. I don't want to cause her any more."

"I believe you. However, these men aren't here to stop you, but to deter anyone who might want to pay a visit for less than savory purposes."

When they were taken to the exercise room the next day for their hour of "free time," and Hawk saw all the other prisoners no longer present, leaving Hawk and his crew the only ones in the brig, he began to understand the Sergeant Major's concern.

"Captain Grey," Hawk heard his name called out from somewhere beyond his thin sleep. "Captain Grey," the voice repeated, this time more forcefully and accompanied by the sharp *clack* of a nightstick striking the cell door. Hawk and the other Knights sat up quickly and turned to the source of the disturbance. The young Marine corporal who had introduced himself as Baldon faced away from the crew and stared down the long hall. He had his hands behind his back and covertly tapped the cell door with his stick. "We have company."

Hawk gazed past his guards and spotted well over a dozen Navy thugs tromping toward them. Hughes led the way, his patented smug smile clearly visible even from a distance. The Senior Chief Master at Arms that held charge at the sham hearing followed on his heels. Neither the Master at Arms nor his minions wore their uniforms.

Baldon, his face young and unlined but possessing an appearance of all business, locked eyes with Hawk. When he saw he had Hawk's attention, he glanced at the floor and let something slip from his outstretched hand. "Oops."

Then the guard seemed to consider the approaching mob before he and his two comrades, one female and one male, spread out and took a defensive formation in front of the two cells.

Before Hawk could react, Ashron jumped forward and scooped up the item the corporal had dropped. Wolf and Hawk gathered close as Ashron rejoined them. "A cell lock override key," Ashron informed them and scooted close to the door, ready to act if it became necessary.

"What time is it?" Laura asked the female Marine, who stood in front of her cell.

"0100, ma'am," she said without taking her eyes off Hughes and his troop.

"I count twenty," Wolf said over their shoulders. "If you count us, that's three to one, and several have guard poles with them."

Guard poles were an electrified polearm, three meters long so they could reach the back of a cell. A pain charge generator capped the end of the rod. They were used for unruly prisoners and allowed the guards to subdue without entering the cell and going toe to toe. It relied more on pain compliance than stunning, but it provided satisfactory results. The pain level could be set to match the size and tolerance threshold of the recipient.

"Anyone want to bet those sticks are set to 'medium-well?'" Ashron said.

"Corporal Baldon, you might want to call for backup," Hawk said.

"I already tried," he said without turning. His tone indicated frustration and anger but, Hawk noticed, not a hint of fear. "Not surprisingly, our communications are down."

"That's far enough," Baldon commanded, pointing his nightstick at Hughes and the Senior Chief. The three marines stood at the ready, each holding two batons, one in low guard position and the other locked for a rapid strike. They handled the weapons in a manner that told Hawk they were well practiced in their use. The Colonel should be proud.

"I said, that is far enough," Corporal Baldon repeated in a firm voice that slowed and then stopped the crowd. Hawk suspected the young corporal would rise quickly in the ranks.

Still pointing his stick at Hughes and the Senior Chief, Baldon said, "You two need to stand down and disperse your men."

Hughes offered a false smile and spread his arms wide. "Come now, Corporal, I have twenty men to your three. I hold you no ill will. Why don't you and your men take a break for a while? The Senior Chief will keep an eye on your prisoners while you are gone. I simply want to have a conversation with Hawk. There's fresh coffee up in the mess; go and enjoy a cup."

"Not a chance," Baldon said, shifting his right-hand baton from quick strike to high guard. He glanced back at Hawk and the others and nodded. Hawk returned it. A grim smirk formed, and Baldon turned his attention back to Hughes. "We may not win this fight, but I can assure you one thing. You will damn sure know you were in one. Now!"

As one, the three marines launched themselves into the crowd, spinning and striking as if performing a choreographed dance.

Ashron leapt for the door and ran the card key over the lock. "Didn't see that coming."

Hawk pushed through the door, and he and Wolf ran to the aid of the three young marines as Ashron darted to Laura's cell door. The Marines took a quarter of the thugs down in the surprise and ferocity of their attack, but the weight of numbers began to work against them. The Navy men also had batons, and the Marines took hits from all sides.

Hawk arrived first and jumped at the Senior Chief as the man grabbed a guard pole from one of his fallen soldiers and struck the female marine across her back. There was the *crack* of a discharge and the smell of ozone. She yelled and went down in a heap. Hawk jumped over the fallen marine, grabbed the pole with both hands, and landed a knee into the chief's groin. Dropping back with a shout of pain, the Chief released the stick. Hawk grabbed it as it fell and brought the lightweight but sturdy weapon up, catching the Chief under the chin. As the Chief fell backward, Hawk swung the staff with both hands and delivered a smashing blow across the man's face. But Hawk didn't have time to admire his work; he was looking for Hughes. He did notice the young female marine give the Senior Chief a kick to the head as she pushed up from the floor, her legs wobbly.

Wolf was a step behind Hawk when he waded into the fray. He grabbed the nearest sailor he could reach, picked him up, and threw him into the others, knocking three more off their feet. He pushed his way toward the center, swinging his massive fists at any person in striking distance, which was nearly all of them. There were cracks and screams as the things he hit broke. Numerous shouts of panic rose as the attackers realized the odds had changed drastically. Wolf's attack accomplished the desired effect: much of the group focused on him. The men with the guard poles concentrated on bringing him down. He felt the stunning strikes when they connected, but they weren't designed for Uraxian physiology. His naturally armored skin absorbed the discharge. The hits hurt but fell well short of debilitating.

Ashron and Laura were moments behind Wolf and recognized immediately that he was drawing fire to allow them to harry the flanks. Laura grabbed a dropped baton and quickly went to work on the first brute she reached. She swung hard, striking him in the back of the head, and he collapsed at her feet. She reversed her swing and hit another in the temple while kicking the man beside him behind the knee, sending them both sprawling to the ground. She fell on the one she had kicked as he spun around to lay on his back to defend himself. She slipped the baton past his guard and heard a loud, satisfying crack as the metal rod slammed into his nose, sending blood spraying and stunning him. When his hands reached up to his face, she turned the baton vertical and jabbed him in the throat. He wheezed in pain and pulled himself into a ball as she stood and, with a predator's grace, moved on to her next foe.

As devastating as the rest of the team was, Ashron lived for battle. Few could match a Lorothian in hand-to-hand combat, and Ashron was a pinnacle of his race in that respect. It soon grew clear the Senior Chief and the rest of his team had never seen a Uraxian or Lorothian involved in a real fight. Of course, Wolf and Ashron were supposed to be contained in their cells. The fear in the attackers' eyes as they saw the assault turn against them was something Hawk would always savor.

Ashron moved in a blur of motion and momentum, a whirling torrent of speed, grace, and fury. He knew not to kill anyone in this fight, so he curled his hands to keep his claws from accidentally eviscerating somebody, but the carnage was no less severe. Bones broke, and joints got dislocated. In a move that would have made his ancestors proud, he drove one man's compound fracture through another's thigh; once both lay on the ground writhing and screaming, he moved on. The odds began to dwindle from three to one, to two to one, to one on one. The sailors still standing broke and ran, led by Hughes. Ashron paused, his heartbeat barely elevated.

Hawk had been unable to reach Hughes through his wall of guards. He mused that substantial bonuses must have been promised to each sailor to make them protect Hughes like they did. Hawk continued to hold the guard pole taken from the Senior Chief. Thinking quickly, he activated the charge and threw it like a javelin, arcing it to fly over the running sailors. It struck Hughes directly between the shoulder blades. The charge fired, and Hughes went down with a scream. The others continued their retreat, stampeding over the Earl in their haste to get away. One of them accidentally kicked him in the face as they ran past, sending blood down the side of his cheek.

Hughes flipped onto his back and tried to get up but froze when he saw Hawk standing over him. Hawk reached down and grabbed him by the front of his fine noble's shirt and dragged him back toward the others.

"Help me," Hughes shouted. "Help. Double pay to anyone who gets me—"

Hawk punched him in the mouth. "Shut up," he said as Hughes's head rocked back and blood ran down his chin.

"Get out of here," Ashron shouted at the sailors. He flexed and stretched his hands, extending his claws to their full glory. He dropped his voice and filled it with menace. "Unless you want some more."

With eyes filled equally with panic and pain, the sailors began a slow retreat under Ashron and Wolf's watchful gaze. Those who could still move assisted those who couldn't, but they didn't have the numbers to retrieve everyone and had to leave six of their fellows behind.

"Help," Hughes said feebly through his bloody mouth. No one paid him any attention, and Hawk held up a fist, daring him to say it again.

Laura moved to the three marines, one of whom lay unconscious.

"You okay?" she asked Baldon, who sat on the floor against the cell bars.

"Yes, ma'am," he said in a dazed voice.

"What's your name, and what ship are you on?"

He offered a weak smile. "Aeric Baldon, and I serve on the marine contingent on the *Noble Sacrifice*. I'm fine." He closed his eyes and shook his head. "Give me a moment."

Laura turned her attention to the female, who had blood running down the front of her face from the top of her head, where she held her hand. "How about you?"

"Name's Jansa, and I'm on the *Noble Sacrifice*." She pulled her hand off her head and stared at the blood on it. "It looks nastier than it is.

I'll be fine. I'm glad you showed up when you did. Would have been a lot worse."

Laura nodded. "Happy to help." She went to work on Kackson, the unconscious marine. He was going to wake up soon with a massive headache. A fist-sized knot formed over his right eye, and it appeared his collarbone had been separated. With a quick push, she re-inserted his clavicle. He screamed and woke briefly, then passed out again. She secured his arm with a shirt, unceremoniously ripped from one of their attackers. She looked over to the corporal. "He'll be okay."

Filled with fury, Hawk picked up the dazed Hughes with both hands and pulled him close so only he could hear. "When this is all over, you and I will have some unfinished business."

Some life returned to Hughes's eyes. Before he could say anything, Hawk grabbed him by the throat, cutting off his air. Hughes' eyes widened in fear, and he clutched Hawk's hand.

"I won't disgrace this ship by killing you here but know that I intend to fertilize the royal field with your blood. Nothing less will do. Choose the time of your death wisely."

Hawk held Hughes at arm's length and punched him in the side of the face. Hughes rocked back, dazed. Hawk let the man fall to the floor. "If he moves," Hawk told Ashron, "stomp on his head until he stops."

Ashron smiled. "Happily."

Hawk turned to Corporal Baldon. "We need damage control, and quickly. Those others will report back and frame this as a prison break gone bad, with you and your team as accomplices. And I suspect there will be zero footage of this incident. We need the Colonel here ASAP."

Baldon's eyes cleared in recognition at the seriousness of the situation. "Shit." His eyes locked with Jansa's. "Frida, are you good to move?"

Jansa checked with Laura, who nodded. "Yes, Corporal."

"Then go get the Colonel."

"On it." She stood and jogged down the corridor.

The corporal spoke to Hawk. "What's our play here?"

Hawk scanned the scene. "Our play is to move fast and get our story straight."

A stern Colonel Graf'eel walked purposefully through the door and down the corridor toward the cells, flanked by Sergeant Major Bishop and Private First Class Jansa and followed closely by half her security detail. As she approached, she initially spotted drops and lines of blood on the floor, and as she drew closer, witnessed a complete mess. Hawk and his crew stood in front of the bunks in their cells. The two guards held parade rest at their post and looked like they had been on the losing side of a bar room brawl.

Six sailors were scattered around the hall. Three of them sat along the far wall, dazed and tending various wounds and bruises. One more lay on the floor unmoving, and two seemed to be stuck together. The Colonel winced when she saw why. She glanced at Ashron, but he gave no indication that he noticed. Her eyes fell on Hughes, sitting along the far wall, slumped over in a daze, head in his hands. *Had he wet himself?* A stain ran down his left pants leg.

Astounded and more than a touch curious about what had transpired, she came to a stop in front of her guards, where Corporal Baldon rendered a sharp salute, wincing at the obvious pain it caused him. She noticed PFC Kackson also stood at his post, although unsteadily and with his arm in a sling.

"At ease, Baldon," she said as she returned his salute. "I'm waiting with bated breath to hear your report."

The corporal started to speak when a noise at the far end of the hall caught Graf'eel's attention. Suspecting what approached, she held up her hand. "Place a talon on that."

She turned to spot Admiral Dillings striding down the corridor, face red and frowning. A contingent of his Masters at Arms followed. Unlike the colonel, the Admiral's uniform resembled an unmade bed, and his gray hair was uncombed; clearly, this incident had caught him unaware and asleep.

Admiral Dillings came to a brusque halt and didn't return the colonel's salute. He glanced around, taking in the damage until his eyes settled on Hughes. His frown deepened. "Son of a bitch," he muttered. "What in the hell happened, Colonel?" he asked, his voice full of accusation.

"An excellent question, Admiral. I was about to receive a briefing from the corporal in charge when you arrived." She turned to Corporal Baldon. "Please continue, Corporal."

"Yes, ma'am." Corporal Baldon came to attention. "It seems Captain Grey and his crew decided they wanted to leave, and we had to stop them. It was a good thing the naval personnel showed up when they did, or things might have gone much worse." The corporal returned to parade rest.

Colonel Graf'eel's snout creased downward in a frown. "That's it? You would have us believe all of this carnage is due to a foiled jailbreak?"

"Yes, ma'am," the corporal said, face impassive, eyes straight ahead and gazing at nothing.

"And that Lord Hughes, accompanied by..." she glanced around the room and considered the blood she had seen leading here as if a group of injured people limped away, "an unknown number of security personnel, came wandering through the brig at one o'clock in the morning, just in time to thwart an escape attempt by Captain Grey?"

"Yes, ma'am. And his crew."

"Yes, and his crew," she repeated. She turned her attention to Hawk. "Is this accurate, Captain?"

Hawk came to attention. "Yes, ma'am. We were out of coffee." He pointedly stared at Admiral Dillings. "The security recordings should confirm Corporal Baldon's summary of events, should it not?"

Colonel Graf'eel considered. "I should think so." She turned to Dillings. "Admiral?"

"Yes, well, it would seem the security cameras were down at the time of this incident." Admiral Dillings glared over at Hughes and his master at arms.

Graf'eel nodded slowly. "I see. It seems your security system could use some updating, Admiral, both here and in the conference center."

Hughes tried to stand. "This is bullshit. I'm…"

"Shut up, Hughes," Admiral Dillings barked. He glared at his chief master at arms, "Chief, see to your charges. I commend you for your assistance here." His tone changed. "We *will* speak more of this in my office at 0900. I suggest you be there promptly."

The Master Chief's demeanor paled. Admiral Dillings returned his glare to Hughes. "You and I have much to discuss. And we'll do so immediately."

Hughes opened his mouth to speak and seemed to think better of it. He nodded. Admiral Dillings turned his attention to Colonel Graf'eel. "I am glad my men came along when they did, to assist in thwarting this," he waved his arm around, "escape attempt." His tone showed he believed the story no more than Colonel Graf'eel did. "Your guards should be commended. I will see something is put in their files, noting their actions."

Colonel Graf'eel nodded. "Thank you, Admiral."

Admiral Dillings scanned the area one final time. The flush had left his face, but his expression showed nothing but extreme disgust. He shook his head. "Chief, take charge. Hughes, I'll see you in my quarters…now." He wheeled on his heel and stormed out.

Colonel Graf'eel waited until all the naval personnel had been extracted, and Hughes, a mournful expression on his face, left before she nodded to Sergeant Major Bishop. Indicating the guards, she said, "See that these three are well cared for and taken out of the rotation until they are fully healed."

Corporal Baldon started to speak, but Colonel Graf'eel cut him off. "You are to be commended, but I need you and your team whole and in fighting shape."

She considered Kackson for a moment, his arm in a sling. "That's some nice work there. Didn't realize our field medical training was that comprehensive." Her eyes slid over to Laura, who simply stared back with a neutral expression.

"You did well," Gref'eel told the guards. "Thank you. Sergeant

Major, double the guards from now on. I don't want any more rogue coffee runs."

"Yes, ma'am. With your permission, I would like to move my operations down to this level. This area will provide excellent training opportunities, and my staff will maintain an ample supply of coffee at all hours."

She smiled despite herself. "Permission granted."

Bishop straightened and turned to Corporal Baldon. "Job well done, Marine. You are relieved. See to your charges. Report to sickbay and get some rest."

Corporal Baldon came to attention. "Thank you, Sergeant Major." He eyed the others. "Come on, you two, let's go get cleaned up." They nodded and followed him out.

Colonel Graf'eel placed a stern eye on Hawk, "Captain Grey, may I have a word with you?"

Hawk nodded. "I'm not going anywhere."

Sergeant Major Bishop opened the cell door, and Hawk followed the colonel to the room's far side. They stopped and spoke low, so the rest of the crew couldn't hear. Hawk considered activating his mic to let them listen in but didn't. He suspected they could figure out the gist of the conversation.

"I want to thank you for your assistance," Colonel Graf'eel said. "That could have ended poorly."

"Your marines acted admirably and decisively," Hawk said. "If Corporal Baldon hadn't taken the initiative to drop his key to us, it would have been an entirely different outcome. For all of us."

"Well, your safety is my responsibility. I should have anticipated something like this. I've forgotten how the gentry thinks rules and consequences don't apply to them. I've been away too long."

Hawk nodded. "That's why I disassociate myself entirely from their games. I never would have anticipated Hughes would attempt something so bold."

She gave a toothy Lorothian grin Hawk recognized from his years with Ashron. "Disassociated or not, you are, as we like to say, tail deep in it now. Hughes and his family will never let this go. Nor, I suspect, will the Diplomatic Corps."

"One and the same, really, but I get your meaning. Do you believe me now?"

Her face hardened slightly. "About the events that transpired back on Alonis Ceti Three? I never doubted you. Your team's and the scientists' documentation are undeniable."

She held up a hand to keep Hawk from speaking. "So, I will tell you, I hold Prince Ashron's safety entirely in your hands. I recognize his work back there." She pointed to where the fight had ensued. "He was never in any danger, but with you—I can't say. Know this: he trusts you; therefore, I trust you. But know this also: if anything ill befalls him, I will hold you personally responsible."

Hawk considered for a moment. "I'm not sure if I deserve him or his trust, but I have it none the less." He paused. "However, I will give him no special treatment. He is one of my crew, nothing more. We are in a dangerous profession, and he is a combat specialist. I can only protect him so much. Your retribution for his loss would pale in comparison to any price I paid myself. All I can say is, I'll do my best."

"Very well. That's all I can ask. Again, thank you for your help. Sergeant Major Bishop will have an entire team down here from now on, so I don't foresee any further problems."

"Still not sure which tail is wagging the dog, but I think after Admiral Dillings gets through with Hughes, our trip from here on out will be uneventful."

A roaring Admiral Dillings slammed Hughes against the wall. On the table beside Hughes, two glass snifters fell and thudded against the soft carpet. Hughes tried to pull himself away from the wall, only to find himself slammed back again and the Admiral, his face beet red and eyes braziers of fury, inches away.

"You can't—" Hughes began.

"Don't tell me what I can't do," Admiral Dillings shouted, loud enough to hurt Hughes's ears. "This is my ship, and I'll damn well do what I want to do."

Dillings grabbed Hughes by the shoulders and tossed him again. He stumbled across the room, helpless to stop himself, and ran into the Admiral's desk. The force bent him at the waist and slammed him against the furniture's surface. His solar plexus landed on the jutting half-circle of a holographic projector, and he huffed, all fight leaving him. He fell to the floor. His injured mouth, which had stopped bleeding, began again. He could taste copper on his tongue.

The door to the Admiral's quarters opened, and the blue-skinned Reeksus walked in, his large ears spread wide, his mouth crumpled in concern. "Admiral, what—"

"Get out of here," Dillings commanded, his voice reverberating through the quarters.

No, don't, Hughes thought but had no breath to say.

As the adjutant turned to leave, Dillings said, "Belay that. I need you to stay in here and make sure I don't strangle this son of a bitch."

The man turned back around, and relief spread over Hughes. He had been worried about the same thing.

The Admiral marched over, looming over Hughes, and knelt. He was broad and imposing, his face flushed. "Now you listen to me and don't say another word, or I'll kill you whether Reeksus is here or not. If I had known what you had planned, I would have never let you ride back on my ship. You are confined to quarters until we reach Berol. There will be a pair of Colonel Graf'eel's Marines outside with orders to punch you in the face if you open the door. When we reach Berol, they will escort you off the ship and ensure you make it back to yours. You will leave with nothing but the clothes you are wearing. Leave everything else. What you do after you leave my ship, I don't care. You can challenge Hawk to a duel or attack the *Flaming Star* with your bare hands. But I will not be involved. I won't be at the trial, and I will not testify."

Dillings paused to take a breath. Hughes opened his mouth but said nothing when Dillings raised a meaty fist and cocked it back. When he saw Hughes's change of mind, Dillings nodded. "My debt is now your debt. Within a week, you will have legal documents sent to me stating you will take over all burdens, and I am free and clear."

"I can't," Hughes croaked out. "My father—"

Without warning, Dillings slapped Hughes. Hughes's right ear rang from the impact.

"You will," Dillings said, eyes glowering. "I will explain to your father exactly why, and you can deal with him."

"If you don't do this, I will have you brought up on charges of reckless battery, assault, and attempting to incite mutiny on a Galactic Council warship. I don't care how many friends or how much money you have. You won't be able to fight against a score of witnesses. I will drag you through the mud, and your family, too, if necessary. Those were my men you bribed. And trust me, when I'm done with them, nothing you offer them will make them your pawns ever again."

Again, Dillings paused. This time, Hughes knew better than to speak. Dillings seemed to consider if he wanted to add anything. "One more thing. If word leaks to any of my superiors about our arrangements, you will find that being of Blood is no protection against my wrath. I may go down, but I'll send you to hell." Dillings sucked in several breaths, calming himself. After a few moments, he stood. "Now get to your quarters. Thank your father when you see him. He's the reason you aren't visiting an open airlock right now. Reeksus, make sure he gets where he's supposed to go."

"Yes, sir," Reeksus said.

Dillings turned and left.

As Hughes sat up, tears of rage burned in his eyes. He would do what the Admiral said, but if Dillings thought this was over, he didn't know the Hughes family. This wasn't over by a long shot.

16

FATHERS' DUEL

Colonel Graf'eel was right; the remainder of the trip to Berol passed without incident. Hawk only knew they had arrived when they were told to lay in their cots in the brig so the vessel's automated injection system could put them into ripsleep. As the needle stabbed into his arm, he had a brief thought of poisoning but got no further with the idea before the medication put him under.

Now he stood at the cell door and watched as a contingent of seven soldiers dressed in the green and gold of Council Security came down the hallway, led by Colonel Graf'eel. As the Colonel arrived, the six marine guards came to attention.

"At ease," Colonel Graf'eel said, and the guards fell into parade rest. She looked at Hawk and the crew, her face impassive. "Commander Grey, it is my duty to formally transfer you to Council Security, where you will stand trial for stepping outside your prescribed mission, thereby potentially causing an interstellar incident with an unknown race."

Again, Hawk thought. He suppressed his instinct to offer a caustic remark. Colonel Graf'eel was only doing her job, and she had been more than fair and gracious to the Knights. "Of course," Hawk said.

She nodded and turned to the Sergeant in charge of the Council detail. "The prisoners are yours."

"Thank you," the Sergeant, an older Tandorn woman with mottled gray skin and numerous wrinkles, responded. She was obviously career military and regarded the crew with a practiced eyed. "I trust you will give us no trouble."

"You have my word," Hawk assured her.

"Very good."

They left the cell behind and moved briskly through the carrier, reaching the flight deck where they were boarded on a twenty-crew transport shuttle. The *Noble Sacrifice* had other orders and would not be transporting them to their destination. It didn't make much sense to have a carrier group move four prisoners.

So, the shuttle would take them over to the cruiser *CS Marizon Bay*, which would take them to Creron G9P, a prison planet that also served as a military black site where high-level prisoners were held before trial—if they ever made it to trial. Individuals sent there tended not to return. Hawk half expected to see Hughes somewhere nearby, gloating at his cleverness in getting the Council involved, but the Earl did not show himself.

The shuttle proved more spacious and better apportioned than Hawk expected. It had two cabins, so it must be used for dignitaries quite a bit. Hawk would have been flattered if he hadn't determined this was simply the most expedient way for Admiral Dillings to be rid of them. They were placed in one of the cabins. The door couldn't be locked from the outside, but the Sergeant made it clear there would be armed guards should they decide to try something stupid. A few minutes later, the cruiser departed the carrier and headed for their rendezvous.

"Welcome back, Captain," Ship said in his head once the shuttle had cleared the *Sacrifice*. "Glad you arrived safely."

"Glad to be back," Hawk said, keeping his voice low, pleased to hear from her. There had been no contact since Gerard fled. He saw from his crew's expressions she also spoke to them. "Although I don't think we're going to be here long. How are things?"

"Quite the mess," Gerard said, adding his voice to Ship's link. "We've stirred things up."

"We're good at that," Ashron said.

"It's more than you think," Gerard continued. "We're at the school. The Council—or more likely, Hughes—demanded we turn ourselves in; we, of course, declined. After your arrival here, Hughes and the Diplomatic Corps, with the blessing of the Council, again demanded we turn ourselves in to stand trial with the rest of you. I gather they waited until after the armada arrived, thinking the show of force would accent the request. They also demanded the impounding of Ship. That's why they're bringing you there instead of taking you straight to Creron. After the first demand came through, Dr. Prasam and I explained our reasoning to the Berolian Assembly and showed them the after-action report and accompanying video of the hearing on board the *Sacrifice*. Our government then stepped in and invoked planetary sovereignty to offer asylum to myself and the scientists, claiming the charges were spurious and invalid. It was quite the dust-up, and the Council is still fighting it, but we're free for now. I suspect the trial will be over, for good or bad, before our status gets settled. However, as a condition, they forbade communication with you until you returned, hence us not getting in touch until now. Something about an escape attempt."

"We'll have to explain that to you later, but you're right," Hawk said. "Quite the mess."

"There's more," Gerard continued. "The Lorothian government is getting involved too, claiming that, as Ashron is a prince, charges against him must be presented formally to the King before he can stand trial. He will remain in custody until the King makes his ruling."

"Boy," Ashron said. "Who would have thought a couple of explosions would cause so much trouble?"

"We did the right thing," Laura added. "But it's naïve to think that will matter."

"Our best hope right now is that Force 13 can step in and intervene on our behalf before this all spirals out of control," Hawk said.

"You mean more than it already has?" Ashron asked.

"We always knew it was a possibility," Hawk responded. "But I underestimated how much anger Hughes has toward us. Have you contacted Grendarin?"

"He has been made aware and is trying to figure out the most political way to respond," Gerard answered. "He's not going to let us hang out to dry, but he has to make sure he doesn't upset anyone, or at least not the wrong people."

"This is why I do demolitions and didn't stay at home and be a prince," Ashron said. "Politics are too damn annoying."

"Any chance your government can offer asylum to us?" Laura asked.

"Doubtful," Gerard said. "They can do it for me because it's home, Trey because he's a minor, and the scientists because they were tangentially involved. It would be much harder to press the case for the four of you. Sorry."

"It's okay," Hawk said. "We'll have to take our chances and hope the evidence is strong enough to exonerate us."

"We also have the recording of the board of inquiry," Ship said.

"That was good for cowing Hughes and the Admiral," Hawk said, "but any good Council lawyer can get that dismissed or never entered."

"Well," Laura said, "I guess we'll have to strive to make our case better than they do."

Elliot Hughes stormed off the tiny four-person military shuttle, his face hot with fury. He was safely back on his own ship now. He rounded on the naval pilot and guard that stood at the top of the ramp, looking far too smug for his taste. "You have one minute to get off of my ship, or I will burn your shuttle where it sits and jettison you all into the void."

He gave a wicked sneer when their smug expressions disappeared, replaced with fear and anger. Either way, they quickly retreated into their vessel and retracted the ramp.

He stood in the landing bay of his luxury yacht, the *Greystar*. Originally named the *Ellipsis,* he deliberately changed it to combine Hawk's last name of Grey and his vessel, the *Flaming Star.* He liked to imagine it pissed off Hawk to no end. Calling it a yacht was a misnomer; it was more the size of a small destroyer. The Hughes family never did anything halfway when it came to flaunting their wealth and power, exactly how Elliot liked it. The *Greystar* exuded opulence, its interior crafted with exotic materials, and the décor as exquisite as the most prestigious decorators could make it. Elliot carefully picked luxury items or rare baubles from almost all the known planets and placed them in his ship. There were some races he avoided because he saw them as uncultured at best and barbarians at worst. The Lorothians fell into the latter category. He spat in anger as remembered the night of the ceremony and how Ashron had humiliated him. He would pay. *Prince, my ass.*

He turned to his yacht captain, who had come to the bay to greet him. "Head for Creron G9P. And make sure you beat that cruiser there, or it will be your head." Before the captain could respond, Hughes pushed past him and headed for his cabin.

How dare Dillings treat him that way? His family owned the Admiral. The sole reason Dillings had advanced as far as he had and not ended up rotting on some backwater shithole was because of his father. Oh yes, he was going to pay too. Hawk and his crew would pay also, but that seemed to be handled. They would rot in prison for the rest of their lives. At least Hawk would, and maybe a couple of the others, but Hawk was the one Elliot cared about. Anyone after that was a bonus. Knowing his actions also put some of his crew away for life would eat at Hawk more than his sentence.

Hughes arrived at his stateroom and almost knocked over the exiting steward. "Damnit Stew, watch where the hell you're going." He called all his stewards Stew. He didn't bother to learn their names since they never lasted long anyway. They were all morons, as were most of his servants. "Get out of my way." He pushed Stew to the side. "Did you get my snack and cider?"

Stew looked down and nodded but didn't say a word.

"Good. Now leave me undisturbed for an hour. I have to make some calls."

After a sonic shower and a change of clothes, Hughes ate the light meal Stew had left for him, a charred cut of Beldonia lamb with garlic-infused asparagus, and enjoyed his favorite Dolan Apple Cider with spritzer added. It was the one alcoholic drink his stomach tolerated.

It was also the only way he could speak to his father without losing his temper. His father, Duke Elliot Hughes, whom he was named after —he was Elliot Hughes Junior, but he despised the junior designation —was one of the nobility's most potent heads and commanded vast resources and wealth. His father made his fortune from the military-industrial complex, mostly by providing raw materials from the numerous mines he owned to the starship manufacturing industry. It would all belong to Elliot Junior one day. Still, the current era of mostly peaceful relationships was detrimental to the family's bottom line, and his father had no intention of stepping down any time soon. Elliot joined the Diplomatic Corps to see if he could gin up conflicts, but it surprised him how difficult it was to diplomatically get species to want to kill each other.

Elliot drained the last of his glass of cider and poured another. With a heavy sigh, he called up his father's private number. His father must have been waiting on the other end because he appeared in the holo right away.

Elliot stared back at an older version of himself. People always remarked on the uncanny resemblance and commented to the Duke there was no denying his child. The difference, in this case, was the anger on his father's wrinkled face. Hughes took a careful sip of his drink as he recalled his father's anger wasn't all that unusual. "Father," he said as a greeting.

"Son of a bitch, Junior. What the hell is wrong with you?"

His father's use of the diminutive suffix irritated Elliot, and he expressed it with a glare. "What do you mean? Hawk and the Knights are ruined. They are being transferred to a transport destined for a secret military prison. They—"

"How stupid are you? Do you know how many favors I had to call to make that happen?"

Elliot went to offer a protest when his father cut him off. "Shut your trap, *Junior.*" His father enunciated the word in such a way to leave no doubt he wished to deride and belittle his son. "You have no idea of the powers in play here, both within the military and the gentry. King Ateron has demanded a full inquiry." His father leaned in. "An *open* inquiry." He waved his hand as if shooing away a minor annoyance. "Fortunately, it was labeled a secret military operation, and all of your actions are after the fact. Stupid as they might have been, I can spin them as childish hot-headedness." His father looked thoughtful for a moment.

"I'm a grown man and—"

"And yet you act like a spoiled, petulant child! Not as someone ready to move in the complicated layers of deception that is the royal court or the Diplomatic Corps." Elliot felt his father's burning stare through the holo. "Now, for once in your miserable life, shut up and listen. Any inquiry will be just that, secret. Meet our legal team, keep your mouth shut, and do exactly what they say. Do not engage any of the Knights. Bite your tongue and keep your head down. This can be salvaged if you don't do anything stupid, hard as that may be for you. Do I make myself clear?"

"What about Dillings?"

"You didn't answer my question. Do I make myself clear?"

Hughes dropped his eyes slightly. "Yes, Father."

"Good. I'll take care of Dillings; his debt is nowhere near paid."

His father terminated the connection. For a moment, Hughes stared with loathing at the space his father's image had occupied, then threw his half-full glass at it. The glass shattered against the far wall, leaving a stream of liquid running down and pooling on the floor. "Fuck."

As he reached for another glass, his holo gave a soft three-note chime, indicating an incoming encrypted message. Hughes let out a long breath, filled up his new glass, and hit play.

A stunningly handsome figure appeared before him, dressed in white with an ageless face and kind, old gray eyes. His voice was harmonically perfect, persuasive in its calming gentleness. "My child, I need you to perform a small task."

The image of a young woman, no older than her teens, appeared before Hughes. "Find out where I can locate this girl. This mission is of utmost importance." The image changed back to the enchanting presence. Elliot would have thought of him as an angel if he thought such things existed. The handsome face beamed with a smile. "I know I can count on you."

The holo went dark as the message finished. The comm pad on his belt vibrated. He opened to see the image of the young woman staring at him. How was he supposed to find her in all the known universe with no clues?

Hughes finished his cider and realized he needed something more robust, stomach be damned.

17

FORGED ALLIANCES

Hawk sat in his cell, which, in all fairness, was not bad as prisons went. Certainly a far cry better than the brig on the *Noble Sacrifice*. Here he had a comfortable bed, a holo-screen, and a sizable bathroom with a vibroshower.

The trip to Creron G9P on the cruiser *CS Marizon Bay* had been as exciting as a trip inside a windowless suite could be. Hawk had again expected Hughes to show himself and cause trouble of some sort, but he didn't. Hawk assumed the diplomat was saving all his plays for the trial. At least there hadn't been any more nighttime visits from armed thugs.

Once they reached Creron G9P, a preliminary judgment panel immediately saw the case. Hughes finally appeared there, flanked by a cadre of Diplomatic Corps lawyers. Both Hughes and the panel members seemed surprised when two people pushed their way into the room, claiming to be lawyers for the defense and that they had video and audio evidence exonerating their client—The Knights of the Flaming Star. After some wrangling and legal jargon Hawk didn't understand, Hughes declared he saw no need for counsel to be present for a preliminary hearing. The board ruled against him, saying that if the Corps saw fit to have counsel, so could the defendant. It was all Hawk could do not to gloat.

It wasn't all good news, though. The panel felt there was enough information to go to trial, and the defense would have to wait until said trial to present their "exonerating evidence."

Hughes didn't bother to hide his pleasure at the ruling, but Hawk noticed something else about the man. Hawk couldn't place it, but Hughes's demeanor was somehow different. He had always been an insufferable ass, but beneath that stood an easily browbeaten coward. However, this Hughes projected real confidence, not false bravado. He relished the challenge presented, and his glances at Hawk had something…sinister was the best Hawk could manage. Whatever it was, it didn't bode well.

How the hell did I end up getting wrapped up in their little games? Hawk thought. He shook his head. He could do nothing about it at the moment, and it looked like he had plenty of time in the future to ponder it over.

So here Hawk sat, alone. The other bad news from the preliminary judgment was the crew's separation, to not cause "undue stress and present a danger to remanding personnel," whatever the hell that meant. He couldn't see any of his crew, but the prison didn't have communications scramblers, so he could still talk to them via their internal headsets.

Not that they had much to discuss right now. For the past four days, they stewed in alternating boredom and worry. Hawk knew they could present a solid case for their actions, but that meant little while he sat here, and Earl Hughes and Admiral Dillings remained free to taint evidence and shift opinion. Daily briefings with the lawyers assured him they were exhausting all efforts to gather evidence and make a solid case, but it took all of Hawk's willpower to not attempt to break out of his cell and take things into his own hands. The only thing that kept him sane was knowing Gerard and Trey were helping too. Another request by the Council to have them sent from Berol to stand trial had been rebuffed by the Berolian government.

Hawk picked up a reader to take his mind off their predicament and searched for something to distract him. He settled on a history of the Cabalonian Revolution, one of the incidents leading to the Galactic Council's formation. He had reached the Secretary of War's assassination when there was a chime at the door, and it opened.

Grendarin, the crew's Force 13 handler, entered the room. Startled, Hawk almost dropped the reader as he stood to greet the Lokathi. Hawk wouldn't have been more surprised if an elephant had sauntered in instead of the thin humanoid. When he saw the look on Grendarin's face, his thin lips pressed so tight they were a mere black crease in the orange face, Hawk began to have an inkling of why the man came. There was only one thing important enough to drag the Lokathi out here personally instead of sending a communique.

They shook hands. "Grendarin," Hawk said. "I'd say it's a pleasure to see you, but I'm guessing you aren't here to tell me good news."

"No, I'm not," Grendarin agreed in his reedy voice as he regarded Hawk with pupilless black eyes. "May I sit?"

"Of course," Hawk said, indicating the simple wooden chair while he took a seat on the bed. "What's happened?"

"A distress signal has come in from the Quintaris sector, planet Falador."

Hawk considered this a moment. "I don't quite know what to say. 'I told you so' doesn't seem entirely appropriate." He thought about it some more. "Sorry?"

"Based on the preliminary reports from your science team, which were largely disregarded or ignored, I believe 'I told you so' is the exact appropriate response. Two days ago, another Serian vessel established orbit around Falador and constructed a platform array like the one described in your report."

Hawk leaned forward on the bed, hands clasped. "I'm not going to like where this is going, am I?"

"The Faladorians responded as expected and sent an emissary vessel with a military escort. As your encounter with the Serians is currently classified, the Faladorians had no idea what to expect. As soon as the Faladorians hailed the Serian vessel, the Serians opened fire. This time, the Serians also came with an escort, so the battle was short and one-sided."

"Did the tunnels collapse like Trey said they would?"

"Do not jump ahead. As soon as the Faladorians realized they were in trouble, they sent out a distress signal. A nearby tactical group responded. The Council convened an emergency session and activated a carrier group. As soon as they up-fitted, they launched."

"Please tell me we didn't lose two full groups…"

"No, but we lost the first one. The second one was still too far away to get caught up in the collapse."

"What's the word from them?" Hawk asked.

Grendarin shook his head. "We have lost all contact with Falador. With the collapse of the tunnels, communications are destroyed."

"Dammit. I'd rather have been wrong and spent my time in jail," Hawk said.

"Keep in mind, no one knows your whereabouts. Secret team, secret mission, secret court," Grendarin waved his arm around the room. "Secret prison. Your encounter with the Serians is a Council secret and need to know only. Although considering the number of personnel involved so far and recent events, I am unsure how long it will remain secret. But the people who need it have both plausible deniability and," Grendarin nodded at Hawk and gave a wry grin, "a scapegoat."

Hawk snorted. "Glad I could be of service."

Grendarin scooted up in his chair and locked his solid black eyes with Hawk's. "You knew this was a possibility the minute you locked horns with Hughes. He may be despised by the gentry, but he is powerful and has numerous allies. And thanks to his father, many of them are in well-placed government and military positions, including your new friend Admiral Dillings. Now that you have killed off Moran and become an Earl, you can no longer ignore your place in the nobility."

"Moran's not dead."

"Whatever. Non-recoverable vegetative state, then. And if he ever does recover, Tasha will certainly finish what you started; the only reason she hasn't done so yet is out of respect for Sara. Either way, you are an Earl, and you better get used to it. That means you need to start paying attention to the happenings of court and forming your own alliances. Hell, you have a prince on your crew; start there. People respect the Lorothians, they…"

"People are afraid of the Lorothians."

"Respect, fear, political nuances, the result is the same. They have a place at any table they want. You should start there. Let Ashron guide you; there is much more there than he lets on."

"I know. I'm not sure I deserve his trust or loyalty. He'll make a damn fine king one day if he's ever called upon to serve." Hawk ran his hand over his mustache and stared at Grendarin. "But you didn't travel all this way to give me a lesson in Galactic politics, did you?"

"No, I didn't," Grendarin confirmed. "Let me tell you what happened."

<hr>

Trey and Sam walked down the math building hallway, heading for their next class: Secondary Equations for Trey and Metaphysical Dynamics for Sam. With everything he had gone through, Trey found it weird to be back to something as mundane as classes, even after four days. He had wanted to hold off until things had been resolved, but Gerard insisted, saying it was important for Trey to return to something resembling normalcy. Trey didn't argue with the idea, just the timing. With everything going on, how was he supposed to concentrate on learning? He worried about what would happen to Hawk and the others. For that matter, he still had no idea what might happen to him and Gerard.

And now there was the matter of Falador and the surrounding collapse in ripspace, which Gerard told him about this morning. Hawk's intuition, backed by the scientists, had been right all along, and their warnings went unheeded. Unfortunately, they hadn't been able to tell anyone about it. There was no way to know how many people died and how many more would die as the days passed. Trey had to keep the idea abstract to stop it from overwhelming him. He knew too much about death and suffering, and if he dwelled on it, he would end up in a corner crying incessantly. In that way, it made him thankful Gerard had returned him to school. It served as a good distraction.

The Kuthrallie also diverted his thoughts. He still had them in his mind. They weren't "there" in the sense of bothering him with questions or demands, but he sensed them sitting quietly in the dark corners, observing and learning. And although he knew he had no reason to fear them, it was weird knowing they perched there, possibly reading his thoughts, some of which he wouldn't want anyone knowing. He reflected that with Ship and the Kuthrallie traveling along, his brain was as crowded as Dark Matter on the weekend.

"Sam to Trey," Sam said, breaking into his musings. "the Porgons are attacking, and I need backup. Can you read me?"

Trey gave her a wan smile. "You're strange, you know that?"

"I do know that," she answered with her own grin. "And I consider that a compliment from someone who disappears and reappears on a whim." Her happy expression disappeared. "Look, I know you can't talk about what happened, but if you ever want to talk about anything you can say, I'm ready to listen."

Like about how much I really like you, he thought. "I know," he said. "And when I figure out what I can say without sounding like an idiot, I will."

"Good luck," she said, giving him a light punch in the arm. Her smile came back.

Trey wanted to melt into that smile. He wanted—

His entire back started to vibrate as if someone had placed a sheet of metal over it and hit it repeatedly with a hammer.

"Ouch, ouch, ouch!"

"What's wrong?"

The pain disappeared, replaced with numbness. "My back is tingling. Like when your foot falls asleep."

"Ooh," Sam said. "Let me see." Before Trey knew what was happening or could offer a response, Sam spun him around, pushed aside the strap that held his reader, and pulled his shirt up to expose his back.

Several of the other students walking through the hall gawked at this strange occurrence. One of the students, a senior based on the bright violet clothing, said, "You two need to get a room."

Trey's face warmed in embarrassment as some of the other students laughed. Trey gave the speaker a withering stare, which, for some reason, made him stop laughing and increase his speed. The other students also quit, as if something had cut their vocal cords. Sam shook her head and turned her attention back to Trey. "Your back is moving," she said, her voice somewhere between awe and disbelief.

"Yeah, it does that." Trey faced Sam and pulled his shirt back down. "I think I need to talk to your mom and Gerard."

Once again, Trey found himself sitting with several people staring at his exposed back. This time it was Gerard, Dr. Mobem, Master Genray, and three other people Trey didn't know. Sam, despite her protests, had been told to return to class by her mother. Dr. Mobem promised she would let Sam know if anything important happened, up to and including Trey's disappearance. Sulking, Sam had left.

They all gathered in a large office Gerard and Dr. Mobem had converted into a temporary research station under the auspices of the Berolian government. Gerard's ongoing vital research was the reasoning to the Galactic Council for keeping him on the planet. Though it served a purpose, it kept Gerard confined to the school grounds. Elliot Hughes had managed to get a platoon of Council Security outside the school, ready to apprehend Gerard or Trey if they stepped or flew outside the school. The Berolians lodged a formal protest but knew they could push sovereignty only so far, and Gerard didn't want them facing any more repercussions than they might already. He was content to stay there and research the Kuthral-lie; he would have been doing so on Ship anyway.

The three scientists accompanying the Knights were absolved of all charges without a trial, having no direct participation in the action. Gerard suspected this drove Hughes insane, but the noble could do nothing about it. Drs. Prasam and Griid had returned home to continue their research with promises to provide updates as they made new findings. Dr. Mobem chose to stay and help Gerard and be close to her daughter.

After several minutes in which no one spoke, and Trey felt distinctly uncomfortable, one of the unknown scientists said, "What does it mean?"

Trey glanced over his shoulder as Dr. Mobem compared the swirling star chart on Trey's back with the holochart floating before her. She made some gestures with her hands, and an image of Trey's map superimposed itself on hers. She traced one finger along a faint gray line. "It looks like a rip tunnel to Falador, although it isn't on any of my charts."

"That's because it isn't there yet," Trey said.

"What do you mean, 'not there yet?'" Gerard asked.

Uncomfortable with his current position, both physically and under the microscope of the adults, Trey spun his body on the chair. "They haven't made it yet. And before you ask, it's because they told me. The Kuthrallie create these pathways as they travel through the *aether*, going from place to place. As they learn the easiest paths, they continue to use them. As they continue to use the same path, space becomes—" here he paused, trying to figure how to interpret and explain the images the Kuthrallie placed in his mind.

"It's like being in a forest," he finally said. "The first time through, you might cut enough branches so you can get through. Then the next time, you cut down the trees so you can get through faster. And after that, you clear the weeds and make a path. That isn't exactly right, but it's close enough. The point is, we don't discover the tunnels until the Kuthrallie have passed through enough to 'clear the weeds.' When they've done so, we have a tunnel."

Master Genray studied the chart over Dr. Mobem's shoulder. "And you are saying the Kuthrallie are showing us a tunnel they haven't made yet."

"Correct," Trey confirmed. "When the Serians collapsed the tunnels, they severely disrupted the *aether*. The Kuthrallie are having to seek out new paths, which is something they haven't had to do in a while." Trey pointed at the holochart. "The path there is the one they think they will be able to make the quickest."

"And how long will that be?" Dr. Mobem asked.

"Under normal circumstances, quite a long time, but they sense our urgency, which is a new experience for them, by the way. The link they share with me is helping them understand us."

"How goes our work in the other direction, Gerard?" Master Genray asked.

Gerard shook his head. "Slower than we would like. We don't know much more about them than we did before, but we have far more questions. I'm afraid we don't have the intelligence to know what questions to ask. Trey, what are we realistically looking at? Can we get aid to Falador in a timely manner?"

More images flashed in Trey's mind. The Kuthrallie presented the information in a way that made more sense, and he frowned. "For a tunnel to stabilize, or be clear of weeds, it takes several years. If I'm understanding correctly, as they travel the path, the tunnel slowly folds back on itself after the Kuthrallie pass. The longer they travel the same route, the less it folds. It effectively gets larger until it is large enough to become stable. Then we can use it."

"We don't have years," Dr. Mobem responded. "Falador is almost completely dependent on trade from other planets."

"The more pressing matter," Gerard said, "is we still don't know the Serians' intentions. The tunnel collapse may be an unexpected consequence of which they are unaware, but given how they've acted so far and Dr. Prasam's observations, we're dealing with a conqueror race. The Faladorians need help now. If we arrive in years, we might find ourselves facing an extinct race, a fortified Serian armada, and full-out war."

"We can get to them," Trey said. All eyes turned to him. "There is a window of time before the tunnel folds back in. If a vessel follows the Kuthrallie closely along their path, they can get through before the space collapses."

"Like following an icebreaker," Gerard added.

Trey frowned. "I don't know what that is, but the Kuthrallie are clear that the ships must stay close and not stray or lag behind. Otherwise—" Trey shrugged and frowned. "You know."

Dr. Mobem continued staring at the holochart. "Trey, how many ships can follow along this path of theirs before it collapses behind them?"

"Under normal circumstances, one or two at the most."

Hawk considered Grendarin's story. He wasn't entirely convinced the Kuthrallie were allies no matter how much they helped. It felt to him like the Knights, and especially Trey, served as pawns in whatever game this alien intelligence wanted to play. "Considering what the Serians launched against them, one or two ships won't be much help to the Faladorians."

"Not much," Grendarin agreed. "Even if one of them *is* your ship."

"My ship," Hawk scoffed. "Good luck getting her to agree to that. With me, Laura, Ashron, and Wolf locked up here, I doubt she'll be in a charitable mood. Besides, despite who and what she is, she's still the size of an advanced scout ship; she's formidable but no match for an assault group of any size. We simply don't have the magazine capacity for a sustained fight."

"I'm aware of this, and Admiral Strong agrees with you. Limited to two ships, he would send one of our new dreadnaughts and a carrier."

"I always liked that man, and I like the way he thinks. But again, that's not why you're here. Get to the point."

"Why? Do you have somewhere to be?"

Hawk gave him a wry smile. "I'm thinking I do. Otherwise, you wouldn't be here."

"You never let me savor the surprises, do you?"

"You know I'm not a fan of surprises."

"Fine. According to Trey, the Kuthrallie have suggested a rather risky endeavor. They will travel as a group, forming a cone through the *aether*. In theory, this will expand the area behind them to allow for much more mass. After crunching the numbers, they figure it will allow for almost a full carrier group instead of only two ships. Due to the size of the disturbance through the *aether*, it should collapse at a much slower rate, allowing the larger number of ships and mass. Gerard's people are sending their best navigators, along with two of their most advanced dreadnaughts and a carrier. Admiral Strong has finished out the armada with some of our newest and most deadly vessels and has insisted on commanding the effort. As pretentious as it all sounds, it is a solid and well thought out plan."

"I notice a lot of 'should' and 'in theory' in there. So, the Kuthrallie aren't a hundred percent on this either?"

"They aren't. At least according to Trey. Who, by his own admission, is an imperfect translator. I did say it was risky."

"And I'm to infer the only way to safely get said armada to Falador is by having them follow Trey through the *aether*? That means Ship and crew with Trey at the helm. I'm positive Sara and Laura have already weighed in on whether they'll allow Trey to undertake such an endeavor unsupervised."

Grendarin grinned. "As always, you have an excellent grasp on the current situation."

"So how does this all play out with the four of us lounging around in this country club? I can't imagine Hughes and his sycophants will simply sit back and allow us to walk out of here. And by sycophants, I include the preliminary panel who decided there was enough for a trial, which they seem to be deliberately dragging out to annoy me."

"Yes, well," Grendarin pulled out a slip of paper and handed it to Hawk. "It seems the trial has been canceled, and all your sins are forgiven due to extenuating circumstances."

Hawk took the proffered sheet of paper with a wary eye. He slowly unfolded it and read the contents. After several seconds, his right eyebrow raised, and he looked up at Grendarin.

Grendarin's wide-mouthed grin got wider. "Yeah, I couldn't believe it either. Who knew Ashron's father, King Ateron, is also a Vice Admiral in the Galactic Navy? I did, of course, but Hughes and his family clearly didn't. They should do better research. This satisfies both the military aspect and the aristocracy."

"Sure, I get how a king satisfies the gentry, but this was a military proceeding. How was he even read in to Force 13 operations, much less made aware of a trial at this level of secrecy?"

"Remember when I told you there was more to their family than met the eye?"

"Actually, you said there was more to Ashron, but go on."

"Don't split hairs. Anyway, King Ateron is not an Admiral in the traditional sense, a commander of fleets and military adventure. Instead, he is a learned man."

"I think some Admirals might take insult at the implication they aren't learned men."

"Of course they are when it comes to military matters. However, Ateron is a different sort. I suspect he recognized the need early on with Ashron. Anyway, the King is a legal scholar with the Galactic Navy, specializing in intergalactic law. When Ashron was accepted into Force 13, his father pulled some strings and got assigned to the task force that oversees your group's operations. In effect, he is my boss. The powers that be agreed having someone of his caliber on the team, both as the King of Loros and an admiral who is a scholar of intergalactic law, was a good move."

"So, he's been behind the scenes with everything we've done since Ashron joined the Knights?"

"Yes."

Hawk gave a low whistle. "I'll be damned. Considering what he must know and has seen, he's demonstrated amazing restraint in not interfering in our affairs." Hawk paused again. "Or has he?"

"You tell me," Grendarin said, raising his singular eyebrow. "Did you have any inkling of his involvement?"

"Obviously not."

"Then, there you go. His family is a firm believer that 'steel is forged in fire.'" Grendarin pointed a finger at Hawk. "And you, sir, have provided a forge worthy of greatness. But I will tell you this: if those tunnels hadn't collapsed like you said they would when the gates activated, you and your whole crew would rot in here. It also didn't hurt that Hughes was the catalyst for this whole thing; King Ateron loathes Hughes and his family."

"Then he's in great company," Hawk said. He considered how closely his team's reputation had been held in the hands of a group of other-dimensional aliens they knew next to nothing about. Though he told the truth when he told Grendarin he would rather be wrong. He considered a few years in jail, even a lifetime, an easy trade for the numerous people lost when the tunnels collapsed and the additional lives hanging in the balance. He didn't know the space around Falador well, but he suspected it wasn't the only planet affected by the tunnel collapse.

He looked back to the sheet of paper in his hands. Five signatures and five seals. He recognized them all—five of the seven council members who oversaw the operations of Force 13. *A quorum*, he thought, *but not unanimous*. They still needed to tread lightly, even among such overwhelming evidence of the justification for their actions. "What's our play here?"

"As we speak, Colonel Graf'eel is escorting Ashron and the others to Port Six, where you all will catch up with Ship and the other two members of your crew. From there, you will join with Admiral Strong and the armada. Then I would imagine it is up to Trey and the Kuthrallie."

"I have a condition: I want a one on one with Hughes before we leave. He and I need to have a frank exchange of ideas."

Grendarin hesitated. "I'm not sure that's the best course of action."

"Possibly not," Hawk conceded. "But it's no good to let him think he can pull a cat's tail and not get scratched. I promise nothing physical, but he's going to be made aware of the foolishness of pursuing his imaginary vendetta."

Grendarin nodded, though he still didn't look particularly happy. "I will see it done."

Hawk paused a long moment before he stood, considering Grendarin's hesitation. "On second thought, let's take care of the apocalyptic matters first. My little tiff with Hughes can wait until we get back. After all, if we don't survive, it won't matter, will it?"

"Wisdom almost uncharacteristic of you," Grendarin said with a wry grin.

"I'm trying to do better. Waiting will also give me a chance to seek council with a certain prince I know."

"An even better idea," Grendarin said with a slow nod.

"We'll see," Hawk said as he walked toward the door. "You don't know Ashron like I do. Thinning the gene pool is on his short list of solutions to most problems. And in this instance, he and I will be closely aligned." He stopped at the door and gestured to Grendarin. "Lead the way, sir. I have a ship to catch."

<hr>

Hughes stared at the blinking "Send?" prompt on his pad. It surprised him how easy it had been to find the person his benefactor sought, and he wondered why the angelic-looking patron hadn't done it himself. But Hughes learned early not to question motive or method, only to acquiesce. Obedience begat reward.

He tilted the glass back and winced as the last of the strong brown liquid poured down his throat. He shuddered and poured another. His stomach was going to give him hell for this abuse, but perhaps it was penance for the sin he prepared to commit. Penance also brought reward, and he was going to be well-rewarded for this simple task. The suffering it might bring wasn't his problem. Others suffered, not him.

He took one final look at the encrypted message, which simply read, "Sterling Arch School on Berol." He downed the third drink and grimaced.

Obedience begat reward.

He sent the message.

18

WELCOME BACK, CAPTAIN

As the door opened, Hawk stepped out of the tube that took him and Grendarin to Port Six. He gazed across the expanse of the platform, surprised at the lack of activity. Though the bay could contain at least six vessels of cruiser size or smaller, Ship was the only one currently docked there.

He smiled as he regarded his vessel, enjoying her graceful cerulean lines. The rest of his crew stood at the lowered cargo lift waiting for him, along with Colonel Graf'eel and a small contingent of her marines. Hawk glanced over at Grendarin, who stood beside him.

"This looks like something out of a holoshow," the Lokathi said with a grin on his orange face. "I'm waiting for the music to start."

"Should I amble across the platform in slow motion?" Hawk asked.

"Better not, the crew might leave you. Stay in touch. Go save the galaxy again." With that, Grendarin re-entered the tube. The doors slid shut, and the tube car left with a rush of air and the smell of ozone.

"I'll do my best," Hawk said to the retreating car. He turned toward his crew and marched across the platform. Despite the size of the bay, landing control had been kind enough—or they had been lucky enough—that Ship sat docked in the berth closest to the tube, so it was a quick walk instead of a ride in one of the wheeled transports.

When he was five meters away, the entire party suddenly spun toward him, came to attention, and crisply saluted. This took him by such surprise that he stopped in mid-stride. Regaining his composure, he realized they weren't going to drop their hands until he returned the gesture.

"You going to stand there with your mouth hanging open?" Ship chided over their secure comm.

Who are you people, and what have you done with my crew? he thought. Aware of Colonel Graf'eel's scrutiny and their previous conversation, he smartly came to attention and rendered his sharpest salute. "Carry on," he said, dropping his hand. The others followed suit. "At ease."

Laura relaxed, smiled, and winked. "Welcome back, Captain."

As the group started up the ramp, Colonel Graf'eel held up a long-fingered, scale-covered hand to him. "Captain, may I speak with you a moment?"

Almost as one, the entire group turned back with varied expressions of puzzlement. Colonel Graf'eel tilted her head toward them with a frown. "Carry on," she commanded. "We should be along shortly."

It amused Hawk to see his crew jump to obey the authority in her voice.

"Take us up, Ship," Ashron said. As the lift activated and trundled upward, he smiled. "Come on, let's see what there is to eat."

Once the lift was far enough toward Ship that Graf'eel could be heard without shouting, she turned to Hawk. He waited, intensely curious about what she might have to say and hopful it wasn't anything dreadful.

She scratched her eye ridge with a talon as she regarded him. "Let me begin by saying when I first heard about you, I did not approve."

Hawk opened his mouth, instinctively ready to defend himself, but stopped when she pulled the talon from her face and held it toward him. "Please let me finish."

He closed his mouth and struggled to keep his face neutral, despite the less than promising start to the conversation—or monologue, if Graf'eel didn't let him respond.

"For the life of me," she continued, lowering her hand, "I couldn't understand why King Ateron would allow an heir to the throne to sign on with such an undisciplined..." she paused and frowned as her light green eyes roamed the platform as she frowned. She was looking for the right word.

Hawk assumed she was searching for the right word. "Rogue? Scallywag?"

Her eyes came back to him, the cat-like slits locking him in place. "Substance abuser," she said.

Ouch, Hawk thought, though her assessment wasn't incorrect. At least over the last couple of years.

She continued. "Assigned to the royal protectorate, I had limited access to your files. Because of Prince Ashron's royal status, I maintained a partial level of need to know, but not as much as I might like. Most everything about you and your team is classified, but the majority of what isn't paints a less than flattering image."

Hawk knew that as a true statement. Force 13 let nothing get out if they could help it. The corporations that occasionally hired the Knights rarely wanted their exploits made public. And if she had seen the various inflammatory and inaccurate stories that came out during the fiasco with Moran, he could see why she would find the Knights undesirable companions for her prince. Hawk wouldn't want to hang out with that group of people either.

"Then came this incident with Hughes and Admiral Dillings, and I saw a glimpse of what your team and, more importantly, *you* stood for. I thought there might be more than what the public face revealed."

"Isn't there always?" Hawk asked.

Graf'eel nodded. "Yes, but it's a scale flip as to whether the truth is better or worse. I reached out to my king and requested a dispensation to acquire higher-level access to your files. I wanted to learn more about you. I would never contradict my King's reasoning, but I wanted to better understand it."

She paused and again locked eyes with him. Her pupils had

widened and gone rounder, which gave her a softer, less dangerous look.

"I was wrong about you. I will follow your lead in this upcoming endeavor, as will my troops. There is an honor about you that is rare, and I know you would willingly sacrifice your life for your crew, which includes Prince Ashron. For that, I am grateful. But know this: as I said before, and it bears repeating, if anything should befall my prince and I find out it's through your negligence," she again pointed her finger at him, "you and I will have harsh words."

Hawk offered a wry grin. "I accept, as I did the day I took on the mantle of leader. I alone am responsible for every action and the outcome of every decision one of my crew or I make, right or wrong." This time it was Hawk's turn to point his finger at her. "I know you feel the same way, Colonel. But I want you to know one thing, and if you ever tell Ashron, I will deny it; I consider Ashron my friend—family even. I might willingly die for my crew, but I will kill for my friends..." Hawk narrowed his eyes.

She nodded in understanding of his statement and offered a toothy grin Hawk recognized as one Ashron wore anytime battle was imminent. "You and I are more alike than I realized." Her tongue flicked slightly. "I believe the prince is in good hands, and I look forward to serving under you, Captain." She rendered a sharp salute.

Instead of returning it, he held out his hand toward her. "We are a team, Colonel, with shared interests." He smiled coyly. "And I hope one day we can become friends."

She lowered her hand, accepted his grip, then wrapped her other hand around it, keeping her talons retracted. "Time will tell. I hope both of us can live up to others' expectations."

"Again, challenge accepted."

Wolf, Ashron, and Gerard watched the exchange between the Colonel and Hawk on the monitor inside Ship's cargo hold. They let them keep their privacy by not turning on the audio, but they didn't need to hear it. The body language was clear.

Wolf jovially clapped Ashron on the shoulder and laughed as he turned to walk away. "That doesn't look good for you, my friend."

Gerard smiled as he placed his non-mechanical hand on Ashron's other shoulder. "If those two develop a friendship, your royal anonymity will become a thing of the past."

"Well, I like her," Ship chimed in.

Gerard laughed and walked inside, leaving Ashron at the top of the ramp, tongue flicking thoughtfully.

Trey joined the others in the room, having shown Colonel Graf'eel's Marines to the cabins and lower berth areas they would be sharing.

"You okay?" he asked Ashron. Trey studied the monitor as Hawk and the Colonel shook hands. "They seem to be getting along."

He returned his gaze back to Ashron, who hadn't answered his question and seemed as if he was somewhere other than on Ship. Trey recognized the expression. It was the same way he gazed at Sam when she wasn't looking. "You okay?" Trey asked again, louder.

Ashron blinked his eyes rapidly, and his tongue flickered. "Yeah," Ashron said. He turned to the young ensign and must have seen the confusion on his face. "The sworn protector of my family and my boss becoming pals might become problematic."

"Why?" Trey asked, cocking his head to the side.

Ashron sighed.

Ship chimed in. "He's afraid he might have to grow up and start acting like the prince he is. To corrupt an old saying, Colonel Graf'eel doesn't seem like the type who will gladly suffer carefree reckless abandon from someone who might potentially rule her people."

"I didn't get all of that, but for the record—as you all like to say—I like Ashron the way he is." Trey grinned up at Ashron.

Ashron's mouth split to reveal his mushroom-colored, sharp teeth. "And that, my boy, is why you will have a seat on my advisory council." He waved a hand toward the screen, where Hawk and Colonel

Graf'eel waited for the elevator that would take them up to Ship's interior. "And those two will be my jesters."

Hawk and Colonel Graf'eel suddenly looked up. Their eyes found the camera, and they seemed to stare directly at Ashron and Trey. Ashron took a step back, his smile disappearing. "Ship, please tell me the audio isn't on down there."

"It isn't," Ship said with a giggle.

"But your internal microphone is broadcasting," Hawk said, so Ashron and Trey heard it. "You need to learn to turn that off if you want to keep things secret."

Trey gave a joyous teenage laugh. "Good luck with your court appointments," he said as he grabbed Ashron by the arm. "Come on, let's get ready to leave."

Several hours later, they reached the rendezvous point suggested by the Kuthrallie and found Admiral Strong with his carrier, the *Strongbow*, two dreadnaughts, and seven cruisers. The Kuthrallie had explained the size limits to Trey, who did his best to convey to the people in charge that it wouldn't be possible to take a full carrier group. The Kuthrallie could not create a tunnel large enough for that many ships. Without his full command at his disposal, the Admiral, after discussion with his advisers, chose the maximum firepower possible within the constraints. Relying on a swift punch instead of a prolonged siege, they took no support vessels, and the Marine transport was off the list, too, much to Colonel Graf'eel's annoyance. Her entire operation would be run off the carrier once they arrived. Hawk offered the Colonel and her security detail passage on Ship until they reached their destination. Despite their mostly stoic manner, Hawk noted the less than excited expressions on the Marines at the prospect of the tight quarters and having to bunk in the storage areas. Hawk didn't care for the crowded conditions either but felt he owed the Colonel at least that much for her support.

Trey walked on the bridge, his body alight with nervousness, his left hand clenching and unclenching while his cybernetic arm rested at his side. Laura was preparing Colonel Graf'eel and her crew for ripsleep, since the additional personnel required her, with Wolf's assistance, to create an improvised administration rig. Hawk did last-minute checks of Ship's systems while Ashron pulled multicolored crackers from a bag and ate them. Gerard sat in his unique chair, starting to rig himself for the jump.

Trey swallowed and cleared his throat. When no one reacted, he tried again, louder. He overdid it, and the noise reached through the quiet space like a gunshot in a warehouse. Trey's cheeks burned as everyone turned and stared at him, Ashron with a cracker halfway to his mouth.

"Did you need something, Ensign?" Hawk asked.

"Yes, sir," Trey said, his voice cracking and turning into a mousy squeak. He cleared his throat yet again, but this time because he needed to do so. He sounded better when he spoke, if still a bit higher-pitched than he would have liked. "I need to speak to Gerard."

"Privately, or can we all hear it?"

Trey considered this briefly before he said, "Everyone can hear it. Everyone probably should hear it."

"Oh, now I'm interested," Ashron said as he set down the bag of crackers.

Gerard had paused his preparations and regarded Trey with a curious expression on his pale face. "What is it?"

Trey swallowed again and blinked a few times, his stomach in knots and his face flush. He wasn't sure how Gerard would react to the news and what would happen if he refused to listen. Considering the many horrible things Trey had experienced, this should be simple. Feeling a sensation like he was about to jump off a cliff, Trey said, "The Kuthrallie told me that—" he paused and gathered himself. "They said that—" he stopped again. Why couldn't he get the words out?

While Hawk and Ashron simply stared at him, offering nothing, Gerard gave him a gentle nod. "If the Kuthrallie have told you, it has to be important. They've done the right thing so far. Whatever you need to tell us, you don't have to be nervous about it. We'll listen."

Comforted, Trey took a deep breath and spoke in a rush to get it all out before he lost his nerve. "The Kuthrallie have said that because it's a new tunnel and not stabilized, you won't be able to pilot through it, and also you need to be asleep like everyone else, and I'm the only one who can be awake, and they will use me as an anchor as they take us through."

He pulled in a breath when he finished and stared at them as they stared back. Silence reigned for several moments.

Ashron chuckled. "Bet that wasn't what you were expecting, was it?"

"It wasn't," Gerard said. "But it makes a certain amount of sense."

"It does?" Hawk said.

"It does," Gerard confirmed. "It has a lot to do with the substance of the *aether* and neuro ripple patterns." He offered a whimsical smirk. "Want me to go into details?"

"My eyes are glazing over already," Hawk said. "As long as you understand and believe them."

"I do."

"Okay, then." Hawk looked at Trey. "Was there anything else, Ensign?"

The astonished relief Trey felt must have been plain as sunlight on his face because Gerard laughed, a rare sound for the Berolian. "Are you okay?"

"Yes," Trey answered. "Just surprised. I thought you would be more upset."

"Because I don't get to pilot this historic event? I'll admit to some disappointment that I won't be able to see how it all works, but even if I were livid, I wouldn't blame you. Unlike those in the ancient past, we don't blame the messenger for the message." His gentle grin disappeared, and Trey almost jumped back at the rapid change. "However, Ensign Julien, I expect diligent observation and a full report of what you see and experience."

"I'll do my best," Trey said.

"And I'll be there to help you," Ship said.

"Thank you."

"I assume this goes for the rip pilots on the other ships, too," Gerard said.

Trey blinked in surprise. He hadn't considered that, but it made sense. He was glad Gerard had thought about it. "Yes. I guess we need to let them know, so they don't get a nasty surprise."

"Ship, can you do the honors?" Hawk said.

"Yes, Captain."

Gerard regarded his arm with some of the wires sticking out and said, "I guess I should unhook and go down to see Laura with the rest of you."

"We'll all head down with you," Hawk said, and then he stared at Trey. "We'll see you on the other side. Wait until you get the all-clear from the rest of the fleet, and then get us there. You have the bridge." He saluted, and Trey saluted back.

As they left, Trey's nervousness at Gerard's reaction, which had disappeared with his laidback response, returned as he considered the magnitude of what he prepared to do. It was one thing to witness the amazing immenseness of ripspace, knowing Gerard had control and they traveled down established "safe" paths. It was quite another to realize he was going alone through uncharted territory. It terrified him.

But you won't be alone, he thought. *Not really.* And it was true, he wouldn't. The Kuthrallie would be guiding him, and he had come to both understand and appreciate them in a short time. He wondered that they ever scared him.

And Sara would be there, too, traveling the unbroken trail with him. The Kuthrallie warned him that what he saw as they traversed the *aether* might still frighten him, but they would protect him and the vessels if the starcraft stayed in the proscribed area. That was the true danger; that the ships would lag and be caught in the *aether* as it collapsed behind them.

Trey didn't understand how the Kuthrallie would use him as an anchor. They tried to explain it using their evolving but still limited mutual vocabulary, but he didn't have a frame of reference to grasp the concepts they presented to him. Eventually, frustrated with his lack of comprehension, he simply told them he trusted them. As long as he didn't need to understand for them to utilize him, he wouldn't worry about it right now.

He sat in the pilot chair for several nervous minutes, waiting to hear from the various vessels. He took deep breaths, working to calm himself.

One by one, the nine vessels reported all crew members were in stasis, the *Strongbow* being the last, an automated message in Admiral Strong's voice saying, "All crew asleep and secured. Prayers said for a safe journey."

I'd pray if I knew who to pray to, Trey thought. Considering the things he had done on Kel, he wasn't sure any deity would answer. He flexed his fingers, both the flesh ones and the metal ones, and realized he wasn't sure what to do next.

A trio of images appeared in Trey's head, in the way the Kuthrallie communicated with him. *Let us control you*, Trey interpreted from their pictures.

He closed his eyes. *I'm yours*, he projected to them.

The Kuthrallie dug into his mind, ethereal fingers reaching through the crevices of his brain. He had to willfully fight his body's rejection of this invasion, had to force himself to accept them, knowing to repel them would doom the mission before it started. It was one of the hardest things he had ever done. It felt like roaches crawling through his skull. His body went rigid, and his jaw clenched despite his attempt to relax. To accept.

He succeeded in lowering his guard, and the tendrils latched on. He shuddered at the alien feel of it, the primal part of him wanting to run screaming.

Then, suddenly, he no longer had control. The Kuthrallie took over, and he became a passenger in his own body. The confines of Ship disappeared, and the vast nothingness of space lay before him. He knew he should be frightened but had no way to express it.

Calmness settled over him. *Relax*, the Kuthrallie said. *You are safe. Your ships are safe.*

Trey relaxed.

The void changed. It tore open, splitting like a shirt ripped at the seams. It revealed a smoky gray mist. Six Kuthrallie hovered in the fog, one larger than the other five. Their octopus-like bodies, so deep gray the tentacles drifting behind them completely disappeared in the haze, pressed in front of him, shaped like a wedge. Pressure built on Trey, or rather his brain, as the Kuthrallie pushed with the effort of breaking through the *aether*. He sensed no movement and could tell they made progress only by a faint shifting of the miasma, shades of gray swirling past him.

He couldn't determine how long they went, and he understood now that time functioned as a different force here. He would never be able to explain it to anyone, and didn't think he would remember when they finished, but at this moment, he saw time was as much a construct as a force of nature. It existed because physical laws demanded it. But when nothing tangible existed, there was no need to measure the passage from birth to death, from rise to fall, from blossom to decay. It was nearly more than he could comprehend.

The pressure continued to build as the effort to forge a path carrying so much with them began to wear on the Kuthrallie's reserves. They kept Trey protected from the extent of their exertion, but it leaked through anyway. They burned themselves to accomplish this, and he had a sense not all six transporting them would survive.

Something else gnawed at the edges, a lingering dread. Other creatures, things not the Kuthrallie, tearing at the fringe. Fear shivered through him. These, not the Kuthrallie, were what had haunted his earlier visions, in the time when the world of ripsleep was a living nightmare to him. Similar to the Kuthrallie, but not. These were darker, more malevolent. They wanted the Kuthrallie to fail. Wanted all the lives intruding in their realm to die screaming.

They are shadows; ignore them, the Kuthrallie said, straining to communicate as they expended themselves. Again, Trey focused forward with a will, resisting the urge to glance toward the flitting phantoms on the periphery.

The longer he felt they traveled, the more detached Trey grew, until he floated in gray. He sensed only the effort of travel, the labored "breathing" of their escorts. Unease flowed through him. Would they make it? What would happen if the Kuthrallie gave out before they reached the destination? Would they die in ripspace, nothing but a lost mission, mourned but unfound?

The concept dragged on him, and no amount of comforting thoughts from the Kuthrallie could displace it. Not that they tried hard. Worn to the point of exhaustion, they had nothing to spare to soothe him further, so they left him to fight the ever-growing terror on his own.

Images of Kel flashed through his mind, visions of the destruction wrought there, the horrors he witnessed. Others followed, things he had experienced with the Knights. A woman's stomach melting through her hands. The loss of his arm. The daily onslaught of emotions Sara endured as Ship.

Despite the dread of those images, they comforted him with the understanding that his experience now was nothing he hadn't encountered before. It was unknown, but unknown didn't immediately mean dangerous. *All in your mind*, he told himself. The others had been physical dangers, and this was mental. He could handle that. He had survived worse. He would survive this.

I've got this, he told the Kuthrallie, and what meager support they gave him left. Some measure of his resolve must have reached them, for they redoubled their efforts, and the frightening shadow images disappeared, left behind as the vessels moved forward in motionless space.

The gray disappeared, the black of space slammed back in on him as if someone had slapped a blindfold over him. He was back on Ship, in the pilot's chair, whole and intact. The first thing he noticed was he had wet himself.

And before he knew it, he was on the deck on his hands and knees, puking.

———

Thankfully, Trey managed to get the deck cleaned and his clothing changed before any of the crew came out of ripsleep.

"Your secret is safe with me," Ship said.

"Thanks," Trey said, blushing.

He stood on the bridge when the crew arrived.

"What was it like?" Gerard asked, an unusual note of excitement in his voice.

"Hard to explain," Trey said. Already the experience felt as much like a dream as anything that really happened. "Let me think about it, and we can talk later."

"Understood," Gerard said.

"I'm pleased to see you didn't kill us," Ashron said as he walked on the bridge, followed by the other three crew members.

"So am I," Trey said, smiling.

"Did you change clothes?" Ashron asked.

Before Trey had to answer or explain, Hawk interjected.

"Well done, Ensign. We'll celebrate and pass out medals later. Right now, we need to get over to the *Strongbow* and get ready to do what we came for."

19

BIG ASS TROLLS

Admiral Strong's voice came across Tactical Two, the communications channel shared by Colonel Graf'eel's Marines and the Knights. "Thirty minutes out. Colonel Graf'eel, are you ready?"

"Aye, Admiral."

"Commander Grey?"

"Yes, sir," Hawk said.

"Godspeed to you and your teams. Switching back to Comm one."

Hawk and his team, except Trey, stood in the *Stronghold's* landing bay designated for *Graf'eel's Gremlins,* the Colonel's three hundred entity Marine detachment. She and Sergeant Major Bishop stood at the head of that impressive troop gathering. Their wing of *Operation Blazing Campfire* was organized around a group of light and medium attack shuttles, one assigned to Hawk's team. While the *Gremlins* attacked the nexus array's defenses on a frontal assault, the Knights would pull a covert HALO jump and work to secure the nexus from within without destroying it. Although a scan of communication satellite archives revealed that much of the civilian population fled before the Serian attack, the crew still wanted to avoid a repeat of their last encounter with a nexus. An explosion in the middle of the small city would devastate the surrounding area, most likely killing any remaining population.

"Good luck, Colonel," Hawk said.

"Luck has little to do with it, Commander," she retorted. *"Fortuna fortes adiuvat et parati,"* she said with a wink, then turned toward Bishop. "Load them up, Sergeant Major."

Sergeant Major Bishop snapped to attention. "Yes, ma'am." He wheeled toward the assembled Marines. "Team leaders, you heard the Colonel. Take charge of your command and mount up!"

Orders echoed throughout the bay area as junior officers relayed commands to their charges. It was organized chaos to the untrained eye, but the Marines' discipline impressed Hawk. Everyone knew their task and performed it with the efficiency brought from years of repetitive training.

Within three minutes, the entire detachment had loaded into their waiting shuttles.

As the ramps raised on the other transports, the Colonel and Sergeant Major walked up the ramp of their shuttle. When they reached the top, Colonel Graf'eel rounded in the doorway and stared down the ramp at Hawk. "Take care of my prince."

Hawk spread his hands. "The die is cast."

The Colonel's eyes narrowed as the shuttle door closed.

"I believe the Colonel is used to getting in the last word," Wolf said over Hawk's shoulder.

"I would agree." Hawk smiled over his shoulder at the large Uraxian. "And so am I."

"I think I'm in love," Ashron said.

"Cool your jets, Romeo; we've got work to do. Let's load up."

"It sounds better when she says it," Ashron told Hawk.

Hawk glanced over to him. "Yeah, it does. Let's go."

"Approaching jump point, two minutes out," Ship said over their commlinks. She remote piloted the *Little Star* as this was an all-hands-on-deck operation. Trey stayed onboard Ship as "acting Captain," but the rest of them had suited up in heated and pressurized light combat suits in preparation for their HALO jump. They had little opportunity to scout for landing areas, having started the attack as soon as possible after leaving ripspace to give them some element of surprise.

Ship, along with the Marines, who were crammed into several shuttles from the carrier, broke away from the main body as the fleet moved to intercept the vessels guarding the array platform. As they approached, a quick survey by both Ship and the Marine tacticians had revealed several suitable landing sites near the nexus. Hawk chose a wide-open space that seemed to be an athletic field near a school, as it avoided the possibility of hitting the numerous buildings, including a few skyscrapers.

It was still early morning planetside, and the sun hadn't broken the horizon. Recalibration of the ship clocks, required after their unusual journey, showed seven standard days since word of the Falador assault. Unless the Serians had some unknown technology, the time-frame gave them little time to both pacify the planet and set up observation posts. That's how Hawk saw it anyway. And even if the Serians were aware, they would soon be too busy dealing with the Marine attacks to pay much attention to Hawk and his small group.

"One minute out," Ship said.

Hawk nodded to Ashron. He slapped a button, which started lowering the back ramp. Wolf adjusted his hold on a container beside his feet. Gerard checked on another box next to his. Laura glanced up and smiled. Hawk gave her and the rest of them a thumbs up, which they returned in kind.

"Thirty seconds," Ship stated.

Hawk watched Gerard, whose arm began to emit a slight glow. Gerard placed his foot on the package beside him and pushed it out the back ramp. Hawk watched as it paused in mid-flight, then took off in a dive.

"Ten seconds."

They stood as one. Laura had her eyes closed and swayed slightly back and forth, as if to music.

"Five…four…three."

Wolf tossed his container out the back of the shuttle. Hawk watched as it tumbled into the darkness.

"Two."

Laura opened her eyes as they all faced the opening.

"One."

"Move," Hawk commanded.

Ashron turned to Hawk, grinned, and jumped backward out of the open hatch. Still smiling broadly while falling toward the planet, he saluted smartly, then rolled over headfirst and plummeted, accelerating as he folded his arms and legs together. Wolf, Gerard, and Laura immediately followed without the fanfare. Hawk shook his head and jumped into the darkness.

"And be careful," Ship whispered to them all.

"They are away," the voice they all called Ship came over Colonel Graf'eel's commlink. It was easily the most advanced AI she had ever encountered.

"Understood," she responded. "Ten minutes," she barked over her tac channel. She checked her screen as four *Speartip* medium attack craft moved to formation, flanking her landing craft. Designed to soften up an area and make it unfriendly to hostiles, the *Speartips* were a welcome addition to the planned assault.

Sergeant Major Bishop glanced over at the Colonel's screen. "Still going to be a short trip if Hawk and his team don't get there in time."

"Agreed. Or a very long one if Admiral Strong fails. Hawk's crew and their craft seem to be survivors, but I have a feeling we're destined to be in this sector for an extended time if something happens to their ship and that young Ensign. Capable as they are, they'll be no match against the Serian fleet if the good Admiral loses."

"*Fortuna* then," he said, grinning.

She smiled, "Luck indeed." She glanced at the timer on her display. "Into the breach."

As Hawk fell through the night sky, plummeting toward the planet with the crew around him, he stared at the landscape through his contact lens HUD, which showed everything in vibrant hues as it compiled and assembled information from infrared, night vision, and echo sounding. For an occupied city, the area showed little damage. The attack must have been swift and unexpected, meeting little resistance.

To his right, Ashron did flips and spins in the air as if he were some circus acrobat. Hawk kept an eye and ear out for incoming fire, wondering if the Serians kept any observation on the sky for a counterattack. The Knight's suits were matte black, reflective, and heat-dampening, making them as camouflaged as possible against known technologies. But they still had no idea how advanced the Serians might be in warfare. The accidental destruction of both the orbital platform and the ground shelter had limited their ability to discover and study their enemy. He had to hope they were as invisible as they should be. Plummeting like a stone with the wind whistling past him, he felt naked and vulnerable.

The ground drew closer. When they passed three-thousand meters, Hawk's HUD pinged as a bright red dot became visible on the athletic field: the supply crate they had dropped earlier. Guided remotely by Ship, the coffin-shaped box had landed near a stand of bleachers within twenty meters of its target. The crate landing intact without attracting any attention made Hawk breathe easier.

It was early morning local time, and he saw little activity on the streets. Lights gleamed in a few of the houses surrounding the field, and no vehicles traveled the roads. Whether this was normal or a result of the occupation, Hawk didn't know. It was okay with him, either way. Fewer people meant less chance of discovery or unintended casualties.

At a thousand meters, the energy "chutes," also black and non-reflective, deployed, and the crew floated toward the field.

"Beautiful sunrise, isn't it?" Ashron said as they drifted.

Hawk had to agree; the sky glowed vibrant yellow as the sun broke the horizon and glimmered on a pair of glass skyscrapers clustered among a handful of taller buildings in what Hawk guessed was the downtown area. He was thankful they weren't going that way. The towering structures allowed for way too many hiding places. Bad enough the nexus sat in an industrial area with massive warehouses, some of them three stories tall, which made it easier for sensors to read everything in open, squat buildings. Snipers twenty stories up amidst a jumble of structures could be much more of a problem.

As the athletic field stood less than half a klick from their primary target and they had taken no incoming fire, Hawk surmised the HALO jump kept them out of Serian detection, or the invaders expected no resistance from an external source.

Hawk landed, flexed his knees, and ran forward to absorb the impact. He felt the chute dissipate behind him as the energy expended. Without a word, the crew assembled at the supply crate, which had opened as soon as they landed. Everyone geared up and took a knee as they waited for Hawk to give the go-ahead.

He glanced at Laura and nodded. She nodded back, stood, and loped off. She had a different destination than the rest of the crew; they had identified a prime overwatch location for their operation. It would also make an excellent fallback and rally point should things go to shit. "Ship, how much time do we have?"

"Three minutes thirty-eight seconds."

"Damn," He looked to Ashron, who bristled with both weaponry and anticipation. Hawk waved a hand across the field. "Point. Move."

Ashron leapt ahead, moving with deadly grace and fluidity. Hawk took up position behind, followed by Gerard and Wolf as rearguard. Despite his size and the massive Minigun of Awesomeness he carried, Wolf kept pace effortlessly with the rest of the team. Though slight and lacking natural stamina, Gerard could use his magical abilities to run at speed for hours on end if necessary. Ashron was just a freak of nature. Following Ashron's blistering pace, Hawk could already feel the burn, and they hadn't left the field yet.

"HUD, medical."

Within seconds, his muscles relaxed and stretched out. His stride grew longer and more measured, even as his breathing slowed. He hated using enhancements as much as Laura did, but this was no time for scruples about such things; they had a job to do, and lives depended on their success.

"Ship, how is your uplink to *Spy Wing*?" Gerard asked. His arm glowed in a strange golden purple color that was difficult to see even in dim light. *Spy Wing* was Gerard's pet name for his reconnaissance drone he launched earlier from *Little Star*. It allowed Ship to coordinate live information to his team from a position that extended her line of sight.

"Excellent," Ship answered. "We are up and running. Updated information should be uploading to your HUD now."

Hawk studied the new information. It didn't appear the Serians had activated the shield protecting the nexus in response to Admiral Strong's assault on their fleet. This also meant Colonel Graf'eel and her detachment had yet to be detected. *Good,* he thought, *we still have a little time.* Hawk checked positioning and time appraisal on his HUD. "Sixty seconds out, Colonel," he said.

"Copy sixty seconds out," Colonel Graf'eel answered Hawk. "Air assault one, go weapons hot and prepare to drop in sixty."

She listened as the commanders of the four *Speartip* attack craft answered in the affirmative. Once they sounded off, she spoke to her troops over the tactical net. "Get ready, everyone. We hit the ground running in ninety seconds." With the firepower backing them, thirty seconds should be an ample softening period.

"Commander," the communications officer of her shuttle said. "I've got a reading at mark seven. Looks like a hostile contact."

"Hawkeye one in position." Laura worked to control her breathing after her scramble to the roof of the eight-story building. She had taken the stairs rather than risk the elevator and running into curious civilians, or worse, a Serian patrol.

She studied the scene from her position on the building roof thirty meters above the street. From this vantage point, the tallest building in a three-block area, she could see both of the newly constructed buildings, formed of the same materials they had seen in their last encounter with the Serians. The buildings a block around the construction had been knocked down or destroyed, forming clear fields of view while providing some measure of cover for any defenders.

The buildings appeared deserted, but Laura suspected plenty of occupants resided inside, doing whatever they did to power the array. Heat scans showed a few people at this early hour in some of the warehouses and offices near the Serian structures, but the alien buildings blocked both thermal and ultrasonic, so they were black holes in her survey.

A flash above caught Laura's eye. She turned her gaze toward the sky and saw more bright bursts as Admiral Strong's fleet engaged the Serian armada. She wondered if Serians occupied the surrounding buildings, hiding among the Faladorians. Though alien, the Serian thermal signature and build were close enough to the locals that there was no way to tell on casual inspection. She had not brought any additional scanning equipment besides what her contacts provided and had to assume they had outposts and defenses ready to prevent the type of incursion the Knights were attempting.

"Sixty seconds out, Colonel," Laura heard Hawk over the comm.

"Copy sixty seconds out," Colonel Graf'eel responded.

Laura scanned the streets for her team and spotted the furtive movement as they dashed from building to building. Sixty seconds seemed optimistic to her, but she didn't have the same telemetry information as Hawk.

She said a little prayer that the team got inside the shield's assumed perimeter before things fell apart, as combat plans inevitably did. They had only a vague idea of what it would take to get past the barrier once it activated, or what would happen if they tried to breach it. The first one had been destroyed before they had any chance to determine anything about it. Gerard had been investigating the problem using what little debris they gathered. She hoped his proposed solution would work if push came to shove.

She focused her attention back to the Serian outpost and willed her team to move faster. A sudden gut feeling told her things were—

What the hell is that? Laura thought as movement caught her eye near the team's approach line. "Contact front, a hundred meters," she warned. Ashron and the team quickly stopped and took cover. She adjusted the magnification on her contacts to bring the beings into sharper focus. "Holy shit," she said to no one in particular.

"What you got, Laura?" Hawk asked.

"Best I can say is they look like Serians on steroids. Bigger, more muscular, and they are on your line of approach and prepared to ambush. Can't tell you anything about their weaponry other than it's big and ugly." She scanned the area, thankful the creatures weren't as stealthy as they were large. "I've spotted three, two at your front and one to your two o'clock. Based on the attitude, they haven't spotted you yet, but they are alert."

"Keep an eye on them," Hawk told her. "Let me know if—"

"Tac break," Colonel Graf'eel interrupted. "We've been compromised. Beginning attack."

As soon as she said that, a flight of missiles whistled from the sky and slammed into the front of the larger Serian building, sending gouts of fire into the air.

"Roger that," Laura responded and trained her weapon at the base of one of the Serian's skull.

"Shot out," Laura called. She watched as the back of her target's head imploded through the front, and the creature pitched forward to the pavement. "Target down."

As she transitioned her attention to the other two, she was surprised as her targets' weapons fragmented and exploded, knocking the hostiles backward. One slammed against a building hard enough to shatter a chunk of stone. The other reeled into the street and rolled across the ground like a ragdoll.

"Looks like *Spy Wing's* ordinance did the trick," Laura said. "Targets are down. Move."

At Laura's command, Ashron jumped up and continued toward their destination, the rest of the team falling in line behind him. "I want those," Ashron said, impressed with Gerard's new, remote-controlled anti-personnel devices. Ship had kindly targeted the creature's weapons, taking both firepower and enemy combatants out in one swipe. "I'm jealous I didn't come up with them."

As more missiles poured from the sky, Ashron's skin tightened, and a sonorous hum vibrated through the air. The missiles streaked downward, heading for the Serian structure. They exploded in midair, two blocks away, and twenty meters above their target. A glimmering silver haze briefly radiated from the impact points and dissolved away.

"Shield's up," Ashron said as he reached the two Serians lying on the ground. "That kind of sucks."

He studied the two bodies as he waited for the others to reach them. Laura was right; these boys were big. With their dull green skin, they resembled the other Serians the crew had seen but stood easily a meter taller than their smaller brethren and rivaled Wolf in mass.

They also still writhed on the ground despite dark red blood leaking from several spots on their bodies.

"These are some tough sons of bitches," Ashron said as Hawk stepped up beside him. "No way they should have survived."

Wolf and Gerard joined them and took up defensive positions, scanning out. More explosions rocked against the shield above the stronghold.

"Shield's up, Colonel, in case your scans haven't told you," Hawk said as he knelt to inspect one of the oversized Serians. "Head for your secondary target."

"Copy that. Good luck."

Hawk stared at one creature, then glanced at the other. The explosives had done their jobs; the heavy weapons lay in pieces of gray metal, shattered beyond recognition. Both Serians had large holes in their bodies, and a black-hued bone protruded outward from the chest of the one closest to Hawk. "Go check the third one," he told Ashron. "We don't need any surprises coming up behind us."

"On it." Ashron vaulted over a crumbled brick wall and ran toward the Serian Laura had shot.

"What do you make of it?" Hawk asked Gerard.

Gerard joined Hawk and studied the still moving Serians while Wolf and his MGoA continued to scan the area for more hostiles.

"It's clearly alive, but how the hell is…" Gerard let the thought hang as his pale blue eyes narrowed. "Amazing, it appears to be regenerating. Look."

He knelt and indicated a ragged wound on the creature's neck. As they watched, the gap knitted itself, the tattered edges smoothing as mottled green flesh flaked away. The Serian's eyes popped open, and its hand tightened around Gerard's ankle.

Gerard yelped and tried to scramble backward as a wicked-looking serrated knife appeared in the Serian's other hand and arced for Gerard's unprotected torso. Hawk fired two rounds from his rifle into the beast's face. The warrior slammed back to the ground, blade clattering as black bone and dark gray brain hit the pavement. Hawk followed up with two more headshots into the other Serian. "If they regenerate from that, we might as well surrender now and hand them the keys."

Lying on his back, Gerard's pale face grinned in relieved thanks as Ashron leapt back over the wall.

"The other one is done." the Lorothian said. "Laura pretty much painted the wall with his head." He pointed at the body nearest them. "Similar to what you did to these two."

"Ship, let the good Colonel know about these new Serians that seem to have regeneration capabilities. Headshots for all my friends. Two if they can manage it."

"Aye, Captain."

"Fire would most likely work too," Gerard said as Hawk helped him to stand.

"Keep eyes and scans open for any more surprises," Hawk said. "We still have a mission to do. Let's see if we can figure out a way past this shield."

Colonel Graf'eel strolled from the rear of her landing shuttle surrounded by her command group. It had been a harrowing descent, pursued by a twelve-ship squadron of Serian light fighters. Though maneuverable and fast, the alien ships lacked any real punch in their armament. And they weren't lithe enough to avoid the *Speartips'* gun crews. At least not for long. Her ship took a couple of hits that rattled teeth and not much else.

The more egregious problem was their premature discovery, which brought the shield up over the nexus structure, making Hawk and his crew's task much harder. It also complicated her mission. The primary plan called for all her *Speartips* to swoop in, unload all ordinance, and pound the structure into oblivion, thus making the space-borne array useless. But like most military plans when it came into enemy contact, it had gone sideways. Now her mission was to take the heat off the Knights so they could covertly access the array and shut it down. They were meant to have slipped inside the shield wall before it activated, but that had gone scales up too.

The best-laid plans, she thought. She didn't much care for the decoy role, but orders were orders, and from Graf'eel's understanding, they needed this operation to be more circumspect and less destructive than the last one. They couldn't allow the possible civilian casualties if this nexus exploded in the middle of the population center.

She grinned as one of her mechs rumbled past, heading into battle, followed by a squad of heavy infantry. Her secondary objective was to move to the main Serian compound and suppress any resistance. That was command speak for assault and destroy, something for which her team was exceptionally well suited. She looked at Bishop. "Sergeant Major, pass on the information Hawk provided to our Squad Leaders. Ensure that any enemies who go down, stay down."

"Contact. Five coming up fast on your left," Laura said as she squeezed off a round, placing it neatly through a creature's skull. "Four," she said, following up for a second shot.

Ashron spotted them as Laura called out the contact. He threw himself in their direction, opening fire as he moved. One collapsed from Laura's shot as another fell beneath Ashron's concentrated weapon fire. The outlier turned into a mist of flesh and shattered bone as Wolf opened fire with his MGoA. The other two ran as a unit to reach for cover, but Ashron launched himself down the road and sprang feet first into the one closest to him. They both landed on the hard asphalt, the Serian ahead of Ashron. He did a forward roll to his feet and fired a burst at point-blank range. The shots pushed the rising creature back to the ground, penetrating the light armor and drawing blood. But Ashron could see that as soon as the wounds appeared, they began to close.

Unacceptable, Ashron thought. He dropped his SMG, and it retreated to his back, pulled there by the harness. He drew his two half-meter blades from his belt, snarled, and launched himself at the still staggering creature. Ashron whirled into his adversary, a blur of spinning knives, claws, and teeth, simultaneously cutting into several vital areas, including arteries, tendons, and nerves. Before the opponent could consider any defense, Ashron finished with a horizontal slash to the throat. He spun away from both the Serian's grasp and the spray of dark, almost black, blood.

Generally, at this point, Ashron took a second to watch his adversary drop to the ground in a dead or dying heap to ensure no further aggression. The Serian surprised him as it advanced on him, although awkwardly, due to its several severed tendons.

"Really?" Ashron said with an edge of disgust. "Trolls?" He sheathed one of his knives, grabbed a smooth metal sphere from his foremost belt pouch, and jumped straight for the advancing monster. He ducked under one of its flailing arms and sliced open a deep gash beneath its rib cage. Before the opponent could react, Ashron shoved his hand into the wound and activated the incendiary grenade. He once again kicked away, ducked under the other flailing arm that reached for him, and took refuge behind a wall. "Regenerate that, bitch!"

The creature, newly classified by Ashron as a troll, clawed frantically, trying to open the rapidly closing gash, defeated by its own abilities. It got nowhere close to saving itself before it burst into an impressive spray of burning flesh chunks and flying bone.

While Ashron danced with one of the remaining Serians, Hawk aimed and fired at the other one, which had turned from the wiser course of retreat and made the mistake of charging Hawk.

Multiple rounds to the chest and head seemed to do the job as the tall creature tried to jump a low wall and caught its foot on the edge. It collapsed and writhed. As the regeneration started, Gerard stepped forward and incanted a formula under his breath. A bright blue flame issued forth from Gerard's cybernetic arm and engulfed the creature. It let out one pitiful wail before the superheated fire consumed it and turned it to ash.

"That was exciting," Ashron said as he returned to the other three. "Although one grenade for one troll is not the most efficient use of ordinance."

CRACK!

Ashron wheeled around, knives in hand, just in time to have a warm spray of gore coat his chest. The troll they had neglected collapsed at his feet, missing most of its cranium.

"You're welcome," Laura said.

"Thanks, you three," Ashron said to the others. "I'm about to be mauled to death, and you don't even bother to warn me."

"Should tell you something of what we think about you," Hawk said.

"Or how quickly it moved and how fast Laura reacted," Gerard said.

"I suspect Hawk's reason is more accurate," Ashron said.

"Ship," Laura said. "Am I to assume you didn't pick those big ass Serians up on any of your sensors?"

"Trolls," Ashron corrected.

"BAS, troll, whatever. Ship?" Laura asked.

"No, I did not. Using all ranges and fields, I am detecting many of the Serians we encountered on Alonis Ceti, but the trolls are missing. Until we figure out why, you will have to go about this the old-fashioned way. Looks like it's on you, Laura."

"Awesome. Stay alert, you four."

"Because Lerts live longer," Ashron and Hawk muttered simultaneously.

"You sure you two aren't from the same parents?" Laura asked. "Anyway, you are clear to the shield on your present route. Get a move on."

A quick jog brought them to the shield wall without incident, where they took cover behind a small office building. The shield enclosed the makeshift Serian structure, barely visible as a shimmering half-dome.

"This one looks different than the last one," Laura said, able to see the entire barrier from her higher vantage point. "It's not as translucent, and the shimmer pattern seems to be different. You think you can pass through it?"

"I doubt it will be easy," Hawk responded. "Or it wouldn't be much of a barrier. We didn't get a chance to examine the last one before Ashron decided to create a small crater where it stood." Hawk smiled and waved a hand at Ashron before he could protest. "I know, we were pressed for time." He turned to Gerard. "What do you think, engineering genius?"

Gerard unslung a dark green backpack from his shoulder and said,

"Remember those items I gathered from the debris during our last encounter?"

"The ones that almost had you peeing your pants with excitement?" Hawk asked.

"I don't think it was quite that, but yes, those." Gerard opened his pack and pulled out two small shining silver disks. "I had an opportunity to study them and the residual materials while you were lounging around in Hughes's country club. I also collaborated with Master Genray and Henna LaRouche."

"You got Henna to collaborate remotely?" Hawk asked.

"It wasn't easy, but I impressed upon her the galaxy-saving importance." Gerard tossed the two disks at the shield. They sat in midair, supported by nothing, the vague shimmer the only indication anything was there. "I may have overstated the case, but it appealed to her ego. We made significant strides in the technology. Fascinating stuff, really."

"I'm sure," Ashron said, rolling his narrow eyes at Hawk and lolling his head back as if falling asleep.

Gerard pulled another disc from the backpack, this one roughly twenty centimeters across, the shiny surface marred by a black strip on the outer rim. He handed it over to Wolf. "Throw this as far as you can toward the top of the dome."

Wolf took the object and hefted the weight, getting a feel for it. With a grunt, he performed a passable discus toss without all the spinning. It smoothly sailed forty meters before it descended and sat suspended in midair.

"Good toss." Gerard ran a finger down one of the wires on his gleaming metal arm. "Once we got past the alien nature of it, the technology was fairly simple, and honestly not much different from conventions we employ."

His arm glowed faintly as he worked the seven metallic fingers in an intricate rhythmic pattern. "I'm almost embarrassed we hadn't figured it out earlier on our own, seeing as it involved bi-material harmonic conversion theories."

"Well, of course," Ashron said as he crossed his eyes. A distinctly odd look, given his elongated snout. "That's what I figured from the first time I saw it."

Gerard smiled as he clacked his fingers together, forming his hand like a bird's beak. He pointed at the closest disk. A soft, low humming emanated from it.

"Henna was incredibly put out when we finally cracked it." Gerard shrugged and repeated the motions with his cybernetic hand. "But you know how she can be."

He formed his bird bill again at the second disk; it also started humming.

Gerard repeated the motions a third time. "Laura, to answer your question, if we tried to pass through the shield, it would kill us like a bug zapper. They have keyed the resonance to recognize either them or something in their equipment. Something we don't have. It's also resilient to our weapon systems, as the pyrotechnics display with the missiles showed. It's highly advanced technology." He closed his eyes, muttered something none of them understood for about a minute, and opened them again. "However, they use *aetheric* energy, which is something my people are quite familiar with." Gerard reached out and touched the shield with his arm, which glowed vibrant blue.

***

"Now," Ship said over Colonel Graf'eel's commlink. The Colonel smiled as the disappearing haze heralded the shield's dissolution, an event confirmed by the readings on her HUD. She was grateful. The Serian's fierce resistance had taken a toll on her Marines. "Engage!" She shouted over the shared channel. "Let's move!"

With a roar of fury, her troops threw themselves forward to engage the now unprotected foe.

Graf'eel switched over to Ship's secure link. "Copy. Units inbound and on the offensive."

She watched as a Medium Assault Mech, painted green and gold, rose from its defensive position and fired a combined volley of missiles from its shoulders, lasers from its torso, and slugs from the cannon on each arm.

All down the line, Graf'eel's Marines opened fire with deadly accuracy. She mused that one advantage of getting your ass kicked while hunkering down in a defensive position was it allowed you to hone your return fire solutions.

A wing of *Sprite*, a light attack aircraft, buzzed overhead and pounded another target with rockets. Having air superiority was a surprise. She assumed the Serians had assessed their resources and determined their air assets were better utilized against Admiral Strong and his advance than hers. No doubt they came to the same conclusion she had: if they lost the battle in space, they lost the ability to retreat. But if they won against the good Admiral, they could focus all their attention on her Marines and the landing force. If that became the case, the battle would turn deadly for her people.

However, that was not her concern. She had given her orders. According to her display, her troops executed the battle plan as effectively as possible against enemy contact. She wanted to get at least eighty percent of her forces inside the shield range in case the Serians had a hidden power supply with enough energy to bring it back online.

So, with air support and mechs pounding on buildings and her secondary teams providing cover, she had one thing left to do; she stepped over the parapet where she and her cadre sheltered. "On me, Marines."

She dashed forward into the fray, her powered armor screaming as she pushed it to its limit.

This was not Sergeant Major Bishop's first dance. As soon as the Colonel moved, Bishop powered up and came to her side. Without armor, Lorothians were fast, agile, and deadly; a Lorothian trained in powered armor became death incarnate. The speed with which the Colonel moved under enhancement was beautiful to behold, but she would rapidly outdistance her troops if he didn't act quickly and get his people flanking her. He and his detail had one priority: protect the Colonel. She knew this and trusted her troops to be where they needed to be and do their duty. Bishop would never hear the end of it if the Colonel had to restrain herself for him to do his job.

The Sergeant Major rarely let that happen, nor did his troops. With practiced precision years in the undertaking, they formed around her as she slammed into the Serian line. To the Colonel, combat was a deadly dance. Once the music started, it didn't stop until the enemy lay vanquished or those above her rank sounded a retreat. She whirled and attacked with a fluid grace few could hope to match, and the Serians didn't measure up. She did not pause and allowed no moments of indecision. Projectiles flew from her arm-mounted weapon as she engaged with others in close combat, her vibroknife a blur of deadly precision.

The Sergeant Major and his detail could not hope to match her in speed or grace, but they made up for it in brutal killing efficiency, and it was time to eliminate the enemies she left untouched in her destructive aftermath. Following their leader, *Graf'eel's Gremlins* plowed into the line of defenders; with their overlapping firing solutions, practiced teamwork, and communications, they flowed over the battlefield like water over a rock, leaving devastation in their wake.

Hawk smiled at Gerard as they took cover behind a single-story building on the inner edge of the shield perimeter. They were delaying their advance on the main structure to allow Colonel Graf'eel's Marines to occupy the Serians' resources and attention. "You've been holding out. That was an impressive accomplishment."

"Like I mentioned, the power supply is *aetheric* energy, something with which I'm intimately familiar and which Trey is beginning to learn. I would hazard a guess the Serians view the nexus as a nothing but a power source, don't understand its true purpose, and haven't encountered anyone who can manipulate it as my people can."

"You mean they're not spellburners?" Ashron asked.

Gerard disliked the term and knew Ashron did it to irritate him, so he ignored it as best he could. That Ashron had gotten Trey in on the act was more difficult to accept. "Henna and I don't believe so. It looks like they are technology-driven and not manipulators. Otherwise, we wouldn't have been able to defeat their shield as easily as I did. Nor do I think our first encounter would have gone so easily."

"Easily?" Ashron scoffed.

"All things considered, yes," Gerard told him.

Having left her perch when the shield collapsed, Laura slid in quietly beside them, her breath coming in quick gasps from her run to join them. She wouldn't use stim enhancements except under genuinely dire circumstances. "Since Ship can't pick up the signature on those new Serians, what do you think about me taking up a position over there?" She pointed to a building off to their left, which, though only four stories tall, was still higher than the surrounding buildings. "I should be able to provide cover and intel as you move into position. Assuming I don't have any issues getting inside."

"I like it," Hawk said. With a flick of his eyelids, he switched his HUD to tactical mode, which showed him the positioning of Colonel Graf'eel's troops. They were making reasonable progress in engaging the Serians. "We need to get moving. We'll start loping toward the target. Let us know when you reach position so Ashron can pick up the pace."

She nodded and jogged toward the indicated building.

"Ashron, shall we?"

With a quick grin, Ashron darted down a side alley; the rest of the team fell into their designated positions, flanking him.

After a couple of minutes of sporadic travel, Hawk's HUD pinged with a large red dot as Ship said, "Hold. There's a group of Serians moving on two. It looks like they're advancing toward the main fighting and will miss you by about a hundred-and-twenty meters."

The Knights each found a spot of shadow and waited. They still had no idea what technology the Serians possessed for enemy detection, and it made Hawk's skin crawl to think his adversaries might know where he was while he waited in the alcove.

A tense minute passed while Hawk watched the red dot move on his HUD.

"All clear," Ship said as the spot cleared Hawk's field of view. He could have zoomed out to track their position but kept to their agreed-upon area of operation setting.

Ashron again took point, and they continued their advance.

"I'm in position," Laura said in Hawk's ear. "I have a clear view of the nexus and the structure they built around it. There is a flurry of activity; it looks like you threw a cross span into their plans, Gerard. Lots of arm flailing and finger-pointing. Every Serian in view is either frantically running toward or away from the advancing marines."

Ship chimed in as another contact appeared on Hawk's HUD. "Captain, there is a group of armed Faladorians approaching from your right. I suspect they are a group of partisans."

"I've got them," Laura said. "They're setting quite the pace, and I think they know where you are."

"Copy." Hawk indicated two buildings that seemed to have taken some fire in the initial assault. The roof on one had collapsed, and the other bore scorch marks and divots blown in the gray stone. "Gerard, you and Ashron take up positions over there, just in case. Wolf, you're on me."

Ashron and Gerard scrambled into position to provide overlapping fields of fire if the need arose. Wolf and Hawk separated to leave space between them. Hawk stepped out into the open and waited.

"They should be in your sight in ten," Laura said. "Looks like they know exactly where you are."

"You are likely being watched and reported on," Ship said. "Although they must be doing it through hand signals or organic messengers. There are a lot of civilians hunkered down in the buildings all around you, but I'm not picking up any communications."

"Organic messengers?" Ashron asked. "Is that computer lingo for 'runners?'"

"Not a computer," Ship chided.

"I guess we'll know in a moment," Hawk said. "Here they come."

The Faladorians emerged from the shadows of the nearby building and strode toward Hawk's position. They were tall, lanky people and wore dull-colored clothing. "I count eight," Hawk said. "A variety of small arms."

"There are ten more taking up positions around you," Ship advised. "It looks more precautionary than an ambush. They seem concerned as much with their flanks as they are with you."

Hawk nodded as the group came to a halt in front of them. As Ship had instructed the crew before they landed, Hawk placed his right hand over his heart and offered a slight nod, a common Faladorian greeting. "*Afata Taia*," Hawk said as he dropped his hand.

The group kept their distance as the tallest man in the group stepped forward, repeated the greeting, and said, "*Afata Taia*."

He switched to the official Galactic Council language. "We have been following your movement but didn't know how best to help." The man's accent pushed heavily to the last syllable of words, giving an uneven cadence to his speech. "However, when the shields came down, we decided it was time to act. Until then, our weapons were completely ineffective against them."

"What about your military?" Hawk asked. "Are they operational?"

"As far as I know, the initial engagements destroyed most of the effective force. I'm sure there are scattered surviving units. Now that help has arrived, they will hopefully rejoin the effort."

"We're heading for the power source structure. The Serians will be concentrating on the marine force attacking their front. If you could provide another distraction somewhere on the flanks, that could be a tremendous help."

"Serians," the leader mused. "A good name." His bronze face turned serious. "Be careful around the building. There is a monster. Large. Like nothing I have ever seen."

"We will," Hawk placed his hand over his heart again. "*Lafadan atar.* Life to your people."

The leader returned the gesture. "*Atar Lafa.* And life to yours." The tall man rejoined his squad, and they ran back in the direction they had come.

"Do you think it was wise letting them know where we're headed?" Laura asked in Hawk's ear.

"I don't know," Hawk answered. "If they were hostile, they would have either attacked on sight or stayed hidden. And if they wanted to know where we were going, they could have easily figured it out on their own."

A far-off explosion caught their attention.

"That was fast," Laura said. "They definitely have some unusual form of communication, and more than one group. That explosion was at least two klicks away. It should provide a nice distraction."

"Well then, let's not disappoint. Ashron, on you."

Ashron bounded up the road, leading them toward the power array.

"Keep an eye out for us, Ship," Hawk said. Speed was critical now, so the open road made more sense than skulking in building cover.

"I've got all of them out," Ship said.

"What do you think he meant by 'monster'?" Ashron asked.

"I hope they saw one of Graf'eel's mechs," Hawk said, loping behind and to Ashron's right. "But I suspect we'll find out soon enough. Stay frosty."

20

DEVIOUS SPELLBURNER SHIT

shron led the team to a small rise overlooking the array, located next to an abandoned warehouse building. Hawk checked his HUD. Laura had again repositioned to keep up with their advance and currently sat on the roof of a four-story building, covering their approach to the array. Ship had plotted all the known Serians and transmitted them to everyone's HUD.

"Keep in mind, those are the ones showing up on my sensors. I have no idea if any of the ones that don't show up are around."

"First trolls," Ashron muttered. "Now invisible Serians."

"We'll assume tactical movement, full-spectrum scans," Hawk said. If Ship couldn't spot them, he didn't know that they would fare any better on the ground, but he had to do something. "Gerard, anything you can do?"

"I'll send an occasional thaumapulse wave."

"I'll take that as a yes. Anything, Laura?"

"Nothing other than what's already on the display. There is a guard post to the front and a flurry of technicians coming and going from the array itself." Laura paused as she caught movement off to the left of the guard post. "Hold on. It looks like you have a couple of trolls hunkered down on a second-story landing over the guard post. If that's all there are, I should be able to cover your approach." They sat deep within the alcove to provide surprise cover for the two guards below. It would be a short leap off the ledge to put them in the fray.

"Copy that." Hawk looked over to Ashron and Wolf. "You two take care of the guards and any other surprises that might be waiting for us. Gerard and I will find the control room and neutralize the power source."

Wolf and Ashron nodded agreement and headed up the road. Hawk turned to Gerard, "Ready?"

"On you."

Hawk took point for the two of them and flanked Wolf and Ashron on their right. The three of them adjusted their pacing to Hawk's so they would arrive at their designated objectives at approximately the same time.

Ashron and Wolf moved as close as they thought they could manage without being observed, a one-story wooden building now the only thing between them and open ground. Ashron peered around the corner to study the guardhouse. He spotted the landing above the Serian guards and could make out two giant figures in the shadows, despite their attempts to hide deep within the recesses. "Laura, do you think you can get both of them?"

"One for sure and maybe the other if he doesn't react quickly enough. How do you want to play this?"

"Wolf and I will move on your shot count, take out the guards, and be ready to assist if the second one is tricky. Ready when you are."

"Copy that. Hawk, are you in position?"

"We are. On your mark."

Laura focused on one of the Serian trolls lounging closer to the edge. Closer being a relative term, as they both hunkered deep within the three-meter depth of the landing. She judged that, with a little bit of luck, the shot would bounce him off the back wall and make him fall forward in such a way as to slow the other one down enough to give her a good follow-up shot.

She started her count. "Three...two...one...move."

The projectile ripped through the bridge of the troll's nose and out the back of his brain stem. He staggered back, but his mass kept him from bouncing as she had hoped. Instead, he dropped like a sack of grain thrown from a loft.

Fortunately, the unexpected violence startled the other one so much that, rather than seeking cover, he jumped back in alarm and hit the wall. This gave Laura all the advantage she needed. Her follow-up shot plowed through his left eye, dropping him on top of the first.

On Laura's move command, Wolf stepped around the corner and opened fire with his MGoA on the Serian guards' station. Using the covering fire, Ashron sprang from his spot and ran toward the guard post, ready to deal with any survivors. He should have known better since there were only two of them. He made it no more than a half dozen paces before slowing as Wolf's weapon left a pile of devastation and a pair of smoking, slug-riddled Serian corpses. Nothing ever prepared Ashron for the effectiveness of Wolf's modified firearm, but anytime he went into battle with the Uraxian, Ashron was glad they were on the same side.

They took up position in the guard post, seizing the spots recently vacated by the former occupants to cover Hawk and Gerard's advance on the array. Unlike them, Ashron placed himself behind the metal extension that acted as a shield, although the still smoking holes from Wolf's attack didn't give him much confidence. All he could do was be ready. Laura sat in an excellent position to warn them of any approach from the battle raging off in the distance. Once Hawk and Gerard shut down the array, things would get exciting in a hurry.

As Laura shouted her command and Wolf and Ashron went to work, Hawk popped up from a deserted vehicle and fired at the guard standing outside the array building entrance. The Serian never had a chance to react.

As he fired, Hawk moved for the doorway in a deliberate crouch, firing on another guard that appeared in the opening. Gerard followed close with his hands poised to launch energy attacks at anything Hawk missed.

Ship had tagged all the Serians in the structure and identified four guards; two at the door and two more near the power source. The rest she identified as either technicians or laborers, but that couldn't account for any trolls lurking about or any other beings that were invisible to their scans. That development bothered Hawk, but he couldn't do much about it in the thick of the battle—that was something for Gerard and Henna to tackle later. Hawk hoped most of them had been sent to the fighting at the front. It was the best explanation for why such a presumably important structure was so lightly guarded.

In the cold calculus of war, he also decided that any technicians, laborers, or scientists who didn't flee upon their approach would be neutralized. For all he knew, their "non-combatants" would happily kill him if he turned his back on them, and he wasn't going to take a chance. But he would let them flee if they decided to take that more prudent choice.

Hawk stepped through the door into an alcove designed as a guard post, which now provided him cover as he studied the area ahead. Through a short hallway, he saw the control room, several blocky machines covered with readouts, and beyond that, a large glass wall, which separated the control room from the mechanics surrounding the nexus. The room gave off a low hum, and the machinery, all the dull gray of carbonited steel, nonetheless glowed faintly yellow. The smell, earthy and sweet, reminded Hawk of roasted corn.

Satisfied there were no waiting guards, Hawk strode into the room. Several technicians rounded on them in surprise. Hawk fired off several rounds into the ceiling, followed by several more through the glass wall, which crashed to the floor in a spray of shards.

"Everybody out," Gerard yelled in Serian at the crouching, frightened technicians as Hawk leveled his weapon at them. No one moved; one of them fainted.

"Now!" Gerard commanded. The paralysis broke, and the workers dropped any equipment they held and dashed for the door, leaving their unconscious companion behind.

"Running out the exit," Hawk said so Wolf and Ashron would be aware. Once the fleeing techs had cleared the doorway, he turned to Gerard.

"When did you learn to speak Serian?"

"Ship and I worked on it during our trip back to Berol. She analyzed the recordings of them from our time on Alonis. It's a software issue mostly." He smiled at Hawk. "I picked up a few phrases that might come in handy at bars or if I smash a finger."

"When were you going to share that information?"

"I just did."

Gerard stepped over the shattered glass and dropped the half-meter into the room. He stood by the machinery, his arm extended over a panel and glowed a dark golden-red.

That's new, Hawk thought. Gerard's eyes were closed, his face scrunched in deep concentration. Hawk quickly checked the room for stragglers or any other entrances. Finding none, he stationed himself out of the way, next to the door, so Gerard could work in peace.

Gerard took out one of the discs he used earlier, spoke a word, and the disc started glowing the same color as his arm. He placed the disc in a small opening on the side of the array.

When the whole room gave a gentle shake, he turned and winked at Hawk's worried expression. He walked to the other side of the array, pulled out another disc, and spoke a different word. This time, the disc glowed dark blue. Gerard took it and placed it in an opening opposite the first one. The room shook even more. Gerard pulled out a slightly larger orb from his pouch and returned to the front of the array.

He spoke several words, his voice resonant and reverberating through the room. The orb glowed bright white.

"Ship," Gerard said as he held up the glowing orb. "Tell Admiral Strong he should see a distinct improvement in a few moments."

Gerard released the orb. It floated in the air briefly and glided over the top of the array, its white light increasing in intensity. The machinery thrummed, and Hawk caught a burning smell, like ozone set on fire. Gerard took out another disc, this one as large as his hand, and placed it against the front of the array. There was a clunk as the magnetic circle latched to the metal machinery. He raised his cybernetic arm and, with two fingers, traced an intricate pattern over the disc. Trails of red followed through his fingers and hung in the air, the form visible and floating before Gerard.

The pattern pulsed, the crimson growing brighter and illuminating the room, which continued to shake as the rhythm of the design vibrated faster and faster.

After thirty seconds, the pulsing stopped, and the pattern image hung in the air.

Gerard smiled and walked over to Hawk. "As I said earlier, the tech is fascinating, but I don't think the Serians have encountered anyone who uses the power from the nexus like my people do." Gerard moved his fingers for another ten seconds, and the image of the pattern faded, leaving an afterglow floating before Hawk's eyes. "That should help Admiral Strong out."

Hawk raised his eyebrows and cocked his head. "What did you do?"

Smugness covered Gerard's pale face. "I reversed the shields."

"What, exactly, does that mean?"

"It means they can't shoot out, but we can shoot in."

Hawk's face lit up with a smile as understanding came to him. "Holy shit. That. Is. Brilliant."

"That's some devious spellburner shit right there," Ashron said over their comm system.

***

Things weren't going well for Admiral Strong's small fleet. Though aware of the Serians' advanced offensive capabilities, thanks to the Knights' initial encounter, the Navy had no time to develop effective countermeasures, much less implement them to the multitude of ships throughout Galactic Council space. The one thing that kept the Admiral's reduced fleet in the fight this long was that, for all their superior weaponry, the Serians seemed to understand little in the way of tactics. Head on assault was their preferred method of engagement, which gave the Admiral's fleet a chance to counter with superior maneuvering and more advanced ploys.

Nonetheless, the fleet had sustained almost fifty percent casualties, while the Serian fleet had taken less than twenty-five percent. And the alien fleet outnumbered the Galactic by a substantial margin.

"Execute Delta Seven Six," the Admiral told his communications officer, who began to relay the order to the fleet. Perhaps if they spread the fleet, they could work on the Serians piecemeal. It was a desperate option, but that's all the Admiral had right now.

"Admiral," the secondary comm officer said in her lilting voice. "Commander Grey is hailing us; he says it's urgent."

What in the world? Strong thought. *Right now?* "Put him through."

"Admiral," Hawk said. "Stand by and hold your fire. I think you're going to be pleasantly surprised."

"Hold my fire?" the Admiral replied. "What are you talking about?"

"Several energy spikes, Admiral," the weapons officer said. "The entire Serian fleet is—"

He didn't finish. On the battle monitoring holo floating above the bridge's command center, the Serian ships launched weapons as one unit. They fired in coordination, and this predictability was one of the things that had kept the Admiral's fleet from being more damaged, since he could maneuver around their launch schedule. But the Serians had begun to adapt.

"Brace for impact!" the *Strongbow* damage control officer called out, more out of reflex than necessity, as everyone on the bridge was already strapped in and wearing their battle suits.

This time, however, the missiles came nowhere near the fleet. Indeed, they barely got away from the ships that fired them. Blossoms of blue and brief flashes of explosions filled the sky. When the displays cleared, the Serian ships were heavily damaged. Every one of them.

"What in the hell?" Admiral Strong said.

"Told you you'd be pleasantly surprised," Hawk said over the speakers, and the admiral could all but see the satisfied smile on Hawk's face.

"How did you manage that?"

"Gerard reversed their shields, and the computer at the nexus sent the information to all the Serian ships. Gerard can give you the details later, but right now, we've got a ground battle to finish."

"Allow me to convey my thanks to Gerard and your team. There will be a little something strong and rare for you when you return."

"Thank you, Admiral. Hawk out."

***

"Admiral," Lieutenant Barton said. "Our weapons are having a devastating effect on the Serian fleet." The weapons officer kept his attention on the display.

Admiral Strong studied his display with an experienced eye. His fleet's last salvo of missiles had just struck the Serian armada. Hull breaches spewed debris as the artificial atmospheres inside the ships escaped. Having lost all power, several larger Serian ships were rolling off course and maintaining, or more accurately, not accelerating. It was also evident from his sensors that a considerable bulk of the debris being expelled was organic, meaning Serian casualties. "Very well, Lieutenant. Cease fire. Have all hands cease fire." To his communications officer, Strong said, "Commander, send word to the Serian commander and offer quarter."

"Aye, Admiral."

Lieutenant Kalra, the tactician, looked up from her display, her wide eyes settling on Strong. "Admiral, the Serians have faced their remaining ships in our direction and are accelerating. They have also dropped their shields."

"Is there any indication that they copy our transmission?"

"Affirmative, they are receiving our signal, Admiral but have not acknowledged," the comms officer told him.

"Multiple missile launches," the weapons officer called out. "And they are still accelerating." Lieutenant Barton and his team worked furiously at firing solutions and countermeasures, or at least ensuring their computers had all the information to work out the complex equations to those firing solutions. Without their shields, the Serian ships were as vulnerable as any other ship. "We will be in beam range shortly."

Admiral Strong shook his head. "Suicide," he said to no one in particular. He looked over to his executive officer. "Apparently, they have a 'with your shield or on it' mentality, and I certainly do not intend to find out about their beam weapon capabilities. So be it. Open up with everything we have. Fire at will."

Admiral Strong's captains and commanders knew their business. A massive salvo launched at the Serian fleet with devastating effect. The Serian forces launched their countermeasures, but it became clear their primary defense had been their shields. With those out of commission, they were simply overwhelmed. By the time the Serian fleet entered beam range, it was a mopping-up operation. All of Admiral Strong's remaining ships suffered damage to varying degrees but remained operational. He turned to his second. "As soon as we are secure, commence search-and-rescue." He stood and started toward CIC. "You have the conn. I'm going to check on Colonel Graf'eel and her offensive."

Laura watched from the rooftop of the building she stood on, a block away from the array structure, keeping an eye out for any surprises. Her HUD revealed nothing in the vicinity, but she was well aware that the lack of heat signatures from the newly discovered "trolls" meant there could be any number of them waiting in the nearby building.

She did her best to watch everywhere in her field of view at the same time.

"Coming out," Hawk said over the comm. She watched him and Gerard exit the array building while Ashron and Wolf stepped out from their cover, and the four converged toward the center of the square.

Something wrapped itself around her right ankle. She kicked and spun, but it was too late. The rifle fell from her hands as she got yanked across the roof, the rough surface tearing her outfit. As she stared at the nightmarish creature towering above her, she drew her pistol and fired. "I'm in trouble," she yelled.

Hawk and the others looked in horror at the beast that stood four stories above them. Hawk now realized what the partisan leader had meant by "monster." Though his HUD did not pick the creature up, his visual put the beast's height slightly over six meters. Its body resembled the trolls they had encountered earlier, but whereas those beasts had been vaguely "normal," this was anything but. A cluster of six tentacles, purplish and glistening, protruded from its back, whipping around in a frenzy. It stood on two treelike legs, thick, bulging, and bunched with muscles. Its rubbery, ropey arms hung to the roof, each ending with a clawed hand. Its mouth most closely resembled a bird's beak. At least twenty wispy tentacles surrounded a dull yellow bill. While most of them flailed as if enraged, two wrapped around Laura's leg and dragged her across the roof. The beak opened as the slender limbs lifted her into the air, and the creature's beady eyes examined the prey.

"No," Hawk and Ashron said in unison. Ashron ran toward the building as if shot out of a cannon. Hawk suspected the warrior would reach the roof far too late to help.

"See if you can force it down here," Hawk told Wolf.

"On it," Wolf lifted his massive MGoA and pulled the trigger. He aimed wide to both avoid hitting Laura and to get the monster's attention. The creature wheeled its head at the vibrant light of the tracer rounds.

Gerard closed his eyes and raised his non-cybernetic arm toward the monster. He turned sideways, aimed his metal arm toward the array building, and began speaking.

Hanging upside down with two of the tentacles wrapped around her leg, Laura quickly assessed her less than ideal situation. It had stopped trying to drag her to its mouth, enraptured by the rounds coming from Wolf. She dangled at least two meters off the deck, but it was better than hanging off the roof and over the ground. Not able to get a shot at the eyes, she aimed her pistol and fired at the thing's mouth. Maybe she could make it too painful for it to eat her.

She had gotten no more than a few shots off before more of the tentacles reached out and wrapped around her.

Wolf grunted in frustration as the thing's attention returned to Laura. Hawk considered shooting but knew he would have little effect from this firing upward from this distance.

"Clip it," he told Wolf. Wolf adjusted his aim, sending a hundred rounds into the tentacles writhing on the back. With a high screech that rebounded over the buildings, the creature lurched forward and dropped toward the road.

In a blind rage as he dashed toward the building, ready to climb the side, Ashron sensed more than saw the creature plummet toward the ground. He stopped his headlong rush and barely missed getting flattened by the thing's massive feet. Air washed over Ashron, redolent with a scent like rotting plants and coal. The jolt of impact shook

Laura like a doll and almost knocked Ashron off his feet. Her weapons dropped from her hands, and her head lolled back. Ashron had no idea if she was unconscious or dead. He launched himself through the air, drawing his two long knives as he did. He landed on the beast's knee and slammed the blades into the rubbery skin of its thigh. Tentacles lashed out at him, but he rushed upward, using the knives like a climber scaling a mountain, heading toward the helpless Laura.

Hawk wasn't far behind Ashron. As he approached, the wounds Wolf inflicted were nowhere to be seen, and the punctures of Ashron's blades disappeared as soon as he pulled them to strike another spot.

It pulled Laura toward its mouth. The dull yellow beak opened, revealing rows of bone-colored teeth. Laura was too close for Hawk to take a shot.

If it has a mouth, it must have an ass. He didn't like the thought, but it was the best he could come up with in this tight situation. It could regenerate wounds from the outside, but if he did enough internal damage, it might stop the beast.

He sprinted at the monster, knocked away a reaching tentacle, and dove headfirst, landing between its two bandied legs, and slid to a stop. He rolled onto his back and looked up. *There it was,* he thought. He aimed and fired.

Ashron clawed his way toward Laura, slicing at random, intent on destroying the monster.

He wasn't going to make it.

Wolf abandoned reloading his weapons since he couldn't fire at the creature. Too many of his people were around it. "We're out of time, Gerard." He drew his knife, a sword to most people, and ran for the creature.

"One more moment," Gerard whispered.

Laura awoke in immense pain. Thick tentacles had surrounded her, pinning her in place, and the smaller limbs around the beak had barb-like hooks that dug into her chest. Blood soaked her shirt. The creature's open mouth drew close, ready to engulf her head.

The creature shuddered and let out another screech, which nearly deafened Laura. The tentacles loosened their grip. She had no idea why the monster suddenly lost interest in her, but she took advantage and yanked her right arm free. She reached down and retrieved another blade tucked in her boot.

Hawk smiled as his well-placed shots punctured through the soft opening under the creature, causing it to scream and shudder.

A low gurgling noise made his smile disappear. Before he could get out of the way, the monster's bowels let loose, and a spume of rancid muck poured down on him. He gagged at the stench. A mass of tentacles from the creature's back lashed out and grabbed his legs. They yanked him from beneath the beast and lifted him into the air. He tried to draw his knife as more tentacles wrapped around him, engulfing his arms and starting to tear him apart like a wishbone.

Gerard opened his eyes and pointed at the monster. "Release." A surge of power flushed across his skin as power flowed from the nexus, passed through him, and sizzled toward the creature as a blast of blue energy.

Completely entwined and unable to move, Hawk clinched his eyes and grunted in pain as he felt like a rope in a tug-of-war contest. He found it difficult to breathe.

His hair stood on end, and the creature's grip loosened. What had been solid monstrous muscle turned spongy. The beast released a cry of pain as the green skin began to bubble like cheese on a hot plate. Flesh sloughed off bone, releasing a smell worse than a hundred sewers.

Before Hawk could begin to escape, the entire creature collapsed, skin and skeleton reduced to the consistency of mush. Hawk fell to the ground with the disintegrating creature, landing with a painful thud on the concrete that knocked his breath out of him. He lay on the ground in a noxious pile of gore, attempting to suck in a breath as every part of him wanted to keep the rank air from his lungs. His stomach flopped at the smells. He felt it was adding insult to injury that both Laura and Ashron had landed and rolled with acrobatic grace, avoiding the worst of the mess.

Hawk still lay on his back, trying to catch his breath, when Laura leaned over him, her face scrunched in disgust, her clothes spotted with blood but almost free of the monster's gunk. With a wrinkled nose and upturned lip, she said, "That was easily one of the most unpleasant experiences I've ever been through. Let's ensure nothing like that happens again."

Hawk closed his eyes as he sucked in the shallowest breath possible that would allow him to speak. "You two had a picnic. I'm the one covered in shit and melted monster." He opened his eyes and reached out a hand. "A little help?"

Laura stepped back, holding up both hands as if stopping an attack. "I think not. We all need a bath, but you need some serious decontamination."

He swiveled toward Ashron, who shook his head and said, "I like you, but not gonna happen."

With a loud grunt, Hawk sat up, trying to ignore the pain in every part of his body. "What in the world?" he asked Gerard as the preter-natural scientist walked up.

Gerard glanced at the pile of gore as his nose wrinkled. "This would have been much tougher if I weren't so close to a power source. I could have stopped it, but not in time to save all of you. As it was, we're lucky its size inhibited its speed."

He pointed to a cluster of five severed but still writhing tentacles that survived consumption by his spell. "Ashron, would you collect one of those for me? We have some serious research to do."

"Will do." Ashron took a leap to catch the edge of a nearby awning cover, ripped the cloth until he had a large swatch, and used it to pick up one of the appendages.

Hawk stood, holding his side. He added ribs to his list of aches. "Ashron, burn the rest."

Ashron smiled. "With pleasure."

SASALEE

While the others stood guard and kept watch for any more attacks, Laura took time to retrieve her gear from the rooftop. Ashron planted an incendiary charge in what remained of the monster, being careful not to touch it. They heard the occasional chatter of distant combat, and flashes from the sky above told them the battle still raged.

Once Laura returned, Ashron fired the charge, and they watched as the beast went up with a satisfying *whoosh* and burned with bright red flames. Within minutes, nothing remained but ash.

"That one was way too close," Hawk said to his team. He thoughtfully regarded Gerard. "Thanks. We would have lost if not for you."

Gerard nodded, "Much too close. Sorry it took so long, but that was the only formula I knew that was a foolproof method of stopping the thing without also killing the rest of you." He glanced among the group and returned his gaze to Hawk. "What's our next play?"

Hawk studied his haggard team, all of them at least splatted, if not coated, with numerous forms of nastiness. That fight had taken a lot out of them. Even Ashron looked less than full bore. "We need to grab a quick rest, get patched up, and re-up on some gear. Ship, warn the others about these things." His eyes followed the sound of battle in the distance. "Then we get back in the fight."

The Serians had Colonel Graf'eel and her team pinned down behind a small building. Their advance so far had been steady but grew slower as they approached their objective. The enemy had set up an emplacement in a bunker twenty meters away, and it was pouring crushing fire upon her team. From recon and sat maps, the Colonel knew other shelters lay spread out at regular intervals, placed by the Faladorians in a ring to protect the spaceport. The recon hadn't told her that they would find the Faladorians displaced and the Serians occupying the fortifications.

She looked over to Bishop, ducked behind a low wall next to the building. He crouched to avoid the debris raining down on them as enemy fire chewed up the building.

Graf'eel watched as one of her mechs, five meters tall and encasing a Lorothian pilot, thundered past. The pilot trained their dual particle guns on the bunker, giving the Colonel the most resistance. There was a whine and shimmer as twin blasts of green erupted from the long barrels that formed the mech's arms. They stuck the fortification and flashed in a brilliant display of power.

Graf'eel had no idea what materials made up the bunker, but it held up to the mech's cannon fire, deflecting the energy with little more than scorch marks. The Serians turned and aimed their energy beams toward the machine with almost as little effect. The reflective coating on the armor dispersed the bulk of the energy, and what little got through did nothing more than chip the paint. It was a close support mech and a tough customer, but Graf'eel knew it could only take so much punishment before the reflective armor burned away.

The fire from within the bunker paused. Graf'eel wondered if the Serians, used to having the upper hand due to their technological advances, were trying to figure out what to make of this development. First, their shields no longer worked, and now their weapons didn't immediately destroy their target. She imagined they felt like she would if she suddenly found herself unable to wield a long knife.

Whatever the reason, it gave the mech, fondly nicknamed the *Lava Spitter*, a chance to draw close enough to employ its primary weapon. Colonel Graf'eel shook her head, saddened. She was not fond of this tactic, but she understood the necessity.

The armor in the mech's center opened like a door and revealed what appeared to be a small nozzle. A loud whoosh followed, and liquid hell sprayed from the opening. Clumps of phosphorus coated with burning liquid plasma poured forth. The nozzle ranged back and forth, covering the structure and penetrating any and all breaches. The Serians might be unknown aliens, but to Graf'eel's ears, the dying screams sounded like those of any other sentient creature.

* * *

Hawk looked over to Wolf, who was shouldering his MGoA, having refilled the magazine. He seemed none-the-worse for wear. Of course, he rarely did. His thick, saline-based skin shrugged off a lot of attacks that put most out of action. Wolf returned his gaze and nodded.

Having applied antibiotic sealant to her wounds and reloaded, Laura sat on a low wall beside the resupply crate with Gerard. She was making some adjustments to her load-bearing gear that had been damaged in the fight with the ridiculously large, tentacled troll.

Gerard tinkered with his golden arm, using what Hawk thought of as a dental tool that gave off a soft, green glow. Unlike Wolf, they both looked fatigued and in need of a long rest. Laura, Hawk knew, would like a long soak with a good bottle of wine. He thought that sounded good, too; his whole body felt twisted and bruised.

He closed his eyes, shook his head to clear the fuzzies, then glanced over to Ashron. The Lorothian broke into a grin, gave him a scaly thumbs-up, and said, "Back in the game, boss. Ready when you are."

"Of course you are," he said, shaking his head. The only one more resilient than Wolf was Ashron. Hawk stared in the direction of the battle raging off in the distance. "We'll be making our way to rendezvous with Colonel Graf'eel in a few." He pointed over to a taller structure. "See if you can make your way up there and get the lay of the land."

"On it," Ashron said, as chipper as if he had recently stepped fresh off the shuttle.

With Ashron taking point and observing from his higher position, the Knights sprinted toward the Colonel and her unit, picking up their location on the HUD.

They found the Marines less than a klick away. The battle appeared to be over for the most part. Scattered fire sounded in the distance, but here several bunkers burned, and two mechs stood guard. A squad of Marines surrounded several Serian prisoners who sat on the ground. Colonel Graf'eel stood in front of them. Blood covered her uniform, but unlike Hawk and his team, none of it appeared to be hers. It was darker, most certainly Serian. Hawk wished they had had a chance to clean up, but time simply didn't permit the opportunity.

The Colonel wrinkled her nose as they approached. "What is that smell?"

"Close encounter with an alien colon," Hawk responded.

"Yes, well, stay downwind." She waved her arm at the desultory group sitting before her. "We are conducting mopping-up operations now. Once the shields came down, the locals, who were already behind the lines, joined in with a vengeance, creating a tremendous force multiplier."

Hawk saw several armed Faladorians scattered about. One of them walked their way, and Hawk recognized him as the leader who had approached his team earlier. Hawk stepped his way over and greeted him with the traditional Faldorian greeting, hand over heart, and a slight bow. "Good to see you again. We were a little preoccupied the first time. I'm Hawk, commander of the Knights of the Flaming Star."

"And I am Haskin," he said, returning the gestured greeting. He smiled. "I am a builder, unwillingly thrust into the role of partisan." He glanced around at Hawk's crew. "Quite a diverse group you've brought to pull our collective asses out of the fire." He looked questioningly at Ashron and Colonel Graf'eel. "I've never seen a Lorothian before, other than in books." He turned to Wolf with raised eyes. "And I'm afraid I have no idea about this one."

After Hawk introduced his team, he indicated Colonel Graf'eel. "This is the Marine Commander in charge of ground operations."

She strode over and offered the same traditional greeting Hawk had used. "Colonel Nassara Graf'eel at your service. You and your people were most helpful and pivotal to the success of this operation. You have my admiration and thanks."

"Thank you for your praise, but if you hadn't arrived, we would still be hiding in the rubble." He pointed over to some of his peers, who were gathered around a defeated yet defiant-looking trio of Serians. "I thought you might be interested in one of the captives. She is apparently a technician or scientist and would like to speak with the leader of the conquering force."

Hawk looked at Colonel Graf'eel. "That would be you. Mind if I join you?"

"Please."

They followed Haskin over to the prisoners, and a tall Serian who appeared to be female approached them. She was clearly not a warrior, having none of the ancillary gear of that group, but she was solidly built and carried herself with the confidence of leadership. She started speaking as soon as they approached.

Haskin held up his hand, and the Serian stopped. Haskin reached out and placed a small device on the Serian's neck. He spoke to Colonel Graf'eel. "We have one translator for now, and it seems to be working relatively well. One of our team members is an engineer and designed it."

He turned to the tall Serian. "This is who you asked for."

The Serian nodded and spoke again. "I am Kaptcha, lead scientist for the colonizing force for this sector." Though Kaptcha sounded from the translator chip, it was clearly not what the Serian had said. Hawk thought the algorithm most likely mangled the name like it had the first translations of the Uraxians, Wolf's people. For now, Kaptcha it was. At least it was easily pronounced. He wondered what the Serians referred to themselves as and if the translator would mangle it as severely as it had Kaptcha's name.

"I am Colonel Graf'eel, commander of the marine expeditionary force sent here to liberate these people from your invasion. You will be treated with respect, but make no mistake: you are prisoners of war and will be treated as such."

She indicated Haskin. "The commander of the Faladorian Planetary forces stated you wished to speak with me." She gave no indication she saw Hawk's smile or Haskin's upturned eyebrow at his battlefield promotion. "What can I do for you?"

Kaptcha glanced down at Colonel Graf'eel. Though her alien face was difficult to read, Hawk thought the expression held an air of superiority. She cocked her head and reminded Hawk of a dog that was uncertain on how to proceed. Finally, she said, "I'm not usually on this side of the conversation. We are destined to control and subjugate all we encounter, take what we need, and enslave those who oppose us. But our strategists have made an unexpected, critical error. We are stretched thin and not prepared for the expansion we have undertaken."

"It seems you're giving an excuse for your defeat—"

The Serian cut Hawk off with a dismissive wave of her hand. "You misunderstand my intent. These things, these disgraces you fought, are not Sasalee."

At least we know what they call themselves now, Hawk thought. He found it interesting how close the name they gave them was to the one they called themselves. He wondered if the translator amalgamated the two terms or if they had just been that lucky.

"Several years back, our ruler died, and his physician assumed command. This power transfer is normally accomplished through trial by combat between our most powerful clans. But in this instance, the two leading clans supported the physician and conspired to place him in power. This was unprecedented. Never have the clans been ruled by anyone but the strongest warrior. But this physician was creating his own army out of genetically modified Sasalee. This is an outrage. He is taking our pure warrior form and making it an abomination." The translator's flat voice did little to hide Kaptcha's agitation.

"Why are you telling us this now?" Colonel Graf'eel asked. "Unless I'm missing something, we've beaten you, and this information could wait until interrogations."

"You've beaten us, yes. But we are simply a supply location. This planet was a strategic location to be used as a jump point for the rest of this quadrant. Our job was to establish a logistical gate for resupply and repair. Our main force is on its way to a location with multiple power sources in sector 62. And I'm telling you this because we, meaning my team and I, are dishonored at the direction our glorious race is going. These genetic mutations are not science or evolution. It is some strange blasphemy the physician is using to mutate our people in an evil way. A dark power that is not for the good of the clans. His motivation is power and control. He is Sasalee, but—not." She paused, and her bony brows folded in, confused. "I can't explain it. He is something different, something more powerful than anything we have ever seen. We can't stop him. He has too many allies and has grown too powerful, but our hope, that is, my clan's hope, is that you may be able to."

Hawk and Colonel Graf'eel glanced at each other, but it was Colonel Graf'eel who spoke. "So, your leader, this physician, has created an army of these mutations?"

"He is working to do so. Those you encountered with us were experimental and brought along as a trial."

"And this army is en route to sector sixty-two?" Hawk asked. Knowing the Sasalee mapping system most likely didn't match Galactic's, he said, "Where is that exactly?"

"If you can arrange a chart, I can show you."

Hawk spotted Gerard standing off to the side with the rest of the crew. "Gerard, would you come over and supply a sector map for us?"

"Certainly," Gerard walked over and held out his cybernetic arm. A glow sprang up and resolved into a holographic display of the planet

Falador and the surrounding systems. Falador glowed bright red. "We are the red dot," Hawk told Kaptcha.

The Serian studied the map for a moment. "Can you pull back and display the area that would be over here." She indicated to her right.

Gerard manipulated the map to encompass the indicated area. "Here?"

"Yes, that's it." She pointed to a sphere planet near the edge of the map. "This is where our fleet is headed. It is a lightly inhabited planet with moderate defenses and a major power source."

Gerard closed his hand, causing the map to disappear, and quietly said, "That's Berol."

WEAPONS FREE

"Still no word," Ship said as the crew, cleaned and dressed in clothing borrowed from the Faladorians, disembarked *Little Star* and took the elevator to the main deck. "As long as the tunnels are down, communications are non-existent."

"Has Trey worked out a return trip with the Kuthrallie?" Gerard asked.

"Yep," Trey responded. "As long as it's just us, they will send us back with one of their 'adolescents,' or smaller ones, if I understand right."

"That's great," Ashron said. "Being led by a couple of kids."

Laura grinned. "You should feel right at home."

The elevator stopped. The crew departed and made their way to the wardroom, where Trey met them with a platter of small sandwiches and drinks. Several mugs steamed, and Hawk caught the fragrant smell of coffee. Wolf smiled in pleasure and wrapped his hand around his oversized mug.

"I think once we enter ripspace, I'll be able to make communication with Berol," Ship said.

"But you mentioned the tunnels..." Hawk said, letting his words trail off into a question.

"Yes, but once we are in the *aether*, it doesn't behave the same for me as for everyone else." She paused, then added, "And now I guess Trey is the same. None the less, I will try to get word to them of the pending invasion and should be successful."

"When can we leave?" Gerard asked.

"As soon as you are all asleep in chambers," Trey said. "The Kuthrallie escort is standing by."

Hawk nodded. "Alright. Everyone stow your gear and meet in the chamber room. Laura will set us up for a long sleep. Eat and drink up on the way there." Hawk grabbed a sandwich and a cup of coffee from Trey. "Good work, Trey. And I don't mean the food…"

"Although it is a nice touch," Ashron said from across the room, finishing off his third sandwich and reaching for another.

Hawk ignored him with a smile. "We are in good hands. Take care of Ship while we are out. She's not as strong as she…"

"Stronger," Ship chided.

"See, touchy too," Hawk winked at Trey. "Thanks, you've done the Knights proud." Hawk turned and went down to the sleep chamber with the others, as Trey, blushing furiously with pride, strode toward the bridge.

Larilla Marin, Berolian captain and owner of the heavy freighter *Jankle*, entered the bridge, groggy from having recently come out of jump sleep. The sharp, antiseptic smell of spray-on synth-skin still hung in her mind. She had no idea why she associated that smell with jump. As far as she knew, there were no doctors or medical personnel in her family. She walked across the room, acknowledging crew members with nods, and stood next to her navigator.

The brown-haired man, his skin paler than the captain's, nodded to her as she approached. "Smooth exit from jump, Captain. We should be receiving docking confirmation shortly."

She smiled back at him, "Thanks, Dail. It's good to be home."

Tarla brushed a strand of light brown hair from her forehead, read the time display, and sighed. 0210. Captain Marin's ship was running later than anticipated. Tarla turned up her lip at the lukewarm *tachi* as she took a sip of the sweet drink. The anticipated arrival of the heavy freighter was the only reason she remained awake so late.

She rechecked the display: 0211. *Damn,* she thought as she flopped back in her chair. *I should have never booked this shift.* She took this watch on the commercial district docking station because they had one anticipated arrival at 0130. Someone still needed to staff the docks, but other than when there was an arrival, she could nap in the duty rack until the shift ended. Everything was automated, but protocol required at least one person to be on station in case something unanticipated occurred.

She opened her eyes when she heard the computer announce, "Heavy freighter *Jankle,* hull number CZX-2442 arriving."

Tarla checked the time: 0214. *Better late than the alternative,* she thought. She spoke, knowing the ever-present voice monitoring system would broadcast to the incoming ship. "This is Berol Station 12, Dockmaster Tarla hailing heavy freighter *Jankle.* How do you copy?"

"Heavy freighter *Jankle* to Station 12, loud and clear."

It surprised Tarla to hear Captain Marin's voice instead of the navigator's come across the comm at this hour. Although she guessed it shouldn't have since Captain Marin's reputation indicated she ran a tight ship and would undoubtedly want to be present for docking. "Thank you, Captain," Tarla responded. "Transponders are functioning properly. Take your sweep through lane six, and then you are clear to dock in bay three."

"Thank you, Dockmaster," Captain Marin said. "My apologies for the late hour. We had maintenance delays."

Tarla smiled. "That's alright. Sleep is—"

The automated computer interrupted her. "Unscheduled, unidentified heavy cruiser arriving from ripspace."

Ensign Howrith stifled a yawn as he watched the *Jankle*, freighter CZX-2442, make its slow turn toward lane three like a bloated whale, like all heavy freighters. He and his crew, stationed on the military outpost that monitored the ripspace arrivals and departures for Berol, were pulling the mid-watch or "the mid-ride" as more seasoned sailors liked to call it. The "outpost" was little more than the living quarters and command center for the personnel assigned to the massive firing battery guarding the rip tunnel.

Howrith's responsibility was the squad of sailors who maintained the Combat Information Center, or CIC. The rest of the personnel on-board were civilian maintenance crews that ensured the weapons and delivery systems stayed in top working order. The civilians and military got along well enough, even if they didn't exactly hang out for drinks. Howrith looked over to one of the crew standing watch with him. "Might as well work out your firing solutions on the freighter, Cy. Nothing else is scheduled until after we leave."

"You read my mind," replied Cy. "Anything to stay awake till 0600."

They gaped at each other in shock as a strident alarm rang through the station, followed by a sonorous computer voice that announced, "Unidentified heavy cruiser inbound."

Dail frowned as the screen poured information across his view. "Captain, we have a military vessel closing in from our rear. Appears to be a heavy cruiser." He paused, puzzled. "And it's accelerating."

Captain Marin walked up and peered over his shoulder, equally curious. "Must be on some sort of unannounced maneuvers, although it seems damn rude to not let the dock know they were going to be zipping around commercial lanes. Are we on a course to intercept?"

Dali studied the calculations for a few seconds. "Negative."

"Then keep a steady course. They can maneuver infinitely better than we can."

"Holy shit," Dail exclaimed as his screen lit up with bright red dots. "There must be at least a hundred more that just came out of rip. All unidentifiable."

Captain Marin grimaced. "There is nothing normal or good about this. Sound the collision alarm."

"Collision?" Dail asked. His training took hold and he followed the order, hitting the panel. A loud whooping sound echoed across the ship.

She nodded. "If we had a battle station alarm, I'd sound it. This is the only way I can think of to warn the crew. Berol Station, are you getting this?"

Tarla stared slack-jawed at her monitor. Where once there had been the signal of the *Jenkle,* she now saw well over a hundred vessels. They poured out of the rip gate like water from a sluice. She had no idea where they came from or who they belonged to, but it didn't take a genius to see the majority were military. She needed to let someone know, but who? Her training had never foreseen this kind of situation.

"Berol station, are you getting this?" Captain Marin said over Tarla's headset. Still in shock, she didn't answer.

"I repeat, Berol station, are you getting this?" The strain in the Captain's voice edged up a notch. "Are you seeing what we're seeing?"

"Yeah, I see it," Tarla replied. "I just don't know what the hell to make of it."

"Get word to the Planetary Council," the Captain told her. "The naval outpost will notify the military; you need to get word to the civilians planetside."

"How the hell do I do that? There's no procedure for this. Who do I tell?"

"Anyone who will listen." Captain Marin's voice softened. "This is an invasion, and we are at war. You and I are simply the first to know;

we need to make sure others know as well. Godspeed, Berol station. Godspeed to all of us."

When the initial cruiser appeared, Ensign Howrith figured it must be one of Command's preparedness operations. They occasionally threw one at the station to test its readiness in an emergency. Although they usually gave them at least some warning—not necessarily the exact time such a drill would happen, but a week-long window of opportunity when it might.

Cy clearly ran on the same thought process. "You think this is some sort of drill?"

"Has to be, or the ship's transponder was damaged in transition." As he looked at the specs on his monitor, he realized he didn't recognize the ship model or even what race might have built it. A small tingle of fear ran up his back. "By the book, Cy. Scan, hail, and lock on."

Howrith reached out and activated the general quarters alarm. He knew that throughout the base, irritated sailors and civilians would be rolling out of their bunks and headed to their assigned duty stations, no doubt cursing whoever had hit the button.

Commander Lightel appeared on a holo above the console, disheveled and sleepy-eyed. "What you got, Howrith?"

"Not sure yet, commander. An unidentified heavy cruiser just transitioned out of rip. Cy is scanning and hailing now. We figure it to be some sort of drill."

The commander rubbed sleep out of his eyes. "Not any drill I was informed about. I'm on my way. I'll—"

"Sweet mother of God," Cy exclaimed. "A shitload more just popped in."

"How many, Cy?" Howrith found himself asking, though he stared at the same display as her.

"Targeting shows one hundred thirty-one, all unidentified and alien in nature. And they're accelerating. This ain't no drill."

Ensign Howrith watched the color drain from Commander Lightel's face. "Any response from your hailing frequency?"

"No, sir."

The commander thought for a moment. "On my way. Let all stations know this is not a drill. Free the computer, all targeting, all scenarios. Weapons tight for now."

Lightel's image disappeared as the holo dissolved away. After freeing the computer, Ensign Howrith met Cy at a small, unassuming table in the middle of the room. Two biometric panels sat opposite each other with a ridiculously ostentatious red button in the middle. They always joked that it looked like something you would see in a bad sci-fi movie.

"Are we really doing this?" Cy asked as she placed her palm down on the reader.

Ensign Howrith followed suit with his palm. "Yeah. Never thought I would be doing it for real."

"Scan complete," the computer acknowledged. Two panels opened, one on each side of their prospective scanners. A green key sat in each recess. Commander Lightel walked into the room as Howrith and Cy removed the key. The Commander approached. "You two ready?" At their nods of affirmation, he said, "Carry on, then."

They each inserted their key into the receptor in front of the large red button and leveled their eyes at each other. "On three," Howrith said. "One. Two. Three."

They each rotated their key until they felt a click, and they stepped back from the panel.

Commander Lightel called over to the technicians sitting at the command panel, "Any change?"

Without looking up, the technician said, "No change, Commander. They are ignoring our commands and accelerating toward Berol. Sixty-three of the ships are capital vessels, the rest are transport and support."

"Thank you," the Commander said. He turned to the communications tech. "Any luck with command?"

"Affirmative commander," she said. "The OIC is aware and live.

They advise weapons tight for now until they can inform the CNO's staff."

Commander Lightel sighed. "For the love of…"

"Multiple missiles launched, calculating firing solutions," a too calm computer voice informed the room.

"Confirmed," the technician chimed in, in a slightly elevated tone.

"Target?"

"This station and all of our batteries."

Commander Lightel reached out and pressed the now glowing red button in the middle of the table, "Weapons free. Computer, fire at will. All solutions, all scenarios." He looked over to Cy and Dram. "CNO be damned."

A loud pounding on the door awakened Master Genray.

"Come," he grunted, rolling over and sitting up on the overstuffed couch in his office. Lately, he spent more time sleeping on it than he did his bed at home. The deeper he dug and the more he learned about Sam's unique nature, the more disturbed he became.

At least if he chose to believe what he was learning. He still couldn't quite come to grips with what he suspected, despite the evidence. It was outlandish—a fairy tale straight out of old tomes and disproven superstitions. And if the volumes were correct, she wasn't the only one. There was—

Professor Allax stepped through the door, interrupting Genray's thoughts.

"Sorry to disturb you, Chavad, but we've got problems."

Genray motioned to a chair across from him. "That sounds ominous; please sit."

Allax sat on the edge of the seat and leaned forward. "I have a niece on Berol station…"

"I remember you telling me about her. An exciting promotion, if I recall. Tara, right?"

"Tarla," Allax corrected. "She contacted me with an urgent message. Said it would be hours before anyone in her chain would be available, and she didn't know who else to call." Allax held up a hand as Master Genray started to speak. "She told me that as she was clearing a freighter for arrival, a heavy cruiser appeared on her screen, and then several of them and then a whole armada."

Master Genray listened intently. He had initially believed Allax awakened him for a problem with one of the students. Obviously, this was way more than he had expected.

Allax continued, distress on her pale face. "While we were speaking, she said a group of support vessels along with what appeared to be troop carriers transitioned—that's when I heard an alarm sound in the background. When I asked her what the alarm was, she was quiet for a moment. Then said that it was a missile launch warning." Allax looked intently at Genray. "Our connection went dead." He shook his head, "I have no talent and never served, so I came to you. What do we do now?"

A demure gray creature resembling some type of rodent with a gray nose and thin, twitching whiskers peaked out of a ceramic box. The rectangular door on the front slid open, revealing a floor of glass and artificial light. It explored its environment from the entrance, sniffing the air as it did. Sterile, antiseptic death was what the creature's senses returned, though the surroundings did not match what the atmosphere foretold.

She nervously inched her way further out and saw she stood on some sort of large table with a clear, smooth surface brightly lit from underneath. A slight movement caught her attention, and she noticed the man sitting behind the table, staring down at her. He wore all white and had kind, gray eyes; he smiled at her and held out his hand. Cautiously, she sniffed his outstretched fingers and smelled...life. In her whole long existence, she had never scented anything like it. He made her think of the sun, the dirt, and growing plants all at the same time; the odor of her children, long since grown and having left the nest. His eyes twinkled at her as his smile deepened. Safety and warmth were what they conveyed. And power. Deep, unimaginable power.

She reached out a small paw and touched his finger; energy radiated through her. She felt young again, as alive as a newborn kit. Her vision cleared, and her muscles relaxed, relieving joints long stiff with age. She gleefully jumped into his open hand, basking in the glow of existence. She purred, rubbing her face along his palm, and felt something stir within her womb. New growth, radiant life, and a bright glow of...pain?

She stopped rubbing his hand as the pain intensified. She doubled over and writhed, squeaking at the agony that roiled through her. Her eyes locked with his gray orbs. They hadn't changed. He still projected a caring, fatherly warmth, as if he wanted nothing more than to help her. Something grew inside her. Something ugly. Something that didn't belong to her. She screamed and...

Sam started awake, a cold sweat tickling her skin, the covers tangled at her feet.

Damn, she thought, *that was the strongest, clearest one yet.* She didn't believe in visions or omens, being of a scientific and mathematic bent as both her mother and teachers had instructed her, but this sure seemed like a warning or premonition of something dire. It was on par with the visions Trey told her about, messages from the Kuthrallie. And those turned out to be real, so there was no reason these shouldn't also. Her recent dreams held a common thread: life, death, and renewal, but renewal with painful mutations. She had no idea what they meant, but they frightened her. She rolled over in her bed; *I've got to stop drinking Tyler's coffee so late at night,* she thought wryly.

A distant, muffled thud drew her attention from her thoughts on the dream. It reminded her of being on her uncle's farm when he would use explosives to remove stumps. She sat up with a frown as she heard another, louder thud. *That definitely sounded like an explosion,* she thought. She stood, slipped a robe over her nightgown, and headed for her door. As she reached for the handle, screams stopped her hand. The sound of running footsteps drawing close caught her attention. More screams, followed by a series of erratic *whirring* sounds—some sort of energy discharge.

Sam jerked open her door to a scene of madness. Kids screamed and ran down the hall in a panic. Several more discharges whined through the corridor, and blue laser light brightened the hallway. Sam recognized her classmate Aritka as the girl fell in a bloody heap at her feet.

Strange clicking and chittering sounds caught her ear, and she turned to see the source of the panic. She recognized the Serians from her mother's description as they worked their way down the hall, firing randomly into the walls and ceiling, driving the students before them in the direction of the courtyard as if herding animals. Occasionally, a Serian would lower their weapon and fire into the backs of the fleeing students, sending one to the floor, dead or wounded.

Sam could discern no reasoning for the attack until one of the creatures looked directly at her. She shuddered at those cold black eyes.

The Serian pointed at her with its long-fingered hand and chittered. The others stopped and focused all their attention on her. Every one of them made a hideous expression she related to a satisfied grin. They had found what they sought.

Sam joined the fleeing students, running through the hall as the Serians gave chase. Over the panicked cries of the students, she heard the excited chirps of the aliens. She had no idea why they wanted her, and she had no desire to find out. With another *whirr* and flash of blue light, a second-year student fell in front of her, his orange robe catching fire. Sam jumped over his body and almost fell when she landed. As she recovered her balance, Professor Calanan stepped from a hallway on her right. She ran past him as he lifted his hands and fired off a powerful arc of magical blue flame. It arched over the students' heads and slammed into the Serians. Sam glanced back to see several of the aliens crumble into ash.

"Run for the courtyard," the professor yelled over his shoulder as he strode toward the ash, preparing another equation as he moved.

Sam fled toward the courtyard with the mass of screaming and crying students. They poured through the archway and into the central square, which was nothing less than pandemonium. Students streamed from all the perimeter buildings, pursued by Serians. Teachers attempted to bring order to the madness, but they were corralled as efficiently as the students. The entire school was being led to either slaughter or capture. Considering the intensity with which the Serians pursued her, Sam didn't know which she would prefer.

Amid all the chaos, Master Genray stood, the eye of the storm, calmly poised in the middle of the square, right arm aloft, emanating a golden glow that extended from his hand up to twenty feet in the air, then spread out in an expanding dome shape as Sam watched. Several of the enemy concentrated fire on him, to no avail. The shield absorbed the blasts, growing brighter where the bolts hit. None of the attacks came anywhere close to Master Genray.

"Run to the shields and take cover," another teacher Sam didn't know yelled over the din. She didn't need to be told twice. She spotted a first-year student who was clearly in shock, his face wide-eyed and streaked with tears. She grabbed the boy's hand.

"Come with me," she said and ran toward the faint metallic glow that showed the perimeter of the protective barrier. The boy followed.

"This way," Sam shouted to the others around her, although she had no idea if anyone could hear her or would pay attention if they did. She had barely gotten the words out when someone grabbed her from behind. Her hand pulled free from the young boy she had in her grasp. He wailed in alarm as a looming Serian warrior yanked her off her feet and tucked her under his arm like a loaf of bread. She struggled violently, but the effort had as much effect as a moth trying to escape her closed hand. She looked at the boy she had tried to rescue. He stood there like a lost puppy.

"Run," she screamed, tears filling her eyes. It was too late. As casual as if hitting a fly, a Serian soldier backhanded the boy across the face. He stumbled back and fell to the ground, his eyes rolled up, blood running from his nose. Sam had no idea if the boy was dead or unconscious.

As the anger grew in Sam, she felt a surge of power she had long suppressed. Rage burned inside her, wanting to get out. A desire to put everything right. All she had to do was reach out and—

No, she thought as she shoved it back to the depths of her soul where it belonged. *Not now, not ever!*

She couldn't help everyone, but she had to try to help herself. She wriggled and thrashed with all her might, twisting her body back and forth. She flung her arms, striking at the creature's chest. It didn't put up with her antics for long. It paused, growled at her, and slapped her on top of her head with its open palm. The strike dizzied her, and she stopped struggling.

That's odd, she thought as her senses returned. Though they still fired on the growing shield that surrounded staff and students in the courtyard, the Serians appeared to be retreating.

Before her captor rounded a corner, Sam caught a glimpse of one of her teachers speaking to Master Genray and pointing in her direction. She didn't see his reaction as several other Serians joined her abductor, surrounding her and cutting off her view. They picked up the pace and, although she couldn't see where they headed, she guessed they were aiming for the gates to leave. She tried again to wriggle but stopped when the soldier raised his hand. She feared he might hit her harder this time and truly hurt her.

The squad of Serians left the courtyard. Through a brief gap in the formation, Sam spotted the main entrance. One of the large ornate gates hung by its hinges, twisted like an insane person's sculpture; the other lay flat on the ground thirty meters from the wall. Smoke still drifted up from it.

More important and hopeful to Sam, she spotted a tall woman standing before the Serians. Her opalescent skin and long silver hair gave her away as a native Berolian. She held a staff of dark wood inlaid with mathematical symbols—a master preternatural scientist, like Trey's friend Gerard.

The Serians never slowed. They raised their weapons and fired.

Barely moving, the woman gave her staff a slight twist and uttered a word. Three symbols on the wood flashed dark blue, and the bolts of energy rebounded on their shooters, striking them in head or chest. They crashed to the ground.

Unable to stop in time, Sam's kidnapper stumbled over one of his compatriots and fell, releasing Sam. She rolled forward, landed painfully on her back, and wasted no time pulling herself up. Her captor also recovered quickly and ran toward her. He got no further than three steps when Sam felt a wave of heat rush past her. The alien's green head disappeared into vapor, blasted from its neck. The body fell forward and lay still.

The woman moved toward her. Recognizing that close proximity to such a powerful person had its benefits, Sam ran to her. She slid to a stop and was about to say thank you when a tumult caught their attention.

Dark shadows poured over the walls surrounding the school. Hundreds of them, at least. At first, Sam thought they were large dogs, but as they drew closer, she thought they looked more like nightmarish daemons. Her stomach clenched, and a cold wash of fear rooted her. Black greasy skin stretched over knobby bones, the joints and spine covered in short spikes. A tail half as long as the body trailed, ending in an elongated sphere, also bearing spikes like a mace. The reptilian mouths hung open as the creatures released low howls and revealed yellowish, triangular teeth.

"Oh, shit," Sam wheezed.

"Oh shit is right," the silver-haired woman said, although she didn't seem all that concerned to Sam. But she reached out and grabbed Sam's robe with a surprisingly firm grip and spun her back toward the courtyard. "Quickly, you must get behind Master Genray's shield. Run!" She roughly pushed Sam toward the common and faced the oncoming monsters.

Sam ran until she reached the alley between two of the buildings that led to the courtyard. Overcome by curiosity despite the danger, she stopped and turned to see what the mysterious woman was going to do.

She held her staff horizontal above her head as the daemon dogs closed the gap, their mournful howls filling the air. The woman's voice reached out over it all, speaking a complicated formula Sam couldn't begin to comprehend. Her heart hammered as the creatures drew ever closer. The woman wasn't going to get the equation completed in time.

With the dogs less than ten meters away, the woman threw the staff down at her feet. It disappeared in a flash, and from the ground, a shimmering barrier of blades sprang up; they were twice Sam's height and extended on either side toward the distant walls. As they rose, the blades spun, the whirring as loud as a ship's engine. The air whipped past the woman and blew her hair back. Her arms still raised, she worked them in a circular motion, and the blades swirled faster.

Sam could no longer see the beasts on the other side, but she knew when they hit. Chunks of meat and viscera poured through, and ichor coated the silver of the blades. The woman remained pristine, not a drop of the gore touching her. Sam's stomach lurched at the vile sight even as her heart soared. After five seconds, the hell hounds must have wised up. The sluice of shredded meat stopped though the blades continued to whirl.

As if she sensed Sam still behind her, the woman peered over her shoulder and shouted. "Run. I can hold them off until the shield reaches me. Tell Master Genray to hurry."

Even at this distance, Sam could see sweat building on the woman's pale forehead. Fearing the woman might be wrong, Sam fled for the courtyard.

She hadn't gone four steps when she saw the golden shimmer of the shield. It passed her within a second, standing her hair on end and making her skin tingle. The shimmer continued growing. Sam could tell it would reach the woman within fifteen seconds and felt more confident in her savior's survival.

When she reached the courtyard, she saw the reason for the rapid growth. Several other teachers had joined Master Genray in his endeavor. The radiant glow grew more robust and energy vibrated through the air. Sam saw her chemistry teacher, Professor Allax, dash across the courtyard carrying a thin iron spike pedestal with a glowing blue orb affixed to the top. He stabbed the spike into the ground next to Master Genray, then joined the other teachers in formulating the equation.

The formula's complexity astounded Sam. While other students cried and stood near teachers, she watched in amazement as the dozen manipulators spoke expressions and moved their hands, laying equations over each other like beavers creating a dam. The golden glow of the shield above grew stronger even as the perimeter expanded beyond where she could see. After a minute or so, Master Genray reached toward the orb that had been spiked into the ground. A gold beam fired from the sphere and toward the sky. More gold light shot out from the globe in a wave and rushed past Sam. The tension went out of the air and left her body. Only with its absence did she realize how much the energy focused on the equation had pressed against her. Breathing grew easier, and her shoulders straightened.

Studying the surrounding area, Sam could see the other students, and some of the teachers, felt it too. Calm reigned for the moment. No Serians assaulted them, and she realized she could no longer see the perimeter of the shield. It must have extended beyond the school grounds. The power and skill used astounded her.

Sam scanned the courtyard. She saw quite a few wounded students and teachers lying around while others tended their injuries. There were also several that didn't move. She saw no sign of the silver-haired woman from the courtyard.

As she took in and registered all of the bodies, tears welled in her eyes. She wondered if this was somehow her fault. Did all this destruction happen because the Serians had come for her? She didn't think she was that important, but the aliens had begun their retreat as soon as they grabbed her. If it hadn't been for the powerful woman stopping them, they would have gotten away with her. *And then what,* she thought. *What did they want with me?*

You know why, another part of her mind said, but she dismissed it.

They had no way to know about her abilities. She hadn't used them since—

Master Genray broke through her thoughts, projecting his voice so everyone in the courtyard could hear him. "The shield will hold. Every student that can should gather in the dining hall and wait there while the staff helps the wounded and sees to our losses. Understand we are most likely on our own for now but stay calm and know that you are protected. We'll give you more information when we have it."

Dazed and confused, Sam and the rest of the students shambled to the building that contained the dining hall. She flopped down at a long table with several others who straggled in with her. Someone sat beside her, and she glanced over to see it was Gin. The older, larger girl stared straight ahead with her eyes focused on some unseen distance. Sam wondered if Gin was in the early stages of shock. She put her hand gently on the other girl's shoulder. "You okay, Gin?"

"They killed Thapany," Gin said, her voice soft and slow. "She pushed me through a door, and they shot her."

Sam knew Thapany was one of Gin's group, a shy girl who liked to belong on the fringes. She never actively participated in the belittling or bullying of others but would be there just enough to make her presence felt. It kept her safe from the ridicule she would have otherwise received had she not joined. Sam liked Thapany. At least as much as you could like someone who was part of a group that made life miserable for the most vulnerable students. "I'm sorry, Gin."

Gin stared at Sam as if surprised at the sympathy. Sam hoped maybe this would be a way for them to bridge a gap, a chance to put aside animosity. She should have known better.

Gin raised an eyebrow, and a sinister gleam came to her stare. "They were after you, weren't they? I saw them grab you and run off."

"I don't know what you're talking about," Sam said, her face heating up at the lie even as she said it.

"No, they grabbed you and backed off." Gin raised her voice. "They wanted you."

Nearby students turned at Gin's statement, faces curious. She continued. "One of them grabbed you, and then they stopped shooting and surrounded you, and Master Genray was able to push the shield out."

Gin cocked her head, her black eyes glittering with malice. "They wanted you," she repeated. Louder, she said, "You brought them here." Her broad face bunched in confusion for a moment. "Why?"

"You're in shock," Sam said, worried as the students, several she thought of as her friends, had less than friendly expressions. "You don't know what you're talking about."

"Shut up," Gin screeched. This got some of the teachers' attention, and Sam wanted to run and crawl into a hole. Gin, now realizing she had an audience, stood and pointed an accusing finger at Sam.

"Thapany would still be alive if it weren't for you. They wanted you for some reason. What is it?" Gin thrust her finger closer until it was only centimeters from Sam's face. "What's so special about you? What makes you worth killing the rest of us? Are you cursed like everyone says? Are the rumors true? Does death follow you?"

"You have no idea," Sam whispered as she lowered her head, and tears rolled down her cheeks.

Gin had warmed up and had a bully's favorite weapon: an audience. "I don't know why they want her, but I say we get rid of her. Throw her out the front gate. Then they can take her and leave us alone."

Sam had her head in her hands, uncertain what she was going to do, so she didn't hear Master Genray walk up. "That's quite enough, Ms. Attawn," he said in his grave, firm voice. Sam lifted her head to find the headmaster staring at Gin, who still had her arm fully outstretched and finger pointed.

"But it's true," Gin protested in her strident voice. "They were after her, and everyone knows it. I say we give them what—"

Master Genray flicked his finger and muttered a word, and Gin's voice suddenly ceased.

"I said that's enough."

Wide-eyed, Gin reached for her throat. She had been struck mute. She tried to speak, but nothing emerged. She looked around desperately for support, but people averted their eyes and found better things to do. A student was not going to win over a teacher, especially one as respected as Genray.

Master Genray waved his arm at the gathered group. "All of you are better than this. We are a school, and we take care of our own. Ms. Mobem is one of us as much as any of us, and this attack is not her fault any more than it is Ms. Attawn's." He stared at one of the teachers who had been entranced by Gin. "Attend to your duties."

Genray placed a hand on Sam's shoulder. She now cried openly. Gin's words had gotten to her, and she wondered if she was responsible for all this.

"Walk with me, Sam."

She let Master Genray lead her across the dining room until they stood in a quiet corner of the room. He gently lowered her into a chair and knelt in front of her. "I'm sorry, Sam. I've failed you."

Sam raised her eyes and wiped the tears away. "What do you mean, you've failed me? I shouldn't be here. I should be back on my father's farm. That way, people would be safe. Gin is right. They came for me..." Sam started to stand.

Master Genray gripped both her arms and gently stopped her from rising. "You stop this right now. You are exactly where you need to be. Your mother and father agonized about their judgment to send you here, but in the end, they made the right decision."

Sam stared at him and tilted her head. "You knew?"

Master Genray nodded, "About your gift? Yes. We've known for a long time now. We brought you here to train you to control it, understand it, and see that it's not a curse. Not something evil inside you." He paused and turned to scan the rest of the room. "I thought we had much longer, but I'm afraid we have run out of time."

Sam started to say something, but Master Genray stopped her. "There is much to do, Sam. The shield will hold, and I have other responsibilities for now." He motioned Allax over. "Allax will stay with you until we can talk more." Sam saw extreme sadness in his gray eyes. "Again, I'm sorry, Sam." He squeezed her arm, stood, and walked away.

Sam wondered what else he wanted to tell her. She looked up at

Allax, who watched her with both worry and fear in his eyes. Sam pulled her knees up to her chest, put her chin down, and stared at the corner. More than anything, she wished Trey were with her. She reached for the communicator pin and realized she had left it in her room when she rushed out. She lowered her head to her knees. She felt more alone than ever before.

2 3

SAM'S AWAKENING

aster Genray turned up from his desk when he heard the knock on his office door. It had been two days since the attack on the school and their planet Berol. Things were going poorly. The initial attack had decimated the planetary defenses, and the Planetary Forces could not match the Serians' advanced technology.

And the Serians appeared interested in extermination, not conquest. Any attempts at surrender or truce were met with death. They killed everyone and everything in their path.

So far, the shields around the school had held off every attack to date, but it was only a matter of time. It was the same around the planet, where enclaves of preternatural scientists resisted the invaders at great cost.

The same could not be said for the shield around the city. The battle there was now house to house. As with the other four Prime schools in Berol, this school had been purposefully built over a powerful nexus, allowing for extraordinary breakthroughs in manipulations throughout the years. Master Genray attributed the success of the shields to being directly over the school and its power source. The military, recognizing the strategic location and tactical advantage the schools gave them, placed a contingent of troops around each one so they could rest and resupply from safety. Though it made everyone feel safer to have those troops around, it drew undue attention. And in the case of the Sterling Arch school, there was Sam.

It was late. Genray was fatigued worse than he could ever remember as he finished the final touches to a letter he fretted over writing. He sighed sadly, read the note one last time, folded the paper carefully, and sealed it in an envelope. He carefully wrote Sam's name on the face of the envelope. He traced his finger on the edge and sealed it with a formula only Sam would be able to break, giving her, and her only, access to the letter inside.

He placed it next to several old scrolls he had been reading, neatly arranged on the desktop. Despite all the technology surrounding them, preternatural science still clung to paper and parchment, since technology wasn't always their friend. He mused on the irony that math had created many of the universe's great inventions but also didn't allow most "magic" to interact with it.

He shook his head to clear the errant thought, too tired to focus, and placed his hand on an ancient book beside him. He had recovered it from his private archive when the Serians arrived, and the ensuing war started going badly. *Was it just two days ago?* he thought.

Dread hammered in the pit of his stomach. He knew this time would arrive one day but didn't expect it nearly so soon. He slid a worn yet simple scroll out of the pile, folded it, and slipped it in his pocket.

The knock on his door repeated. He sighed heavily. "Come in."

A tall woman with glossy silver skin and glimmering silver hair to match entered his office. She wore a loose-fitting black shirt and tight black pants. As she walked across the office on long legs, she offered a friendly smile Genray didn't bother to return.

As she drew closer, Master Genray stood and extended his hand. She took it in both of hers, silver engulfing pale white, and gave a slight nod of her head. Her shoulder-length hair drifted forward and back. "Hello, Master Genray," she said in a voice surprisingly light for such a tall woman. "My name is Mia, and I'm from—"

"The Agency," Genray interrupted. "I know."

The smile never faltered as she released his hand. "Sounds so ominous, doesn't it? The Agency. Like something from a spy thriller. But I see you have your sources."

He finally offered his own tired smile. "I've been out of the game a while, but not that long. I still have friends." He gestured for her to sit in one of the chairs in front of his desk.

Mia sat on the edge of the chair, back straight, hands neatly folded in her lap. "I need to speak to Sam."

"She is not ready, nor does she know. Nor do her parents."

"I would hope not," Mia said. "Or we would have been severely remiss in our work. But I'm afraid we have no choice."

"It will destroy her."

Mia shrugged."Again, we have no choice. Better her than the entire planet, yes? Indeed, the entire system."

Genray sighed again. Why did the fate of worlds always have to fall on the noble sacrifice of the innocents?

The ground shuddered as a deep rumbling sound echoed through the school. Mia looked at Master Genray. "The time is now. Your shield is failing."

***

Sam woke out of deep, dreamless sleep as someone pounded on her door. She rubbed her eyes and stared at the dim green glow of her clock: one in the morning. Dread ran through her as she wondered who would be bothering her this time of night.

"Hold on," Sam said. The holo beside her bed lit up and revealed Master Genray standing outside with another woman. Sam almost jumped out of bed as she recognized the woman who had saved her in the courtyard in that frightening attack two days ago. *What in the...?*

"Just a minute," she called out. "Holo off." She crawled out of bed, threw on her soft yellow robe, and walked to her door. She opened it to the two adults standing in the hallway.

"Master Genray...what...um...why..."

Master Genray held up his hand to Sam and gave her a sad smile. "Sam, I want to introduce you to Mia. She works with a group of people who need your help. She is with the government and specifically working with the military on our current situation."

Sam furrowed her brow and regarded Mia's deep black eyes. "Um, okay."

Mia offered a warm smile that nonetheless made Sam wary. "May we come in, Sam?"

Sam had no doubts she would regret saying yes, but what choice did she have? Besides, Mia had saved her life. "I'm sorry, yes, of course."

She opened the door and stepped aside so the two grown-ups could pass. Master Genray followed Mia into the room but gave Sam no response to the inquisitive look she slipped him behind Mia's back. Master Genray had promised to tell her more about what he knew on the day of the attacks, but he had been understandably busy since then. On the rare occasions she saw him, he gave her little more than a cursory acknowledgment, seeming to continually be needed elsewhere. She would think he was avoiding her if she thought she was that important.

Sam closed the door and crossed the room to sit on her bed. Other than her desk chair, there were no other seats in her cramped dorm room. Sam had a single room because no one else agreed to be her roommate. She had initially felt the stigma unwarranted, but rumors being insidious, even first years had heard of the fiery red-headed girl everyone avoided. Now she knew the stories were not so unfounded.

"You might want to get dressed," Mia told her.

"Why?"

"We'll explain once you're dressed."

Sam looked at Genray, who offered an apologetic shrug. Worry gnawed at Sam. She had never seen Master Genray so cowed. "Excuse me," she said.

Sam grabbed a pair of jeans and the shirt she wore earlier that day, making sure to wrap her hand around Trey's communicator pin. She slipped into the tiny bathroom, closed the door, and put on the shirt. She activated the pin and turned the volume all the way down, so if Ship spoke, they wouldn't hear. She wouldn't either, but she wanted it on so someone on the other end could know what was happening. The shield over the school had prevented her from contacting Ship, but she knew the shields were weakening, and she hoped a transmission might go through now, assuming Ship was even in range to pick it up. *What was the range anyway?* She didn't know why, but she felt like she needed an ally now.

Dressed, she left the bathroom and returned to the bed.

Mia had taken the lone seat at the desk chair, leaving Master Genray to stand beside her. She moved the chair closer to the bed and leaned forward with her elbows on her knees, across from Sam. "Sam, as Master Genray stated, my name is Mia. I work for a group with the rather silly name of The Agency, and we have need of your particular talent."

Fearful of what she meant, but putting some vain hope in playing dumb, Sam said, "But I don't have any real talent to speak of. I mean, I'm no slouch, but I'm no standout either."

Mia held up her hand to stop Sam from any further comment. "I have been following your progress to date and think you are doing an excellent job of hiding your true talents. Except for that little demonstration in the bathroom with Gin, you are doing quite well."

Master Genray's eyebrow rose slightly at Mia's reference to Sam's encounter with Gin. *If he didn't know,* she thought, *then how did this woman?*

The exchange didn't escape Mia's attention. "Yes, I know Gin and her little group of miscreants will no longer bother you and Trey." Mia leaned in a little closer. "And I know why. We've known ever since you came here."

Trey, do you have a moment? Ship thought to him through their newfound link.

Of course, what's up? He sat up in his bed, where he had been lying and reading.

Ship flew safely tucked in behind the adolescent Kuthrallie, a full day into their travel through the newly created tunnel, which folded in behind them. Though they were vastly different beings, Trey and Aphrilaosarn, the name the young Kuthrallie gave itself, as near as Trey could make out, had a connection based on age respective to their species. They were both teenagers and young teens at that. Why its elders trusted Aphrilaosarn with this species, the young one didn't know, but Aphrilaosarn relished the freedom of the task. The youth was far more playful with getting concepts across, a nice change from the frustrated information dump Trey got from the older Kuthrallie.

Almost as soon as they transitioned into ripspace and the crew was awake, they reached out and contacted Berol. Ship was correct in her assumption she could manipulate the *aether* and establish contact despite the lack of a conduit. Unfortunately, they discovered their message arrived too late. The planet was already under attack, and the planetary shields cut down heavily on communications planetside. Ship theorized that the surrounding communication satellites were either destroyed or damaged. Their attempts to contact Sam met with similar results.

What do you know about Sam's talents? Why is everyone afraid of her? Ship thought to him.

Well, I haven't asked her directly, but the rumors are that she is an evil witch who kills for fun. Kind of a 'death follows her, and she can't control it' thing. Why?

Her commlink is open and set to transmit only, I assume so we can listen in on her conversation with Master Genray and a woman named Mia who works for The Agency. She knows a great deal about Sam but is being extremely vague about it.

Trey sat up straighter. *What do they want with Sam?*

I don't know. I'll patch you in; maybe you can shed some insight.

Trey grew quiet as he heard Sam's voice come through the connection.

"... just used these stupid rumors to my advantage. I didn't mean anything by it. I would never hurt anyone."

Once again, Mia held up her hand, apparently her way of getting attention. "Sam, I know you swore to never use your power again after the incident with the intruder at the farm, but we need you to put that aside." Mia stopped when she saw Sam's eyes widen.

Sam covered her mouth, and her eyes started to water. She couldn't believe it was all going to come out. "How could you possibly know?"

Several years ago, a drifter arrived at Sam's family's farm searching for work. He seemed capable enough, and they needed help. Not liking the way he always watched her, Sam kept her distance. After about a week, the herd had been cut, and he said he would move on. Two days after he left, Sam headed down to the family pond to catch some fish. Sam loved to fish. Shortly after she set her pole in the water, he stepped out of the wood line behind her.

Sam never told anyone. Not even her parents. And she never went fishing again.

Mia's face softened, her silver skin almost seeming to glow. "You are a unique and wonderful girl, Sam. But your power is also unique. And formidable. So unique there are no others known to possess it. You came to our attention when you were tiny. Actually, your parents brought it to Master Genray's attention, which in turn brought it to ours. We have been watching you since you were a toddler."

Sam turned to Master Genray, whose face had taken on a sad, pained disappointment. Not in her, but in himself. "I'm sorry, Sam. When you were young, still a baby, and you became scared or angry, things would—happen. No, that's not fair." He locked his brown eyes with hers. "You are no longer a little girl, and you deserve an honest account. But before I continue, I need you to do one thing for me. Turn off your communicator."

Emotions churned within Sam, anger foremost. Was her life nothing but an activated tablet to these people? She included Master

Genray in this. She had thought of him as a trusted grandfatherly figure who would protect her. Currently, she wasn't sure about anything. Trey was the only one she could depend on, and now they wanted her to cut him off. She reached up to her lapel and hesitated, thinking.

"Please, Sam. I'll tell you everything and answer all your questions, but this is for no one else's ears. What you do after that is up to you."

She hesitated a moment. Then saying a small prayer Trey would forgive her, assuming he was even listening, Sam turned off her pin.

"No, no, no!" Trey shouted out loud. "Ship, override it."

"I can't."

"What, why not?" Trey jumped to his feet and paced in his cabin. "You were able to get around the Admiral's jamming and safe room. Why can't you do it now?"

"For two reasons. First and foremost, because Sam terminated the conversation on her end. It sounds as if she has had a lot of trusts betrayed today. We won't add to the list. If she wants us to know, she'll tell us. Secondly, I get the feeling that if we attempted to reopen communications with her, they would know and would successfully thwart our attempts. I can circumvent most any technology, but magic is a completely different story. Another reason Gerard is such a vital addition to our team."

Trey slumped back down on his bed. "What do they want with Sam?" he asked, more to himself than to Ship.

"I don't know," she answered anyway. "But I think we need to let the others know when we can, especially Gerard."

Trey jumped up. "Good idea, have them meet me in the wardroom."

"Excellent idea, Captain," she said with humor in her voice.

Trey blushed. "Sorry. I'm just worried about my friend."

"So am I."

Sam glared at the two of them. "Alright, it's off."

"Thank you, Sam." Master Genray said as he sat down on the bed beside her. "This is one of those times when adults have a hard subject to tell a child or family member, but struggle for the right time to tell them. It never seems like a good time until the time has passed. Then it is too late, and the telling leaves anger and resentment for not having been forthcoming earlier." He sighed heavily and ran his hand through his hair.

"This sounds a little ominous," Sam said warily.

"When Mia said you were unique, that wasn't an exaggeration. You are indeed one of a kind, Sam. My research indicates there is never any more than one person with the power you possess in existence at any one time. And usually, hundreds of years separate them. As I said earlier, when you were a child, you would become scared or angry, and if the target of your anger was living, it—well—died. We, mostly your parents and I, were able to contain it magically. When you grew more aware of your difference, you seemed able to contain it yourself, either consciously or unconsciously, to the point of full suppression. We thought maybe it had been a temporary fluke, and the power was so deeply subsumed it wouldn't return. That was until the laborer at the pond attacked you."

Sam's hand returned to her mouth. "He turned to dust and blew away," she said in a shaking voice. "I didn't mean to do anything like that, but he was going to...going to..." She couldn't bring herself to say it.

"We know what he was going to do," Mia said, moving forward and taking Sam's hand. "It's okay."

"He said if I told anyone he would come back and kill my family." Sam had never told anyone, but not because of the man's threat. She still had no idea how anyone knew. She barely let herself think about it since it happened. "I kicked at him and pounded on his chest, but he was too strong. I closed my eyes and screamed, and he screamed a deep horrible scream, like it came from his soul. Then he simply burst into dust and blew away with the wind." Tears ran down her face. "I'm a monster."

She stared up at the two of them, having to focus through the tears in her eyes. "Is that why you're here? To take me away. To keep everyone safe?"

She recoiled as Master Genray reached out and gently touched her arm. "No, Sam," he said softly. "I'm afraid it's much worse."

"What do you mean?"

Mia grabbed a tissue from the desk and held it out to Sam. "Tell me, Sam, have you used your power? Do you have complete control over it?"

"Yes, I think so. I mean, I've never had it get away from me again like it did that time."

"Yes," Mia leaned closer. "But that's not what I asked. Have you used your power since then?"

Sam sat back and frowned. "You seem to know everything else about me. What do you think?"

Mia's face became less friendly, edging toward frightening. "Answer the question, please."

"Fine, yes. I eventually wanted to see if I could do it again. So, I tried it on some insects."

"And what happened?"

"Well, they didn't turn to dust, but they did die."

Mia glanced over to Master Genray and back to Sam. "Go on."

"Over time, I found I could do the same thing to the slaughter animals. I never told my mom and dad, but it seemed better for them —the animals, not my parents." Sam smiled slightly, remembering the pleasant days there. "It seemed more humane in some way."

"How does it work?"

"It started out that I had to touch whatever it was I killed. I mean, I didn't do it all the time. We live on a farm. We eat what we grow and raise." Sam felt horrified at herself when she heard what she did out loud.

Mia stepped in. "Sam, I know all about farm life. I also grew up on a working farm. I understand, and there's no judgment. We simply want to know how far your power has progressed. Please continue. When did you find you didn't need to touch them anymore?"

"It was the stingers. It was late spring, and I was moving a pile of old barn wood when I must have disturbed a *tezzen's* nest. I pulled a board from the bottom, and all of a sudden," Sam waved both arms out. "Poof. The air was full of angry *tezzens*. I screamed and ran, but you can't run faster than a swarm, so they caught me pretty quick. I was running and screaming and getting stung when suddenly they weren't stinging me anymore. They got me eighteen times. When my father and I went back to find the nest, there were no more insects, just a large nest at the bottom of the woodpile. He thought it was odd but never said anything else about it. I guess I know why now. They knew all along." Sam started to softly cry again. "I wish they…" Sam let her thought linger. "Anyway, I didn't have to touch anything again after that."

"Don't be too hard on your parents, Sam," Master Genray said. "They have struggled for you at every turn. Your dad wanted to take you away, but your mom thought it would be best if you stayed here and learned to control your power. Unfortunately, there is no manual. Just know your parents love you unconditionally and have ached over every struggle you have undertaken."

Master Genray offered an angry glance at Mia. "And the Agency may have had influence over some of the decisions made on your behalf."

Mia didn't back down from his challenge. "The Agency does what it thinks is best." She dismissed his concern with her eyes and turned back to Sam. "How does it work? How do you tap into your power? Is it like the formulas used here at the school, or something else?"

Sam considered for a long moment, then gazed into Mia's black eyes. "You want to learn how I do it so you can teach others." She pointed a finger at her. "You want the formula to turn it into a weapon."

Mia started to offer an angry retort when Master Genray held up a hand. "You are correct that The Agency would like nothing more than to learn how to mass-produce your power—"

Sam crossed her arms. "Well, I won't do it."

Mia's eyes glittered with anger, and when she opened her mouth once again, Genray stopped her with a sharp gesture. "Mia doesn't know, or chooses not to accept, that you can't teach it in a formula, can you? The power you have has nothing to do with formulas and the ways we know of magic, does it?"

Honestly surprised, Sam wanted to ask him questions, like how he seemed to know more about it than she did. She gave Mia a defiant glare. "No, it doesn't."

Master Genray continued. "You were right when you said you are no slouch when it comes to your studies here at the school, but you aren't holding back either, are you?"

"No."

"Then how?" Mia asked cautiously.

Now it came to the point when Sam had to confess. "I don't know."

"But I do," Master Genray said. He reached into the pocket fold of his robe and pulled out an old scroll. "This," he held it up before them both, "is something I found after Sam arrived at our school. It was folded up in an old tome, hand-written, almost like an afterthought. It speaks of a power like hers and says that it is her power. Not given or learned, but *hers*. And it has a name." He watched for Mia's reaction and said, "*Asdrahu*."

Sam saw Mia's face change. Her dark eyes widened, and her mouth gaped—a strange look on the silver-skinned woman. "It can't be. That's ancient mythology."

"What is?" Sam asked. "What does that mean?"

Mia ignored her. "You're saying it to try and frighten me like I'm a child, and you hope I'll go away and leave Sam alone."

Master Genray offered a sad shake of his head. "I say it, so you know what I believe we are dealing with."

Obviously shaken, Mia turned back to Sam. As she spoke, her voice quivered. "You're correct, Sam. The Agency sent me here to learn the formulas to your power. We knew you weren't ready and likely had no idea the extent of your ability, but our hope was we could glean something from you with the help of Master Genray.

Though it is only a few days old, Berol is losing this war, and the Agency fears that if this planet is lost, it's only a matter of time before the Sasalee, the invaders, take over every Council planet. It would be a long, protracted war, but we would eventually lose. And this planet will fall in hours."

2 4

ASDRAHU

Sam stared out at the burning city. She stood on the Power Tower's twenty-meter-wide platform, twelve stories above the ground and directly over the nexus. From here, she could see everything.

Battles raged in various quarters, evidenced by the sounds of weapons and explosions. Several buildings burned, tiny figures moved, and Sam thought she heard occasional, faint screams.

She gazed up and saw a separate battle in the skies above, flashes of light and debris that flared as it hit the atmosphere.

Sam's parents had joined them, and they each held one of her hands in theirs. It was one of the strangest moments in Sam's young life as she stood there watching the death of her planet while holding her parents' hands and being told she held the power to stop it all. She turned her eyes to her father and saw strength in his pale, chiseled face and worry in his bright green eyes. Looking over to her mother, so recently returned from her adventure with Trey, she saw the same strength in the fiery red hair they shared.

From behind the trio, Mia spoke. "They dropped a device on the city that worked against both our physical defenses and many of our magical ones. Then their ground forces—those dog-like creatures—

334

swarmed in and started devouring everything in their path. This was followed by their real troops, who began the real battle. We've done the best we could, but we are lost…"

"But the Council—" Sam started to say in desperation.

"Couldn't arrive in time even if the ripspace tunnels were intact. Without them, it will be a lifetime before any ships arrive."

Also standing behind her, Master Genray whispered, "This could destroy you, Sam."

"I know," Sam said, still staring out at the city, tears gathering. "You made it clear earlier. It seems to me if I don't do this, we'll all be destroyed." She reached out and hugged both of her parents and whispered so only they could hear. "I'm really scared." The gathered tears finally broke free and ran down her cheeks.

Her father, a big man with muscles produced by years of hard work on a farm, gathered them both in his arms. He squeezed so tight that Sam heard her mother suck in a little gasp of air.

"I love you, Pumpkin," he buried his face in her hair, and she could feel his tears on the top of her head. "I wish I could take this from you."

Sam locked her eyes to his and kissed his damp cheek. "Me too, Dad, but you can't."

Her mother pushed her out to arm's length and pleadingly looked over to Mia and Master Genray. "There must be another way."

Master Genray shook his head sadly. "I'm afraid not, and unfortunately, our time is short. As we linger, people die. We can't force you, Sam, but you must decide soon."

Sam wished she had time to talk to Trey. He could tell her what to do. They both had shared hardships. He would—but no, she couldn't put that burden on him. This had to be her choice, and hers alone. And in the end, it wasn't a choice, which she suspected Master Genray and Mia knew all along.

Sam pulled away from her parents' embrace but held on to their hands a moment longer before she let go and walked over to Master Genray. He seemed older to her than he ever had, and for the first time, she wondered how old he was. There was something in his eyes she couldn't place: sadness, regret maybe, she wasn't sure. "I'm ready," she told him, though she wasn't.

He nodded and spoke in a distant voice. "You're not, really," he said, and it startled her to hear her thought spoken aloud. "You're not powerful nor strong enough to do this on your own, so I'm going to assist you. The first phase will be a strong empath formula. It will give you the capacity to feel the emotions of the people of this city, perhaps even beyond." Master Genray gestured to a woman who stood on the other side of the platform, dressed in a dark blue robe and possessing short black hair. Sam hadn't seen her before. She must have arrived while Sam watched the dying city.

"This is Mistress Donnallan," Genray said as the woman approached. "She will be the caster and will help you focus. This is her specialty, and I can think of no one I trust more for this task."

Donnallan smiled at Sam. "I will help you gather the energy of the people and let you feel their thoughts and fears." She lowered her hazel eyes and studied Sam. "I understand your power manifests itself mostly through fear, so this is where we will place our attention. Other people's fears can be crippling, so I will be here to try and help you maintain your concentration."

Master Genray continued. "I'm going to draw from the Power Tower and focus the nexus energy toward you."

The look Sam offered must have been comical because Master Genray smiled. "Yes, it was called that even when I was a student here." The smile disappeared, and again the sadness flashed through his eyes, but it passed as he took her hand.

"This power will be raw, and like nothing you have ever experienced. It will rise through you, warming your very soul, but will soon burn." He locked eyes with her. She flinched from the intensity in his gaze but recovered and held the stare. "You must keep it in for as long as you can. Then when you can no longer handle it, release your power."

He squeezed her hands so tight they hurt, but she didn't complain. "Be careful; the power can consume you. If you hold it in, you will feel as if you are a god, with the ability to move mountains, worlds, even galaxies, but this is a fallacy—a corruption. No matter what happens, release your power."

The Master's intensity confused and frightened Sam. She wanted to run, to refuse, but the plea in his eyes, the understanding of what she would be saving, stopped her. "Sure," she heard herself say. "I promise."

His eyes softened, and another thin smile came to him. "You are exceptional, Sam. When this is over, allow yourself the time to forgive. Lean on those who care for you."

Before she could say anything in response, he released her hands and turned to Mistress Donnallan. "Let us begin."

Mistress Donnallan reached out with a long finger and touched Sam on her forehead. Just before the ensuing flash of light and wash of emotions, she heard her mother call out, "I love you, Sam!"

Sam felt like she swam in a warm churning sea that fought to pull her under. She gasped. The warmth of her mother and father's love poured over her. She briefly considered how different their love was, not better or worse, but different. Her father's was strong and protective, her mother's equally strong but tempered with the understanding of what must be done and fierce pride at Sam's willingness to do it. She felt Mistress Donnallan work the equations; the complexity was stunning, artisan, a brilliant mix of power and subtlety. She also felt profound fear, not only for her people but for this endeavor. Sam realized this had never been attempted before, and the thought terrified the Mistress more than the Sasalee did.

Before Sam could linger on that thought, she picked up Master Genray's feelings as he began his part of the conjuring. His equation made Mistress Donnallan's seem elementary. In comparison, she was finger painting on paper, and he was creating a masterpiece in the stars.

But she sensed something else: fear mingled with a sense of inevitability, not for her, but for himself. She felt his concern for her, his worry she would survive physically but not mentally. His care for her was real and genuine. However, there was an end to his anxiety and understanding that it would not be in his power to help her through the coming trial, and then she comprehended.

He knew he would not survive this conjuring.

"No!" Sam screamed as she reached out for him. But he finished his computations, and the power overwhelmed her.

Sam sensed the people of the city, then she felt them. All of them. Their worries, shattered dreams, and hopelessness. Babies and children cried out as the war raged around them. Her power warmed her. She felt the desperation of parents knowing they could not protect their children, and her power grew. She felt the soldiers as they fought for their lives and those of their families. She was hot now, burning from within. She felt the love that would never be, the sadness of lives unfulfilled. And the burning grew. Her hands were clenched so tightly her fingernails dug into the palms of her hands and drew blood.

Now came the fear. She could smell the terror, feel it, ache with it. She thought she heard Master Genray cry out, but the power consumed her, engulfing, crushing—yet irresistible.

And then the pain came, the pain of death, the pain of suffering, of wounds, of the lost, friends, family, and loved ones. Children in the arms of their dead parents and parents holding their dead children. Wives and husbands crying out to each other. She held the power close to her.

She became aware of the Sasalee. Their emotions, though alien, were still immediately recognizable: glee and joy at the suffering of their enemies. No cares for the loss of their comrades, only pleasure and lust in the misery they inflicted. She burned with the fires of hell. And the fear turned to anger. It boiled inside her, and Master Genray cried out.

She understood now. What she felt up until then had been a candle to a volcano. Master Genray's power combined with the power of the nexus and poured through her. She felt Mistress Donnallan close to her; what the woman experienced was fear, not of the Sasalee or the situation or even her own end, but fear of Sam and what she had become. *Asdrahu.* Not the power of death, but the incarnate of the concept. She was death. Now even her parents feared her.

Energy pulsed through her body and radiated from it. Her long-submerged power slowly rose, its darkness growing. It clawed its way to the surface. Hungry. This is where she would always push it back down—but not today.

She opened her eyes as the force grew. She saw the world differently through the darkness. She saw life, all life...but...not. The malevolence of her power engulfed her, and the anguish grew. She threw open her arms and reached out, drawing in the energy surrounding her. She saw it clearer now; it swirled around her, pouring from the tower through Master Genray and into her. It felt as if thousands of threaded hooks pierced her flesh and pulled her apart from every direction. Life forces clung to her, tore at her; desperately, she cut some loose.

"No, Sam," she felt more than heard Master Genray whisper to her. "Hold on to them dearly. The ones you cut loose die."

Master Genray's power and life force continued rushing through her. Through vision blurred by her trembling body, she saw Master Genray reading a formula from a scroll. The thread from his soul that had hooked itself deeply into her flesh suddenly tripled in intensity. The thread thickened, and the power flowed through to her. She felt near overloaded and marveled that she didn't glow.

But as he worked the incantations, she saw something else. His skin withered before her, his flesh sinking as if water was being sucked from him. His hair went so white it grew transparent, and his face turned gaunt.

"Please, no." Sam pleaded softly, reaching toward him as he finished reading.

Master Genray completed the formula and opened his eyes. He was tired. So tired. For a moment, her power backlashed to him, and he saw what Sam saw, felt what she felt. He wept at the death the Serians brought to his people, cried as they gleefully killed in the throes of battle. He experienced the pain, suffering, loss, and fear brought on by their actions and knew Sam felt it more keenly than he did.

His last thought was regret that he had to make her do this and that he wouldn't be there to help her recover. "I'm so sorry, Sam."

Sam watched in helpless terror as Master Genray arched his back and shrieked. He collapsed to the floor, dead.

Anger, hatred, and something else, something darker, flared inside Sam. It was a malevolence she could no longer contain, an evil she no longer wanted to control.

Energy coursed through her, longing to erupt out of her. It burned every nerve ending in her body, but she held it in, focusing on the hatred inside her, her anger at the loss of Master Genray. The destructive force boiled up, consuming her. She could see the threads making up all the living things around her. Every creature, being, and plant lay before her interwoven in a living tapestry.

Where before the information overwhelmed her, the power provided by Master Genray's sacrifice let her understand and decipher everything. She could separate the strands and decide to hold or release them, strengthening the tapestry or cutting away loose threads. She gathered the parts she wanted and separated them from the others before the energy consumed her. She snagged the last thread, trapping all the invaders, and screamed as the dark volcanic energy inside her exploded, and the strands dissolved.

And the Sasalee died. All of them. She watched in her mind's eye as the ones on the ground and in the ships above simply turned to dust.

Sam fell to the ground on her hands and knees. She saw the others through the sweat-soaked red hair that had fallen in front of her eyes.

And what she saw on their faces was abject terror.

Asdrahu, she thought. *Death.*

She collapsed lifelessly to the stone floor.

2 5

AFTERMATH

Transition complete, Ship told Trey. *The crew is waking up now.*

Trey stared at the destruction on the monitors. Berol was in the throes of recovery, having won a war but at a high cost. And the problem was that in the larger scheme, this was one small battle in what was apparently a much bigger war.

The crew gathered in the wardroom and rehydrated as they watched the monitors. The news feeds were split between the destruction and the relief efforts. Various pundits speculated on the invaders' motivation, where they were from, why they choose Berol, and what Galactic's response would be. All of them noticed the focus had been on Berolis, which was both the capital and the city where the School of the Sterling Arch resided. They spent an inordinate amount of time speculating and theorizing the reasons for this. All were equally sure of their philosophies, and the higher the pedigree, the more confident they felt about their particular concept, what Gerard called "the arrogance of over education."

"I'm going to land in a large clearing near the school," Ship said. "It looks like some sort of beam weapon leveled everything near the northern wall."

"Thanks, Ship," Hawk said. "Let me know as soon as we can depart."

"Will do," she replied. The destruction of the orbital platform necessitated a landing planetside, something Hawk didn't like to do but that Ship was perfectly capable of handling. The decision was made more complicated by the level of debris and the ongoing rescue operations. Hawk felt the last thing anyone needed was another ship cluttering up things.

Fortunately, the military already had their transponder and clearance level in the system—Hawk was amazed it even worked after all the carnage—so they were able to travel down to the planet with little effort. It was agreed they could assist with the recovery efforts.

Gerard shook his head softly. "I still don't understand how Master Genray was killed in all of this. He would have been one of the last shield-bearers for the school." He glanced around at the others. "Grand Master Zehesel, my old mentor, has been brought out of retirement to oversee the school's reconstruction. He said to come by his office when we arrive, and he would fill us in on what he knows so far."

"Grand Master," Laura speculated. "I didn't know there was such a thing."

"It's mostly an honorary title. He doesn't like it and just goes by Zehesel. He is the most powerful manipulator I have ever encountered and easily the humblest." Gerard paused a moment, looking up at the ceiling in thought. "And his equations are flawless."

He sheepishly lowered his eyes back to the group, realizing he had been lost in thought. "Sorry. He said we should come on up. He is expecting us." He glanced over to Trey, who had a troubled look on his young face. "I'm sorry, Trey, they still have no idea where Sam has gone."

Trey shook his head. "We can't raise her on my communicator..." He let the thought trail away and continued to stare at the monitors.

Laura reached out her hand and gently rested it on his back. "We'll find her."

He leaned into her comforting arm.

Gerard was the first through the door to the reception area outside of Master Genray's old office. To his surprise, Zehesel sat at the reception desk. He was older, his long curly hair gone gray, and wrinkles lined his dark face. He stood immediately and stepped from behind the small desk. "Gerard, good to see you again. I wish it was under better circumstances."

Gerard extended his hand, but Zehesel brushed it aside and grabbed him in a hug, pounding on his back with vigor. "It's been too long."

Gerard hesitated for a moment, then returned the man's hug with equal strength. "Yes, it has."

As the rest of the crew piled in, Gerard turned and introduced them all.

Hawk was the last to shake Zehesel's hand. Though bony and thin, it was not frail. "Glad to finally meet you. Gerard has told us much of your exploits."

"Lies," Zehesel said with a gentle laugh. "Gerard has a way with words that put everything in a better light." He indicated several chairs and couches set around the small room. "Humor an old man and take a seat. I'll fill you in with what I know."

They all took seats around the small desk Zehesel used in his temporary role as headmaster. There was even a chair suitable for Wolf's size. Gerard noticed his old mentor didn't move like he remembered; he was more careful in his steps and held back some pain as he slowly sat down. However, his eyes were crystal clear; the body may certainly be failing, but the mind appeared sharp as ever.

Zehesel waved one arm around the room. "I apologize for the sparseness of the accommodations, but it didn't seem appropriate to move into Master Genray's old office." He looked over to the closed door. "My position is temporary. I'm going to let the next headmaster deal with all of that."

"I don't know where to begin," he said as he regarded the group. His deep-set eyes studied Trey. "I suppose I should start with you,

Trey. I know you are worried about Sam. We all are. I'll start around when the shields began to fail and bring you up to speed with what I know."

As Zehesel filled them in on Sam's last hours at the school, the gravity of the situation washed over them all. Trey was clearly distraught but did a good job of holding back until Zehesel got to the point of Sam's collapse.

"Then she's alive," Trey exclaimed excitedly. "So, where is she? We haven't been able to raise her with the communicator we gave her."

"I'm sorry, Trey, I didn't know you weren't informed she was still alive. Physically, she's fine." Zehesel leaned forward, a frown on his old face. "But I'm afraid that spiritually, she has suffered greatly. The effect of her power has left her broken inside."

Trey stood up. "I need to see her. Where is she?"

Zehesel put up a wrinkled hand. "Peace. We don't know where she is. Her parents are beside themselves. She was in the infirmary, like I said, physically fine, but empty inside. She wouldn't speak, just stared off in the distance, not seeing anyone, more looking through them." He sighed. "Then one morning she was gone. Her parents were at her bedside all night and were asleep in their chairs when they woke and found her missing."

Trey thought for a moment. "May I see her room?"

"Of course. I thought you might make that request. You know the way. I'll have Allax meet you there and let you in."

Trey looked down at Laura, who nodded her head. "You go on. We'll be here when you're ready."

Trey let out a heavy breath, "Okay…yeah…" He glanced around as if to say something else but decided against it before quietly walking out.

Zehesel watched as the door closed. "Those two formed quite a bond while they were here, but I'm afraid he won't find any answers down there. She left without a trace." He held Gerard's gaze. "We're still piecing together all the information, but I believe she is somehow connected to all of this." He paused for a moment and slowly scanned the rest of the crew. "As I think the rest of you suspect that young man is."

Trey sat in Sam's old room on the corner of her bed, holding the communicator pin she left on her pillow. Her room was amazingly neat, which was unlike her. Everything was clean and meticulously placed, except for a small bean plant in her window; she had told him it reminded her of home, a simpler time back on the farm. It was now a pile of dust in the pot. Trey stood and tested the soil with his finger. *Still damp.* He glanced around her room once more. She had no intention of returning, her effects were in order, and there was nothing for anyone to do. Trey recognized this behavior. He had seen it on Kel, during the war, when people began to lose hope and decided to kill themselves. Everything in order, so no one had to take on the burden. She wasn't going to return, but she hadn't killed herself. He didn't care how broken she was; she wouldn't do that. He had to believe that was true. He rolled the pin in his fingers. "We have to find her, Ship."

"Working on it, dear."

EPILOGUE

I*t's my birthday*, she realized as she walked across the beautiful field of golden grass and wildflowers covering the valley. Winter snows still covered the mountain range in the distance, waiting for the spring melt. In the valley, spring had arrived; birds were busy chasing the insects as they gathered nectar from the blossoming flowers. Spring had come early this year, and Sam could feel the warmth of the sun as she slowly walked through the grass. Her arms stretched out beside her, softly brushing the tops of the stalks. She raised her face to the sky as she moved, taking in the heat. Several small animals skittered out of her path, not seeming to mind as they gathered seeds for their newly arrived young. She closed her eyes, feeling the life before her. She felt the bees seeking out the juices of the flowers; she flew with butterflies, light as the wind; she was the caterpillar, hungrily eating the fresh young stalks, fattening up for the coming metamorphosis. Tears streamed down her face as she moved. The life before her was overwhelming. All this living potential had no idea that a monster came for it, she thought, a monster of unbelievable evil.

Trey paced his steps across the meadow toward her. He both saw and felt the agony of her soul, but he could also sense it inside himself too. There she strolled, almost calmly, arms extended, face to the sky. But the tears running down her face belied that façade. Trey couldn't help but weep for her as he moved her way. "I found her, Ship."

"How is she?"

"Not good. I won't be communicating for a while. I have a feeling it will take everything I have to get through to her."

"I thought that might be the case. You may be her last hope."

"You have no idea," Trey whispered, stopping about one hundred meters in front of Sam. She hadn't seen him yet; her eyes were closed. "Sara?"

"Yes?"

"I love you. Tell the crew I love them, too, even Ashron." He smiled. "And Hawk…I…I don't know, just tell them, okay?"

"Trey, what's going on?"

Trey cut off the communication. Ship could reach him through their unique link, but he knew she wouldn't. She loved him too.

Trey moved so he stood in Sam's path. She still hadn't seen him, and if she didn't open her eyes soon, she would run into him. Trey's tears were flowing as much as Sam's. He choked back a sob as he looked at the path of destruction behind her. In almost a perfect V emanating from her arms and flowing out behind her was nothing but death. Everything living had turned to dust, exoskeletons from insects, and bones from animals. There also extended an odd absence of light. Not darkness, but more like the sun shone through a filter of fine debris, except nothing floated in the air to diffuse the light. Trey shuddered. "Sam."

She stopped when she heard her name. *That's impossible,* she thought. *This area is uninhabited.* She opened her eyes. Trey stood not three meters from her, tears streaming down his face.

"Sam, please," he said again.

Anger roiled through Sam. "How did you find me? How did you get here? Are the rest with you? Are—"

"I'm alone," Trey said softly. "I came through a gate about a kilometer from here. And no one knows where we are. I found you with the help of the Kuthrallie, the uh, worms."

Sam dropped her arms, but Trey could still see the anger seething in her. "Go away, Trey, I'm a monster." Sam dropped her eyes, and her shoulders slumped. "A monster," she whispered.

"I'm not going anywhere without you."

Anger flashed in her blue eyes again, but her voice softened. "I am death, Trey. Everywhere I go, death follows. Everything I touch dies."

"Not me," he said as he stepped forward.

"No!" She shoved out her arms out to stop him.

Trey gently pushed her hands aside and wrapped his arms around her. She stiffened at his embrace, but he held on tight. "And I'm not going anywhere without you."

THE END

FRIENDS OF FALSTAFF

Thank You to All our Falstaff Books Patrons, who get extra digital content each month! To be featured here and see what other great rewards we offer, go to www.patreon.com/falstaffbooks.

PATRONS

Dino Hicks
John Hooks
John Kilgallon
Larissa Lichty
Travis & Casey Schilling
Staci-Leigh Santore
Sheryl R. Hayes
Scott Norris
Samuel Montgomery-Blinn
Junkle

ACKNOWLEDGMENTS

Steve and Paul would like to offer a special thanks to their beta readers: Cheryl, Gary, and Bob, for pointing out the flaws and saying nice things about the good parts.

Also, much love to our editors, Erin Penn and Alisha Grace, for keeping us honest, cutting the unnecessary words, and making the timeline work, a monumental task.

ABOUT THE AUTHORS

Steve Murphy put on his first uniform at age 19, starting with four years in the Navy and a stint in the Army National Guard. Steve then spent 23 years as a police officer, 14 on the SWAT team and 9 as a sniper. After retiring from the force, he swore his next job would allow him to dress however the hell he wanted to. So he became a writer, which can be done in pajamas while drinking bourbon.

Steve currently lives on a 12-acre farm somewhere in North Carolina with his wife, two dogs, and a cat. That is about to change and he may soon be homeless, living under a bridge with the people mentioned above, and a troll named Sam.

Paul Barrett has worked a variety of jobs in his life, but the two that make him happiest are writer and motion picture producer. He has produced four films and worked on a variety of cool television shows. His films include *Cold Storage* and *Night Feeders.*

When he's not writing, Paul enjoys board gaming and watching great TV shows. He lives in North Carolina with his graphic artist husband and three cats.

Steve and Paul have known each other since 1982, when Paul bribed Steve with a roll of quarters to give him a ride home on his motorcycle. Paul really wanted to ride a motorcycle. Somehow, they became instant friends, which speaks to either Paul's winning personality or Steve's love of quarters. Combined, they have written five novels and four screenplays.

You can email the guys at info@twomenandatypewriter.com